THE TRIALS AND TRIUMPH TRILOGY:

THE RISE

THE REBELLION

THE RETURN

THE REBELLION

BOOK TWO OF
THE TRIALS AND TRIUMPH TRILOGY

KENNETH E. NOWELL

Vero House
Publishing, Corp.

Vero House Publishing, Corp.
5460 Corsica Place
Vero Beach, FL 32967
www.VeroHousePublishing.com
Telephone or fax: 888-292-7160
Email: admin@VeroHousePublishing.com
Paperback Edition:
ISBN-13: 978-0-9828279-6-3 ISBN-10:0-9828-2797-0
Digital Edition:
ISBN-10: 0-9828-2797-0 ISBN-13: 978-0-9828279-7-0

Library of Congress Cataloging-in-Publication Data:
Nowell, Kenneth E.
      The Rebellion – Book Two of The Trials and Triumph Trilogy / Kenneth E. Nowell.
            p. cm.
1. Suspense fiction 2. Christian fiction 3. Historical fiction 4. Prophecy
            I.   Title
813.6-dec22   LCCN: 2012935621
(pbk.)ISBN-13: 978-0-9828279-6-3 ISBN-10:0-9828-2797-0

The author and publisher recognize and accept that the final authority regarding apparitions, miracles and prophecies rests with the Holy See of Rome, to whose judgment we willingly submit.

FOR THOSE WHO HAVE
EARS TO HEAR
AND EYES TO SEE.

THE
REBELLION

October 13, 1884

Pope Leo XIII was finishing the celebration of Mass in the Vatican Chapel when he suddenly stopped at the foot of the altar. He stood there for about 10 minutes, as if in a trance, his face ashen white.

When asked what had happened, he explained that, as he was about to leave, he heard two voices – one kind and gentle, the other guttural and harsh. They seemed to come from near the tabernacle. As he listened, he heard the following conversation:

The guttural voice of Satan boasted: "I can destroy Your Church."

The gentle voice of Our Lord: "You can? Then go ahead."

Satan: "To do so, I need more time and more power."

Our Lord: "How much time? How much power?"

Satan: "75 to 100 years, and a greater power over those who will give themselves over to my service."

Our Lord: "You have the time, you will have the power. Do with them what you will."[1]

Concerning the coming of our Lord Jesus Christ ...
[that day will not come] until the rebellion occurs
and the man of lawlessness is revealed,
the man doomed to destruction.

2 Thessalonians 2:1-3

Woe to the worthless shepherd,
who deserts the flock!
May the sword strike his arm and his right eye!
May his arm be completely withered,
his right eye totally blinded!
Zechariah 11:17

Chapter 1
Capernaum, Israel
July 10 - The First Day

Seven armored vehicles stormed westward down an empty highway, transporting enough fire-power to challenge a small kingdom. To the left of the fleet of sand-colored Sidewinders stretched the scenic Sea of Galilee. The ruins of Capernaum approached ahead.

The area appeared deserted. Wisely, the small town's residents and tourists had heeded the warning of the Legion of Babylon,[2] and had evacuated. Almost everyone now understood that cooperation insured safety. Defiance, on the other hand, invited destruction.

Evan Thas[3] led the way, roaring ahead without any regard for speed limits or dangers. The small, young man was more concerned with shielding his burn-scarred face from the bright, mid-day sun. Evan wiped beads of sweat off his brow and squinted with his good eye as he adjusted the black and white "bulls eye" patch over his right eye. With warm wind whipping through the open windows, he ran his fingers through his disheveled red hair.

The woman sitting next to him, however, exhibited no discomfort or imperfection. She radiated beauty, even now.

Evan was proud to have her by his side and flashed a smile her way to share his excitement. She did not respond. In fact, he had never seen her offer a serious smile. Behind those stoic but exotic eyes were no amusements or entertainments, only calculations.

For Evan, Faridah Shabaan[4] was more special than any woman he had known in his thirty three years. He had developed a deep reverence for her and called her his blessed mother.

"Here ... this is it!" she directed as they approached an intersection.

Evan slammed on the brakes and began to swerve left, into Capernaum.

"No," she shouted as the following vehicles skidded to avoid collisions. "Turn right!"

Evan slowed to a stop, grinded his gears into reverse, and backed up a bit. His crippled hand gripped the stick shift with difficulty, but he eventually managed to engage first gear and slowly roll ahead, up the hill, away from the sea. The men driving behind him followed without complaint. They knew that they were expendable.

Nearing the crest of the hill, Faridah pointed at a rock formation. "There it is."

So, Evan rolled up to the boulders, next to a bulldozer, as the other vehicles parked, nearby. Two unusual men brought up the rear, transporting a balding, older passenger whose famously bright blue eyes now had dimmed. The men[5] in the front seat were twins, a year younger than Evan, dark in features and wearing black suits that were oddly out of place in this hot climate.

Immediately, Faridah emerged from the Sidewinder and directed the followers. She singled out the soldier in charge and ordered, "Get that boulder out of the way."

"Yes, ma'am!" the officer responded with an unsettling air of zealotry. He had tattooed a bulls eye around his right eye, mimicking Evan's eye patch. "Right away," he promised. Then, when he mounted the equipment, he felt around under the seat and found a key. But when he examined the cockpit, he stammered, "Uh, ma'am... I don't know..."

"Then find somebody who does!" she snapped.

An eager young soldier volunteered, "I can do it, sir." He jogged over and replaced the officer, behind the controls. Before turning the key, however, he offered, "Ma'am, this dozer ain't been used in a while. I bet the diesel's gone bad."

Evan grumbled, "Just do it!"

After a few attempts, the engine sputtered to life and, soon, the large boulder was shoved aside, revealing a hole that was over three feet in diameter. Faridah moved closer to the cavity and, for the first time, almost smiled as she peered into the dark abyss.

"Do you remember it?" she asked Evan.

"Only a little."

"Ohhh," she moaned. "I have longed for this day, sustained only by the faith that I would bring you back to finish what we started."

On the brink of fulfillment, Evan's bloodshot eye sparkled with pride. He realized that, with his mother's assistance, he had overcome all obstacles, centralized his power, and soon would lead the world's struggling masses. Yet, for herself, Faridah only desired to lead her son.

Always cautious, Evan whispered in her ear, "Not so loud. The soldiers ..."

Faridah waved him off with, "They don't matter anymore." Then she shouted at one of the vehicles, "Cyst! Let's go!"[6]

†††

INSIDE THE CAVE OF SECRETS, Faridah descended down the rope ladder, last. After she slid off the altar and brushed the dust from her long, slender pants legs, she scanned the cave and inhaled deeply. In the stale air she could still detect a welcome hint of incense that had lingered all these years, like influenza in a doctor's office, patiently waiting for its next host.

Then, she took charge. "Evan, let's get this place lit up."

Barely assisted by the light that beamed down through the oculus above the altar, her son shuffled across the dirt floor – past a slithering, poisonous viper – and into the shadows. There he groped along the jagged cave walls, occasionally back-handing black-widow spider webs, until he felt one of the tarps that had blanketed a precious secret since the last time they visited this cave, 28 years ago.

"Uncover it, this time," Faridah instructed.

Evan nodded and then threw back the tarp, revealing a large box that, even in this dim light, sparkled with golden reflections.

Then, as Evan felt along the dirt floor, his hand brushed against an old two-way radio, some large candles, and a box of matches.

When the third match finally ignited, he began lighting the candles that were scattered around the cave and on the stone altar.

For Faridah, the golden flames signaled the beginning of their long-awaited ascent to supreme worldly power. She and her son had been delayed and denied for 28 years. She wanted to soak up every sensation and, in the shadowed silence, found herself admiring the flames, yearning to be one with them.

In the flickering glow, Huntington Cyst also seemed trans-fixed by the flames as he stared without expression.

To the masses, Huntington Cyst had become known as a walking miracle, a cause for celebration. Four years ago, his scientific breakthrough had been revealed. After almost a month of cryogenic preservation, Evan Thas and a team of experts from XCyst Industries had raised Dr. Cyst from the dead. Then, in the press conference heard around the world, Thas boasted that he had even replaced Cyst's severed feet, just so that there could be no doubt that he, in fact, had ex-ceeded the miracles of Jesus of Nazareth.[7]

Publications around the globe found the story irresistible and trumpeted the new age of scientific enlightenment that would be led by Dr. Evan Thas, an extraordinary, but eccen-tric, young genius.

Throughout his career, Dr. Cyst had proclaimed that sci-entific advances, someday, would usher in the glorious age of the immortal man. It had been his vision, supported by the genius of Evan Thas, that had made his amazing return to life possible. This scientific triumph had captured the world's imagination and almost everyone eagerly awaited hearing about other breakthroughs that would be revealed from XCyst Industries' biotechnology facilities at Eden Village on the is-land of Nauru.

But Huntington Cyst had changed. The once domineering and flamboyant adrenaline-junkie had been reduced to a faded memory. His genius and daring creativity now seemed to be extinguished. His eyes were no longer bright blue, radiating with energy and imagination. They were weary, fearful and dimmed by post-traumatic stress and drugs.

While the world applauded Dr. Cyst, each passing day of his new life appeared to weigh him down with a deepening sense of foreboding. It seemed his vision of immortality had devolved into an endless, personal hell.

"Now, you know what to do." Faridah spoke with the confidence that their soldiers would prevent interruption. "We will finish the ritual, this time."

The three of them took the positions that they had occupied 28 years earlier. Cyst shuffled behind the altar, Faridah stood in front, and Evan laid on top of the altar's blood-stained pentagram. As the oculus light shone down on him, Cyst read slowly from a sheet of paper.

"It was prophesied: In the twentieth century, by the power of Satan, from a Hebrew nun…"[8]

"No, you idiot," Faridah interrupted. "We don't have time for that. Pick up where you left off."

Cyst skimmed down to the litany of evils and then continued his recitals while Faridah soaked in the memories of their first attempt. Back then, they had been joined by three other participants. Evan's father, B. Abu Ladin,[9] was now dead, after planning and executing a string of terrorist attacks across 20 countries. Lindley, Dr. Cyst's former body guard, had been no less deadly but much more discrete than Ladin. He, too, had died violently when he attempted to kill Evan. Finally, the only living holdout not in attendance was Cyst's early business partner, Henri Blanc.[10] Faridah had once admired Blanc's brilliance, his charm, and his grace under pressure. She had found him very alluring. But he had fallen into religion, in the worst way, and that unforgiveable intellectual failing had caused his professional breakup with Cyst. Now, the thought of Blanc – consumed with self-righteous piety – disgusted Faridah.

Huntington Cyst, hesitatingly, continued reading while extending his hands over Evan. His tone, however, was hollow. "Father of Darkness shine down upon your servant. Let the sins of our ancestors stoke the flames of your servant's passions. Lead him to destroy all that you oppose. God of this world, we reclaim for him all land and property that has been offered to the Enemy. In your name, we reclaim for him all principalities and powers over the masses. Under your authority, we reclaim for him every human life."

Laying there, as he once had done, so many years ago, Evan turned his head to seek reassurance in his mother's exotic, cat-like eyes.

"We call upon," Cyst continued, "every curse, hex, spell, snare, trap, lie, obstacle, deception or diversion to assist him. We call upon every astrologer, channeler, charter, clairvoyant, crystal healer, fortune teller, medium, reader, psychic, witch, witchdoctor and spirit guide to assist him. We call upon every spirit of anger, arrogance, bitterness, brutality, confusion, cruelty, deception, envy, fear, hatred, insecurity, jealousy, pride resentment and terror to assist him."

Thas shifted to his side on the cold, hard altar. "Huntie, can you get through this faster?"

Cyst continued without change. "Make him an instrument of your terror. Where there is love, let him sow hate. Where there is pardon, injury. Where there is faith, doubt. Where there is hope, despair. Where there is light, darkness. Where there is joy, sadness. Father of Darkness, shine down upon your chosen one, so that he shall elevate each of us to greatness in your kingdom, both in this life and the next. Possess your chosen one, perfectly and permanently, so that he and we shall rule with you. Impose all of mankind's iniquity upon this generation and reward your servants, now and forever."[11]

Together, the three of them said, "Amen" and waited for a moment.

Then ... nothing happened.

Thas and Cyst frowned at each other, unable to determine what had gone wrong. Cyst kept his hands extended over Evan's body as Faridah moved closer, nodding at the young man.

"What?" Evan asked.

She nodded again, with an expression that he had not seen from her before. He imagined that she might be regretful, but that would be a first.

Then she spoke. "You have to..."

"You didn't tell me that."

"There is no other way," she responded, revealing the long-kept secret that her inner voices had instructed.

She slipped something out of her sleeve and handed it to Evan.

Dr. Cyst started to pull back his hands.

"Cyst, stay!" she growled.

Everyone now realized that the ritual could not be completed without one more perversion of the sacred. The sacrifice would not be symbolic, from the one laying on the altar. It would be real, from the one standing behind it.

Huntington obediently extended his arms, again.

Evan held the knife loosely. He was embarrassed that he had not anticipated that a blood sacrifice would be required. After all, he had seen blood stains on the altar's pentagram.

As the flames flickered across their faces, Evan apologized to Cyst. "I'm sorry, Huntie. It's nothing personal."

Evan studied the man's lost look as the reflected flames wavered in his vacant blue eyes. *He doesn't seem to care. Maybe, this is what Huntie wants.* Still, Evan's crippled right hand did not tighten its grip.

Thas knew that he never would have accumulated such

wealth, fame and power without his adoptive father's generosity and deference. Huntington Cyst had been the "Prophet of Technology," preparing the way for Evan Thas and everything Evan had, he owed to his mentor. But the certainty of Evan's appreciation became clouded as he began to remember his early years with Cyst and how the man had ripped away whatever innocence that had existed within the boy. The more he thought about it, the more Evan despised how Huntie had abused him.

"Do it," Faridah urged.

Evan turned to examine her wide-eyed intensity. Then he remembered Cyst's warning: "Once I am gone, she will attempt to find and control you. Do not trust her."

Indeed, she had managed to find Evan, after Cyst's death and revival had been reported by international media outlets. But Evan knew that it was he, not she, who was – and would remain – in control.

Unexpectedly, the three of them heard, from above, men shouting angrily at each other. They looked up to the oculus … and then heard a shot.

Suddenly, like firecrackers on New Year's Eve, a deafening hail of rapid-fire gunshots – dozens, then hundreds – echoed from outside the cave.

"Do it!" Faridah screamed. "Do it now, dammit! Conjure the demons!"

Evan froze, still mesmerized by the bright oculus and the unseen violence above. Then he felt her hands around his. Evan did not fight her, but neither did he want this. She groaned the growl of a ravenous predator, shoved with all her might and, together, they plunged the dagger into Huntington Cyst's heart.

Evan focused on Cyst's weary blue eyes, as life left them.

He released his hold on the knife and his adoptive father collapsed on the dirt floor.

Taking a moment to absorb what he had done, Evan then inhaled deeply and, as he exhaled, whispered, "It is finished."

Faridah began babbling with delight, but he was too numb to notice anything until, suddenly, he saw a spectacular burst of light and heard a jarring, thunderous roar. Then the oculus darkened, the candle flames extinguished and – unlike any event in human history – the light of the world vanished.

After thousands of years, God's warnings and merciful patience ended.

The prophesied Three Days of Darkness began.[12]

Thirteen
Months Earlier

I tell you the truth,
some who are standing here will not taste death
before they see the Son of Man coming in His Kingdom.
Matthew 16:28

Chapter 2
Tarbuwth Correctional Facility
June 12

Alarms pierced through the warm afternoon air as cantilever gates grinded to a close and electronic devices automatically locked every vulnerable gate and door. With shotguns in hand, guards flowed out of the building and sprinted across the grounds while patrol cars sped to the prison, with sirens blaring. Tension and even a bit of fear gripped every officer because each knew that this was not a drill. For the first time in its history, TCF was entering into extreme lockdown.

Inside, however, a completely different mood was evident. Some prisoners jumped playfully on their bunks, screaming and cheering. Others loudly clattered their steel mugs along cell bars to celebrate. Word had quickly spread: John Eben Malek[13] had escaped in broad daylight, just hours before his planned execution.

Among the inmates, the most jubilant were John's small band of followers. Here, they had found their time together surprisingly transformative. Today, however, would offer them more surprises.

One by one, as they cheered and screamed, select prisoners discovered that their cell doors had become unlocked. As the eight inmates wandered into the hall, no one seemed to observe them. But, there, near the exit gates, they could not help but notice the glorious illumination of a beautiful, veiled woman. She was clothed in purest white, but with a scarlet sash. She motioned for them to come with her. They each silently considered the opportunity that she offered and, because of the warm, loving peace that she seemed to radiate, they followed.

As she led the eight inmates, a sequence of jail doors unlocked and opened before her. Then, when they eventually exited the front door of the prison, they saw Officer D.J. Jefferson on his knees in the empty parking lot. The atmosphere, outside, seemed electrified by sirens, alarms and scurrying officers. But none of them noticed the escaping prisoners.

Jefferson also seemed oblivious as the inmates walked past, carefully observing his odd behavior. To them, it appeared that the guard was in the midst of a breakdown of some kind. He was laughing so hard that tears streamed down his cheeks. He kept shouting, "Praise God! Halleluya Lord! Thank you God! Thank you!" Then he would study the clouds more deeply and start screaming, again, "Praise God! Praise Almighty God!"

The prisoners did not realize that he was single-mindedly focused on a vision of the glorious return of Jesus Christ.

Following the lovely lady, the men watched as motorized perimeter gates rumbled open as they approached. Then, outside the fence, they were joined by three more amazed friends of John: Father Alonzo, Pedro Lopez and Ricky Zipp.

To each of them, as he followed the mystical beauty, those moments seemed like a dream, contradicting all rules of time and space. However, the love and peace that the lady radiated felt not only real, but unforgettable.

When the eleven men reached the Port of New York, they

encountered no delays as she led them through a gate for employees. Then, in the shadows of a large cargo ship, they saw Qurban, looking more alive and happy than they had ever seen him before.

Soon, the twelve men were boarding a cargo ship where John was thrilled to greet them, on deck. He did not see the mysterious lady, at first. But his heart raced with surprise when he heard a familiar sound. It was the joyful, innocent giggle that could only come from Sister Clarita. John gasped and abruptly turned. Then he nearly melted with joy when he watched her raise her hands to cover her veiled mouth, as if she had been caught doing something naughty.

He missed Sister Clarita so much, and her death had been a mystery that he still did not understand. However, he was comforted with knowing that once God creates life, there are no endings, only new beginnings.

As John savored the moment with her, a memory flooded through his mind. It was Sister Clarita's baffling comment, the last time he prayed with her on the day before her death. Trying to understand one of the most enigmatic people he had ever met, John had whispered, "Sister, what saint do you most identify with?"

Completely serious, she answered, "Samson."

John embarrassed himself when he coughed out a laugh in the quiet chapel. To John, she could hardly have picked a saint *less* like herself. Yes, Samson had been consecrated to God from birth to death. But he had killed thousands and had foolishly followed beautiful women down the path to destruction. Even physically they were polar opposites. Samson was one of the strongest men of his time, while the diminutive sister was frail and weak from continuous fasting.

"Samson?" he asked, incredulously.

She simply responded, "Someday, you will understand."

Now, as he gazed at the beauty of the illuminated apparition on the deck of the ship, John finally understood: Just as Samson's self-sacrifice had begun the deliverance of Israel from the power of the Philistines, Sister Clarita's self-sacrifice had begun the deliverance of all mankind from the power of Satan.[14]

John could not believe that God had requested such a violent end to her beautiful life. But he could imagine her becoming overzealous, and storming a path to heaven. The ancient Apostle knew well that even living saints have flaws. He also believed that if there was one imperfection in Sister Clarita's character it was impatience to be with God. To John, her action was repugnant, but almost understandable. In fact, no one could grasp, more than John, the dark night that can descend into the soul of a saint[15] when heavenly reward is delayed.

He now knew why she identified with Samson. He also appreciated why she so often quoted Saint Therese of Lisieux, saying, "I will not be a saint by halves. I am not afraid of suffering for God."[16] So, Sister Clarita exercised her free will, and may have done so foolishly. But God judges the heart, and hers was among the purest.[17]

Regardless, it had become clear to John that his incarceration had prevented him from stopping the events that were leading to God's final justice. With the time that was left, John and his little band of misfit men necessarily would become the Apostles of the End Times, working to convert as many souls as possible.[18]

After all that Sister Clarita had sacrificed for God and mankind, John understood that no person was better suited to send them off on their ministries. She had become their patron saint of global evangelization.

Now, even amidst the dark and dingy surroundings of this India-bound cargo ship, John felt a profound sense of peace descend into his heart. He relished this moment to commune, once again, with such a beautiful saint. But before a tear could roll down his cheek, she was gone.

Chapter 3
Vero Beach, Florida
September 21

At last, some of the guilt was lifting. The young mother grinned as she scrambled eggs and listened to the bacon sizzle. But the sound effects were not quite complete. So, she scurried across the living room and slid the glass doors open, welcoming the rumble of the unseen surf and the light of the dawning sun.

Normally, she would preach, "We eat healthy around here." But today, she had even volunteered a soft drink before her boy started begging for it. This was a special time – a weekend vacation. And even though they would share just three days on the lovely white sands of Vero Beach, she had planned more than relaxation. She knew that it was time to re-establish her relationship with her son and that this would be her chance. His eighth year had been their most difficult together.

She had recently separated from her husband and moved out of their Miami home. He had become increasingly angry as the economy had refused to recover. When his unemployment compensation finally ran out, he felt hopeless and useless. She wanted to help. She yearned to comfort him. She tried to accept his verbal abuse, but when he started to take it out on the boy, she knew that the marriage was over. It was a difficult decision, but her income alone would be enough to sustain them. These days, as rioting had broken out around Miami, emergency room nurses were in high demand. Even violence begets beneficiaries.

Their son, however, never understood why she had taken him away and he blamed her for the separation. He loved his dad, even though, lately, his mother felt only contempt for the man. But she thanked God that their son had been the one thing that they had gotten right, together.

Now, looking down on her little blond boy slurping the last drops of his soda, she couldn't help but chuckle. From the top of his sandy blond hair, to his ever-present glasses, to his little pot belly and his oversized swim trunks, she wanted to hug every inch of him. What a relief it was to see him smiling and full of energy again. She was determined to make sure that, together, they would not only survive but thrive.

She planned that this weekend would be a nature adventure. She wanted to get her son out of the big city, for a change, and uncover the natural beauty of Florida's Treasure Coast. Here on Orchid Island, snuggled between the Atlantic and the Indian River Lagoon, she would open his eyes to one of the most bio-diverse areas in America.[19]

Her optimism, however, faded as she reached for the remote and clicked on a television in the living room. XBC News was airing an Evan Thas press conference, live, from Germany. After all that Dr. Huntington Cyst famously had done to build XCyst Industries, she couldn't believe that Thas was now in charge.

That little twerp!

She had learned to despise Evan after he denied responsibility for the company's stock collapse. Her modest but precious savings had been lost in that "flash crash." Now, it seemed that her loss had become his spectacular gain and, with the help of XBC News, he had been everywhere, bragging on each new accomplishment.

To her, XBC journalists had lost their way. They were covering all the fluff but missing too many important stories. So, she flipped to another news channel.

The boy begged, "Mom, not more news." He tossed his soda can in the trash. "I wanna go to the beach."

"Honey, it's barely light out there. Let's eat breakfast first."

His smile faded. "Ohhh, mom. How long's that gonna take?"

"Won't be long, honey," she said, flatly. "It's almost ready."

She strained to hear the television commentary on how urban centers from America to Europe were evolving away from traditions of faith and family, and into anarchy. The video showed numerous youth riots in the major cities of Europe led by young workers who were protesting the burdens of continued support for the generous entitlements that their retiring parents had been promised.[20] She shook her head, realizing that this was just one more log for the economic bonfire that had started with the recent Saudi sabotage of their own oil reserves.[21] Ever since that jolt to the global economy, it seemed the law of the jungle was starting to take hold.

"Mom," the boy whined. "How long?"

Though she should have realized that even one minute would be considered too long, she suggested, "Maybe ten minutes."

"Mom!" he shouted with alarm. "That's like forever!"

What could she do? There was only one way out of this predicament: surrender.

"Ohhh," she groaned as she turned the heat down on the

stove. "If I treat you like a big boy will you act like one?"

He nodded wildly.

"You're in third grade now. If I tell you to stay on the beach and not go into the water, will you do that?"

He nodded some more.

"Okay, but...." The child bolted for the door. "Hey wait a minute, young man!"

He marched back to her as she reached for the sunscreen lotion on the counter. "You're not leaving without this."

The mother smeared white lotion all over the boy's face and body while he squirmed and smirked his disapproval. When she finished, he sprinted out the door. She shouted, "You yell if you need me."

She removed the bacon from the greasy pan and reflected on her increasingly independent boy. Though she could not afford renting an oceanfront condo, this house was only one lot from the beach. She was comfortable that here, along the quiet Treasure Coast of Florida, her son could have the freedom that she would never dream of permitting on Miami beaches.

She turned the stove fan off when an odd story caught her ear.

TELEVISION REPORTER: "...after three months, the dramatic prison break in broad daylight still remains a mystery. None of the fugitives from New York's maximum security Tarbuwth Correctional Facility has been apprehended. Prison authorities continue to refuse public comment, apparently too embarrassed to discuss how so many prisoners could have ..."

Then she thought she heard something and quickly reached for the remote and muted the TV.

She heard it again.

Instinctively, the mother dropped the pan toward the sink, but it tumbled out, splattering hot oil on the cabinets, the floor and even her leg. Still, she was too focused to respond to the scalding.

Her son was screaming.

The woman sprinted out the sliding glass door, through the vacant lot and over a sand dune before she spotted her boy. He was standing on the beach, alone and crying. "I didn't do it, mom. I didn't do it."

She sighed with relief, comforted that he was safe.

But then her eyes turned toward the rising sun, where the ocean reflected a surreal red and silver sheen on the surface. As she scanned up and down the coast, and out to the horizon, the woman spotted the dolphins that had amused her, the lazy manatees that she loved so much, and millions upon millions of fish.

All of them were floating, dead.

I am sending you out like sheep among wolves.
Therefore be as shrewd as snakes
and as innocent as doves.
Matthew 10:16

Chapter 4
Kumbakonam, India
October 21

Father Antony ended the Mass, leading the congregation
in the most stirring choral version of *The Lord's Prayer*
that the Beloved Apostle had ever heard. As the final
verse rose to a crescendo, resonating through the long, narrow church, John thought, *Surely, heaven must contain such
angelic voices.*

Here, the sublime pleasure of hearing, however, was confronted by a disturbing visual reality. This church was filled
with the refuse of India, and almost all of them were children.
The blind, deaf, disabled and deformed – those who, other-
wise, would be left helpless and hopeless in one of the most
impoverished communities on the planet – were welcomed
at St. Mary's School and Orphanage, where they were fed,
housed, educated and loved.[22]

The orphanage was a Catholic outpost, in a dusty Hindu
land, nestled along the peaceful but polluted Cauvery River,
amidst the dominating Chola temples. In fact, within just a
few miles, dozens of temples could be found, each one dedicated to a different Hindu god and attended by worshippers of
the only faith they knew. Still, the Catholic minority here in
southern India was more numerous than in any other region of

the country and they even had their own local miracle generating Spiritual sustenance.

Not far away, in Kottayam Kerala, a statue of the Virgin Mary had been weeping tears of blood. The image, known as Rosa Mystica, unsettled many viewers, but it followed the pattern of other pictures and statues of Rosa Mystica, around the world in recent decades. Many had been either weeping fragrant oil, oozing a blood-like substance, or even exuding pearls.[23] Over 80 of these events have been witnessed and reported to the Vatican.[24] Witnessing the mystery, most viewers had been moved to wonder: *Why is she crying?*

Some crass skeptics had responded with vile ridicule, claiming that they were far too smart to fall for such simplistic trickery.[25] Still, no one mocked the miracle here, where some were blind, but only physically.

John watched as an orderly procession of the orphans formed to exit the church, down the center aisle, two by two. Some had limbs that were twisted beyond recognition. Others, hunched over and walked on all fours. Still others, had been born without four limbs. It appeared to John, however, that wherever one child was weak, another was there to help. The blind were assisted by the sighted, the lame by the strong, the mentally handicapped by the nurturers.

Two by two, John thought.

Then he reflected on his men, and that they also would need to rely on each other just as the original Apostles once had. John remembered how, during their recent ocean passage to India, he had tried to divert the disciples' attention from the privations that they had been enduring. One day, he even encouraged a competition in which they would debate who had been the worst sinner and, now, was least deserving of the graces that God had made available to them.

Worthington, the gigantic man with flame tattoos across his forehead, still offered an intimidating presence. But he had become an obedient puppy dog ever since John had delivered him from his demons. Now he was embarrassed to admit how he had often scoured the obituaries in the local newspapers. Then he would burglarize the deceased person's house during the funeral.

Ricky Zipp revealed that, for the first time in his adult life, he was remembering that falling asleep is not the same as passing out, and waking up is not the same as coming to. He admitted that he had been such a distracted father that his son had taken his own life.

Qurban told of his terrorist past: his education in a Pakistani *Madrasah Islamiyyah* and subsequent training in a Yemeni terrorist camp. He described his past obsessive hatred for America and Israel and how he had planned and almost executed a suicide bombing of a Metro railcar during Washington rush hour.[26] But his life had forever changed, he claimed, when God blessed him with a glimpse of heaven during his brush with death in prison.[27] Now, he understood the joy of complete love and forgiveness.

Soon, others were confessing their sinful pasts, but Jin's story brought them all to a thoughtful silence.

"I have harmed more lives than all of you put together," Jin claimed, without bragging. It was his time for a full confession. "I told you that I am responsible for thousands of abortions. You know about how I required cash payment and used garbage disposals to avoid reporting the income. You know how I trained my staff to stampede desperate young women into quick decisions, without offering alternatives, and how we even sided with abusive boyfriends to prevent last-minute cancellations. But it was even worse than that."

Some of the disciples offered questioning expressions.

"Yeah, I set them up for a fall. I liked to speak at "sex education" classes in high schools. I told them that modern contraception is virtually fool-proof, leading them to believe that the age of sex-without-consequences had arrived. But I wasn't educating, I was deceiving. I never told them that – even when administered exactly as prescribed – which was rare for these young girls – a contraceptive with a 1% failure rate per month, produces a 70% likelihood of an unplanned pregnancy over a 10 year period.[28] I encouraged teenagers to play Russian Roulette and lied about how many bullets were in the revolver."

"Why'd you do that?" Pedro asked.

Jin shrugged, "It was good for business." Then he thought for a moment and added, "They were more like customers than patients, to me. I was a good marketer and, as long as I continued developing my future customer base, I knew my gravy train would never get sidetracked." Jin snorted at his self-deception. "I guess I miscalculated."

Father Alzonzo said, "It's a real tragedy, Jin. Many of those lost would have benefited mankind."[29] After a moment of reflection, John changed the subject. "You know, I have always managed to travel discretely. But many of you will need to change your ways. We're all wanted men, now. You cannot afford to slip up."

Suddenly, John realized he was no longer the teacher. Each of the accomplished criminals had often contemplated how to live on the run. They were invigorated to now apply their knowledge.

California Rodney took the lead. "Just remember, no more plastic. Credit cards are out. No more bank accounts, either."

"Forget about any kind of registration," Booker added. "I

mean, you don't even wanna get a fishin' license."

"Or a driver's license, or a car registration, or a voter's registration, or a loan," Ozzy added, "or – heaven forbid – a marriage license!"

Some of them chuckled.

Henry said, "Mon, you gotta stay away from that Internet … and forget about cell phones!"

The suggestion reminded John about the hundreds of scrolls he had secretly sent to the Vatican over the centuries. He had always used the most primitive, but safe, delivery system – personal courier.

Not to be outdone, Ricky suggested a ploy he had read about. He said, "if you go to a graveyard and find the grave of someone who was born around the time of your birth, and died as a child, you can request a birth certificate using the dead person's information. Chances are, the boy never would have received important identification documents." So, he claimed, "It's easy to get a social security number, driver's license, passport, or whatever."[30]

John discouraged that plan, first, because he meticulously avoided lying and, second, because he knew that most of Ricky's schemes were half-baked.

"Don't overcomplicate it. Just pray with faith and things will work out for you." John reminded them, "You are leaving your possessions, your loved ones, your lives behind. Remember: Everyone who has left houses or brothers or sisters or father or mother or children or fields for Jesus Christ's sake will receive a hundred times as much and will inherit eternal life.[31] You can't contact your loved ones until I say it is alright. I am sorry to say that they can't be trusted right now."

"Three can keep a secret," big Worthington grumbled, "only if two of 'em are dead."

The group was stunned into silence.

"Come on!" Worthington smiled broadly. "I'm just kiddin'!"

IN THE EMPTY INDIAN CHURCH, John continued kneeling and praying. Then he felt a hand on his shoulder.

John turned toward a frail, dark-skinned Indian who had removed his Mass vestments and was now dressed in black. "Oh, Father Antony, how are you?"

The blind priest responded, "I am blessed. John, please join me for dinner. I don't want you to waste away, here."

John smiled at Father Antony, realizing that he was very perceptive – even without his eyes. In fact, John had lost a lot of weight. But it was only partially from deliberate sacrifice. Most of the loss was because the food here was not appealing to him. John never complained, however, because he did not want to offend Father Antony. After all, he ran the place.

John responded happily, "It would be my honor, Father."

As they walked, arm in arm, with Father Antony's tapping cane leading the way, John could see concern in the priest's face and suspected that there was a serious reason for this escort. Indeed, Father Antony seemed to have a hard time getting to the point.

"How long have you been here, John?"

"Tuesday, it will be three months."

"Very nice ... very nice ...."

"Are you finding your stay here Spiritually rewarding?"

"Yes, Father. I must admit that, at first, I had no idea why I was here. But now I know. I thank you for your hospitality."

"It seems we never know why until afterwards.... But every day, every place, every person is an opportunity.... Very nice ... very nice ...."

Continually tapping his cane, the priest led the pace. But it seemed to John that he was moving deliberately slowly. Then, after a moment of uncomfortable silence, John asked, "Father, is something bothering you?"

"Oh, I have learned not to let anything bother me. I am just a bit confused."

Towering over the blind Indian as they walked down the hall, John patted his hand and said, "Go ahead, Father. Ask me whatever you want."

"Thank you, my friend." He thought for a moment and then added, "Please forgive me if my observations do not seem polite, but I have come to believe that you are not who you say you are."

John reluctantly answered. "That's right, Father, I am not."

Father Antony sighed and said, "Then there is no point in asking. If you want me to know, the question is not necessary. If you do not, your answer would remain a lie."

"Forgive me, Father. I have not lied to you, but only failed to reveal the entire truth."

John could see disappointment in the blind man's face. However, he knew that his story would have been too much for the good priest to comprehend. So, he simply said, "We can leave in a couple of days."

"No," the priest responded flatly. "You must leave tomorrow morning."

John nodded with regret. "Father, I am sorry I violated your hospitality and offended you."

The priest sighed again. "No, John, you have done neither." Then he asked something that seemed completely off the subject. "Do you know the Prefect at the Secret Archives of the Vatican?"

John asked cautiously, "Why do you ask?"

"I received a call from him today ... from a Monsignor Bolaka." The priest stopped tapping and walking. "Imagine that: we can't even get our bishop to notice us, but someone at the Vatican tracked me down. I didn't believe it until I checked him out."

"What did you find?"

"It appears that when someone speaks to Monsignor Bolaka, he might as well be speaking to the pope."

The priest started tapping again and they continued down the hall before John asked, "So, what does this have to do with me?"

"I was told to deliver a message to you.... He said it was urgent."

"Yes?" John asked, warily.

"He wants you to leave tomorrow morning."

"Is that it?"

"Then he said, 'Your time has arrived.'"

THREE HOURS EARLIER, the XCyst communications satellite known as "White Appaloosa" whizzed through tiered algorithms for 1.02 seconds – an extraordinarily long time – as it evaluated a telephone call. The orbiter triggered its first layer of analysis when a biometric voiceprint detected a vocal match for tone, diction and pitch. Clearly, a "whale" was speaking on one end of the line. Then a Cyst-Blanc supercomputer traced the caller's telephone number to a disposable cell phone that had transmitted just one call from a suburb of Rome. That information prompted further scrutiny. Finally, an analysis of each spoken word rocketed the call's priority to the top of the list when the name "Malek" was detected.

To be forgotten.
It is this, I think, which gives Him the most pain.
St. Therese of Lisieux

Chapter 5
White House, East Wing
October 21

President Angela Concepcion reached her hand across the antique mahogany table that Thomas Jefferson had once owned. Then she opened her palm under the bright glow of a tortoise shell lamp. The wide-eyed Haitian immigrant, known as Momma Laudie, adjusted her ample girth in her small accent chair, took the hand and examined the palm.

"Ahhh, yes," the ebony skinned seer sighed with an air of satisfaction. "I can see that you are a very, very special person."

Angela frowned at the obvious.

"Extraordinary, in fact."

"And?" Angela prodded with disappointment.

"Ohhh, let's not rush, my dear," Momma Laudie said with a grandmotherly smile. She ran her forefinger across each major wrinkle. She studied the length and proportions of each finger. Then the woman pressed the president's hand into a fist, opened it again and studied the creases.

Angela was starting to regret this little diversion. She had read about Momma Laudie in one of the tabloids and had wanted to learn more about this rising celebrity. So, she requested that the Secret Service sneak her in, disguised as a maid.

"So, what else? What about Israel, or Russia, or Iran?"

The woman swooned, as if entering a trance. Her large brown eyes rolled back, exposing only a disturbing white emptiness between her lashes. Then she started to tremble and shake.

It was a bit too much show, for Angela. After a trying day in the Oval Office, she was unimpressed and could hardly fight off impatience. She studied the woman's bright, floral Haitian head wrap and glanced around at the bookcases that surrounded her in the reading room of the president's residential quarters.

"Yes!" Momma Laudie shouted as she came out of her trance. "I see now that…"

Suddenly, Fred Whitehead burst in. "Oh, sorry. Don't mind me." Fred wore just a T-shirt and plaid boxer shorts, but he was not embarrassed. "I'm looking for my spy novel."

Angela whispered to the woman, "Just ignore my fiancé." Then she chided Whitehead, "Dear, we'd like some privacy."

He shuffled some books on the shelf, pulled one out and said, "Okay. No problem. I found it." Then he left as quickly as he had arrived.

"Now," Angela asked, "what were you about to say?"

Momma Laudie frowned at the interruption. She stated flatly, "I see an expanding family."

"Oh, please. Everybody knows that Fred and I are getting married. Find something else."

The seer's brow tightened, then she closed her eyes.

"Yes?" Angela urged.

"I see two very divergent paths."

"Okay."

"You must choose one soon."

"So, what? I have to make tough decisions every day."

"One path leads to life … the other to death."

Angela stared at the woman. "Are you sure about that?"

The Haitian opened her eyes. "Absolutely."

"That's not much help. Give me more details."

A moment later, she answered, "The man who was just here will play a role in your decision."

"A positive role?"

Momma Laudie drew a breath and exhaled slowly. "No."

"So," Angela strategized, "I should wait until the dilemma presents itself and then do the opposite of what Fred advises?"

"I cannot say."

"Come on! You're telling me that my life is on the line, here."

"I see four people advising you. Only one is trustworthy. Only one leads you to life."

"Which one?" Angela barked.

Momma Laudie did not like her angry tone. "The one you least expect."

"Okay, but who is it?"

"I cannot say."

Angela jerked her hand away and stood up. "Well, that's really great! As if I don't already have enough issues to deal with. You're saying I've got a life or death decision to make, I can trust just one adviser, and that's it?! I need more details!"

The woman frowned at the shouting. Then, after a moment of reflection, she offered, "I can only tell you…"

"Yes?" Angela urged, "Who is he?"

The Haitian asked, "He? I did not say 'he.'"

Angela drew a blank. She could not think of any woman in her administration that she would trust for life or death advice.

Then the seer added, "You have not yet met this person. She is favored by God."

That was the final straw. Angela's patience with this guessing game had reached its limit. "Well then you obviously don't know what you're talking about. I wouldn't trust life or death advice from someone I hardly know." Then she turned to the hall door and shouted, "Anderson!"

An agent opened the door and stepped in.

"Escort this phoney out."

Momma Laudie did not rise. "I am not a fraud."

"Just leave. I've heard enough."

The woman did not budge.

"Well," Angela prodded, "leave! You're certainly a fake."

"You are certain of nothing," the big woman growled, "I curse your certainty!"

"Get her out of here, Anderson."

The president now saw a different side to the woman. Her facial muscles tightened hideously and her eyes darkened with resentment and hatred.

As the agent approached, the Haitian continued, "I call upon the demons of confusion to steal away whatever certainty you think you have."

"Get out!"

The agent signaled Momma Laudie to stand and she complied, but her eyes still projected a haunting glare.

"I saw more than I told you," the black woman said as the agent led her across the room. "You are surrounded by evil. Forces more powerful than you can imagine. They will destroy most of humanity … because you choose to let them lead you."

"You're a fraud."

When they reached the door the woman planted her feet and would go no farther. She seethed, "You are too stubborn to listen. I could see it in your palm. But I know how to get your attention." Then, suddenly serene, the palm reader said, "My words and my curse are as true … as life is short."

"Are you threatening me?!" Angela screamed. "Get her out of here, Anderson!"

The Haitian turned, calmly, and followed him out the door.

THE NEXT MORNING, the presidential motorcade revved down Pennsylvania Avenue, headed to a conference at the Four Seasons Hotel in Georgetown. Along the way, various pockets of tourists, protesters and supporters had accumulated after hearing that the president would be driven along this route.

Suddenly, Angela was thrown forward as the driver slammed on the brakes. Angela heard a loud thud against the car and, as she dove to the floorboard, felt the car bouncing over rough terrain. Then the armored vehicle slowed to a stop.

Angela's heart raced. *Why aren't they getting me out of here?*

After a few seconds, she heard the limousine's window between her and the driver open.

His voice was panicked. "I'm sorry, Madame President. You're safe. It was unavoidable."

She crawled into the seat. "What happened?"

"Somebody jumped in front of the limo."

Angela raised her head to look out the back window. There, in the middle of the road, was the body of a heavy black woman with a bright floral head wrap.

... I want to do a lot,
but I cannot do it without you ...
Our Lady of Medjugorje
August 19, 1988

Chapter 6
St. Mary's School and Orphanage
Kumbakonam, India
October 21

A
ctivity in the rustic cafeteria quieted when a prayer
of thanks was offered by Father Antony. Then, within seconds, the room was filled with laughter, the
universal language of children.

As the kids proceeded through the dinner line, the priests,
John, and his twelve followers served them their portions. The
nuns, however, remained in line with the children to maintain
order. Then they ate with the kids, sitting on the dirt floor with
the metal plates in their laps.

Later, when the children had eaten and politely returned
their empty dishes to the kitchen, the nuns escorted them
across the grounds to the orphanage.

Now it was time for the priests to eat and, in fact, finally
relax a bit.

But before their food was plated, Father Antony repeatedly tapped a fork on his glass.

"I have some bad news," the priest began as attention
turned his way. "Our friends will be leaving tomorrow morning."

A number of groans were heard as John looked around
his table at each of the twelve disciples who had been led to

this orphanage. Still, the surprising change of plans seemed to invigorate John and the men noticed that he appeared to be in a good mood when he nodded that the news was true.

The blind priest, making the most of his farewell, launched into a lengthy homage to the men who had become such close friends in Christ.

John's mind, however, was not on those words. His optimism and anticipation was tempered by the realization that, after tomorrow, the disciples might never assemble together again. With their time together expiring, he reflected fondly on their arduous journey and their rigorous training.

For months, now, they had grown fond of the orphans and, just as much, the eccentric priests and nuns, here. The disciples had come to know and love each other like brothers. Together, they had matured Spiritually and had endured, under John's tutelage, a boot camp of training for their coming missions. John drilled them with constant instruction, realizing that the internal guidance he was receiving had never before been discerned so clearly from Blessed Mother.[32] Following her requests, he taught them how to pray constantly, from the heart.[33]

Perhaps, that was what had sustained them through their difficulties. Over the past few months, each of John's followers had experienced moments of doubt. Each had witnessed miracles, but everything that was happening to them seemed crazy, at times. Each had followed John on the hope that he could bring them closer to God, but the only thing that they truly understood about their mysterious leader was that he claimed to place himself in complete submission to his Lord and Savior, Jesus Christ.

Still, they had persevered, learning a monastic lifestyle that toughened their bodies for the coming sacrifices. Six days a week, from dawn until dusk, they had worked to improve the orphanage. They trenched and drained a nearby swamp, transforming it into a new garden for the cafeteria. They repaired the leaky roof of the children's sleeping quarters and painted many of the dreary buildings in bright new colors. They drilled for water and found a sparkling flow that ran much fresher than the current supply from the town. They modified the orphanage's waste disposal practices, improving the sanitation and health of the community. By emphasizing the practical arts, in addition to the Spiritual, John and the modern day Apostles had transformed this island of poverty into an oasis of peace and security.[34]

Then, each night, they returned to John's training sessions that prepared them for an endless variety of future challenges.

As Father Antony continued his tribute, John reflected on how much his followers had learned, here, as they witnessed the crushing realities of true poverty and hunger. He prayed that they now would realize how fortunate they had been. Regardless of their past circumstances, they had lived relatively sheltered, affluent lives in America – where even the poorest 5% are better off financially than two thirds of the global population.[35]

To them, India had presented a small but sobering sampling of the world, where almost a billion people go hungry every day; where 1.4 billion live on less than $1.25 a day; and where hunger kills a child every five seconds. Still, John taught them that "overpopulation" was not the problem. In fact, the world's entire population could fit in the state of Texas with no greater population density than what currently exists in the state of New Jersey."[36]

From learning to love the bent and battered refuse of India, John's men understood that every child of God has a purpose.

Even stacking disability upon poverty, these children radiated love and joy. So, the Apostles felt a sad revulsion when John explained to them that in wealthy America, 80% of disabled children are aborted before birth.[37]

They also realized now that the poverty of the world is not financial. It is Spiritual.

Finally, the latter-day Apostles had learned that Christ's Peace is accompanied by something more fulfilling and permanent than wealth or even happiness. In the midst of some of the most impoverished people on the planet, under circumstances that were demanding both physically and mentally, Jesus Christ had made them Joyful.

FATHER ANTONY CONCLUDED his long-winded announcement, "So, in honor of our last evening together, we will suspend our rules and allow our friends in Christ whatever they request."

John's amused glance scanned the felons at his table. "Are you sure about that, Father?"

The priest answered warily, "I think so…"

"Great!" John responded. "Where's your wine?"

John's men erupted with cheers.

AN HOUR LATER, the conversation was loud and lively. Ozzy the Aussie and Samir, the Indian pharmacist, were in the kitchen teaching the blind cooks the finer points of seasonings and sauces. Henry, the dreadlocked Jamaican, California Rodney, and Booker were moving from table to table, socializing like seasoned politicians. Their food was delightful and the jug of wine, that they had opened, never ran empty.[38]

"We need some entertainment," John announced. "Who can make us laugh?"

The rough men searched their memories, but every joke that came to mind was too crude or profane to say. That fact, alone, was a source of amusement for each of them. It also made them realize just how far they had progressed, Spiritually.

As the evening advanced with lively conversation, John savored the moments of this celebration that marked the beginning of their fateful, public ministries.

Perhaps, more than ever, Jesus Christ had comforted John in his prayers. He had also prepared him for the difficult days ahead, showing him that these men would walk in the footsteps of Christ's original disciples. John could never forget the heroic virtue, the tragedy and the triumph of the first Apostles.[39]

He wondered, *Are these men up to the task?*

Appreciating the good natured rowdiness of this strange group, the Indian hosts had no concept of their importance. But none of them complained, even when the boisterous festivities continued until the obscenely late hour of nine o'clock.

WHEN JOHN RETIRED to his cell, his joyful attitude was diminished by the foreknowledge of harsh realities to come. Time on earth was running out for Satan and his demons. So, John knew that their last attempt to prove mankind unworthy of God's love would require a crescendo of conflict.

John lamented the evils he had witnessed over his lengthy life. Through the centuries, he had been cast into the middle of the savage entertainments of the Roman emperors, the confiscations and persecutions of the Reformation, and the anti-Christian outrages of various revolutions from France to Russia to China. Sadly, he also had witnessed Catholics, on occasion, who responded, in kind. He watched, helplessly, as Crusades and Inquisitions lost their grounding in the Faith and returned evil for evil.

The nightmares turned John's stomach and he yearned for the peace of Christ's return. But the ancient Apostle realized that even worse malevolence would arrive soon because he knew that, thirty years ago, an even greater evil had spawned.

I have to attain immortality,
even if the whole German nation
perishes in the process.
Adolf Hitler

Chapter 7
Damascus, Syria
30 Years Earlier

Young Faridah Shabaan was homeless and friendless. She had betrayed her family, her faith and even herself. Shame, however, was not high on her list of priorities. Now, pregnant and needing support, she tried her last resort: returning to her parents in Damascus.

Faridah had hoped that her homecoming might repeat the parable of the Prodigal Son. But when she arrived at her parents' house, they refused to let her in. Then, before slamming the door in her face, her father cursed her existence.

She did not flinch. He was a fool, she thought, and she had always rebelled against his leadership. So, Faridah took some comfort in knowing that her curses would be more powerful than his.

From the earliest times she could remember, Faridah had listened to her inner voices and they taught her the value of blessings and curses.[40] They offered her a small taste of the power she sought and she developed a habit of following their spiritual guidance because they knew what she wanted and how to get it.

Still, as she walked away from the home, carrying her small suitcase down the street on which she grew up, Faridah feared that she had run out of options and, quickly, was running out of time. Doubts began haunting her.

Just nine months ago, she had been a Roman Catholic nun at St. Basil's Convent in Beirut, Lebanon[41] after following an unlikely path to her vocation. A few years before, she defiantly rejected the faith of her ancestors, a long line of Syrian Jews, by careening into Christianity. She became a seemingly fervent Catholic, investing her prayers and waiting for the payoff. But it never came, even after entering the convent.

Soon she began resisting the constraints of her Catholic vows. So, secretly, she sought radical change, again, and began to study *The Satanic Bible.* In those pages she found what would calm the turmoil of her rebellious spirit … or, so, it promised.

It seemed that Shabaan's life had been punctuated by alternating extremes, deliberately chosen.

Her beauty and intelligence had made her proud. In fact, it was her pride that led her to the convent.

Surely, she thought, Christ would particularly favor a bride as beautiful as herself.

But He did not.

Certainly, God would tangibly reward a nun as special as herself.

Wrong again.

Early on, she learned that she did not fit in at the convent. She was better than the others, and her lack of humility made her impatient to lead them. It was a vice that had festered in her soul for many years. Whenever she found resistance to her control, however, Faridah did not have the fortitude to gradually earn the respect of would-be followers. Instead, she defied resistors by lashing out, abandoning course, and striking a new trail in the opposite direction. But with each major turn in her life, it seemed she was moving down a path, ever deeper and darker.

Indeed, she already had reversed course when, one fateful night, an errant Israeli rocket struck her convent. It was just another deadly accident, the stepchild of Syria's never-ending conflict with the Jewish state. Faridah, also, could have died that night, if not for the quick thinking and hard work of John Malek, freeing her from the rubble.

He had arrived in time to save her life, but not her soul.

Just hours before, she had rejected all things holy and, most importantly, her vow of chastity. That night, she followed her inner voice to the safe-house of the world's most vicious terrorist, B. Abu Ladin.[42] Now, she was carrying a most important son.

He has to be the one, her inner voice told her.

Just as Jesus of Nazareth had descended from the tribe of Judah, the Antichrist would descend from Dan,[43] the tribe that her ancestors had claimed. He would be born twenty centuries after Jesus, as prophesied.[44] He would be of Syrian descent.[45] He would be born from an unwed mother,[46] a Hebrew nun, a false virgin.[47] Finally, Faridah was determined that he would carry the name of Evan Thas, as directed by the prophecies.[48]

The prophecies all seem to match.

As the sun disappeared behind buildings, the young Syrian was anxious to find a place to sleep for the night. So, as she wandered down a quiet street, she began checking parked vehicles to see if any were open. One car after another was locked and, with each one, she grew angrier. She was getting desperate.

Normally, she would have broken a window to get in or slit a tire, just out of spite. But her delicate condition on darkened streets necessitated her caution.

After a while, she found an open gray Hyundai, parked in front of an old house. She glanced around to make sure no one had spotted her and quickly slipped into the front passenger seat.

Shabaan was frustrated and worried about her full-term pregnancy but, more than anything, she was tired. So, she cranked the seat back and quickly dozed off.

AN HOUR LATER, an old man knocked on the window and demanded – in Arabic – "Get out! That's not your car!"

Faridah jolted up from her deep slumber and, in her panic, quickly locked the door. Her mind was spinning as she tried to regain her bearings.

He pounded on the window again while the woman next to him started shouting about calling the police.

It was night and the street was not lit. So, Faridah refused to open the door.

Suddenly, she felt a stabbing pain.

"Oh, no," she thought.

Faridah groaned, loudly, "Not now, dammit!"

She had no choice. So, she opened the door and stumbled out of the car. The Syrian couple backed away as Faridah bent over and clutched her midsection.

"What are you doing?" the man screamed. "Stop it! This is not your toilet!"

The old woman moved from behind her husband to see what had upset him so much. Then she realized. "Quiet, Sargon! Her water broke."

The man stepped back in shock.

"Here," the woman directed. "Take her inside. Her baby is coming now."

✝✝✝

THE OLD WOMAN finished wiping the boy clean and then offered him to his mother.

"No, you hold him," Faridah responded, resentfully. "He caused me too much pain."

Shabaan now doubted that this child would be special. He looked … ordinary. His birth was like any other.

As she watched the old woman caress the baby, Faridah frowned at his pasty white skin, certainly nothing like her own golden complexion. She was repulsed for having been deceived. Why would she want a baby? Unless he would be truly extraordinary.

"Look at all this red hair," the woman said, trying to boost his mother's morale.

Faridah began making plans. She would slip out in the middle of the night and leave the baby behind. Or, if the old couple made her take him, she would drop him in a trash bin, along the road.

"Amazing," the old woman said as she ran her index finger along his lips. "He already has a full set of teeth."

"I don't care about…"

Suddenly the baby spoke out, clearly, but in what sounded like another language.

The woman appeared shocked. "I don't believe it!"

"What?" Faridah demanded. "What did he say?"

"It was Aramaic ... clear as could be."

"What did he say?!"

"I won't repeat it."

"Tell me!"

"He spewed a vile blasphemy!"

With that prophecy fulfilled,[49] Faridah's eyes widened and she reached out.

"Give me my baby."

Mary will raise up Apostles of the Latter Times
to make war against the Evil One....
They shall be little and poor in the world's esteem....
But they shall be rich in grace....
They will have recourse to Mary in all things
and they will know the shortest and most perfect way of
going to Jesus and they will belong entirely to Him.
St. Louis de Montfort

Chapter 8
St. Mary's School and Orphanage
Kumbakonam, India
October 22

Moments before dawn, John rounded up the twelve disciples. They had all enjoyed last night's celebration, but now it was time to get to work. He brought them back into the cafeteria and began another lesson. This one, however, would be their most important and their last.

John appeared more somber than the night before and, once the disciples were seated at the candle-lit table, he began. "Through faith, you are shielded by God's power until our Lord returns. So, rejoice! But for a little while you will suffer grief in all kinds of trials. These come so that your faith may be refined like gold in the fire. Still, have no doubt that by remaining steadfast, you shall receive the goal of your faith, the salvation of your souls."[50]

The disciples did not find these words very comforting. So, Booker spoke up. "Some people believe God would never punish anybody. If He really is loving, He'd always forgive and never punish."

John responded, "He is loving and He is merciful. But He

is also just. He knows that when we defy His loving guidance, we not only harm ourselves but we harm and contribute to the downfall of others. At some point, His merciful patience will come to an end."

"Yeah," Ricky Zipp chimed in, "but you'd think He'd tell us before He'd do anything big."

John threw back his head and laughed. "Ricky, Ricky, Ricky ... are you still waiting for the two minute warning before you get into the game?"

"Well ... uh ... I didn't mean ..."

John continued, "The Old Testament prophets warned: love God and man or there will be consequences. Jesus Christ warned: love God and man or there will be consequences. Numerous apparitions of our Lord and Blessed Mother have continued to this very day, warning us to love God and man or there will be consequences. How many times do we have to be told that our choices have consequences, both in this life and the next?"

Ricky asked, "Like what apparitions?" Then he added, defensively, "I mean, I believe you. I just wanna know so I can tell everybody."

"Okay, fair enough," John said. "Most people have always ignored or mocked God's warnings. So, let's go over just a few of the many credible apparitions."

John thought for a moment and then forged ahead. "For example, in 1846 Our Lady appeared to two children, weeping, at La Salette France. She warned, *'If my people will not submit, I shall be forced to let go the hand of my Son. It is so strong, so heavy that I can no longer withhold it.'*[51] He continued, "In 1936, Teresa Neumann quoted Our Lord, saying, *'Sodom would not listen to Me, nor do the people listen to Me nowadays, nor heed My warnings; therefore they will incur the sad experience of My wrath which they deserve.* '[52]

"In 1918, Marie Mesmin quoted Blessed Mother, saying, *'By my tears [at La Salette and Bordeaux], I wanted to make you understand that prayer and penance can keep away the punishments. If one would pray, nothing would happen. God is powerful enough to govern mankind; all would be renewed in peace without the terrible punishments which will extermi-nate three fourths of mankind.'*[53]

"Also, in the 1600s, Venerable Mary of Agreda and St. Louis De Montfort both prophesied that the power of the Virgin Mary over demons will be very conspicuous in the last days.[54]

"I could go on with older prophecies, but let's look at something more recent. Maureen Sweeney-Kyle, a simple Ohio woman, claims she has been receiving heavenly messages almost daily since 1985.[55] On March 12, 1995, she said the Blessed Mother warned of a series of four looming chastisements: *'Dear children, today I invite you to recognize the season of tribulation that is upon you. As in any season there are signs. Recognize the cataclysmic natural events as from God. These occur in order to return souls to God, Who is King of heaven and earth.'* Was she correct? Well, since then, the world witnessed a tsunami kill 230,000 in Indonesia, a cyclone kill 146,000 in Myanmar, a heat wave kill 56,000 in Russia, an earthquake kill 222,000 in Haiti, and an earthquake/tsunami combination in Japan initiate a long-term death toll that is currently impossible to calculate. By these standards, even Hurricane Katrina – the costliest natural disaster in American history – cannot compare.[56] Even in America, the destruction toll continues to mount with record tornado activity, record flooding of the Mississippi River, record cold waves, record heat waves, and on and on."

Jin spoke up. "Yeah, but anybody can predict natural disasters and end up being right."

"Jin, 2005 was the most expensive year in history for natural disasters. Then, just six years later, that record was smashed by 44%."[57]

Jim grimaced.

"But I'm not through with her four prophecies," John continued. "That day, Blessed Mother also warned about the second phase of chastisements, *'In the next season of tribulation you will find money systems failing and collapsing. This will occur as a means of stripping people from the idol of money.'* Now, how many of you wish you had known, in advance, about the greatest financial collapse since the Great Depression?[58]"

Some of the men nodded.

"You see, these are not isolated cautions. When we study credible heavenly messages, reported from all over the world, we find that they typically reinforce each other. In the early 1990s, Austrian seer, Maria Simma, for example, also warned, *"Satan is everywhere today – in the Church, in the law, in medicine, in science, in the press and in the arts. But there is an area where he is, for the greatest part, running the show, and that is in the banks. The West's greed has permitted this, and only God is now strong enough to stop it."* [59]

"What about the third phase?" Father Alonzo asked.

"Blessed Mother also warned, *'The next season I reveal to you ... is the apostasy, which will occur in the Church ... and will take place mainly in the West.'* In this age of demonic ascendency, could there be a more sinister evil than priestly pedophilia to destroy the Church's credibility? Is it any surprise that most news coverage has virtually ignored that this grave evil has permeated not just the Church but every layer of our society and that it is more prevalent among teachers, coaches, Boy Scout leaders, and even Protestant ministers?[60] In fact, rampant pedophilia is also Hollywood's biggest secret.[61] So, for the apostasy to be fulfilled, what could be better than a storm of anti-Catholic bigotry that has placed a cloud of suspicion over every holy priest in an attempt to discredit and even bankrupt the Church that has always condemned that despicable evil?"[62]

John continued, "Think of the Church's scandals and apostasy when you hear that Our Lady of La Salette warned: *'Lucifer, with a very great number of demons, will be unchained from hell. By degrees they shall abolish the faith, even among persons consecrated to God. They shall blind them in such a manner that, without very special graces, these persons shall imbibe the spirit of those wicked angels…. The superiors of religious communities should be alert regarding the ones they take into the community, for the devil will use all malice to bring persons into the orders who are addicted to sin…. '*[63] Puerto Rican visionary, Barrio Rincon, reinforced this prophecy when he quoted the Blessed Mother, in 1953, saying, *"The times will come when the spiritual and moral deterioration of the shepherds of my Son's flock will be a matter of public knowledge. '*[64]

Booker nodded and asked, "And what about the fourth phase?"

John spoke with emphasis. " *'Then [comes] the season of the anti-Christ. He will be in the world and in hearts. '"*

John paused to let the men absorb that message. "So, don't wait for a warning, you have been warned. It is a Grace from God. Our Lady explained: *'I reveal these things to you now, so that as these events unfold, you will recognize God's hand in your midst. Just as in nature, these seasons will overlap one another. There will be no clear line of demarcation, but you will recognize them through Holy Love. "*[65]

John continued, "My friends, our Savior has told us that the harvest is plentiful, but the workers are few. So, I send you out for the final harvest. Two by two, proclaim the Lord's imminent return, but remember that you shall be like lambs among wolves. Do not take money or possessions with you and do not greet anyone on the road. When you enter a town and are welcomed, eat what is set before you. Heal the sick who are there and tell them, '*The kingdom of God is near you.*' But when you enter a town and are not welcomed, go into its streets and proclaim, '*Even your dust we shake off our shoes.*' Wherever you are rejected, I tell you, it was better for Sodom than it will be for that town."[66]

Chippy, the lanky, quiet Canadian spoke up. "Brother John, just tell us where and we will go, for the Lord."

John then explained, in detail, how and where they would be sent. Chippy and Henry would evangelize North America; Worthington and Pedro, South and Central America; Booker and Qurban, Africa and the Middle East; Samir and Rodney, India and China; Ozzy and Jin, Australia and the Pacific Islands; and Father Alonzo and Ricky would travel to Europe and the Former Soviet Union.

John reminded them all: "Everything you will need is revealed in Holy Scriptures. Study them and cling to their wisdom. When it says that with faith you can move mountains, believe it. However, remember Lord Jesus Christ's words: *'If any man would come after me, let him deny himself and take up his cross and follow me. For whoever would save his life will lose it; and whoever loses his life for my sake and the gospel's will save it. For what does it profit a man, to gain the whole world and forfeit his life?'*[67] The time has now arrived when those who refuse to sacrifice anything will lose everything."

Pedro asked, "So, what do you want us to do?"

"First, put on the full armor of God so that you can take your stand against the devil's schemes. For our struggle is not against flesh and blood, but against the rulers, against the authorities, against the powers of this dark world and against the spiritual forces of evil in the heavenly realms.[68] Second, whenever you are welcomed, love. When you are criticized, love. When you are attacked, love."

Pedro shook his head. "That's not much help."

John smiled at Pedro, remembering how much he had loved him from the first time he met the little Honduran. John answered, "Pedro, I am saying, 'Trust God.' Our message is one of hope. As long as we live we can choose to reject our sinful nature, we can choose to use the power of God, and we can choose true Life with eternal happiness. So, when you don't know where to go, pray. When you don't know what to say, pray. When you don't know who to trust, pray. Pray for boldness; the boldness to defend life in a culture of death, to proclaim truth to those who are deceived by lies, to announce God's mercy to anyone who wants it and His justice to anyone who does not."

Father Alonzo, the only disciple who had discerned John's true identity, worried, "What about you? How will we reach you ... to communicate with you?"

John could see the growing uncertainty, even doubt, in the eyes of his followers. "Just pray, Father. Your path shall be lighted."

This was not the rousing send-off that John had prayed for. The men looked confused.

Still, John knew that their days together had ended.

Realizing that it was time to send them on their way, he gave them a blessing and then simply prayed, "Almighty God – Father, Son, and Holy Spirit – give these men what they need to serve You best."

Suddenly, a sound like the blowing of a violent wind came from heaven and entered the dining hall. A rush of joy and knowledge filled their hearts and minds. Now they understood everything: That John was the Beloved Apostle; that with Almighty God, all things are possible; and that they would spend the rest of their lives leading souls to Christ, before the end of the age.

In the humble cafeteria, they watched with amazement as tongues of fire separated and came to rest on each of them. From that moment, they were forever changed, filled with the Holy Spirit.[69]

Finally, after a period prayerful rejoicing, the holy pairs eagerly set out for the far corners of the globe, armed with nothing more than their faith.

> In the middle of difficulty
> lies opportunity.
> Albert Einstein

He was no longer Detective Tim Lassiter. He was not the friendly, fit family man he had once been. Now, he was just another depressed unemployed schmuck, separated from his wife and getting fat.

Around the bar, the flat screen televisions were tuned mostly to various sporting events, but only one had the audio turned up. Lassiter listened without interest as the XBC News reporters segued from the excitement of President Angela Concepcion's upcoming wedding, to the nightmare of the political drubbing that her party likely would take in the coming mid-term elections.

For Lassiter, the over-hyped extravaganza of the President's wedding had come to represent a lot of what was wrong with America today. By now, most everyone was tiring of the once fashionable displays of conspicuous consumption.

He wanted to scream at the TV, *Some of us have to earn what we spend!*

Ever since budget cuts had forced a series of layoffs at the Yahsar police force, Lassiter had been spiraling downward. His home was in foreclosure and his debts were piling up. He deeply resented that politicians and bureaucrats had victimized him in the political crossfire of the budget battle that deliberately slashed the most visible and important public services before any one of a thousand examples of waste, fraud or abuse would be considered. He also suspected that his sacking might have had something to do with his handling of the Malek case.

Lassiter sat alone in a booth, near the back of the bar, sipping his beer and mulling his limited prospects when a young woman asked, "Tim Lassiter?"

He looked up and studied her short, slender form before responding. She was blond, very attractive, and appeared to be all-business. As a cop, he had seen her type many times before. Her slim-fitting suit was one clue, but the briefcase gave her away. She had to be a lawyer.

"Who wants to know?" Lassiter asked, without a hint of cooperation.

She didn't bother to answer. "I was told I would find you here."

"By who?"

"It doesn't matter. May I sit down?"

Lassiter shook his head. "Look, whoever you represent, I'll get you a check as soon as I can. But, right now, we're both outa luck."

"Tim," she paused, "May I call you Tim?"

He just glared at her.

"Okay," she continued, "Mr. Lassiter, I am not here to ask for money." She handed him a business card.

Lassiter read, "Mercedes Dare, Attorney at Law." He snickered, thinking, *Sounds like a stripper's name.*

"I represent a client who wants to hire you."

He perked up. "To do what?"

"To find John Eben Malek…. Now, may I sit down?"

†††

OVER THE NEXT HALF HOUR, the woman explained that she represented someone who requires absolute confidentiality. She claimed her client was willing to pay handsomely for a successful outcome.

"How handsomely?" Lassiter asked.

"A hundred thousand."

"Dollars?"

She smiled. "Twenty now and eighty more if you are successful."

"That's ... well ... that's good," Lassiter tried, unsuccessfully, to downplay his excitement. "But why'd you pick me?"

"Malek has been very good at travelling under the radar. As far as we know, you're the only person who ever conducted extensive interviews with him. We hope you'll be able to draw from what you learned during your investigation. Do you have an interest in catching the one that got away, Mr. Lassiter?"

"Sure but ... uh ... I don't even know where to start."

"We've had a lot of false clues and dead ends. But we finally established measures that allowed us to track Malek to a specific orphanage. Unfortunately, we have reason to believe that he is moving on, now. We need someone like you, hot on his trail.... Look, you questioned him for hours. Mull it over, see if he gave you any clues as to where you might find him."

"Okay. So, where do we go from here?"

"I have a certified check from our firm and a one-page contract for you to sign ... you know, confidentiality clause, that sort of thing ... and, of course, provisions to make sure you get paid when you succeed."

She reached into her briefcase and pulled out the check, two copies of the contract and a pen. Lassiter superficially scanned the agreement but he couldn't stop thinking about the check.

Man, she really came prepared!

As he scrawled his signature twice, the former detective thought, *"Sweet!"*

The lawyer wrote notes on a napkin and slid it over to the former detective. "This is the orphanage where Malek was last seen."

"Kumbak...onam," Lassiter stumbled through the name and then blurted out, "India?"

"Oh, didn't I mention that? You'll love the curries."

The lawyer hurriedly gathered her possessions and then extended her hand. Lassiter pointedly glanced down and noticed something that he liked: she was not wearing a wedding ring. The two of them concealed sly smiles as they shook and, when she left, he couldn't stop watching her all the way to the door.

To celebrate his good fortune, Lassiter ordered a neat little army of vodka shots, six in all, and left the waitress a big tip. With the first gulp, however, his euphoria started to fade as he began to second-guess his negotiation.

Why didn't I hold out for more?

He downed another shot.

Obviously they're desperate. I bet I could've gotten twice as much.

Then one more.

The least I should've done was get travel expenses covered.

Then another.

Man, I could end up flying all over the world and maybe still not find Malek.

And another.

Ohhh, I screwed up!

He threw back the last one.
Idiot! Idiot! Idiot!"

LASSITER STAGGERED across the dark parking lot in search of his car. As he fumbled for his keys, he heard a voice.

"Timothy Lassiter?"

He turned and saw a woman approaching. Then he observed: brunette, slim-fitting suit, briefcase.

"May I speak with you a moment, Mr. Lassiter?"

"Look, I don't have any money right now."

"Oh, no," she said with a smile. "I have an opportunity for you."

Lassiter laughed as he looked her over. Jane Marconi had a few more pounds and a few more years, compared to Mercedes Dare, but she definitely was another attorney.

"Are you kidding?"

She opened her briefcase on the hood of his car. "Look, I won't take up much of your time. But I assure you that you will love what I have to say."

"Okay ..."

"We want to find John Eben Malek and we think that you are the best man for the job. Do you think you could do that for us?"

Lassiter wanted to scream a laugh but, instead, puffed up with inebriated pride. "Well, sure. I think you're right. I *am* the best man for the job. But I'm not cheap."

"How about sixty thousand dollars?" She studied his response and was surprised to see that he did not look excited. Still, she pushed ahead. "Of course, we require complete confidentiality."

Lassiter's head almost exploded, but he made sure his

face showed no reaction. "Well, I don't know. I would have to do a lot of international travel."

"What makes you say that? Where would you go?" she asked, feigning ignorance.

"I'd start with India."

Her eyes tightened and her lips conveyed a slight smile. "You are good, Mr. Lassiter. That's where we lost track of him. How did you know?"

He ignored the question. "Look, if you want the best, you're also gonna have to pay my travel expenses."

She nodded. "Okay. But you only get full payment when you bring Malek to us, alive. We'll pay twenty five percent now and the balance only when we get Malek."

Lassiter shot back, "Fifty percent now."

"Thirty."

"Forty."

"Thirty three and a third."

"Thirty ... uh ..." Lassiter stumbled, "seven and a quarter."

The brunette lawyer sighed and then closed her briefcase. As she began to walk away, Lassiter shouted, "Hey wait! No, I'm just kidding. That's fine ... thirty three and a third is great!"

When she returned to the car, she jotted down a few minor changes on the documents and initialed them in the margins. Then she let him scan the agreement and showed him where to sign and initial.

"What about my money?" Lassiter prodded.

"My, you are pushy."

"Well ... I just ... uh ... ya know ..."

"Our runner will deliver a certified check to your home tomorrow morning ... around ten. Is that alright?"

"Sure ... sure, that's great."

Then a memory flashed through Lassiter's pickled brain and a look of horror transformed his face. "Oh, no," he mumbled. "Ohhh, where'd I put 'em? Did I throw 'em away?"

"Are you okay?" Marconi asked.

"Look," he rushed, "I gotta go."

Lassiter snatched his copy of the contract, jumped into the car and spun his tires out of the parking lot. As he raced home, one thing dominated his thoughts: If he could find the interrogation tapes, they could hold the key to locating John Eben Malek.

Crotona has only two classes of inhabitants –
flatterers and flattered.
From the ancient Roman satirist,
Petronius

Chapter 10
The Breakers Hotel
Palm Beach, Florida
November 1

The most coveted invitation on the planet today was to the wedding of President Angela Concepcion and Mr. Fred Whitehead. Every suite in the historic Breakers Resort had been reserved for guests of the reception, but only 120 lucky souls were invited to witness the vows.

For this fairy tale weekend, the Breakers' 1,800 member staff – fluent in 56 languages – would be pushed to the limit by the president's demanding entourage. The ceremony had occurred in the small but boldly ornate Magnolia Ballroom.

Because of Fred's marital history, a succession of cardinals, bishops and even priests had politely declined Angela's invitation to preside over the nuptials. So, tossing a sop to the masses, a politically correct choice was made and Brother Daniel Mitchum, the rabble-rousing firebrand was chosen.

Mitchum was a white man who had commandeered America's race-relations spotlight. Now he fancied himself as Martin Luther King's replacement. However, across America – from ghettos to barrios to union halls – the charismatic preacher's words usually sparked rioting and looting. Angela had once seen herself as a kindred spirit when his sermons only preached to "covet thy neighbor's wealth." Now, however, he had gained more fame with "steal thy neighbor's wealth" homilies.

Mitchum loved to witness the power of his words, and there was no greater testimony to his effectiveness than the sight of burning buildings.

Angela's hope was that this favor would placate the popular non-denominational pastor and lessen the intensity of his divisive social justice tirades. The decision had been a calculated gamble, accompanied by an offer of four oceanfront suites, chauffeured limousine service, and the use of a private jet.

Sternly, Mitchum had been advised not to speak longer than five minutes. By the thirty sixth minute, however, he had offended every guest within earshot. They could not stop him, and he knew it.

Having already imbibed a bit, and finding the ballsy insults amusing, Fred Whitehead got a case of the giggles, which finally prompted Brother Mitchum to wind down.

Then, Angela and Fred exchanged vows and rings in front of a roaring fireplace and a fine French tapestry. The moment was bittersweet for both of them. She sadly reflected on the shock she felt after her first husband's tragic death. He sadly reflected on the expense of his previous three divorces.

Both of them, however, had perfected the art of publicly exuding supreme confidence, even in moments of private doubt. And ever since her encounter with Momma Laudie, Angela's mind had been full of doubts.

They had worked hard on fine-tuning every detail of the images they would present. Maintaining tradition, Fred wore the expected Armani black tuxedo, and Angela insisted that her lavishly full, flowing gown be Vera Wang and blindingly white. Fred's demanding fitness regime had returned his torso to college trim. Now, however, his distinctive white hair proclaimed the wisdom that only age or chemicals can produce.

Angela, on the other hand, never had to work at maintaining her beauty. Her dark, Latin aura seemed to come naturally. She was never overweight, out of shape, or even in need of makeup.

When she entered the ballroom – orchestrated by three harps, a violin and a cello – Angela's name fit: she looked angelic. Today, this beautiful couple had set a new standard for marital perfection and the production crew, that soon would be marketing her DVD, knew it. In the lead up, fashion reporters had predicted that this mega-event would rival the wedding of Kate Middleton to Prince William. That was how Angela wanted and expected her wedding to be viewed. After all, she had always described herself as a political "Perfective," capable of molding a perfect world for the people. Today should be a lesson for her political opponents. Her wedding was an example of what she could accomplish, if only everyone would get out of the way and let her run the show.

However, her heart was no longer in the daily grind of bad news at the office. This was where she really wanted to be: in the spotlight, setting new fashion standards as America's *Arbiter Elegantiae* of social mores.

The ceremony had just ended and Angela's staff directed the powerful men and beautiful women into a receiving line where every VIP would pay homage and be thanked for their support. Unlike when Angela attended Hollywood functions, she realized that this was not a room full of rented tuxedos and borrowed diamonds. These people were players.

Then it was time to do what Angela and Fred dreaded: greet the masses. When the doors flung open, the guests roared with cheers and applause. But Angela's smile quickly disappeared.

"No, no. I'm sorry … That won't do," she said, trying to quiet the crowd. Finally, when everyone settled down, Angela shouted, "I'm sorry but one of our cameramen was not in place. Let's try that again. And, come on, everybody. Show me how much you love me."

The crowd chuckled as the couple re-entered the small ballroom and, repositioning, Angela and Fred kept rapturous smiles pasted on their faces. They had been practicing perma-grins for weeks, knowing that, today, the slightest frown photo would be woven into a tabloid tale of unhappiness. Angela had sternly warned Fred about the danger and he worried that his facial muscles might not endure the day's charm marathon.

But, when they burst out again, the roar was even louder. Led by the camera crew and Secret Service agents the happy couple progressed through well-wishers who lined both sides of the North Loggia. When they reached the main lobby, another round of cheers erupted. Under the gloriously painted, vaulted ceilings of the 200-foot long lobby the loving pair soaked in the adoration and fondly remembered that this room had been patterned after Genoa's *Palazzo Carega,* one of their own little love nests.

Smiling and waving, but rarely touching anyone, they made their way down the South Loggia and into the Mediterranean Courtyard where cheering guests surrounded the fountain and reflecting pool. Angela surprised even herself when she managed to maintain a pleasant demeanor as the Senate Appropriations Committee Chairman approached with Amy Laugherly – his daughter and Fred's ex-wife. Angela had to work with the snake-oil-selling Senator, but his daughter was as welcome as herpes on a honeymoon.

Why did that troll have to bring her?!

But Angela recovered nicely and was as giddy as a birthday girl when she addressed the crowd. During her remarks, Fred tried to keep his concentration focused on his loving smile. All he heard was, "Oh, my, Gawd! *Something, something* ... amazing! *Something, something* ... fabulous!" Then, when she leaned over and gave him a peck on the lips, her fans went wild.

For the next half hour, the happy couple smiled, nodded and babbled, "Wonderful," and "Marvelous," and "Extraordinary," and every other superlative that Angela's little thesaurus had suggested.

She knew her words had fallen short, lately. She privately had become extremely irritated that Evan Thas and his scripting service had been missing in action, prior to the wedding. Perhaps he was backing away because he knew that it had been his bad idea to put on such a lavish display. He also knew that the public had developed a negative opinion regarding such luxuriously wasteful spending during a time of global depression. The extravagant wedding that he said would propel her party to increasing dominance had now become a symbol of decadence. For that, her party would pay a price at the polls and her power would be diminished in the last two years of her first term.

Increasingly, in recent months, she and Evan had been growing disenchanted with each other. She was irked by Evan's development of a wide range of front groups that posed as "non-partisan" academic, philanthropic, or religious organizations. Ironically, however, each one operated to do the opposite of what its name implied. Reliable Research, for example, was a polling firm that always rigged the questions or the sampling so that Evan's preferred results were achieved. The Faith Preservation Foundation used every tool in its legal and media arsenal to stop public expressions of faith. The Coalition for Ethical Reporting gained widespread media attention as it elevated or intimidated journalists, depending on whether they were compliant to Evan's agenda. Finally, the Life Charitable Trust operated internationally, sponsoring every form of population control including abortion, mass sterilization and mandatory euthanasia.

Each of these organizations was deemed highly credible by XBC News. But Evan's control was hidden and his funding of the groups was circuitous, creating the illusion of independence that was never challenged by weak-willed journalists.

Angela also resented Evan's recent self-promotion binge, contributing to an army of non-profit and non-governmental organizations that would advance his causes and, of course, himself. Week after week, the usual suspects in the media had proclaimed another one of XCyst Industries' medical breakthroughs or another discovery of hidden treasure by the daring adventurer, Evan Thas. No doubt, the man had been on a roll, and his ego reflected the fact.[70] His head was becoming so inflated, Angela thought, that he might even skip out on her big day.

An hour later, she noticed Evan, at a distance, near one of the many tables that had been set up on the ocean lawn. He was very animated, happily gesticulating to a beautiful woman.

Angela knew Evan would not approach her, today. After all, their working relationship was still very discrete and their meetings had continued to be at unusual venues that did not require a Secret Service screening or sign-in. So, she took the initiative and headed Evan's way, with Fred in tow.

She approached with a contrived smile but, inside, she was simmering. "Hello Dr. Thas."

"Oh, Ang… I mean, Madame President. Great wedding!"

Angela paused to take it all in. She had never seen Evan like this. He seemed almost loving.

As Evan exchanged cordialities with Fred, Angela turned to study the woman next to Thas. She definitely was older, but still exquisite. In fact, as the two women evaluated each other, they realized that, for the first time, each of them was encountering someone of equal beauty.

Angela wondered if this woman was the reason for Evan's uncharacteristically good mood.

"And who is your friend, here?" Angela asked.

"Oh," Evan chuckled, "she's not my friend."

"Now, that's not very nice."

"She's my mother."

Angela almost gasped as she extended her hand, musing over the fact that the two couldn't look less similar.

"It is a pleasure, Madame President. My name is Faridah Shabaan."

Evan beamed with pride as they shook hands.

Exotic accent, golden complexion, charming personality, the President studiously observed. They were three attributes that she liked most about Fred Whitehead. But as she responded, "So nice to meet you," she suspected that this woman's qualities might actually be real.

However, the exotic guest did not release the president's hand. Instead, she turned it over and examined her palm.

Angela offered a quizzical grin, but loved indulging the mysterious lady. As Faridah traced her forefinger along various creases and wrinkles, her eyes flared with excitement. Then she looked up at Angela. "I see now why you are so successful." Her studious gaze returned to the revealing wrinkles as she whispered, "It is what your soul demands."

Angela offered a self-satisfied smile. The revelation was appreciated, but not surprising.

Sizing up the unusual woman, Angela thought she observed a mystical aura radiating from her. Then the palm reader's tone changed, she said, "Oh … oh," and gently pushed the president's hand back to her.

"What?" Angela laughed.

"No … not today."

Faridah knew that those were the only words that would entice a woman who is accustomed to getting whatever she wants.

The president thrust her hand back in the Syrian's face. "Tell me. It's not diseased, you know."

Solemnly, Faridah resumed her study. She sighed her hesitation and then whispered, "Your judgment has become clouded."

Angela pulled her farther aside and whispered, "I know."

Faridah said, "You will be confronted by dark forces."

The president mumbled, "That's what a Haitian palm reader told me."

"The instincts that have always served you well will deceive you."

"Yes, I was told that," Angela said, intrigued by the confirmation.

Evan's mother looked up from the palm. "Madame President, rely on your advisors. Trust them, not just when they agree with you, but most especially when they vehemently disagree."

"She said that there is only one advisor that I can truly trust."

"Of course, Madame President," Faridah said, smiling pleasantly, "Evan."

"Evan." She responded without enthusiasm. After all, Thas had been incredibly difficult, lately.

"Does that surprise you?"

"Frankly, yes. The Haitian described a woman."

"Then, with all humility, I suggest that I am the one foretold."

Hmmm, Angela thought. *She fits the prophecy.*

A moment later, Angela asked, "A matter of life or death?"

"Absolutely."

"So … what am I to know?"

There was no hesitation. "Destroy John Malek or he will destroy you."

Angela looked deeply into her eyes, trying to detect any hint of dishonesty. Seeing none, she chose to trust the woman. However, she also realized that her guidance presented a clear conflict of interest. After all, if Faridah became a trusted advisor, she and her son would become the prime beneficiaries.

Angela took the Syrian's hand and led her back to their small group.

Fred joked, "I bet you told her we'll live happily ever after."

They all smiled politely. Then the president glanced at her lead Secret Service Agent and asked Faridah, "May I borrow your son for a moment?"

"Certainly."

"Fred," Angela said, "please entertain our lovely guest."

"Sure," he responded … too enthusiastically.

"Don't forget, dear: You're married, now." And they both laughed like teenage lovers while distant guests clicked pictures.

The Secret Service Agent had politely cleared a section of the ocean lawn, allowing Angela and Evan a perimeter of privacy. As he escorted her to the area, Angela's smile became more rigid.

"I've missed you, my friend," she mentioned as her gown dragged across the freshly manicured grass.

"I haven't seen my mother since I was five. The surprise has kept me busy."

Angela laughed as if Evan had said something funny.

"You've been out of reach for two weeks. It certainly would be helpful if you returned my calls."

"It also would be helpful if you stopped dragging your feet on my NSA[71] clearance request."

"Now, Evan, why do you need NSA access? Doesn't your little CyBot search engine allow you to snoop enough?"

"I'm not here to negotiate, Angela. I want access."

"For what?" Angela asked, surprised that he was demanding rather than requesting.

He did not respond.

"Does this have to do with Malek?"

Again, he remained silent.

"Why are you so obsessed with John Malek? Get over it. He got away. Who cares?"

"I care," he growled hatefully, "and that is all that matters."

"People are watching," she whispered.

Catching the attention of distant guests, suddenly, he declared loudly, "Of course, I will assist you at NSA, Madame President. I am happy to be of service to my country."

She led him a little farther from the crowd. "It seems we've had another fish kill ... near Vero Beach, this time. People are freaking out, Evan."

Thas feigned ignorance. "The water's pretty cold this time of year."

"That may explain the fish, but it doesn't explain the dead birds."[72]

Angela glanced at Fred, who seemed genuinely entranced in pleasant conversation with Faridah. Then she asked, "Evan, why do you always have to be so difficult?"

"Neurotransmitters, Angela," he toyed with her.[73] "My DNA is unique. My sense of adventure is dictated by my extraordinary genome: eight copies of the dopamine receptor 4 gene on chromosome 11, for example. Actually, twice what's normal."

She stared at him blankly.

"Oh, I see. You were asking as a rhetorical question."

She smiled through gritted teeth. But the president still had another card to play. "Evan, I think you're being a bad boy," she said, as if scolding a child. "And if you don't play nice with your toys, I'll have to take them away from you. Now, you don't want time out, do you?"

From afar, Fred noticed that the president's conversation was appearing heated. So, as he dragged Faridah their way, he shouted, "Hey, save business for later."

But Evan wasn't finished. His smirk had disappeared. "Who do you think ..."

Arriving, now, Fred interrupted, "It's happy hour, let's go have a ..."

"I'm talking!" Evan snapped. Fred recoiled in stunned silence as Faridah savored the moment and distant guests turned with surprise.

"Who do you think," Evan growled, "will operate those 'toys,' as you call them?"

No one smiled now.

"I assure you, Evan, I'll find someone."

"If I don't play with them, *you* don't play with them."

She lowered her volume again. "Young man, don't over-estimate your value. Don't underestimate my power. You're forgetting who the star is."

"Angela, you are not a star," Evan whispered as he moved close to her face. "You are a small, lifeless meteor … a cold, barren rock floating aimlessly through space until you crash into a true celestial body. You must learn that *I* am the star, lighting and warming the world in which you live…. Little meteor, you can only be seen when you reflect the brilliance that I shine upon you."

Angela could have signaled for an intervention by the Secret Service, but she was too afraid.

Suddenly, Evan's smirk returned as he proclaimed to the nearby crowd, "This is such a wonderful place for your wedding, Madame President! Isn't this near where you were born on a beach near Miami?" Then, more loudly than necessary, he shouted, "That's right because, definitely, you were *not* born in Cuba."

Evan took his mother's arm. "Come, mother, let's get some free food."

As Evan and Faridah strolled away, Angela thought, *What's he talking about? Of course, I wasn't born in Cuba.*

Then she signaled a Secret Service Agent.

"Give me your phone," she demanded with fear in her eyes.

Angela grabbed it and quickly dialed the Director of National Intelligence.

"Carla … this is top priority. Covert operation. Get somebody into Florida vital records … tonight. They're probably at DOH in Jacksonville. Make sure my birth certificate is still there."

She did not hear a response because she dropped the phone when a wave of nausea hit her. Angela quickly strode across the lawn and into the eastern loggia as two Secret Service agents hurried to keep up. Quickly, she spotted the women's restroom, burst through the door and into an empty stall. Then she dropped to her knees, leaned over and heaved into the toilet.

I looked and there before me was a pale horse!
Its rider was named Death,
and Hades was following close behind him.
They were given power over a fourth of the earth
to kill by sword, famine and plague,
and by the wild beasts of the earth.
Revelation 6:7-8

Chapter 11
South of Luxor, Egypt
November 1

From 22,236 miles above the equator, the orbiting satellite that had been code-named Glass Andalusian[74] scanned a barren desert where a simple man was dismounting his camel. The Bedouin traveler, Mustafa, had separated from his Alagat Tribe in search of new water supplies. But now, it was time for the noon prayer.

Mustafa rolled out his red *sajada* prayer rug, on the sand. While standing, he gazed over the endless ripples of Egyptian terrain – a country where 96% of the land is uninhabited – and felt the wind ruffling his royal blue *thobe* and the beige *sarong* below it. The breeze was welcomed, but it was hot, and soon it would become a windstorm.

Ancient traditions in clothing persist here, more as a reality of survival than a statement of fashion. In the desert, layered robes protect the wearer from the harsh sun, and draped cotton turbans, from the wind-blown sand. In this inhospitable climate, nature is man's most formidable opponent … at least, that is what Mustafa thought.

The prayerful Arab adjusted the curved *Khanja* knife in his belt and fell to his knees before Allah. However, lacking water to perform the traditional purification before prayers, Mustafa struck the desert sand with his palms and recited, "I perform *tayammum* to make my prayer permissible." He clutched the sand and rubbed it over his face. He struck the soil again and rubbed sand over his hands and forearms. Then his prayers began.

Nonetheless, far removed from earthly empathy, Glass Andalusian executed its orders with precision and without emotion or regret. The geosynchronous orbiter cast its beam downward, analyzing not only the visible surface, but also subterranean secrets under the Egyptian sands.

Then, shortly before his prayers ended, Mustafa felt a sudden wave of heat. It was more extreme than anything he had ever experienced before. As he staggered to his feet, his camel groaned. The man threw off his turban and held his head, attempting to stave off the pains of a stabbing headache. The camel shrieked as the Bedouin fell to his knees and examined his hands. They were not only red but blistering. A sudden wave of nausea disoriented him, his vision blackened, and he staggered back to his feet. By now, the camel had dropped to the ground and rolled on its side, moaning helplessly. Mustafa struggled to remain standing but, instead, collapsed on the rug.

THREE DAYS LATER, the bodies of the Bedouin and his camel were mostly covered with sand, unnoticed by the 87 men who drove over them in a fleet of large transport trucks. Then, the caravan circled and stopped. They knew exactly where to go.

Two men opened their doors and hopped down from their massive truck. One checked his GPS coordinates, again, and shouted, "Okay, this is it!"

As if participating in a well-rehearsed stage production, the subordinates quickly took their positions and performed their assigned responsibilities under the hot Egyptian sun. One group moved to the periphery and began setting up camp. Others off-loaded numerous hydraulic excavators, track loaders and articulated dump trucks. Then surveyors flagged the work perimeter: a square plot of land, approximately 500 feet on each side.

Within a week, below them, the excavators would reveal the 3,341 year old tomb and gold sarcophagi of the Egyptian heretic pharaoh, Akhenaten, and his mysterious wife Nefertiti; they would discover 157 burial chambers filled with ornate, priceless treasures, unmatched in craftsmanship and historical significance; and they would find and discard the molten flesh of a lone Bedouin and his camel.[75]

A deception that elevates us
is dearer than a host of low truths.
Marina Tsvetaeva

Chapter 12
XCyst Industries' Corporate Headquarters
West Palm Beach, Florida
One Week Earlier

Evan Directed the young lawyer to one of the leather sofas in his expansive office and slid in next to her. His friendliness made her a little uncomfortable but she was not going to let that get in her way. She knew that Dr. Evan Thas was the kind of client who could catapult her career.

Still, she wondered why he had requested her by name. He was famous. Surely, a man this influential would normally work with senior partners, not junior associates, barely out of law school. But, then again, he did have a reputation for eccentricity and a *nouveau riche* air about him. His red hair made him look younger than his years. Compounding that were the wrinkles on his polo shirt and khaki pants that contrasted against his nicely pressed navy jacket. Then there were those scuffed tennis shoes, one of which was untied. Clearly, this young man needed fashion and style advice, as the tackiness of his office seemed to testify. She scanned the room and quickly determined that Evan's taste in art never quite reached beyond the unclothed female form.

The young lawyer was a guarded woman, rarely revealing the scars – and always concealing the hunger – that were by-products of her childhood in a broken family. On the other hand, Evan, like him or not, really didn't care what anyone thought. He had finally become his own man, living each impulsive moment however he wished.

"That's an unusual name…. Is Mercedes Dare really your given name?"

"Yes, my mother had a quirky sense about her … and, no," she added, pre-empting the obvious follow up question, "I've never been a stripper."

"Well, I wasn't going to bring that up but, I must say, the thought crossed my mind."

Evan liked to test people, to tweak them, just to see how they respond. So, he raised his arm to the back of the sofa and gently extended a forefinger into her blond hair. Evan briefly admired her large green eyes and thin coral lips.

But she signaled that she was here for business: "So, what legal matter do you have for me, Dr. Thas?"

"I want you to help me find a very bad man. He's a convicted murderer who escaped from death row on the day of his scheduled execution."

"Are you talking about that Malek guy?"

"Yes, exactly."

"I remember the news reports. So, what do you need me for? There has to be a million law enforcement officials chasing him. He'll turn up."

"I prefer to find him first."

"Well, I'm not sure I feel comfortable with that, Dr. Thas. I really can't get in the way of an international manhunt."

"No, I understand. We just want you to assist in locating him. I need a confidential middle-man, so to speak. I'll direct you. We have leads."

"What kind of leads? From where?"

"Well … I'd rather not say."

"Dr. Thas, with all due respect, before my firm will take

you on as a client, I need more information. It is privileged communications. Don't worry, what you tell me will never get outside this room."

Thas thought for a moment and then gave in, partially. "We've been monitoring Vatican communications."

She chuckled, "Monitoring the Vatican?"

"Yes, and we have tracked Malek to an orphanage in India."

"What does the Vatican have to do with this?" she asked with a doubtful tone.

"They're the most corrupt enterprise in history, and they're trying to shelter that terrorist."

Mercedes frowned at his surprisingly extreme evaluation. She knew that Evan's XBC News had been on a tear, over recent months, relentlessly pounding the Catholic Church for the evils of a tiny minority. However, she did not think that the sins of a few should invalidate all the good that the Church was accomplishing.

Then a woman's voice interrupted, over the intercom. "Dr. Thas, I'm sorry to disturb your meeting, but "Mammon's Apprentice" just sent a priority communication. It just says, "Bingo."

Evan jumped up and screamed, "Yeah, baby!"

Mercedes found his erratic behavior very disquieting.

"Come with me," he urged as he headed for the door.'

"Where?" she asked as she reached for her briefcase. "Where are we going?"

He returned to the sofa and took her by the arm. "Don't worry. You won't regret it." Then he led her out the door. As they passed Evan's personal assistant, he said, "Rev it up," and she quickly picked up the phone.

Evan pulled the attorney into the elevator, saying, "You're

gonna love this."

When the doors opened again, she found herself walking out onto the rooftop. There, before her, a helicopter's rotors were starting to turn.

"Let's go," he said pulling her along.

"Where are we going?" she shouted over the rumble of the blades.

"You'll see."

"Dr. Thas, you can't expect me to just…"

"Vero Beach. We'll be back in three hours."

"Three hours?"

He was determined, and shoved her through the door. "You're on the clock. Don't worry about it."

Before she could get her seatbelt fastened, they lifted off the roof.

Mercedes was a bit fearful, but the thrill of the adrenaline rush had silenced her resistance. This was a first for her and, as they rose toward the plump, white cotton clouds, she was awestruck by the beauty of the expansive blue ocean below. She did not know much about where they were going, except that the community had been struggling to recover after a mysterious fish kill on its beaches. She knew from recent news reports that tourism had dried up until town volunteers and Mother Nature finally succeeded at removing the carcasses and the stench.

As they flew north, along the coastline, she tried to identify landmarks that she had never seen from this perspective and imagined the jealous spectators below who certainly had to be wondering about her charmed life.

"What's this all about?" she shouted.

"Is this still confidential?"

"Of course."

Then he seemed glad to fill her in.

"In 1715, a fleet of ships – 11 in all – left Cuba bound for Spain. King Philip V was anxious to welcome the fleet because his new bride had refused to consummate their marriage until she received its cargo."

"What was that?"

"Almost a billion dollars worth of gold bars, coins, diamonds, emeralds and pearls."

"Wow," she shouted.

"Anyway, as the fleet neared Vero Beach a hurricane hit and drove them onto the reefs. The ships sank and their precious cargo has not been seen since."[76] Then Evan smiled broadly. "Until now."

"You're kidding," she said as she grabbed his hand with excitement.

"A four million dollar investment is returning almost a billion." He laughed. "Not bad ... even for me."

She giggled, still holding his hand. "How did you find it?"

He knew he shouldn't say, but the excitement of the moment overwhelmed his better judgment.

"We're still lawyer-client, right?"

"Absolutely."

He looked out the window. "Look at that beautiful sky." She did. "But when I look out, I don't see blue, I see green."

"What's that mean?"

"Right now, there are 3,000 satellites orbiting Earth. I control twelve of them. Four of mine are mind-bogglingly powerful, and one of them has just cashed in."

Mercedes found herself giggling uncontrollably. "How? How? Please tell me how?"

We call this one "Glass Andalusian."

"That's a weird name."

"Huntie and I felt that our satellites are like a stable of racehorses just waiting at the gates, anxious to burst out and show what they can really accomplish. So, we decided to code-name our most powerful satellites after the most beautiful beasts on the planet. For five centuries, Andalusian horses have been known for their prowess at war and prized by nobility."

"But why '*Glass* Andalusian'?"

"'Glass' was the code name for the imaging technologies we use. Basically, utilizing technologies such as magnetic resonance imaging, computed tomography, hyperspectral imaging, infrared thermography, and X-rays, my satellites can be directed to cast a focused beam over a specific area in order to evaluate the density of everything in its path.

"You mean like gold and diamonds."

"Exactly. We simply program in the specific density of an element – like gold, for example, We see through everything we are not interested in – such as rooftops, land and sea – in order to find large reserves of exactly what we want. You know, like the way an X-ray detects bones or metal objects. Then, we just have to find a way to extract what we want."

"Wow," she found herself giggling again. "That's amazing!" Then she paused with a thought. "But don't X-rays emit radiation?"

Evan shrugged it off. "Yeah, well ... we're working on that."

FOR TWENTY MINUTES MORE they flew quietly, contemplating what wonders this day would bring. Then, as they neared Vero Beach, Mercedes noticed that the helicopter was descending closer to the ocean. The pilot circled over a wall of sea grapes at the edge of Humiston Park and smoothly glided down to a small area of freshly mowed lawn between palm trees and a large patch of pampas grass. Mercedes smiled out the window as she watched buff surfers interrupt their rituals to gawk at her show-stopping entrance.

Then Evan hopped out of the helicopter and suggested with a wink, "Don't slow me down, now." He took Mercedes' hand and she followed enthusiastically. They ran across the park, down some steps, and onto the beach. There, a high-speed Zodiac Hurricane was waiting for them, with a man at the helm.

Mercedes felt a little silly as she stumbled into the boat, bouncing her briefcase off one of the rubber, inflated pontoons that would soon keep them afloat. Her professional, linen suit and designer pumps were not appropriate for this trip. But she really didn't care … that is, until the boat revved ahead and bounced her over the ocean waves, destined for the horizon.

As they roared along, Evan pulled her close to him, behind a glass shield, protecting her from the wind and salty spray. Silently, together, they skimmed along until they spotted a small ship and, as they circled the ship, she could see "Mammon's Apprentice" sprawled across the stern.

When they boarded, climbing up a rope ladder, Mercedes was surprised at how old and dingy the ship appeared. But when they descended below, she saw that it contained a vast array of electronic equipment. She marveled at what, to her, could have been mission control for a space shuttle launch.

Mercedes observed that Evan was bubbling over, but the crew seemed stoically professional – almost soldierly – discussing their salvage plans. As they evaluated the ocean floor video feeds on flat screen monitors, she heard a lot of jargon that she did not understand. But, somehow, it was clear to her that, under those bumps of sand, there was a billion dollars worth of long-lost treasure.[77]

AN HOUR LATER, they were in the Zodiac again, bouncing back toward the beach. As Evan pulled Mercedes close again, he noticed that she was getting chilled in the brisk breeze. He pulled off his navy jacket and put it over her shoulders as she thought, *What a nice guy.*

When they finally reached the beach, both were damp and rumpled, but still exhilarated. Evan helped Mercedes out of the boat and held her hand as they walked across the bright sand. Thas was explaining the process of salvaging ocean treasure when Mercedes' eyes were drawn to two dark men in black suits, who seemed to be observing them. The matched pair looked oddly out of place at a beachfront park. Then, as they approached the beach steps, she saw an attractive, well-preserved woman staring at them, with a look of awe.

Evan glanced up and gasped. He let go of Mercedes' hand. For him, the woman's distinctive exotic eyes were unmistakable.

"Are you ..." the woman struggled with her words, "Evan Thas?"

Wide-eyed, he nodded.

The woman burst into tears. "Yes! Oh, I can't believe it!" she shouted as she almost tumbled down the steps. She ran across the sand and embraced the stunned young man. "My baby! My baby! I found you!"

"Mother?"

"Baby, baby, it's me. I found you! I found you!"

Tears streamed down Evan's cheeks, but he could not return her embrace. "Why did you give me away?"

She responded with anger, "They took you! They took you from me! They stole all those years from us!"

Hearing the affirmation that he had longed for all his life, Evan burst into loud, moaning sobs and embraced his mother for the first time in 25 years.

"Momma," he sobbed, "I missed you so much!"

As Mercedes wiped tears from her eyes, her heart soared at the sublime beauty of their familial embrace, and she yearned to experience the love that she had never found in her own family.

For Mercedes and Evan, this dramatic reunion was more moving than any film they had ever seen, and Faridah Shabaan's acting was worthy of an Academy Award.

*... a time is coming when anyone who kills you
will think he is offering a service to God.*
John 16:2

itting at the small table, Monsignor Bolaka inhaled the air deeply, realizing that there was none on the planet that had been more thoroughly filtered, conditioned and humidity-controlled. Nor was there any place more safe than in this large vault. As he looked up from a scroll, Bolaka scratched his black chin through his white beard and reflected on the improbability of succeeding at constructing this bunker in complete secrecy. But it had been accomplished.

Hundreds of trusted laborers and craftsmen had burrowed for eight years, constructing the storage facility that would store valuables so precious that, even to the workers, the description could not be revealed. Hidden deep below the Secret Archives, the reinforced steel enclosure was safe, even from nuclear attack.

But the structure was not built to protect the College of Cardinals, not even the pope. The pontiff and his cardinals realized that their lives were not measured in physical terms. Death was not to be feared but, rather, accepted as an inevitable step through the door to eternal Life. In fact, martyrdom was acceptable, even welcome. They knew that, throughout Christian history, the blood of martyrs had been the seed of the Church.[78] That was why the cardinals were clothed in red, as an admission that they might, some day, be called to offer their blood for Jesus Christ and the Church He founded.

The 20th century had repeatedly taught the lesson of evil's determination to silence and even kill the faithful. During that time, approximately one million Catholics had been martyred, and many more had been persecuted, specifically for their beliefs.[79] It had been the unrelenting murderous rampage that few reporters seemed to notice or care about.

Bolaka realized, however, that though his life was fleeting, these scrolls must be protected. Mankind's fate and faith would depend on them.

He rolled the scroll more fully open, on the table, and reread the last words John had sent:

> "The living Church withers in parched, lifeless soil. If it were not so, the world's Shining Darkness could not have dawned. When My Church and My people are persecuted, be not afraid. The rise of great evil shall be confronted by the rise of the Greatest Good. Follow the beloved watchman who shall resolve the transcendent mysteries and crown the conquering monarch. Remain in Rome and prepare to carry your cross. When darkness prevails, victory is near, and no secret shall remain hidden."

Those words did not instruct as clearly as he had hoped, and no further instructions had been received.

Suddenly, Bolaka was jolted by the distant sound at the top of the long spiral staircase. It was the steel door slamming shut. Then foot steps echoed in the enclosed stairway as an intruder descended.

Bolaka knew that no one else was authorized to access this level, at this late hour.

The two Swiss Guards readied their Uzi submachine guns positioning themselves between the stairway door and the entrance to the vault.

"Do you want us to lock you in?" one guard whispered hurriedly.

"No. We don't have time."

The monsignor positioned himself just inside the vault, peeking out toward the stairway door. The guards squared off, pointing their guns at the doorway, ready for anything. Then, abruptly, they dropped their guns to their sides and stood at attention.

Emerging from the darkened doorway was Pope Innocent XIV. "Boys, boys, boys," he said in Italian. "Relax. It's just me."

Bolaka gladly exhaled the breath he had been holding. He stepped into view, bowed and said, "Your Holiness. Why are you up, at this late hour?"

"I couldn't sleep," the pontiff complained as he extended his ring and the monsignor kissed it. "I am worried about the Apostle."

"Yes, I understand."

Bolaka stepped aside and followed the pope into the vault.

Innocent scanned the shelves that stored all 1782 instructional scrolls that John had delivered to popes throughout the two millennia of Christian history. He sighed, "What a treasure we have."

Perhaps it was partly from a restless night, but Bolaka could not avoid noticing that Pope Innocent had become a frail shell of his former self. Twenty years ago, a Turkish assassin had nearly killed him, landing four bullets into the popular pope's abdomen and hand. Since then, he had become susceptible to infections, had a colon tumor removed, dislocated his shoulder in a fall, broke a leg and replaced a hip, had his inflamed appendix removed, suffered from debilitating Parkinson's Disease and arthritis, could only eat through a feeding tube at times, suffered blood poisoning and blood vessel collapse from a urinary tract infection, and was forced to surgically insert a tube into his throat to aid respiration.[80] It seemed the Evil One had been working overtime at taunting this holy man.

Then the pope waved his hand toward the fifteen framed pictures on the wall. He admired each of the photographs that showed a never-changing John Eben Malek, posing with a succession of pontiffs over the past 180 years.

"Sometimes, late at night, I come down here just to study the scrolls and to look at those amazing pictures. Do you think I will be up there, some day?"

"Of course. The Apostle hasn't missed any of the last fifteen Holy Fathers."

"You're probably right," the pontiff exhaled. "But he better hurry. I don't have long."

Then the pope looked down at the scroll on the table. "I see we both have the same man on our minds."

"Yes, Holy Father. We've lost track of him. It just seems odd, after sending such a cryptic scroll."

"I agree…. Do you have the lawyer lady … Marconi on the search?"

"Yes, but she decided to contract it out."

"Why?"

"She found a former detective who had done extensive

interviews with the Apostle. She thought he would be the best man for the job."

"That sounds reasonable. Why do I detect disagreement in your voice?"

"Your Holiness, I'm not too sure about the man."

"Why is that?"

"He does not seem to be a man of faith. He's not a very serious person."

"Give it some time … and pray on it."

Innocent turned to leave but, before he reached the door, Bolaka had rolled the scroll open, on the table.

"Holy Father?"

The pope turned, "Yes?"

The monsignor pointed to a dark smear on the parchment. "What is this? You never told me."

Innocent smiled at the blotch at the end of the message. It was oval, perhaps an inch wide.

The African priest added, "I checked. It's on every one of these scrolls."

Innocent answered the question with a question. "Do you play cards, monsignor?"

Bolaka frowned. "I did … when I was young."

Before he turned to leave, the pope simply concluded, "That, monsignor, is our trump card."

There is a power somewhere
so organized, so subtle, so watchful,
so interlocked, so complete, so pervasive
that they better not speak above their breath
when they speak in condemnation of it.
President Woodrow Wilson

Chapter 14
Bali, Indonesia
December 4

Almost anyone would consider this five-star resort a tropical paradise. But ever since Evan Thas landed, he had been hearing nothing but complaints: "The airport was backed up.... We want the presidential suite.... The spa has a wait list."

The opulent St. Regis Bali Resort offered every luxury imaginable, even a personal butler service. Here, traditionally Asian-influenced architecture – with rooflines thatched by palm fronds – blended tastefully with contemporary onyx statuary and the flora and fauna that only Bali can boast.

Still, there were only 123 lavish suites, at the resort, and some of them did not provide a front row seat for viewing the south Pacific's famously clear turquoise waters.

Like himself, Evan was dealing with people who were demanding, but for understandable reasons. They lived by the gospel of "More" and, on that subject, Evan sympathized. He had expected that this international collection of global powerbrokers would be hard to please. He also realized that the invitees for the Legion of Babylon's annual conference – along with their entourage of invited hangers-on – would overrun not just the resort but the entire island. Evan predicted hearing complaints that this year's meeting was a very inconvenient twelve time zones from New York City, especially considering the price of jet fuel, these days. He even knew that many attendees would be uncomfortable in a country with such a large Muslim population. After all, many Muslim nations were now allying with communist countries in an effort to jointly undermine Israel, America and the other Western democracies. Still, all of that was the way Evan wanted it.

This year – Evan's first as Chairman of the Legion – he was determined to avoid the public relations fiasco of the last meeting. Then, the location of the secret summit had slipped out and protesters had disrupted the scheduled conferences for four days. That prompted some of the attendees to leave the conference early and, within days, the meeting was widely criticized when it was revealed that the Legion had named global depopulation as its top priority. It was an ominous message for the protesters and other conspiracy theorists.

These elites shunned publicity. For most, their names were unknown, around the world. Many held positions of power that few even understood. The members included the President of the European Central Bank, the Governor of the People's Bank of China, the Governor of the Bank of Japan, the President of the World Bank, and the Managing Director of the International Monetary Fund. Other interests were represented by the President of OPEC, the Secretary-General of the United Nations, and the CEO of the investment banking firm, Teppley Thor.

These days, the world had grown even more hostile to the leadership of the Legion's supremely-privileged, supremely-influential members. Spain's politicians, for example, were the first to buy into the Legion's Green jobs proposals. They launched an aggressive policy shift toward alternative energy and, soon, the country's unemployment rate shot up to more than twice the European Union average. Shell-shocked Spaniards started to realize that 2.2 jobs had been lost for every one created. Now, every macroeconomic statistic seemed to shout that Spain would be the next economy to collapse. The International Monetary Fund and other economic backstops had survived through the bailouts in recent months of Greece, Ireland, Portugal, Ukraine, Hungary and Iceland. But Spain was becoming a problem that would dwarf those. The Spanish economy was the fourth largest economy in the Eurozone and the tenth largest in the world. A bailout would likely cost hundreds of billions of dollars. Spain could become the proverbial straw that breaks the camel's back.[81]

Years ago, Fred Whitehead had allied himself with the Green-movement to help establish one of the Legion's favorite programs. He engineered a lobbyist's grand slam for bio-fuels production. Whitehead was able to push legislation through congress that awarded ethanol producers subsidies, a federal mandate, and even tariff protection. Now, however, taxpayers were starting to feel like they had been slammed across the head. After $50 billion had been spent propping up the industry, studies were starting to show that ethanol uses more energy than it produces.[82] Not only is it less energy efficient than represented, it is less environment-friendly.[83] Then, adding insult to injury, the new Green policies had diverted a wide variety of food products – from 25 percent of America's corn crop, to 98 percent of Thailand's cassava produce – to fuel. Literally, the world's food supply was being incinerated and the result was that food riots were breaking out around the globe as food inflation had thrown 44 million people into poverty.[84]

On top of that, the earlier sabotage of the Saudi Arabian

oilfields had introduced to the world "the new normal," including: not enough oil, not enough jobs, not enough health care, not enough food, not enough young workers to support entitlements for senior citizens, not enough control over rioters and terrorists, and on and on. Resistance, now, was starting to come from every country and every demographic.

Though, the Legion had once formed policy in secret – leaving the fame to the political figureheads they chose – recently, computer hackers had exposed how the puppet masters pulled the strings. With those secrets exposed, Legion members felt that bolder strategies had become necessary in order to insure safety and centralize power.

However, other forces also were planning their version of global centralized power. In the Middle East and Africa, radical Islamists had gained control wherever lawlessness prevailed or governments could be toppled. Their reward was a growing control of the world's oil supply. In many Western countries, also, Islamists had spread their influence by taking advantage of the exact freedoms that they hoped to eliminate, someday. The extremists had managed to channel widespread discontent, from city streets to prison cells, effectively silencing the voices of moderate Muslims with threats of violence or death. Their goal had been to establish a global *Caliphate* in which *Sharia* Law would prevail and freedoms that the West had taken for granted would perish.

Likewise, in Russia, neo-communists had rekindled the passions of those who had once longed for global domination of the communist ideal. The trend was a backlash from the recent excesses of Russia's greedy few and was secretly supported by Evan's partner, Vasily Melnikov, one of the greediest of the few.

Back in the 1990s, after the breakup of the Soviet Union, a

lull in East-West tensions had caused a false sense of peaceful coexistence,[85] and the new Russian acceptance of capitalism created a need for Western advice. So, the Russian government developed an economic transition plan based on the recommendations of American-sponsored economists, including Huntington Cyst's hand-picked experts.[86] Soon, frustrated Russians felt powerless against the fire-sale auctions of state-owned assets that eventually made a handful of Russians incredibly rich. In a country that spans 11 time zones, encompasses one-sixth of the world's land mass, and is arguably the wealthiest in terms of natural resources, corrupt cliques quickly devoured national assets like locusts descending on a wheat field. The auctions for Russia's spectacularly valuable natural resources raised less than $5 billion. By 1996, just seven Russian businessmen had gained control of 60 percent of the country's treasures, including its enormous oil and gas reserves.[87]

Today, resentful Russian radicals were no longer satisfied with protesting greed and preaching communist philosophy. Their impatience and anger had come to a boil. Their long list of grievances was balanced by just one proposed solution: violent change.

They did not wait long to strike.

Russian President Anton Nevsky had announced that he would seek another six year term. So, naturally, he knew that Vasily Melnikov's support would be highly valuable, not only because of his immense fortune but also because of his prized membership in the Legion of Babylon.

So, Nevsky arranged a meeting with Evan's partner at his scenic mountaintop estate. Before the meeting convened, however, a small band of heavily armed intruders stormed the mansion. Melnikov quickly made his way to his underground bunker, but Nevsky was not so lucky.

A day later, an Internet video was released that showed the intruders dragging the screaming Russian President out into the snow. There, bound bodyguards and Melnikov's bikini-clad girlfriends watched, helplessly, as the radicals hurled Nevsky off a scenic cliff.

It had been a major publicity coup for the leftists to "redistribute justice" by murdering one of the most powerful men on the planet. The video became a big hit on the Internet.

Here, on Bali, many of the conference attendees had offered their condolences to Melnikov, but they all knew that tragedy, once again, seemed to work in Evan's favor. The power vacuum could be filled, easily, by Evan's partner, Russia's richest man.

One reason for Evan's advancing influence in America was that he had brilliantly cobbled together a variety of tax-deductible foundations that had successfully funneled money to, and promoted, a variety of Evan's pet causes. He could even count on those groups to intimidate anyone who resisted his agenda priorities, such as campaign finance reform. So, channeling $123 million through eight "watch dog" organizations, Thas successfully convinced congress that the American people were insisting that campaign finance reforms be passed into law. His media machine relentlessly reported that the so-called Laugherly Bill would level the playing field of American politics, and take big-moneyed interests out of the political equation. In supporting the Bill, Evan's lackeys offered reams of deliberately faked data. The end result of the law's eventual passage, however, was the opposite of the stated goal. Now, Thas and other like-minded billionaires would be more in control of steering campaign results than any group in history.[88]

Internationally, the rosy scenarios that the Legion of Babylon had predicted regarding their policies were now turning blood-red in the streets. Anger and resentment had risen so significantly against the upper classes that many of these elites had now resorted to employing body guards for themselves and their families. In response to the growing anarchy, those on the extreme right, around the world, were starting to attack anyone who didn't look, think or act like them.

In a statement released prior to the summit, Evan Thas had pointed out that the Legion should not be blamed for the world's current economic problems. The outrageous self-sabotage of the Saudi oil fields, he argued, could not have been predicted and would have staggered the globe regardless of whose macroeconomic policies had been in force.

Still, to Evan and most Legion members, nothing could be more exhilarating than experimenting on this scale. The farther the world had sunk, the more "global solutions" were being demanded, around the world. Every member was certain of three things: The world could be saved, they were the ones who could do it, and salvation comes with a price tag. They also knew that every sullied reputation can be resuscitated by a good public relations expert.

For this year's summit, Evan's steering committee – including 36 members from 18 countries – had agreed upon an island venue so that the Legion would enjoy unprecedented isolation and security. Now, disruptions and breeches of confidentiality would be prevented or, at a minimum, receive swift justice. The tenor of the times demanded it.

Just as Thas had planned, the little island of Bali had no room left for journalists, paparazzi, or other assorted trouble-makers. Now, secrets would be kept, order would be maintained, and the global chess board would be rearranged in private.

Each meeting was by invitation, for Legion members only. Spouses were free to enjoy the pools, golf course or spa amenities, but not the conferences. Each member was sworn to secrecy and every one understood that even spouses – sometimes, *especially* spouses – could not be trusted.

On that point, however, many of the attendees did not have faith in Evan, either. He was simply becoming too powerful, and his global initiative for free, government-provided broadband Internet access was turning him into a bit of a poor man's cult hero, bringing entertainment to the masses. In the Information Age, he had become the king of information.

Worse, still, he seemed unpredictable, was becoming too visible and too often trumpeted the wrong messages. Many of the Members were still disturbed by Evan's previous meltdowns. But, over a span of just half a year, Evan Thas' media machine had transformed him, in the public eye, from late night talk-show joke to cover-story visionary.

After Cyst's death, the uncontested will had made Evan an instant multi-billionaire and the largest minority shareholder of XCyst Industries. That substantial ownership position in the conglomerate, combined with his experience in its every division, made him the obvious choice to become the next CEO.

The investing public, however, did not know what to make of the announcement. To them, Evan had been largely unknown, always working in the shadows of Dr. Cyst, the corporate visionary and technology rock star. Then, soon after being named to the top position, Evan's behavior became bizarre in the extreme. His apparently drunken rants gave rise to rumors of mental instability, drug abuse and even black magic rituals. His outrageous antics were streamed live on the

Internet and, soon, went viral as his name shot up the list of most popular word searches. Investors had become spooked by their first impressions and dumped the stock.

But it was all an act, aimed at commandeering the focus of the popular culture's echo chamber. Evan had staged a deliberate scandal, which provoked the stock collapse that made the world's top technology company ripe for the picking. Then, he and Vasily Melnikov took control of XCyst Industries by snatching every available share.

Soon, when the time arrived for a personal redemption story, Evan's media flaks released a flood of tantalizing fabrications, describing his anguished commitment to rehab, his humbling spiritual awakening, and his heroic decision to become the world's greatest philanthropist.

Evan's "rising out of the ashes" story became almost as popular as his "crash and burn" scandal had been. Many people felt sorry for the young man who had been suddenly thrust into one of the most consequential jobs on the planet. Men respected his feisty tenacity. Women longed to mother him. Still, even with so much sympathy in the air, Evan had gotten exactly what he wanted: Control of XCyst Industries and the most formidable technologies on the planet.

However, there was more than sympathy for the young titan. Nothing added more to Evan's messianic appeal than the amazing death-to-life revival of Huntington Cyst at the XCyst facilities on the Island of Nauru. With that bold announcement, Thas invigorated global dreams of immortality as he promised humanity that human life span is poised for previously unimaginable extensions and that the flaws of inherited biology would no longer dictate destiny.[89]

Legion members, though, realized that Evan's promises of longevity ran counter to the depopulation movement that they supported. Their computer models were clear: If mankind is to advance, then human population must sharply decline. After all, every living person consumes scarce natural resources and adds additional greenhouse gasses to the atmosphere. Consequently, Legion members strongly recommended that XCyst technologies should be reserved only for those individuals – and, of course, their loved ones – who excel economically, physically, and intellectually. So, in a world of limited resources, Evan's operations in Eden Village provided the ultimate perk for Legion members. They would always be first in line for any needed organs, blood or tissue. After all, the goal of immortality for Legion members was consistent with their private population control agenda that promoted human quality over quantity.

Among the most surprising of Evan's talents, however, was that he had developed a Midas-touch for finding gold, silver, diamonds and other precious metals, thanks to the technologies he controlled. He had received widespread attention when his satellites located the long-sought tombs of the ancient pharaoh, Akhenaten and his wife, Nefertiti. However, when covetous Egyptian authorities squabbled with him over the rights to such important treasures of Egyptian heritage, Evan simply renounced his claims on any of the property and simultaneously explained that his intention had been to sell it all to the highest bidders and distribute all proceeds directly to the struggling Egyptian masses.[90] Before long, equally covetous rioters had overwhelmed the streets of Cairo, demanding their "fair share" and revolutionaries in the rest of the Middle East prepared to follow their lead. The point had been well established: Don't mess with Evan Thas, or he will destabilize your regime.

In the media, Evan flaunted the newfound precious metals and antiquities that he discovered, but his surprising new technologies also gave him access to long-sought reserves of strategic minerals and metals. Today's advanced weaponry require very unusual, scarce resources, and Thas was now at the forefront of the companies that could find them.

Shadow owes its birth to light.
John Gay

Fred Whitehead nudged his back pillows, slid his reading glasses higher, and returned to his novel. But he could not focus on the story. He was growing impatient. "Come on, Angela. It's getting late."

Fred listened, but heard no response from the adjoining bathroom. So, he set his book down, pulled the sheet back and slid out of their antique mahogany poster bed. He slipped across an old Persian rug and put his ear to the bathroom door. Fred heard the sound of running water and, just before he moved away, heard Angela gagging.

Disappointed that there would be no sex, tonight, Fred returned to his bed and book.

A few moments later, when Angela emerged to sit on the bed, Fred mildly scolded her.

"Angela, you gotta get a grip. You're bringing your work home from the office."

She picked up some briefing papers from her bedside table and slid under the covers. "Easy for you to say. You have no idea what I'm dealing with."

Fred dropped his book to his lap. "Okay, I'll bite. Go ahead and get it off your chest."

She had to think, for a moment, whether her complaint was worth voicing to an ignorant and unreceptive audience. Then, she spoke. "Nothing is me. It's all so scripted.... Whenever the polling shows that people think I'm arrogant, they script me to express my humility. Whenever Evan's focus groups think that I am unfaithful, I go to church. Do you realize that I had to go out and shoot a bird, on camera, just to prove that I'm not anti-gun?" She frowned with disgust. "I'm serious. You have no idea."

"Oh, come on." Fred tickled her. "You're a charmer. Tell them what they want to hear. They'll love it."

"That's just the superficial side. I'm telling you: the world is coming unglued."

"Angela," he soothed, "you need to chill. Let's enjoy what we've been given. I'm not blind. I know the economy's in the shitter. So what? The stronger the downturn, the stronger the recovery. Just give it time. We'll get through it all, just fine."

His optimistic assessment made her realize that the luxurious lifestyle that she had provided her husband truly had blinded him to the world's harsh realities.

"There's a lot more going on, out there, than just an economic downturn."

He rolled next to her and tried to change the subject. "Come on. Let's snuggle."

"No," she demanded. "Let's talk."

"Oh, no," he groaned as he pulled away.

She tossed her papers into his lap. "Here's an example."

"What?"

"I had an eye-opening briefing from the CIA, today. Do you realize that even after removing prostitution and pornography from the numbers, the sale of women constitutes the third largest industry in the world?[91] Today, human trafficking is the fastest growing criminal enterprise on the planet."[92]

"Oh, come on. Don't judge everything by Bible Belt standards."

"Fred! They're sex objects! The worst kind of slaves!"

Angela began to weep as a hormonal tide rushed through her system.

"Hey, hey," Fred put his book away. He tried to calm her with an embrace. "It's okay. You're safe. What are you worried about?"

"I just ... I just imagine them doing that to our daughter."

"That's silly ... don't worry about things that aren't possible."

"Fred," she paused to work up her courage. "It *is* possible."

He pulled away. "What are you talking about?"

"I'm pregnant, Fred."

"Don't be ridiculous! You're over fifty!"

"I know. The doctors tell me I'm defying the laws of nature. It's weird, Fred, but I already know it's a girl."

"Well, get rid if it."

"It? Fred, we're talking about our baby."

"Are you crazy? We've got a sweet deal going. Let's not screw it up."

"It's a sweet deal for you, Fred. For me it's a hell of a lot of pressure and stress. I need an outlet. I need a pressure relief valve. I need someone to love."

"What do you think I'm for?"

She mulled over her disappointments, of which he was one. Not too many years ago, she had set her sights on a magazine-style existence where high heel shoes did not cramp her feet, staying thin was effortless, and facial wrinkles were conveniently airbrushed away. *Being president should be more fun.*

She mumbled, "It's not the same." Then Angela added, more firmly, "I want this baby, Fred. It's my last chance."

"Oh, that's just great! The fun's just starting. Don't I have a say, here?" Then he added, seriously, "I say get rid of it."

Angela thought for a moment, then mumbled, "Momma Laudie was right."

"What are you talking about?"

"Momma Laudie … she said that my family would be expanding. I just thought she meant getting married. She said a life or death decision would have to be made. I thought it was my life she meant."

"Are you nuts? You're gonna listen to that crazy old bag?"

"She even said that you would give me bad advice and that I should do the opposite of what you say."

"Oh, that's just great," he mumbled to himself. "Really great."

"Fred, she cursed my certainty and – with all these changes in my body – I really have found it hard to keep my emotions in check. I've been so confused, lately." Angela shook her head. "She had it right, all along."

"She was right about one thing. You *are* thinking foggy headed."

"Not now, I'm not."

Whitehead threw back the sheet, grabbed his book and slid out of bed. Then, as he headed for the door, barked, "Well, for what it's worth, I vote NO."

The real rulers in Washington are invisible
and exercise power from behind the scenes.
Supreme Court Justice Felix Frankfurter

Chapter 16
Bali, Indonesia
December 5

When the conference's opening lunch ended, the spouses and other non-invited guests were escorted out of the meeting area. Then, when he was introduced as the keynote speaker, Evan Thas approached the podium.

Behind the stage were 10 flat screen monitors that would display simultaneous translations of each speech. Because of the sensitive nature of the sessions, the words were computer generated. Human translators were not trusted.

Thas stood almost expressionless, even after hearing the glowing introduction that he, himself, had written.

While 120 predominantly male attendees applauded, a few of Evan's most ardent lackeys rose to their feet. However, he did not seem to care. When the room was restored to order, the redheaded young man spoke without notes and with a tone that conveyed a disdainful superiority.

"I struggled with the title that I would give this speech.... I thought, maybe, 'A prayer for the dying.'" Some of the audience members snorted their disapproval. "But then I settled for: 'You're either with us or against us.' I subtitled it, 'And God help you if you're against us.'"

These elites were not accustomed to being lectured to in this tone. Some grumbled, some even laughed.

Evan's eyes flared with unmistakable contempt. He

shoved the podium over and shouted, "Forces are gathering to take what you have!"

Suddenly, the room was quiet.

He continued, "We have uncovered an unmistakable pattern of actionable and predictive information from data-mining CyBot searches, emails and social networks. We know, with certainty, that revolutionaries on every continent have developed a level of global organization and technical sophistication that would have been unthinkable just five years ago. Make no mistake, they have a plan and they are coming after you. President Nevsky is just the beginning. Our research reveals, in detail, the barbarity of what they want. What you own is not enough. They want you, and they want your families. They want your demise to be shown on the Internet, and they want it to be so horribly shocking that no one like you will dare surface again."

The words hit hard because no one doubted the ability of XCyst Industries to eavesdrop on private communications around the globe. Now, Evan controlled a whole range of the world's most sophisticated technologies, including the CyBot search engine and the popular hard drive backup service that XCyst Industries offered for free. The questionable tactics used during the XCyst corporate takeover had launched a hundred investigations. But each eventually would consume years before clearing the Supreme Court.

The Chairman of Teppley Thor, Wall Street's most influential investment bank, could not restrain herself any longer. Agnes Thor's short, silver hair and placid blue eyes, normally presented the image of a loving grandmother. Nothing seemed to unsettle her, after so many years in the trenches of international finance. So, when she spoke out with concern, everyone took notice.

"Evan, have you talked to President Concepcion about these threats? I mean this is the kind of thing that should be handled by ..."

Suddenly, a door burst open at the back of the conference room and the lights went out. In the darkness, deafening gun shots flashed once, twice, then three times. Pleas, curses and prayers floated together in the electrified atmosphere of the darkened room. Some attendees groped their way to a door only to find it barricaded from the outside. Then, the room lighted again.

Four gunmen, dressed in black and wearing ski masks, surrounded the group. All of them had handguns and what looked like vests laden with explosives. One thug, at the front, had his arm around Evan's neck and a pistol to his head. The other three were guarding each of the double-door exits.

"Please don't kill me," Evan pleaded.

"Shut up, pig ... thief!" the gunman shouted. Then he announced to the audience, "We only want Thas. If you cooperate, we will only kill him."

Then one of the gunmen moved away from the barricaded door, pulled out a video camera, and started filming as Evan was dragged down from the podium.

"Please don't hurt me," Evan squealed with tears streaming down his face. "What did I do? What did I do?"

The man with the camera moved in close as the small redhead was thrown to the ground.

"You!" the gunman shouted at a woman as he pointed his gun at her head. "Shoot him!"

She nodded nervously as the cameraman handed her his pistol and the other man aimed his gun at her face.

"Rita, don't! Please don't!"

She paused as she looked down the shaking barrel.

The leader shouted, "Now!" and she pulled the trigger.

The deafening blast filled the room and Evan screamed as he clutched his stomach and moaned.

"He's not dead," the cameraman complained. He snatched the gun from the woman and handed it to another man, nearby. "You! Finish him."

The man did not hesitate. "Okay, just don't hurt me." He quickly took the gun and shot Evan.

By then, the powerful members of the Legion of Babylon were so numb that they almost didn't hear the blast. They also didn't hear Evan's final cries. Nor did they care. They only wanted it all to end.

But when Evan had coughed his last gasp, the leader sneered, "You stupid pigs! Why would we kill just one when we can have you all!" And, as he reached for a rip cord detonator on his vest, screams erupted.

Then he snatched the cord.

But nothing happened.

The leader glared at the group, but just before he and the gunmen sprinted for the back exit, he smiled.

With everyone but Evan now apparently safe, the audience was stunned and silent.

Then they heard a slow, steady clap. It was Evan's partner, Vasily Melnikov. He, alone, had not been fooled. "Bravo, Dr. Thas! Bravo!"

Evan rose to his feet and brushed himself off, but he was not smiling.

"This was not a joke," he said flatly. "It is unfortunate that such extreme measures were necessary. But you had to be shocked into reality. Next time, your enemies will not be firing blanks."

As Thas returned to the dais, some of his audience cursed

him and others thanked God. He set the podium aright, allowing his audience a moment to regain their composure. Then he said, "Churchill once observed that 'an appeaser is one who feeds his friends to a crocodile, hoping it will eat him last.' You had them outnumbered 30 to one and you still sacrificed me to the crocodile."

Some in the group nodded.

Then, with pointed urgency, he added, "I will no longer speak in delicate metaphors. I'm telling you now, without any doubt, that if we do not consolidate our capabilities, if we do not centralize our power, in a year we will all be dead."

Thas paused to let that message sink in. Then, he continued. "Most of you are clueless about the probability that your days are numbered. As unemployment and hunger have increased around the globe,[93] revolutionaries have been harnessing today's technologies to organize, educate and communicate more effectively than at any time in history."

The chairman of the Federal Reserve was aware of the world's increasing instability, but he did not share Evan's dire forecast. He spoke out with mild sarcasm. "To hear you tell it, we're dead already."

"Notice I used the word 'probability,' not 'certainty.' Look … from the beginning, emerging technologies have always tipped the balance of power. The spear, the sling, the arrow, the shield, the stirrup, the catapult – and on and on – each separated the conquerors from the conquered, in their day. The Internet has empowered our enemies. But the Web is a two-way street. I bring you the technologies that offer the advantages of a totalitarian spying regime, the likes of which the world has never seen.[94] I am offering the Legion supercomputers and data-mining technologies that will provide actionable intelligence by isolating and interpreting significant strands

116

of voice and Internet communications around the globe. We cannot lose sight of the fact that our first enemies are communicated words and ideas. So, the first front in the coming war is non-violent; it is a war against words. We must disrupt and distort the communications of our enemies and we must destroy the credibility of anyone who strays from our path. Call it rhetorical terrorism, if you like, but we have enough clout in the media to discredit or humiliate almost anyone.

"My friends, public opinion can be a manufactured product. How do we do it? First, we learn from those who have succeeded ... like Mao, Stalin and – dare I say..." Evan whispered, "Hitler."

He put his hands on his cheeks with feigned concern, "Oh my, I've spoken the unthinkable!" Then, seriously, he added, "But you can't argue with leadership success. They each molded their followers into single-minded armies. Using only the limited communications tools available to them, they overturned tradition and manufactured truth. In fact, Hitler once said that without a loudspeaker, he could never have conquered Germany."

Thas scanned the audience and still detected hesitation. "Look at the simple Hutus of Rwanda. This tribal people harnessed their only technology: the A.M. radio. Effectively harnessing the awesome power of rhetorical terrorism, the Hutus enflamed public opinion, demonized their enemies, and overwhelmed their opposition. Then, using little more than machetes, almost a million Rwandans were slaughtered in three months. That's a lot of people ... for Rwanda."

Evan suddenly realized he needed to tune back his enthusiasm a bit. "A terrible tragedy, of course. But it goes to show the supreme importance of harnessing whatever technology one can access."

Silent doubt filled the room.

"Look," Evan continued, "some of you have heard rumors about the technologies I control. It is up to you whether to believer them. But trust me, you want to be on my side."

Umberto Valdez – a Brazilian timber magnate – voiced his skepticism: "Dr. Thas, with all due respect, I have received reports that you and your various nonprofit organizations are actually funding and assisting the same radical organizations that you are warning us about."

"Quite right," Evan shot back. "I can exert more control over them if they believe I am on their side. But make no mistake, I will crush them when the time is right."

Senator Laugherly, the only politician deemed worthy enough to become a member, attempted to appease the critics by nudging Evan further. "I think you're holding back too much on us, Dr. Thas. I can't reveal classified senatorial briefing details, but CIA and NSA seem to be in awe of what you have developed. Can't you share a bit more with us?"

Evan sighed. "I guess now is as good of a time as any, for this."

Thas stepped down from the dais and into the audience to make his presentation more personal. "Would you all feel more secure if you partnered with someone who has control of satellites with thermal imaging technologies that track human targets even through walls and ceilings?[95] Or what about with someone who commands space platforms, with hyperspectral imagers, that locate undiscovered reserves of every type of strategic mineral or metal that is necessary for 21st century warfare? Those technologies are in my hands. I am the partner you need. In fact, I could go on and describe our newest generation of orbiters, but that program is too lethal to disclose, now, even to you." Evan smiled. "Ah, I have your attention?

Like avenging angels, my satellites will deliver justice from the sky. Suffice to say, these global orbiters will make today's strategic weapons obsolete… and they will drive fear into the hearts of my enemies. Or, should I say … our enemies?"

Evan waited for approving nods. But the information was too much for this audience to fully absorb. So, he spoke even more bluntly.

"Ladies and gentlemen, I set before you today a blessing and a curse – a blessing if you obey, a curse if you do not. [96] I assure you, they are coming after us. We must centralize power and take control now."

Evan saw some frowns. This group was not big on obedience, neither did they take kindly to threats. So, he went back to sugar-coating. "Our plans are for the greater good. We can all benefit. Look, if we act and I am wrong, the world will be safe and under our control. If we act and I am right, the world will be safer and still under our control. Mankind has nothing to lose!"

The iceberg of doubt was thawing. This group realized that a web of evil is not acceptable unless it is spun with pretty words.

So, Evan stayed positive. "We are going to reorganize the world! Isn't that a beautiful responsibility?"

Heads started nodding.

"Join me. Control your destiny. At this conference, we will divide the globe into ten regions. You have power now, but follow me and I will make you kings![97] You want in on that, don't you? Of course, you do!"

Faces in the audience finally reflected growing agreement.

"So, let's get moving!

Legion members started applauding.

At the podium, Evan quietly admired his own rhetorical

maneuverings, but he was not surprised. After all, the Titan technologies he controlled had evaluated the fears and addictions of these individuals so thoroughly that Evan knew exactly which buttons to push. This was Evan's special skill. Whether pitching individuals, groups or legislatures, he relied on the same tactics: Know your audience; Instill extreme fear; Present an enormously intricate plan of action; Stampede powerful but weak-willed individuals into immediate acceptance of his leadership. At this conference his strategy would succeed again.

Some of the Legion's members had been slow to convince. But the stakes were too high. This train was leaving the station, and almost no one was willing to remain behind.

"However," Thas continued, calming the increasingly excited audience. "No one outside the legion is to be trusted." He shouted, "No one!" Evan added, "The stakes are too high. So, our talking points will be distributed. You may recite those lines to your spouses, reporters … whoever. But you must never reveal the truth of our plans."

Evan's eyes scanned the approving crowd. "It is your choice: we cower and die, or take power and lie."

Then, to make them feel less pressured, Evan called the day's conferences to a close.

"If you do not wish to stay," Evan suggested, "your time to leave is now. But for those who remain a part of this great undertaking, we will spend the next three days remaking the world."

THAT NIGHT, at the restaurants of the St. Regis, conversations were muted. Many of the spouses could not understand the somber mood that had suddenly descended on the island.

Only one couple missed dinner. Umberto Valdez and his wife had decided to accept Evan's offer and leave the island. Unfortunately, their plane did not make it far.

The tragedy was blamed on Islamic extremists, but many Legion members had their doubts.

Chapter 17
Semiazas, California
December 20

Sharks understand certain things. They know how to kill about 20 Americans a year and they excel at killing fish for the purposes of eating or self-defense. They are the oceans' most efficient predators, taking life as if there is nothing to fear.

People understand certain things. They know how to kill about 38 million sharks a year[98] and they excel at killing anything and anyone for the purposes of eating or self defense, for sport or territory, for treasure or convenience, over an insult or for attention, for vengeance or fame, over ideology or for drugs, and on and on. They are the world's most efficient predators, taking life as if there is nothing to fear.

But there *is* something to fear … and it is not sharks.

CHIPPY AND HENRY had been faithfully evangelizing the territory that John had assigned to them. As the odd couple – a lanky Canadian and a dreadlocked Jamaican – wandered from town to town, across North America, they knew that they had to strike a delicate balance. On the one hand, they hoped to communicate their message to as many people as possible. On the other hand, they needed to keep an extremely low profile. After all, they were wanted men, hunted for their escape from Tarbuwth Correctional Facility, only months earlier.

From India, they had stowed away on a cargo ship. For nine days they had prayed in the dark, unable to open the doors of the container in which they hid. John told them that these trials would help prepare them for the days of darkness to come. Then, shortly after their arrival at the port of Mobile, Alabama, someone unlocked and opened the container door. When they snuck out, they saw no one, and no one saw them.

NOW, THREE WEEKS LATER, Chippy and Henry found themselves in Semiazas, a scenic city on the California coast. The Spirit-filled pair had accomplished a lot, so far, in Arkansas, Oklahoma and Utah. There, they had witnessed a passionate renewal of faith in a small but significant segment of society. Economic difficulties had already descended upon those communities, but many of the converted had heeded their warnings and had stepped up their focus on Spiritual needs, as well as preparing for a future in which food, clothing and shelter might be jeopardized. For some, the mission of renewed holiness was fully embraced. The more they had witnessed the descent of darkness around them, the more they had desired to return their communities to God. So, the two modern-day Apostles took comfort in knowing that their efforts would insure that the world's increasing evil would not be rising unchallenged.

In every community in the midst of all the anger, the traveling evangelists had encountered small pockets of heroic virtue. There were places of worship emphasizing that we must love the sinner, even while hating the sin. There were soup kitchens, homeless shelters and homes for unwed mothers that provided not only for physical needs but also Spiritual sustenance. There were prison ministries that delivered those

123

who had been broken by addiction or violence. There were prayer groups that instilled in their members a transcendent Spirit of forgiveness, mercy and humility. There were holy priests who continued to serve humbly, even when attacked by religious bigotry that attempted to tar them all with the taint of scandalous evil.

Chippy and Henry had been relying on prayers to find the remnant, the faithful few who could be counted on to shepherd the coming converts through the difficult times ahead. The remnant consisted of people from all walks of life but, it seemed to the evangelists, that they were almost always the least noticed in the world. Left on their own, the believers would be charged with the responsibility to dedicate themselves to prayer and fasting, preparing themselves and their loved ones for whatever would come to humanity, be they blessings or curses.

Across America, they also had found no shortage of blame and anger, and they had found waves of people with legitimate grievances: Workers who couldn't find jobs or felt exploited by their bosses; Bosses who felt overwhelmed by political forces that seemed hell-bent on regulating their businesses into bankruptcy; Women who had been abused by the very men who should have been protecting them; Men who had been betrayed by women they thought they loved; Members of various races, regions and sexual orientations who felt marginalized by bias; Youths unwilling to contribute to retirement and medical systems that would only benefit their elders; Elders who felt betrayed by youths who were destabilizing their promised retirement benefits; And everyone feeling disappointed by the incompetence, or betrayed by the corruption, of their elected officials.

Semiazas, however, had been a tougher nut to crack, so to

speak, than any other community. It was proving to be their most difficult destination. The community was known as the Hollywood of the porn industry and ever since the pair had arrived, they had found nothing but ridicule and disdain. Here, it seemed vice was perceived as virtue, and virtue as vice.

Even though Henry had been amazed at the power of his prayers, they seemed ineffective, here, and this city was becoming a major disappointment for him.

Before now, they had learned to accept the limitations of their ministry. They no longer felt offended or angry over rejection or insults. They had come to view themselves as mailmen with the sole responsibility of delivering an important letter. However, people did not have to read their mail. They were free either to welcome it like a lottery winnings notice or to toss it in the trash like so much junk mail.

Semiazas excelled at the tossing option.

From the crowded beaches, to the urban center of the city, to the rural vineyards on the outskirts of the county, no one had accepted the evangelists' message and the two of them were becoming emaciated and growing weak with hunger. They did not want to give up, but they had been offered no hospitality and the dumpsters here had not been very fruitful.

Henry had always been a bit of a pessimist, but even Chippy's enduring smile vanished as they sat on a boardwalk bench at the beach. The Canadian thought about how, just a year ago, this would have been paradise for him. The beach, bikinis and nearby beer were among his highest priorities in life. Now, however, he had more important things on his mind. He had learned to joyfully sacrifice his temporal comfort for the eternal comfort of others.

As he tucked his dreadlocks into a knitted cap, Henry said, "I don't know, mon. I'm gettin' awful hungry. I'm not sure how much longer I can go."

"Yeah," Chippy said with a sigh. "I know what you mean."

Then, as they looked down the beach, their eyes focused on a big man in the distance. He had a dark complexion and long dark hair. He was wearing sandals, jeans and a dark T-shirt, and was walking toward them.

Henry said, "John?" Then he jumped off the bench and shouted, "My brother? My brother! Oh, dear Lord! It's brother John!"

A couple of attractive sun-bathers looked up from their beach towels with irritated frowns.

More cautious, Chippy just stood back and watched. *Surely, Henry's imagining things.*

But as he watched the Jamaican run, he also saw that unmistakably calm smile stretch across the man's face.

Chippy screamed "John!" and the two of them rushed to their friend with so much joy and Christian love that the reunion baffled many of the nearby sunbathers.

THE TWO MEN walked through the city for hours with John, describing to him how they had been striking out time and again.

"Brothers," John assured "redouble your prayers. I am confident you will find a remnant here."

"So, what are we doing wrong?" Chippy asked.

"I have never seen a town where the demons have total control. It is very rare. But, sometimes, the really tough ones require more prayer and fasting from you."[99]

"Oh, no," Henry moaned. "Don't tell me that. If I fast any more, I'm gonna be dead!"

John smiled. "Okay, brother Henry, let's see if we can find

you some food."

They wandered through the streets noticing what looked like a town in serious decline. In fact, the recent economic downturn had accelerated the area's dimming prospects. A few storefronts had been burned and abandoned. Some others had broken windows boarded up, graffiti and other signs of vandalism.

"These people are clearly going through difficult times," John observed. "Remember to emphasize that if we bear our burdens with hope and love, we will be blessed with eternal reward."

Henry laughed. "That doesn't work here."

John remembered many of the people he had encountered during countless disasters, both natural and man-made. He realized that tragedy can reveal the inner heart and that it tends to either perfect the good among us, or convert or condemn the wicked.[100] While suffering comes to all, one's response to it identifies one's level of Christian commitment.

Over the centuries, John had witnessed a full range of reactions from the one extreme of persecutions in which Christians were quietly resigned to martyrdom, to the other extreme of rioters looting, raping and murdering after a natural disaster. John now believed that there is nothing that reveals the state of a soul more than a crisis and that, oftentimes, only a crisis can convert a lost soul.

The more they walked, the more the three men wondered if vice, here, had completely eclipsed virtue. There were busy porn shops, strip clubs and hookers, even during daylight hours. Trying to find their way out of the area, they took a shortcut that turned out to be "crack alley." There, they even witnessed a mugging that happened so fast that they were unable to stop it.

The cause of the problems here, however, was not economic. It was Spiritual.

Everywhere, John tried to politely strike up conversations with strangers, inevitably mentioning God's loving mercy for anyone who wants it. But his efforts here were uniformly rejected. When the three hungry men finally found a dumpster that contained discarded food, a young punk threw rocks at them and forced them to flee.

Escaping, they nearly ran into a crowd that had gathered, apparently protesting something. Then they noticed "Planned Parenthood" on the front of the building.

"Let's check this out," John suggested as they blended in with the crowd.

The protesters were confined to a sidewalk, outside the clinic property fence. Some of them carried large signs of aborted fetuses and one man even prowled the fence line dressed like the Grim Reaper. A few signs displayed, "BABY KILLER" in dripping red paint.

John attempted to size them up, noticing that none carried Bibles or rosaries. In fact, he saw no indication that this group had faith-based motivations.

Then an old Dodge Neon slowly pulled into the driveway, but it had to stop until protesters were able to get out of the way.

"Uh, oh," an elderly ringleader groaned to herself. "Probably gonna call the cops, now."

John asked, "Why?"

The woman looked at the big, dark immigrant, suspiciously, sizing up the man she did not recognize. Then she explained, "Every time we block a car the least little bit, they call the cops." She snorted, "You'd think they'd wanna protect our constitutional right to protest. But no, they gotta defend the murderers."

When the Neon had pulled into a space at the back of the lot, the protesters behind the fence watched, but no one emerged from the car. The crowd quieted as they waited, one minute after another. Suddenly, a young clinic staffer bolted out the back door. She was carrying a coat and, when she reached the car, the door opened. A girl stepped out – very young, very afraid, and very tearful. Just before the coat was thrown over her head, John felt stabbing empathy as he beheld the terror in her eyes. Then, as the two girls rushed into the clinic, the crowd erupted in cat-calls.

"Baby killer!"

"Rot in hell!"

"We got your license plate! We're gonna tell your momma!"

John was stunned. He saw only hatred in their faces. He had attended many abortion protests in the past. None of them had been remotely like this. John was pro-life to his core, but he cringed while watching these aggressive tactics that he felt would only embolden the opposition and allow them to portray themselves as the victims. John agreed with the saying that for every abortion there are two victims, one dead and one injured. It was not his calling to add insult to injury.

When the two girls disappeared inside, the crowd quieted. But John was boiling.

"What are you people doing?" he shouted angrily.

One man said, "We're saving babies."

"No you're not! Not one baby will be saved by your actions."

One guy grumbled, "Oh, shut up."

"Wait," another man yelled, "here he comes."

The crowd parted as a black Mercedes Benz pulled through

the driveway. The car pulled into a reserved parking space and, when the man got out, the protesters screamed again.

"Murderer!"

"Baby killer!"

But the doctor reacted very differently to the insults hurled his way. The man smiled broadly and took a dramatic bow to the crowd.

"Don't you see?" John shouted. "You only encourage your enemies! You only give them reason to hate you back!"

The doctor smiled as if soaking up adulation, then he flipped the bird at the protesters with both hands. But before the abortionist's hands lowered, the smile left his face. The Grim Reaper had burst through the open gate, rushed toward the man and slammed a knife into his chest.

Wide eyed and gasping, the doctor stood staring into the Grim Reaper's eyes. Then he collapsed onto the pavement and the masked attacker fled.

John, Chippy and Henry were stunned into silence. Around them, however, chuckles and mildly affirming comments soon replaced the gasps.

"I guess he killed his last baby."

Henry whispered to John, "Oh, mon, we're in trouble now."

John's anger was coming to a boil. He shouted, "Don't you see what you have done? You have become what you despise! You condemn murder while you condone murder! Only love can change hearts!"

Two girls from the clinic rushed out of the back door, to assist the doctor.

"Oh my God! He's bleeding! Call 911!"

The other girl ran back inside as one protester shouted,

"Don't blame us. We didn't do it."

"John, we gotta go," Chippy urged as he pulled on John's arm.

"He deserved it!" a woman screamed. "They all do!"

John pleaded, "In the name of Jesus Christ…" but the protesters were repelled by the words. Some of their faces contorted even more hatefully.

"Go away! We don't want you here!" one protester demanded in such a guttural tone that it did not sound human.

John pulled loose from Chippy's tugging, backed into the empty street, looked up to heaven and began to cry. His chest trembled and tears streamed down his red cheeks. He dropped to his knees on the asphalt.

A man looked down on John and sneered, "Still think we didn't save any babies today?"

With the sound of distant sirens, the protesters realized it was time to disperse. So, they left in all directions, with a sense of accomplishment.

As the approaching sirens grew louder, Henry begged, "Brother John, we have to go, now!"

Six patrol cars quickly surrounded the exits and, when protesters started running, officers chased them down and tackled the unlucky ones. One fleeing man was clubbed over the head and spewed venomous hatred at the policeman when he fell to the pavement.

In the midst of the tumult, John slowly rose to his feet, moaning and sighing. Chippy and Henry felt helpless. They suspected John was about to have a nervous breakdown.

John mumbled, "Oh, dear God, there must be someone here worth saving. There must be a remnant here worth saving, Lord!"

John seemed to be listening for an answer but his moans

grew louder and he sobbed, uncontrollably. Then, with a look of dread, the ancient Apostle gazed up to heaven and choked out these words: "Even your dust ... we shake off our ... shoes."

After a deep sigh, John's head lowered and he sadly nodded at Chippy and Henry. The three men walked through the noisy tumult, without interference from anyone, almost as if they were unseen.

An hour later, Chippy asked John how he had known that they needed him in California. He explained that Spiritual discernment had sent him there just as Spiritual discernment was now sending him to Rome. Then, as they headed out of town, John asked the two evangelists to avoid looking back on Semiazas,[101] even when they felt the initial rumblings of the San Andreas fault.[102]

The Lord said,
"If as one people speaking the same language
they have begun to do this,
then nothing they plan to do
will be impossible for them."
Genesis 11:6

Faridah Shabaan clicked the remote control until she found the XBC News channel. When she saw Evan at the podium she sat her vodka and tonic down and called out. "Malphas,[103] Pruflas[104]... he already started."

Faridah stretched her legs across the floral patterned sofa as Evan's brothers entered the family room and stood, almost at attention, behind their mother. The twins looked alike – stoic – they dressed alike – in black suits – and they always obeyed Faridah.

"Huntie?" she called out. "Do you want to see Evan?"

She glanced out the glass doors at Cyst who was sitting on his favorite poolside chaise lounge. He did not respond. His eyes never left the ocean. So, she turned up the volume.

Evan looked pleased to be answering the questions. He was at Eden Village's auditorium on the island of Nauru. Evan had arranged this press junket for reporters from all the major networks and international publications, including the most prestigious science journals.

Evan's family had missed his initial comments, but it appeared to them that the journalists were showing great

133

interest. Perhaps they already realized that they would be reporting on history in the making.

1st REPORTER: "Dr. Thas, can you explain those breakthroughs in layman's terms?"

THAS: "Of course. Chimeras are mixtures of two or more species in one body. They might even be part animal, part human. For example, at Eden Village we have designed pigs with human blood flowing through their bodies.[105] We have even fused human cells with rabbit eggs."[106]

2nd REPORTER: "What benefits do these experiments offer?"

THAS: "Transhumanism extends the research agenda of contemporary biomedicine. It will allow mankind to transcend the limits of nature and overcome the effects of human disease and degenerative illnesses. It provides the promise of engineering human anatomy to battle global warming.[107] We envision the possibility of broadening human potential by overcoming aging, cognitive shortcomings, involuntary suffering, and even our confinement to planet Earth. Here, at Eden Village, we are on the cusp of accomplishments that will allow a future of ageless bodies, transcendent experiences, and extraordinary minds.[108]

2nd REPORTER: "Is it true that your biotechnologists have produced an experimental child whose parents are a pair of mice?"

Other journalists laughed at the question.

2nd REPORTER: "No, I'm serious. I've been told that Eden Village has genetically engineered mice to produce human sperm and eggs and that XCyst Industries has conducted *in vitro* fertilization to produce human offspring. Can you confirm or deny that?"[109]

Evan thought for a brief moment before answering.

THAS: "Most people would find that problematic. Next?"

3rd REPORTER: "Why all the secrecy? Why can't we have more freedom to explore, while we're here at Eden Village?"

THAS: "What do you want to see, my underwear drawer?"

The journalists laughed.

3rd REPORTER: "It's just that we're hearing some pretty crazy stories about what's going on here."

THAS: "That's not surprising. I'm sure Newton, Pasteur and Einstein all had competitors who lied about their work. Doesn't bother me a bit…. Okay, how about you, in the back?"

4th REPORTER: "It appears that the pace of these developments has sped up. Has the new translator feature on the CyBot search engine been a factor?"

THAS: "No doubt. CyBot's universal translator provides simultaneous translations, allowing scientists from every country, using any language, to communicate effectively and immediately via the Internet.[110] Of course, our Cyst-Blanc supercomputers also get some of the credit…. Did I mention that they're sixteen times faster than any other?"

Evan pointed to someone near the door but a bald, old reporter in the front stood.

OLD REPORTER: "Aren't you trying to play God?"

THAS: "You're joking, right?"

Hunched over from age and a lifelong spinal problem, the old man spoke without anger, and with sadness in his voice.

OLD REPORTER: "No sir, I am not."

THAS: "I am leading humanity to a quality of life that has never before existed. I have put years of blood, sweat and tears into these breakthroughs… and Dr. Cyst, too…. Look, earlier this year, my team successfully injected human neurons into the brains of embryonic mice. At Eden Village, we now have mice with brains that are 100 percent human. Imagine what doors that will open for our studies into treating diseases like Alzheimer's and Parkinson's?[111] I am putting humanity on the path to immortality."

4th REPORTER: "But what about the possibility of unintended consequences on Nauru ... like, disturbing fragile ecosystems ... endangering human health ... disrupting species integrity?"

THAS: "Of course, those are the first priorities for any serious scientist. Rest assured that we have integrated unprecedented security and safety systems into our operations, with multiple layers of redundancies. Trust me, it's all safe. We're not dummies, you know."[112]

The journalists laughed at Evan's calm understatement. After all, their host had paid for this trip. He deserved a friendly audience.

THAS: "Now, let's get to the big announcement."

The room filled with the sounds of mumbling and shuffling. No one had suspected that something even bigger was to be announced.

THAS: "So, you thought those developments were the breakthroughs that I am here to announce? No, not at all.... Of course they are all historic biological milestones. But I want to speak to you about something far more important.... To those who are here, to those who are watching on television, to those who are listening on radio, I say that you will never forget this moment. I announce to you today that I have created synthetic life."[113]

Some of the journalists grumbled their disbelief.

THAS: "I have created organisms with manmade DNA. I give to humanity designer organisms that are built rather than evolved. This is a defining moment in biology. Imagine: I am designing microbes that will clean up after offshore oil drilling disasters. I am reconstructing algae that will absorb carbon dioxide from the atmosphere and convert it into fuel. That alone is worth more than a trillion dollars."

OLD REPORTER: "Is that what it's all about: the money? You developed Eden Village on an independent but economically desperate island that offers no regulatory scrutiny. You say your work is for the good of humanity but you've applied for patents on more than 300 genes, raising concerns that you're claiming intellectual property rights on the building blocks of life."

THAS: "You're Goldstein, right?"

Faridah grunted her disgust.

The old man refused to yield.

OLD REPORTER: "You're creating life that could never have existed naturally. Are you trying to usurp the role of God?"

THAS: "Do you want me to halt the development of bacteria that will soak up carbon dioxide from the atmosphere and end global warming? Do you condemn humanity to be without the vaccines that I will soon bring to market? If so, that blood will be on your hands."

Faridah burst out, "Stupid Jew!"

THAS: "You're a Luddite, Goldstein, and people like you are holding us back! I'm really sick of your kind. You're a misguided ... no, let me correct myself ... you're an evil man. Yes, evil people stand in the way of progress. And we will all be better off when your kind is snuffed out from..."

Abruptly, back in New York, a quick-witted XBC News producer switched Evan off the air and scrambled to replace the broadcast with a taped segment. The producer knew that

Evan's rants had become venomous in recent months and hoped to protect her boss from the consequences of his fury. Still, as she cued an old report, she worried that her career was now over.

"What happened?" Faridah asked.

Her sons, as usual, did not answer.

The television had switched to a report that was describing John Eben Malek as a fugitive from justice, a man who had viciously murdered a nun and had escaped from prison, with other inmates, on the day of his scheduled execution.

"Wait," Faridah shouted as John's mug shot displayed on the screen. She knew who he was: the enemy. From the first time she saw him, peering out from the rubble that had entombed her and might have killed her, he agitated her to the depths of her soul.

"He's the one," she continued. "Study his face."

Malphas and Pruflas focused their attention on the image.

As the program went to a commercial, she added, "He can stop us."

Just then, Cyst yelled from the pool. "Medicine … I need my pills!"

Faridah growled her disapproval and clicked off the television.

*Choose a job you love,
and you will never have to work a day in your life.*
Confucius

Chapter 19
Over the Atlantic Ocean
December 22

Tim Lassiter stretched his long legs, kicked off his shoes and nestled into his comfortable recliner. He had never before flown first class and he was determined to take advantage of every luxury it offered.

These days, a little bit of rebellion was in order for Lassiter. After eight years on the police force, subject to all their rules regarding proper dress and behavior, Lassiter had relaxed many of his standards. He had let his hair grow long and had not even bathed or shaved for a couple days.

As the jet reached cruising altitude, the man sitting next to Lassiter asked, "You gonna keep those off?"

Lassiter looked at the frowning passenger and then at the aromatic tennis shoes he was pointing at.

"I think so."

Not happy with the answer, the man cranked back his seat, turned away, and put a blanket over his head.

This would be a long flight to Mumbai.

Lassiter was still giggly about his good fortune and negotiating prowess. So far, he had received over $86,000 from his two mysterious clients. So, even if he eventually failed to find Malek, he already felt like a winner. In some ways he even hoped he would not find John. Perhaps the man was a delusional lunatic, but he truly seemed harmless. The former detective had developed a respect for the enigmatic drifter and was thrilled when he heard about the escape. Still, that respect could not compare to the additional $213,000 he would collect if he captured the fugitive. But, no matter what, this would be the job of Tim's life: nothing but the best, paid for with other people's money.

So, he settled in, reflecting on the past tumultuous week.

Then a word nagged at him: *Alive.* He remembered that the brunette attorney, Jane Marconi, had emphasized bringing Malek back alive and unharmed. But he did not recall lovely Mercedes Dare expressing that requirement.

Lassiter wondered who had hired them and he suspected that it might even be the same client, one who had mistakenly thought he would have twice the chance of success if he used two different law firms as intermediaries. *The poor sucker doesn't realize that all roads lead to me!*

Then he chuckled to himself as he recalled speeding back to his apartment, that night, tearing up the place in search of the audio tapes of his interrogations. It was one of his sloppy habits that had contributed to his firing. He never had been very organized and had developed an inconvenient habit of losing evidence.

Finally, after four hours of frustration, storming through his apartment like a destroying tornado, he remembered that the tapes might be in the trunk of his car. He ran outside and woke the neighbors when he hooted with delight upon seeing the 18 hours of taped clues to where John might go to hide.

By the time the flight attendant made the rounds, Lassiter's neighbor had dozed off under the blanket.

"Sir, would you like a drink?"

"Uh, is that included in the ticket price?"

"Of course," she said, smiling.

"Yeah, well, sure. Bourbon on the rocks."

Then, as she pulled out a mini bottle he added, "Can I make it a double?"

She assured him pleasantly, "Sir, whatever you want."

"Well then, what the heck, let's make it a triple."

She set him up with three miniatures and started to roll her cart away when he added, "Oh, I'm sorry. I almost forgot." He pointed at the sleeping man next to him. "My friend wanted a triple, too."

HOURS LATER, Lassiter felt stuffed from the large, lovely meal he had just eaten. Hoping not to miss out on anything, he had ordered each of the selections: Trout Almondine, Beef Wellington and Chicken Kiev.

Then, making a final round, the attendant suggested, "Coffee or tea?"

He asked sheepishly, "Both?"

Of course, with all that caffeine, Lassiter eventually needed an after-dinner liqueur to settle his nerves. Soon, as most passengers slept in the darkened cabin, Lassiter reclined under his little spotlight, sipping an Amaretto and immersing himself in a travel magazine.

As he flipped through page after page of glorious luxury on the French Riviera, Lassiter was beginning to relish his perks. Soon, he imagined living the life of these lovely pictures: reviewing priceless artworks under the ornamented dome of Nice's fabulous Hotel Negresco, then heading out to take a sunny stroll along the beachfront *Promenade des Anglais*.

And, of course, an adoring blond would be on his arm.

No, he thought, *make it a French brunette.*

Then, Lassiter's heart raced as he dreamed of revving

the engine of a red, convertible Porsche along the Mediterranean's cliff-side *corniche,* destined for a day trip to the Monte Carlo Casino and, of course, an unforgettable evening with his new friend at the medieval, mountaintop village of Eze.

But then Lassiter put the magazine down and remembered that this trip would not be so luxurious.

After refueling in Ankara Turkey, he would catch a connecting flight in Mumbai India that would take him south, along the Western Ghats, before connecting in Bangalore. Then the weary traveler would head for his final destination in Kumbakonam. All totaled, the trip would take 32 hours.

Just the thought of it forced him to order another Amaretto.

A DAY LATER, the blind priest's face revealed his deep suspicion. Lassiter had managed to find St. Mary's Orphanage and had quickly discovered that Father Antony, if anyone here, would have the answers he needed. But after ten minutes of cordial conversation and gentle prodding, Lassiter could tell that the priest was hiding what he knew.

"Look," Lassiter pressed, "I'm just gonna be straight with you. John Eben Malek is a convicted murderer."

"Oh, my Lord."

"He murdered a nun, Father. And we believe he helped to execute the biological attack on the Saudi Royal Family. He escaped from an American prison on the day of his scheduled execution."

Lassiter pulled a wrinkled clipping out of his pocket. "Look, here's a news article about him." Then he remembered, *Oh, yeah, he's blind.*

Stunned into silence and realizing the gravity of the

situation, the priest's face tightened with pain. "Ohhhh, I had no idea."

"So, where do you think he might have gone?"

"I'm telling you sincerely, I really do not know. He never talked about it with us. But I know he talked a lot with his friends."

"Friends? What do you mean, friends?"

"The men he was with. There were twelve of them."

"You gotta be kidding me! They were here, too?"

"Yes, he had twelve friends. But, I must say, none of these men had evil in their hearts. In fact, I believe quite the opposite."

"Well, ya know. It is what it is…. You sure you don't know anything … anything at all. I gotta find him."

Lassiter studied the priest's face as he seemed to sincerely search his memory but remember nothing. "I am sorry. I do not know," the priest answered as he wondered, *Why would the Vatican protect a criminal?*

After Lassiter made a cordial departure he searched for a quiet place to gather his thoughts. The area outside the orphanage was crowded, noisy and dusty, just like what he had experienced on his way there. Lassiter maneuvered around cow dung on the street and did not like the smell in the air. As he quickly hustled across the busy avenue, he dodged an old yellow taxi, but was almost hit by a bicycle driven rickshaw.

Then, on the other side in the distance, Lassiter found a quiet spot next to a spring, where he sat on a short wall, oblivious to the historic Hindu Temple behind him. He missed home but, soon, his thoughts returned to the job at hand. This arduous journey had produced nothing. Still, something was nagging at him. He recalled the interrogation tapes and remembered that John had repeatedly spoken of his fondness for the mountain-top Monastery of Monte Cassino. John had explained that the historic, holy site was where St. Benedict had established the Benedictine Order in 529. It is just 80 miles south of Rome, and John claimed he had visited there many times.

Lassiter mulled over that destination but, first, he knew he had to focus on other important matters. He pulled out his cell phone and, just as directed, sent progress reports to attorneys Mercedes Dare and Jane Marconi. The text messages read: "Malek left India. I got xlent tips here. Trail leads to Nice France, Hotel Negresco."

He clicked off his phone and smiled.

Ahhh, yes. Christmas on the French Riviera.

The closer we get to the reign of Antichrist,
the more will the darkness of Satan spread over the earth,
and the more will his satellites increase their efforts
to trap the faithful in their nets.
Jeanne le Royer (Sister of Nativity)
18th Century

Chapter 20
XCyst Industries Headquarters
West Palm Beach, Florida
December 24

Today was expected to be a whirlwind for Evan. Since he had turned 30, however, every day had been spent this way.[114] He had scheduled a full load of meetings with his division heads, one on one, at his corporate headquarters. All of these managers were highly accomplished in their fields, capable of leading large companies, on their own. But each felt a special honor to be at XCyst Industries and to meet, today, with their legendary boss.

The international conglomerate had always been successful. However, at a time when most companies were struggling to survive, every XCyst division had become a steamroller under the new leadership of Evan Thas. Though many of the division heads had doubted Thas when he initially took the reigns, now, no one questioned his leadership.

Still, working for Evan was not easy for any of them. He was brilliant but mercurial. He demanded the highest standards of excellence and commitment. Also, even though he was a master delegator, his genius and experience allowed him the credible threat that, if he had to replace any one of them, he could manage their division without skipping a beat.

145

These very accomplished leaders each understood the amazing breadth of Evan's knowledge.

Just as Huntington Cyst had been known as "The Prophet of Technology,"[115] the media had now dubbed Evan Thas "The Tech Titan."[116] Where Cyst had spent years, methodically preparing the way for technology to dominate human existence, Thas was now lunging ahead, reaping the benefits. However, some of his envious competitors more accurately described Evan's hyper-aggressive style as "raping the benefits."

Every endeavor was war, for Evan. The metaphor for his approach was not "take no prisoners." Rather, it was more like "execute the prisoners in full view of the enemy just to instill fear." For that reason, in whatever industry Evan chose to expand, competitors had learned that they would soon be purchased by, or crushed by, XCyst Industries.

The company's success, however, had as much to do with rewards. Increasingly, XCyst's corporate generosity was reaching into the upper echelons of twenty seven national governments and the United Nations. Also, Evan had moved quickly to leverage his leadership of the Legion of Babylon into significant relationships with the central bankers of the G-20, whose countries comprised 85% of global gross national product, 80% of world trade (including EU intra-trade) and two-thirds of the world's population.[117]

Today, the mood in Evan's reception area was jovial and triumphant. Though the global economy had been hammered, the assembled division heads had delivered record profits. So, they each expected that a generous Christmas bonus would top off a great year.

The first scheduled to meet with the boss was the head of XCyst's advanced weaponry division. The former general had recently received the Forrestal Award from the National

Defense Industrial Association for his outstanding contribution to global security. From his acceptance speech, he had received widespread media attention when he described the world as having "one of the most complex and demanding" global security environments anyone has ever seen because "the number and velocity of events and the volatility of their consequences have never been greater."[118]

Proud of his recent accolades – and secure in the belief that a world on the brink made him the man with the plan – the bulldog general entered Evan's office on a high. Within seven minutes, however, Thas had explained that he would be initiating a strategic shift, that the company was moving away from advanced weaponry, that the division was being sold, and that the transition would take six months.[119]

"I'm ... well, frankly ... I'm shocked," the general stuttered.

"Haven't you read about my spiritual conversion, general?"

He snorted, "Of course, who hasn't? But I thought that was all P.R."

"You thought wrong. Frankly, what XCyst has been offering through that division is yesterday's news."

The general laughed. "What? Those are the most sophisticated weapons in human history."

"Not quite."

As Evan stood to signal that the meeting was over, he offered his hand and his best wishes for whatever the executive chose to do after that. The man rose, shook Evan's hand and left the office quietly, still trying to absorb what had just happened.

The next executive on the list had been leading Evan's XBC News division. With her decades-long record of reporting from every major hotspot, she had earned her colleagues' respect from when she had been held captive and tortured during her last reporting assignment in Afghanistan. The harrowing adventure lasted a grueling three weeks as Taliban warlords interrogated her as a spy. Her eventual midnight escape in a black burka soon became the poster image that advertised the eventual movie that told her story. So, this journalism icon was revered in every newsroom.

To Evan, however, she had become a woman of ambition and her Titan profile had indicated that she was not a trustworthy lieutenant. Somehow, she had developed the idea that her supposed "journalistic standards" conflicted with the stories, facts and slants that Evan wanted XBC News to report.

In recent months, she had quietly simmered as Evan fanatically demanded stories that sensationalized the sins and shortcomings of people of faith. She resented his bias against Christians and Jews, in particular, and mocked his interest in promoting hate-speech prosecutions for some Biblically-based sermons. She could hardly hold her tongue, at a recent meeting, when he pushed his agenda for taxing and marginalizing churches and charities so that America's social support network might become monopolized by the federal government.

Her working relationship with Evan finally boiled over, however, when she adamantly refused to run a Thas-scripted "news" story that stereotyped Catholic clergy as sexually obsessed perverts. In fact, as she correctly observed, it was not the priests who were obsessed, but Evan.

However, she did not understand the roots of his compulsion. Thas had projected the sins of Huntington Cyst – the adoptive father who had treated him so horribly but rewarded him so generously – upon all priests. It was a crutch for him, the only solution to the dilemma of psychologically managing his love/hate relationship with Cyst.

After that confrontation, it did not sit well with Evan that her supporters in the news division now knew that she had defied his orders and emerged unscathed.

So, understanding the prickly nature of their relationship, the news executive entered Evan's office warily.

"Please sit down," Thas suggested before he got right to the point. "I don't think it is a secret that I am not satisfied with your performance."

"Oh," she feigned surprise, "but XBC News is first in the 25 to 54 demographic for every hour except 7:00 PM."

"You see," Evan shook his head, "that wouldn't be good enough for me. If I were in your shoes, I would be asking, 'How can we be first every hour?'"

Of course, she had to accept that perfection would be an improvement.

He continued. "No. We can't let the News division continue its death spiral."

She snorted a laugh of incredulity.

"So, for the good of our great network, we have to let you go."

"Wow," she marveled. "You're a real piece of work.... After all I've done for you." Then, barely containing her contempt, she asked, "So, who's replacing me?"

Without missing a beat, Evan responded flatly, "Trixie Stapleton."

The executive burst out a laugh, "You're joking! She's my secretary!"

"That's right."

"She's a kid ... never made more than $35,000 a year! She doesn't even have a journalism degree!"

"And your point is…?" Then Evan raised an eyebrow as if to ask, *Any more questions?*

She stood, spouted a sarcastic, "Merry Christmas to you, too, asshole!" and bolted for the door.

As the former executive left the office, Evan savored the trade that he was making. It would give him exactly what he wanted: A figurehead for the news division, who would be immensely grateful and completely subservient.

Outside, the mood in the reception area was changing. When the general had departed, speechless, the laughter subsided. But, now, after watching the news executive storm out, cursing Evan under her breath, an ominous silence filled the waiting room. The remaining division heads wondered what this meeting was all about. *Maybe Thas is looking for something more than profits.… But what?*

The theatrics had worked. Now, Evan's management team would be entering his office exactly how he wanted them: Shaking in their hand-made John Lobb loafers.

Always unpredictable, however, Thas changed the schedule and announced to the receptionist that he wanted to see Amy Laugherly, next. The leggy, young blond had been Fred Whitehead's old flame when they built their partnership into Washington's most powerful lobbying firm. Their marriage, however, had not been as successful. But as the daughter of the Senate Appropriations Committee Chairman, she was still quite a power-player in Washington. Now, even without Whitehead at her side, she had managed to build on her firm's lobbying successes, particularly in the area of tax laws.

As Amy sat down, Evan reflected on her record: Based on XCyst's international profits of $14.2 billion for the preceding fiscal year – $5.1 billion of which from operations in the United States – the company's annual tax liability had totaled zero. But not only that, XCyst had even earned a tax benefit of $3.2 billion to carry forward in future tax years.[120]

"Bravo," Thas applauded as Amy sat down with a smile. "Excellent work."

"Well, I wish I could say I did it all. Fred deserves some of the credit."

"I'm sure he does," Evan said. "Speaking of Fred, you still have the hots for him?"

She squirmed a little in her chair. "Oh, you know: Once a flame, always a flame."

"Well, who knows? Maybe you'll be seeing more of him."

Amy thought the comment sounded odd. *Fred's married now.*

Evan passed on to more pressing matters. "Your next lobbying priority will be the most important one you have ever tackled."

"How so?"

"Amy, you remember how most of the Saudi Royal family was wiped out."

"Of course ... a biological attack from unknown perpetrators."

"No, that's just the cover story."

"Then what happened?"

"What I am telling you cannot leave this room."

"Certainly."

"The cause was actually the most virulent virus the CDC has ever encountered," Evan lied. "They did not release that information for fear of panicking the public before a vaccine could be developed. We've been lucky it has not spread outside the Kingdom ... yet. But it's coming."

"How bad can it be?"

"The 1918 influenza pandemic killed up to 100 million, worldwide. Adjusting for population growth, we're looking at 370 million, assuming this virus is not more lethal. However … we know it is."

"Dear God."

"I want you to clear your schedule for the next month. We need a full court press on this priority. We must move fast, but Angela doesn't want a panic." Evan tossed a thick folder into her lap. "Here are the studies that validate where America stands and where we must go. Our researchers at XCyst have found the vaccine. We're working triple shifts to produce enough of it. Now, we just have to educate our politicians in order to quickly mandate that every citizen receives immunization shots."

"Shots?"

"Yes, we can do it on the hand but we prefer the forehead."

"That's strange."

"No big deal. It just leaves a little mark … three small, concentric circles, kind of like a bulls eye. And, soon, we'll roll the immunization program out globally."

"Why do we need to lobby for this? It sounds like a no-brainer."

"It is. But some congressmen may try to delay … you know debate, read the bills. But, Amy, this is a crisis. Everything must be implemented immediately. The world can't afford to have them play politics when lives are at stake."

"So, what do you want me to do?"

"I have you scheduled to meet with our top scientists for the rest of the afternoon. They'll get you up to speed fast."

"What about the people who won't go along?"

Evan slammed his palm on the desk. "We can't have that. Not only will they face likely death but they will be endangering the lives of others. Amy, the highest levels of America's security and enforcement entities are being briefed today. Everyone will low-key this thing for the next week until the president makes the announcement. Then, if the shit storm hits, they'll be ready for it.... But, frankly, I think everyone's so beaten down, these days, they'll all just go along with the plan." Thas snorted a suppressed laugh. "We've got a doozey of a public relations campaign planned."

Then Evan switched gears. "You know, I could picture Senator Laugherly in the White House. He's the only congressman I've trusted with the advance data. You think your Dad's interested in higher office?"

"Uh ... 'interested' is probably too mild of a word.... Still, he's not as young as he used to be. Too bad he has six years before that possibility opens up."

Evan pondered, "Well, you never know."

THE REMAINING EXECUTIVES continued to file into the office, one at a time. The energy division head explained that, after the loss of the Saudi oilfields, the global shortages of oil and natural gas supplies had produced record profits for his division. With Evan's urging, he reluctantly agreed to continue to drag his feet in the search for new oil reserves.

Later, Evan expressed general satisfaction to the technology division chief who oversaw the developments in Cyst-Blanc supercomputers as well as the CyBot Internet search engine, and the popular hard-drive backup service that XCyst Industries offered for free. His primary concern was that they needed to continue to tweak their data-mining algorithms in an effort to better manage information overload. This had become necessary because, with the Legion of Babylon, he had set an unalterable deadline for the Titan program to be fully integrated into XCyst's satellite program within six months.

Then, to the marketing and public relations head, Evan directed a detailed and ambitious new publicity plan. He said he wanted everyone to understand his commitment to relieving the global food shortage and resulting food riots. So, he would sell the XCyst Industries' advanced weaponry division. From those proceeds, he would fund an unprecedented food bank for the poor. Unmentioned to the public, however, would be that most of the money would be channeled into marketing his image.

Next up, Dr. Trip Weston entered the office. He was the head of XCyst's Aerospace Technologies Division.

Evan greeted Dr. Weston with extraordinary deference. The young man had a mind that even Thas admired. More than that, however, was that this brilliant scientist had been trusted as Evan's only backup for control of the XCyst satellites. A series of biometric triggers had been devised, that required either of them to authorize and initiate any significant satellite maneuver. His assignment to this position demonstrated Evan's extreme confidence in the man's loyalty.

Weston was one of the very few scientists who understood the full capabilities of Evan's four most powerful satellites, most importantly, the one code-named Glass Andalusian. Each of them had proven extraordinary capabilities, whether utilizing thermal imaging to detect and pursue individuals, even inside buildings, or monitoring communications across the globe, or even detecting gold under the sands of Egypt or at the bottom of the Atlantic Ocean.

When the man sat down, Evan asked, "So, Doctor, how's that baby girl doing?"

Weston was surprised and pleased that, for the first time,

Evan showed a friendly interest in his personal life.

"Thank you for asking, Doctor Thas. She's great. Not really a baby, anymore. Definitely a toddler. You know, scooting around so fast that it's hard to keep up."

"That's wonderful," Evan chuckled. "Maybe someday I'll have children. I'm looking forward to it."

The long day was wearing on Evan. There was an uncomfortable silence, for a moment, until Evan continued. "Doctor, I want you to know that I have some real concerns about the program."

"Concerns?"

"Yes. Not about you, mind you, but about White House interference."

"Oh? How so?"

"Well, they've threatened to remove satellite control from us."

The scientist was blushing with embarrassment. "Dr. Thas we're working on correcting the problem. I know we've had some unexpected problems: widespread fish kills, bird kills, you know."

"That's not what I'm …"

"But our team feels that we can tweak the radiation exposure down …"

Evan tried to interrupt his blathering. "No, that's not what I …"

The scientist defensively refused to yield. "We can decrease the lethality of the radiation beam if we just …"[121]

Thas' tone became angrier. "You don't understand what I am …"

"With reduced radiation levels, I believe you will still find the treasures you are looking …"

"No!" Evan shouted, cutting him off. Then Thas took

charge, in rapid-fire mode. "Look, Trip, I have a really packed schedule today. So, I'm sure you'll forgive me if I get to the point … or, actually, two points. First, I don't want you to decrease the lethality of our radiation beam. I want you to increase it."

"Increase?"

"Yes, dammit! Increase and focus it as much as..."

"Well, I guess we can …"

"Stop interrupting me! Second, I have entrusted you with backup control of my satellites. Your absolute loyalty is with me. You are never – Do you hear me? Never! – to let those satellites fall under anyone else's control!"

"Well, I guess …"

"You guess?! You guess?! Listen to me," Evan shouted. "If you even think about relinquishing control of my satellites, that little girl of yours is dead!"

Weston winced.

"Now, get outa here."

As the stunned scientist left the room, Evan's receptionist entered with a telephone message she had just received.

"I'm sorry, Dr. Thas, but your last appointment is a no-show."

She could see that he was about to explode, so she quickly added, "But there's good news."

She handed him the message that she had been given. It was from the chief bio-engineer at the Eden facilities on Nauru.

Evan read, "Sorry I can't make it, Dr. Thas. You will understand when you see. We've made amazing progress. You have to see to believe. Come ASAP."

Thas lowered the note, thought for a moment, and smiled.

In the center of hell, I saw a dark and horrible
looking abyss and, into this, Lucifer was cast...
God Himself had decreed this and I was likewise told,
if I remember right, that he will be unchained for a time
50 or 60 years before the year of Christ, 2000.
Venerable Anne Catherine Emmerich[122]

Chapter 21
Near Atlanta, Georgia
December 28

John woke with a start when a stream of rainwater touched his face. Rising from his midnight slumber, he sighed as he reevaluated his choice to sleep under the bridge that he had chosen as his makeshift bedroom for the night. The comforting sound of rain had lulled him into a deep state of sleep, and he dreamed of the many times that God had sent miraculous signs and wonders to warn and to guide His people.

One time, in particular, repeatedly had returned to John's dreams.

In the 1st century, Emperor Domitian had been conducting a reign of terror against Christians. He was a vain man, even by royal standards, who had taken to wearing wigs over his balding scalp and he was outraged when John ignored his demands to stop evangelizing in Rome. When the Emperor finally ordered John's arrest, he decreed that the execution would be presented as an entertainment for the Roman people.

On that fateful day, a large vat of oil – five feet high and wide – had been placed over a roaring fire on the bloody sand floor of the Colosseum. With the Emperor and his entourage watching, a variety of gladiators first proved their skill against wild beasts as they slaughtered hundreds with the encouragement of over fifty thousand cheering spectators. From a nearby cage, John observed the bloodbath with his wrists and ankles tied together. Then, when all saw that the oil was sufficiently boiling, the Emperor gave the signal, and two gladiators dragged the Apostle out of the cage, jerking a rope that had been tightened around his neck.

As John stumbled repeatedly from the rough treatment of the Gladiators, the jeering crowd screamed blasphemous obscenities at the determined Christian until the Emperor stood. Then, over the rumblings of the large crowd, Domitian shouted, "John, son of Zebedee, Jew from Galilee, follower of the one known as Christ, you have been tried and sentenced to death for failing to profess my divinity."

The spectators hissed their disapproval.

Domitian continued, "However … I am a forgiving god."

The crowd grumbled that mercy would not be entertaining.

"My vengeance might – and I emphasize "might" – be placated if you will now grovel in the dirt, beg for my mercy and worship me."

Throughout the arena, angry viewers shouted their disapproval, demanding death. Then the Emperor raised his hand, commanding silence, so John could speak.

But John did not respond.

"Go on … beg for mercy."

After a moment, John shouted, "I *do* beg for mercy."

The spectators laughed until the Emperor quieted them.

Then John continued, "From the one true God, from our Lord and Savior Jesus Christ."

Angrily, Domitian punched his fist into the air – signaling the execution – and the crowd screamed with delight. The

Gladiators dragged John by the neck, closer to the vat and threw the loose end of the rope over scaffolding that had been constructed high over the bonfire. Then they pulled the loose end until, choking and coughing, John dangled over the bubbling oil.

Domitian shouted to the crowd, "What do you want?"

Almost in unison, thousands screamed, "Death!"

So, the Emperor's fist punched into the air, the Gladiators released the rope, and John's body dropped and disappeared into the boiling oil.

Thunderous cheers and laughter erupted throughout the arena and Domitian visibly celebrated his satisfaction ... until John's head emerged out of the oil.

Suddenly, as if a switch had been flipped, the Colosseum became quiet.

Shocked, Domitian rose to his feet.

Then, when John spoke, everyone could hear. "Romans: Worship the one true God. The God of Abraham, Isaac and Jacob. The Creator and the Judge of all. He is a jealous God, desiring that you worship no other."

"Kill him!" Domitian screamed. But the rope had fallen from the scaffold and the embers and red-hot vat prevented the Gladiators from subduing the Apostle.

"Almighty God, alone," John continued, "has the power to deliver you from death. His Son, our Lord Jesus Christ, has given you the Word of God. Follow Him, so that you may truly live."

"Kill him! Kill him! Kill him!" the Emperor demanded with the frenzied scream of a spoiled child.

By now, the oil that had splashed out had extinguished the bonfire. With minimal effort, John lifted himself out of the vat and emerged completely dry.

Standing in front of the smoking symbol of Domitian's vanity, John shouted, "Romans: Will you now accept Jesus Christ as your Lord and Savior?"

The stunned crowd did not know how to respond.

"Will you place no god before Him?"

The Roman spectators were witnessing a convincing contrast between the power of John's God and the impotence of their Emperor.

"Do you now choose to worship the One True God, the One who has delivered me from certain death?"

Slowly, rumblings grew into cheers and then into an echoing roar of approval. Domitian turned and quickly exited with his entourage, fearful that the crowd might turn on him.

This humiliation had accomplished the opposite of what the Emperor had wanted. Within days, so many Romans had converted that he knew he had to get John out of view. He couldn't kill him, so he chose to end the bothersome Christian's evangelizing by exiling him to the island of Patmos. There, again, he accomplished the opposite of what he wanted. On that island, in exile, the Apostle wrote The Revelation, the book that would intrigue future Christians until the end of the Age.[123]

AS JOHN LOOKED OUT from under the bridge, he mourned that the examples of evil through history seemed endless. But as the rain grew worse he pulled out his new Rosary and began praying for the rain to stop. Soon, however, he realized how petty those prayers were and changed to praying for the conversion of the hard-hearted people he had left in Semiazas, just eight days ago.

Back then, the ancient Apostle had separated from Chippy

and Henry so that they could journey into Canada, while he headed east, across America. John felt urgently drawn to far-away Rome, but his hitchhiking progress had been very slow. Earlier, as he neared Atlanta, John had wondered how an escapee, convicted of murder and suspected of terrorism, could possibly get to Rome quickly. He knew, however, that answers to his prayers always seemed to materialize.

Suddenly, from the shadows, John heard something and stiffened with fear. Through the centuries, he had experienced more than his fair share of pain, and he had studiously learned how to avoid it, whenever possible. But he also did not want to escape, unnecessarily, into the downpour.

A man stepped out from the darkness. It was the buck-toothed bum that John had shared his sandwich with, earlier that evening, after a successful round of scrounging for food. Even though John never carried anything of value, he remembered other times when he had been mugged after showing generosity. Now, the bedraggled stranger was probably coming back for whatever he could take.

The man stepped out of the shadows and John saw that he was carrying a large black bag.

"What do you want?" John asked with as much calm as he could muster.

The bum moved closer, prompting John to stand up and prepare to defend himself or to run out, into the rain.

"These are for you, old chap," the bum responded with a distinctly English accent as he extended the bag toward the Apostle.

John took the gift. Then the man handed him a note and walked away, into the dark rain.

John folded the bag over his arm and opened the note, which read, "Hartsfield Airport, Alitalia Airlines Flight 1389,

Gate 29B, 4:30 p.m., tomorrow…"

John was baffled. He peaked under the plastic bag and could see a dark, freshly dry-cleaned suit. John threw the plastic off and realized it was a pilot's uniform, on a hangar. He felt around and found another bag dangling from the hangar that contained neatly polished black shoes. Then he discovered a passport and an airline identification in the coat pocket. He opened them up and saw his picture on each I.D. above the name, John Michael Gabriel.

John looked out into the rain, but the bum was gone. He raised and read the rest of the note: "Get a haircut."

Then, when he understood, John threw back his head, belted out a loud laugh, and exclaimed, "Angels!"[124]

THE NEXT DAY, John was clean cut and shaven after happening upon a homeless shelter where they took care of his grooming needs. As requested, he waited in his crisp pilot's uniform at Gate 29B. He had no idea of what would come next, when three pilots approached him.

"Captain Gabriel?" the apparent leader asked.

John studied the lean Italian who had extended his hand.

"Uhhh, just call me John."

The pilot shook his hand and introduced him to the other men. Then he added, "Look, John, I realize you're going through hell, right now. Don't worry. We'll try to make this flight easy for you."

John answered tentatively, "Okay."

Then one of the other pilots asked, "Where's your luggage."

John stammered, "I … uh … don't have any."

The third man responded sympathetically, "Yeah, you

have more to worry about than luggage, right now."

"John," the leader added, "in ten hours we'll have you in Rome. Just take it easy for this one."

Then the three pilots led him through the check-in, down the boarding ramp, and into the cockpit of their Airbus 380. There, they directed John to a backup pilot's seat as they stowed their luggage. While they prepared for the flight, John watched to imitate them as they strapped on their seatbelts and secured their headphones.

John studied the baffling array of keyboards, joysticks, levers, pedals and digital monitors in front of the two lead pilots. He had no idea what any of it meant. After all, this was not just his first time in a cockpit, it was his first time in a plane.

As they prepared for departure, the three Italian pilots spoke loudly and gesticulated emphatically while John just sat back quietly, trying to hide the fact that his mind was racing with prayers.

"You okay, John?" the other backup pilot asked.

"Yes ... yes ... I'm fine." Then John inquired, "You mentioned the hell I'm going through."

"Oh, man, that was terrible."

"Uh ... what do you know about that?" John asked, trying to figure out what he was talking about.

"Yeah, everything, pretty much."

John pressed on, "What ... exactly?"

The pilot reluctantly added, "About James, your brother."

A flash of bittersweet memories ran through John's mind as he remembered his beloved brother. Then he wondered, *What have the angels worked up, this time?*

John confirmed, "Yes ... James was my brother," with an increasingly uncomfortable tone. "What about him?"

The pilot showed extreme reluctance. "Oh, man."

John felt he had no choice but to push. "Yes … go ahead."

After a pause, the man spit out, "The bastards chopped his … well, you know."

John wanted to roll his eyes, but knew he shouldn't. Yes, his brother's tragic beheading had been one of the worst memories of his long life. But it had happened almost two thousand years ago. Now John understood that God was determined to get him to Rome quickly and that the angels had set up this elaborate scam to protect him from telling lies. Once again, he knew to just go along and keep his mouth shut.

Then the embarrassed pilot added, "If you want to sleep this one out, go ahead. We can handle it."

So, comforted by the knowledge that Jesus and James were smiling down upon him, that is exactly what John did.

Ambition is not a vice
of little people.
Michel de Montaigne

Evan Thas sat quietly, deliberately diverting his thoughts to a pleasant subject: his new girlfriend, Mercedes Dare. The coming meeting, however, would not be so pleasant. He was waiting for the president like a schoolboy who had been called to the principal's office.

Evan did not like that the receptionist had directed him away from the sofas and, instead, insisted that he sit on an uncomfortable chair across from the president's desk. That requirement had signaled that this was not to be a social visit. But he suspected that, already.

There had been numerous warning signs. For example, this was to be his first "on the record" meeting with Angela. Normally, they had always met at odd locations, off site, so that the Secret Service would not make an official log of the visit. Now, Angela seemed to be planning a publicly confrontational conference. One of her staffers had even leaked that prediction to the press.

But Evan comforted himself with the thought that some disasters cannot be blamed on him.

Thas listened, without amusement, to the muzak that was being piped into the most important office in the world. It was a kitchy remake of a 1960s hit. *So much like Angela*, he thought regarding the lyrics. *Naïve, self-absorbed, passe'*.

Then Angela stormed in with Vice President Everson Blight following close behind. Over the past few weeks, she had started to rely on Blight's loyalty more than ever, hoping that he could soon eclipse Evan's influence.

"What the hell are we going to do, Evan?" she asked as she plopped down in her leather desk chair.

Evan studied the desperation in her face and responded calmly, "Can you be more specific?"

Blight had stepped in next to Evan, towering over him. "Look Thas," he demanded, "don't play stupid. We got panic spreadin' from Seattle to El Paso because *your* radiation is spillin' out over half the west coast. What's your damn plan?"

Evan slowly turned to look up at the Vice President. Then he asked, condescendingly, "And why are you here?"

Blight pulled his fist back and growled, "I oughta…"

"Stop it, Everson!" the president shouted. "We need answers, not fights."

Indeed, Thas understood exactly why she was upset: the San Andreas Fault had been ripped open by the earthquake that everyone knew would some day come. Over forty thousand had died in the tumult and subsequent tsunami. Now, however, the San Opollito nuclear power plant – designed and built by XCyst Industries – was leaking radiation and might be melting down. The potential long-term human and economic impact of this disaster could eventually dwarf the tragedy of the initial earthquake. So far, over ten million California residents had been forced to evacuate without any assurances that they would ever return. As radiation had spread into the atmosphere and ocean, many evacuees sought comfort from their gods: The proud looted; The humble prayed.

Evan also understood why Angela had wanted Blight to attend the meeting. He would be her witness and, more

166

importantly, her bodyguard. Evan knew that she was becoming more paranoid every day. He liked to play on that weakness, just to tweak her, occasionally.

But most importantly, he knew she was upset that her honeymoon had been interrupted. Evan inwardly celebrated that misfortune because it had been at her wedding that she had threatened to take control of his satellites. That was an unforgiveable mistake. The more she had defied his wishes, the more he had withdrawn his support, and the inevitable consequence was that her incompetence would soon be revealed. Now, the responsibilities of the office were dogging her wherever she went and the stress showed on her face and in the polls. She was becoming bitter by the distractions and seethed at the thought that her long list of global problems now included a catastrophe in her own back yard.

Angela waved Blight to take a chair. "This is an XCyst nuclear plant, Evan. It could single-handedly destroy my presidency."

"Yes, it is my plant and there was nothing wrong with it."

"What?!" Blight asked incredulously.

"The regulators requested a facility that would withstand a 9.2 quake and that is what we built."

They all knew that this quake had registered 9.3 on the Richter Scale.[125]

"That difference is a minor technicality," the Vice President charged.

"That difference is a 52 percent higher seismic energy yield ... moron!"

Angela sighed. She wanted to jump over her desk and strangle the little redhead. But she realized he had gained the upper hand. After all, they both knew the secret that her birth certificate was mysteriously missing from the archive of

Florida's Vital Records. It was one more of Evan's clever little tricks, another blackmail noose that he had strapped around her neck. The last thing she needed now was a media firestorm claiming her entire presidency had been a fraud. Still, she had never discussed the subject with Evan. She realized that he feasted on fear and anger. So, even though she was boiling inside, she knew she had to present a cool exterior.

"Look, Evan," she reasoned, "I know we have hit some rough patches in our relationship, lately. You want me to admit it? I will: Everson, I wouldn't be president today if I hadn't received Evan's assistance."

"That's no surprise," Blight complained. "He promised I'd be president, too.... I always knew he was a two-timin' bastard."

Evan showed no response.

"Come on, let's stop arguing," she urged. "We have problems to solve."

Evan took control, "XCyst has assembled 3,742 experts – more intellectual talent than has ever been mobilized for any natural disaster. Our emergency response team has been arriving from around the globe and is working 24/7. They are integrating seamlessly with FEMA, NRC, Homeland Defense … you name it. We have in transit the world's largest cement boom pump that will start encasing the rupture in concrete as early as tomorrow afternoon. It is one of a kind."

"What about the workers?" Angela asked, accepting the hard reality that this tragedy would get worse before better. "Do you have an estimate of … long-term fatalities?"

"That's not a major issue. We've imported our labor pool from Sub-Saharan Africa. When the job is done, we'll pay them well and ship them back, out of the public eye. So, we don't have to worry about headlines and lawsuits concerning irradiated Americans."

The thought turned her stomach. "That doesn't solve much."

Evan added, "Look, our public relations department has prepared an information packet that will be distributed throughout the international media. It contains a detailed crisis response plan and provides ample evidence that neither XCyst Industries nor your team are at fault. This tragedy easily can be pinned on the last administration."

"Evan," she groaned, "I'm focused on the problem, right now, not politics."

"Angela," he shouted, "wake up! Haven't you learned anything, yet? This crisis creates opportunities for you. Dammit, you're the president! Next election, your opponents will be handing the voters Rorschach tests on blank paper, while yours will be printed on hundred dollar bills. Just stick to our scripts and you'll be fine."

She didn't respond.

"Angela, everything is moving in the right direction. Nobody can blame you for tragedy. It's your chance to centralize power and seize control!"

"I don't want control!" she screamed.

Thas responded flatly, "It's a little late to be deciding that."

Blight inserted, "Madame President, this guy's got some kinda crazy agenda going on. The scientists I consulted say even his immunization program is a pile of crap."

Evan persisted. "They elected you to supply their wants, Angela. Give them what they want or they will turn your life into a living hell."

She sighed, "How?"

A good start would be at the FCC. I can do a lot with the Internet but the public owns the airwaves. So, the government should take control of them. You have a national emergency that requires strong leadership. Issue an Executive Order to rescind all FCC licenses. Then you control the news that is reported. I assure you, Americans will be much more cooperative when we are telling them what they need to know.

The president was frozen in thought. So, Evan added, "Angela, don't you understand that the worse things get, the better? Where else will they turn? They need you, Angela, and you need me. They'll be begging us to take charge of their lives.... Need is good. The time to centralize power is now."

"Who elected you?" Blight complained.

Evan continued, "Look, Angela, what's done is done. We can't cry over spilled milk. However, within three days, the radiation leaks will end. Still, the civil unrest will not. You think you have problems on your hands now, just wait. So, I and my strategists have developed a detailed crisis response plan for American governmental reorganization. I tell you, Angela, your life is at risk. You have to get things under control. You must rid this country of the checks and balances on government action that have only hindered effective change. This plan will set in place the mechanisms that will allow you to restructure from top to bottom ... declare martial law ... suspend elections ... temporarily place all authority in the Executive Branch. In other words, no half measures."

Exasperated, Blight asked, "What is this, a *coup*?"

"I don't know, Evan," she hedged.

Evan snapped. "I'm losing my patience with you!" Blight gasped at his audacity. "You keep pulling away from me and where has that gotten you? I am offering you unprecedented power! Follow my plan and I guarantee you that the vast majority of your media coverage – the contemporaneous record that historians will some day review – will report that

President Concepcion's handling of this crisis was on par with the greatest of American presidents. This quake was bad, but just be glad it wasn't "The Big One." Angela, there is always a way to profit from disaster. Now, you have an opportunity for greatness. I assure you of this..."

Blight interrupted, "Ahhh, your assurance don't mean..."

"Enough!" Angela shouted, with increasing claustrophobia.

She had hoped Evan might have offered some magical fix that would make the problem go away quickly. With all the unrest that had been percolating around the globe, the growing budget deficits, the worsening inflation and unemployment rates, street riots and falling governments, she had already reached her limit. None of her advisers were solving the problems and, in fact, they all seemed to be growing. In desperation, she had even resorted to her old means of spiritual support: psychics, palm readers, and trance channelers. But nothing seemed to work.

Evan turned toward Blight slowly and resumed where he left off: "I was saying: I assure you of this..." then he added with emphasis, "as long as nobody pisses me off."

"Who the hell do you think you are?" Blight growled. "You're talkin' to the Vice President of the United States, you little punk."

Evan remained stoic as he stared at Blight. He remembered how much the pompous blowhard irked him from the first time they met. Elevating him onto the ticket had been one of Evan's most regretted miscalculations.

At the time, Thas had believed that maneuvering someone from the opposition onto the ticket would allow him an additional level of control over the president, since the threat of impeachment could be manufactured with this particular congress. But, before long, Vice President Blight had alienated so many legislators, from both parties, that no one was inclined to impeach Angela no matter how badly she led. Surprisingly, both of them had worked out a cozy relationship in which his two most demanding responsibilities required knowing how to cut a ribbon and how to sit in a funeral pew.

Regardless, as long as Blight had been given access to Air Force Two, the spotlight, and top-shelf booze, he had presented no threat to Angela. That didn't sit well with Evan because he knew that a paranoid Angela was far easier to control.

So, Thas seemed to change the subject with, "There once was a wise and worthy monarch."

"What are you jabbering about?" Blight grumbled.

"It's called a parable," Evan answered. "something a simpleton like you might understand."

President Concepcion had reached her limit, and finally erupted at Thas, "What the hell are you talking about?! I need solutions!"

Thas resumed, "There once was a wise and worthy monarch."

"Look," she shouted, "skip the fairy tales!"

He continued, unperturbed, "His kingdom was the envy of the world."

"I'm the President of the United States, dammit!"

"But the king was not happy, because the world had not yet benefitted from his enlightened leadership."

"Shut up!" Her voice had become shrill.

"So, the monarch called his two children into the throne room. As they stood before him, he evaluated their limited abilities and numerous flaws."

"I am ordering you to shut up!"

Evan returned an intense stare to Angela. "The young princess was attractive, bright and clever. However, she was arrogant and had dedicated her life to learning everything about anything that is inconsequential."

Then his hollow gaze focused on Blight. "However, the fat and lazy young prince was too dim-witted to learn anything..."

"Do I have to take this?" Blight asked Angela.

She demanded, "What is your point? Dammit, get to the point?!"

"Ohhh," Evan groaned, "I hate to leave out the wise leader's warning that cooperation insures safety and defiance invites destruction.... But, okay, since you're in charge, I'll skip it."

Evan pulled a large silver coin out of his pocket and then continued. "So, the king was forced to choose. Who would rule his kingdom when he left to conquer the world ... and who would have to be tossed into the moat?" Thas studied the coin. "Would it be heads, for the ungrateful and disobedient princess whom he once had named as the temporary head of his kingdom while he travelled?" Evan turned the coin over. "Or would it be tails – the ass end of the coin – for the ungrateful ass of a son..."

"That's it," Blight said as he rose out of the chair and headed for the door. "I don't have to put up with this crap."

Just as the door slammed, Evan tossed the coin high into the air. The bright silver disk flashed brilliantly as it caught the sunlight from a nearby window with each revolution.

"Little man, you listen to me," Angela screamed. "If you push me, I will push back!"

Evan caught the coin effortlessly and flipped it over, onto his forearm. But he did not look down at it. Instead, his eyes locked in on hers. Then, with an unwavering stare, he asked, "Who do you think loses, Angela?"

†††

THAT NIGHT, Fred had to move to another bedroom because Angela kept waking him as she struggled to get comfortable and fall asleep. The day's confrontation had stolen what little peace of mind she had left. However, at least she had drawn some satisfaction from the fact that Blight had witnessed Evan's treachery. For the first time, she felt she had gained the upper hand, because Evan had violated his own rule: Never allow more than one witness when admitting incriminating facts.

Soon after she dozed off, in the early morning hours, the phone rang. The polite and professional military voice on the line gave her two reports of tragic news. The second account was that "The Big One" had hit – a 9.8 magnitude earthquake centered on a small California town called Semiazas.

Angela, however, could hardly pay attention to those words, because the first report was that Secret Service protection had been breached and that Vice President Everson Blight's naked body had been found in a dumpster.

Poor is the pupil
who does not surpass his master.
Leonardo da Vinci

Chapter 23
Cyst/Thas Estate
Jupiter Island, Florida
December 29

Waiting ... waiting ... patiently, Dr. Huntington Cyst reclined in his chaise lounge, gazing over the infinity pool and past the tumultuous ocean. For two hours, he had focused on the horizon. But now, the anxieties were returning. His heart was beginning to race and his breathing was becoming labored. Cyst's medications were wearing off.

"I need my pills!" he shouted at the house.

But there was no response.

A year ago, Huntington Cyst had returned from a trip like no other. Staring into the crystal waters of the pool, he remembered that it was there that Evan – his adopted son – had drowned him. But that wasn't what bothered Cyst.

His murderer had not only escaped justice but had managed to commandeer everything Dr. Cyst had owned. Thas had even claimed total credit for Cyst's revival after simply applying the life reviving technologies that Cyst, himself, had pioneered. However, those details didn't bother him, either.

Now, Cyst was a prisoner in his own home, forced to live in a fog on a diet of narcotics. Still, even that did not bother him. In fact, Huntington Cyst now treasured the fog.

Indeed, Evan Thas had learned well ... perhaps, too well.

No, what bothered the once-brilliant, internationally

renowned "Prophet of Technology" was something far more disturbing than Evan's manipulations. He was haunted by the knowledge of something unimaginably horrendous.

Hell.

After experiencing a month of death, Cyst returned with unrelenting waves of depression and hopelessness. He was not certain that he had actually experienced hell but, whatever it was, he dreaded it with every fiber of his being.

He remembered seeing a great sea of fire which seemed to be under the earth. Plunged into the fire were demons and souls in human form, like transparent burning embers, all blackened or burnished bronze, floating about in the conflagration, now raised into the air by the flames that issued from within themselves together with great clouds of smoke, now falling back on every side like sparks in a huge fire, without weight or equilibrium, and amid shrieks and groans of pain and despair, which horrified Cyst and made him tremble with fear. The demons could be distinguished by their terrifying and repulsive likeness to frightful and unknown animals, all black and transparent. The vision had lasted only an instant, but the fear and terror it produced continued to haunt Cyst's mind.[126]

Still, that was not the worst of it. There, he had realized that he was profoundly and completely separated from God, the source of all life and joy. Suddenly, he fully understood that he had freely and definitively chosen his course. Cyst also knew that, regardless of the seemingly miraculous revival capabilities of Eden Village, his death had sealed his fate in hell forever.[127]

"Pills!" Cyst screamed. "My pills!"

He heard a glass door slide open, followed by a sarcastic, "Coming, dear."

176

It was Faridah Shabaan with a tray in her hands. She looked almost Floridian, gliding by in her stylish beach cover-up, splashed with floral reds, yellows and greens. But her Syrian accent gave her away. Regardless, in just a couple of months she had settled into Cyst's estate like a conquering princess, and Evan had welcomed her conquest.

She sat at the foot of the chaise as Cyst sat up. She doled out his Zolofts, Vicodins and Percocets, and then handed him a glass. He gobbled them down as fast as he could, spilling water on himself in his haste.

"Oh, Huntie, slow down. I'm taking care of you." She patted him on the back as he resumed his gaze out to the ocean. "Poor old man. You thought you could keep me away from him. But I just bided my time."

Cyst's mind had cleared a bit. He remembered how he had never really liked or trusted Faridah. He and his former partner, Henri Blanc, had done the research that had identified five-year-old Evan as the one who had been prophesied. Then the deal that Cyst had negotiated with the boy's mother had been for life. So, upon Cyst's death, Faridah felt free to find Evan, and the search had proved relatively easy. She simply listened to her inner voices.

Through the years, the financial arrangement had cost Cyst millions. Still, he had always seen it as a worthwhile investment ... that is, until his death.

Cyst's cash pipeline had allowed Faridah to enjoy a depraved lifestyle, privately, while publicly presenting an image of holiness. In fact, she had become something of a Middle Eastern Rasputin, a mystical guide to foolish followers.[128] Mostly, however, she spent her income not on buying things but on purchasing influence, and her revolutionary teachings were gaining international popularity. But while her public image had become that of a philanthropist, feeding hundreds, her private support had often enabled anarchists and other revolutionaries to kill thousands.

Cyst craned his neck back at the house and noticed, again, two dark men in dark suits behind the glass doors.

"Who are those guys?" he mumbled.

"Don't you remember, Huntie? They're my sons. They're Evan's younger brothers. We're all family here."

Cyst did not remember that explanation and the thought of those strange men in his house stoked his pangs of paranoia. He wondered why Evan wasn't around and why he had been left alone. His anxieties began to peak, again.

"Huntie, calm down. I have something very special for you. It will make you feel very, very good."

"What?!" he demanded.

"Let me show you." She pulled a fentanyl patch out of her pocket and cut it open with the scissors that she had brought out on the tray. He had never seen it before, but he thought he knew what it would do. "Here," she handed the pain patch to him, "suck it all out."

Cyst went after it like a hungry dog.

Within seconds he would be hit with a jolt 50 to 80 times more powerful than morphine.[129]

Faridah put her arm over his shoulder and pulled him close with pretended affection. "Don't worry, Huntie. I'll take care of you. You have work to finish."

He refused to look at her.

Then she added, darkly, "You shouldn't have kept me from my son."

Just before the fog returned, a wave of anxiety sent a shiver through his limbs. Huntington Cyst wanted to drive the unwelcome memory out of his head. But it stayed, lurking in the darkest corners of his mind.

As long as Cyst lived, he would never forget that eternal damnation is waiting … waiting … patiently.

The hellish vapors rise and fill the brain,
Till I go mad and my heart is utterly changed.
See this sword? The prince of darkness sold it to me.
For me he beats the time and gives the signs.
Ever more boldly I play the dance of death.
From "The Player"
By Karl Marx

A ll summer long, Huntington Cyst and Henri Blanc had called and written to Israel's National Library, attempting to convince the Custodian of Ancient Codices that he should grant them access to the archive. They had claimed that they needed access to his collection in order to complete their M.I.T. doctoral theses on the unique geological aspects of Israel's caves. While it was true that they wanted to learn more about Israel's caves, their true purpose had nothing to do with geology. So, after being rejected repeatedly, and with time running out, the two decided to take matters into their own hands.

One afternoon, in the library's reading room for the general public, Cyst created a diversion by loudly accusing an innocent bystander of stealing his wallet. When the security personnel focused on the commotion, Blanc stepped back to the door of the secured archives and studied its electronic locking system. Immediately, he recognized it as an XG-1 electronic card swipe device, sophisticated for his day, but no challenge for Blanc. While Huntie loudly badgered the blameless young man into defensive explanations, Henri pulled out his mother-of-pearl pocket knife and used it to pop off the cover of the card reader. He quickly evaluated the circuitry and then touched the knife blade to two exposed terminals. The door opened with a buzz.

He snapped the cover back on and then, standing in the archives' open doorway, Blanc yelled, "Give it up, Huntie. You must have left it at home."

Cyst grumbled a few more choice words at the accused and, still feigning righteous indignation, followed the security guard to the door of the archives.

"It's okay," Blanc assured the watchman. "He's with me."

Fearing another tongue lashing from Cyst, the guard let them through, without delay.

HUNTIE SLID the newfound codex down the long research table where his college buddy was engrossed in an ancient book of maps. Henri's ravenous dark eyes shifted to the new prospect. As he dragged his long fingers across a broad forehead and through wavy brown hair, he studied the tattered cover, finding ornamentation but no words. He opened the delicate book and examined its contents while his intense stare tightened over an eagle-like nose and prominent, unshaven cheeks.[130]

Cyst moved closer, behind him. "Be more careful with these old books, Huntie," Blanc mumbled. "They're fragile."

"What do you think, Henri?"

The Frenchman closed the book and handed it back to Cyst.

"This is Aramaic. See if you can find one in Hebrew."

As Cyst headed to the shelves, Blanc leaned back in his chair and added, "Better yet, why don't we call it a day? It's almost happy hour."

Behind the towering books, Cyst dismissed the suggestion with, "Naw, let's keep going."

"Huntie," Henri snorted a laugh. "Maybe we'll never find it. Maybe it doesn't exist. Did you ever think of that?"

Cyst turned deliberately and marched back to the table. "Look," he demanded, "stop trying to discourage me. I can find another linguist, ya' know. I'm not giving up."

Blanc threw his hands up amiably. "Hey, I don't mean to throw a wet blanket on your theory. I'm just saying that, sometimes, even the best research can lead you down a dead end."

"It's here."

"But what if that brilliant brain of yours got it wrong, this time? Is that impossible?"

Cyst moved in close and glared down at Blanc as he whispered, "I don't know it in my brain." He lightly pounded his chest with his fist. "I know it in my soul."

"Okay, okay," Blanc surrendered. "You keep paying the bills, I'll keep translating."

Cyst shook his head as his glance noticed a particular codex in a stack of Blanc's rejects, on the table. "That one's Hebrew."

"No, I've already…" Blanc looked closer. "Wait, maybe I didn't see this one."

Huntington studied Henri's reactions as he examined the cover, opened it carefully, and turned page after page. Near the middle of the aged collection of pages, Blanc moaned, "Ohhh, yeah."

Just then, another researcher walked past the table and Blanc defensively jerked his forearm over the map he was examining.

Cyst smiled, realizing that they may have found something big.

Last spring, they had completed their PhD dissertations at M.I.T. Though they both had delivered stellar academic performances, in a variety of disciplines and at a few Ivy League universities, they agreed to spend the summer in the Middle East, before settling down with jobs. It was a chance to test Cyst's wild theories, and as long as Cyst was willing to foot the bills, Blanc was willing to tag along.

The two had become close friends and their skill sets complemented each other. Cyst was the gregarious socializer, always adept at meeting attractive girls – the salesman, so to speak. Blanc, on the other hand, had the rugged masculinity that drew them in and closed the deal. Still, underneath his attractive exterior, Blanc was introspective and shy. Also, above all, he was disciplined, both physically and intellectually. In fact, each day before dawn, he would jog ten miles while contemplating innovative but obscure computer architecture design issues like symmetric multiprocessing and non-uniform memory access. Only a handful of people on the planet could understand those thoughts. They were the scientifically transcendent meditations upon which he would build his fame and fortune.

Together, the two friends shared charismatic popularity, extraordinary intelligence and unlimited ambition. They also shared a sense of adventure, enjoying life on the edge.

It was Cyst's research on Christian prophecies and Black Magic that had brought them here. Blanc had followed for the adventure but had been relentlessly skeptical, forgetting the fact that Cyst's hunches usually proved true.

Blanc moved his forearm and examined the deteriorating page. This book had intriguing aspects to it. Code words were written on the margins, signaling that something had been hidden, something too important to divulge publicly. Then he turned to a page that folded out. It displayed a detailed map, hand drawn.

"What do you think, Henri?

Blanc did not answer. Instead, he ran his finger along the map, whispering to himself various Hebrew words. Then his finger stopped over a spot that looked like it had been deliberately scratched out.

"Look at this, Huntie."

They both leaned over and tried to make out what had been written there. It appeared that the marred area on the map was indicating elevated ground, not far from the Sea of Galilee.

Cyst had to rely on Blanc's superior language skills. "Where is it?"

Blanc whispered, "Capernaum."

"Can you make it out, with the scratches?"

Henri squinted as he leaned over. "Looks like *Me'arah shel seter.*"

"So, what's that mean?"

Blanc smiled. "It means we're getting drunk tonight."

CYST CONVINCED BLANC to delay their planned return to America if his hunch panned out. He claimed that the potential for success in Israel was far too important to abandon. Their future jobs, he argued, could always wait. When Huntie reflected on his research into the Dark Arts, his mind reeled with possibilities. The suspense was driving him into a state of frenzy.

The morning after their discovery at the library, they left

for Capernaum. Driving west, along the Sea of Galilee, Cyst lectured his skeptical partner about the power of the Prince of Darkness. Blanc, the agnostic, preferred to put his faith in science. But Huntie had always possessed a special intuitive gift. His instincts had proven their value time and again.

Huntington slowed as their Jeep entered the ancient town, and skidded to a stop when two oblivious pedestrians walked in front of their vehicle. It was the peak season for pilgrims who had made their way from around the world, seeking to learn more about the historic fishing village that had been the center of Jesus Christ's early public ministry in Galilee. This was where brothers Simon-Peter and Andrew lived, and where many of Jesus' first miracles occurred.

Blanc ignored the tourists and, instead, studied the rocky terrain. The quiet adventurer had translated the cryptic notes in the margin of the codex map. Those scribbles identified the location of a particular group of boulders, there.

As they rumbled through the narrow streets, Cyst could not keep his eyes on the road. He hoped to be the first to spot the identifying rock formation. Then, when he almost grazed a parked car, Blanc yelled at him to pay attention to driving.

A moment later, Blanc said, "Okay, I think that's it." Then he instructed, "Turn right here…. There … at the top of the hill, you see it?"

"Oh, yeah," Cyst said as he shifted into a lower gear and revved the engine up the rocky slope.

When they neared the rock, Henri groaned, "It's too big. We'll have to get more manpower."

Cyst snorted his disagreement, turned to Blanc and deadpanned, "Wimp."

The driver rolled up to the capstone, shifted into first gear, and gunned the engine. The tires spun, throwing pebbles and dirt down the hill. But the rock did not budge. So, Cyst hit the brake and tried again. This time, he accelerated the engine slowly, trying to maintain tire traction. The bumper crumpled as the rock slowly slid but he ignored the damage. Once the rock had moved a few feet, Cyst backed up, revealing the large hole that his tires had straddled.

The men got out and stood over the cavity.

"Me'arah shel seter," Blanc said with satisfaction.

"What's that mean?" Cyst asked.

"The Cave of Secrets."

WHEN BLANC LET GO OF THE ROPE, he thought he was standing on solid ground, in the dark. But as he stepped ahead, he fell another three feet, hard onto the cave's dirt floor. He staggered to his feet, brushed himself off and realized that he was lucky to remain uninjured, after falling off a stone table.

Blanc looked up, through the oculus, and shouted, "You coming down?"

Cyst, more accustomed to eating than exercising, responded, "No way. Just tell me what you see."

"I need a flashlight."

Under the light of the oculus, Blanc waited in the dark cave, fearing that he may have encroached on the home of a vicious animal. Only his eyes moved as he crouched, perfectly still, squinting into the darkness, listening for any sound of animal movement.

He jumped slightly when Cyst yelled, "Here it is," and tossed down the flashlight.

Blanc caught it and, as the light flitted around the cave, the beam revealed jagged rock walls and large, loose stones scattered on the floor. Then the light hit something that flashed back brilliantly.

Outside, Cyst heard a gasp. "Henri?" he shouted. "You okay?"

He could only hear soft sounds, like whimpering.

"Henri, what's going on?"

He heard no answer.

Cyst ran to the Jeep and retrieved gloves and a knife. He sprinted back, put on the leather gloves, slipped the knife into his pocket, and grabbed hold of the rope. Immediately, however, when he started to repel into the abyss, he lost his grip and fell eight feet, landing hard on a flat, stone surface.

Blanc did not budge. He and the light remained fixated on the object of his amazement.

Addled, Cyst sat up and slid off the stone table. He staggered on his feet, asking, "Why didn't you answer? I nearly killed myself." Then as he straightened up, Cyst's eyes followed the flashlight beam. At the end of it was a large, golden box. He estimated it to be about four feet by two feet by two feet. He sputtered out, "What the…"

Henri Blanc moved closer, analyzing every detail in the light.

Huntington's eyes widened. He shouted, "That's it! That's it!"

"Stop shouting," Blanc whispered.

Cyst ignored him. "I told you we'd find it! I knew it…. This is the place. Now is the time."

"How can you be sure?"

"The prophecies, dammit!"

"So, what does this all mean?"

"He's here, somewhere near."

"What do we do next?"

"We find him."

"How?"

"The prophecies tell us everything we need to know." Then Cyst laughed.

"What's so funny?"

"The saints," Cyst answered with unveiled sarcasm, "have been *so* helpful."

Dismissing the attempt at humor, Blanc returned his gaze to the ancient relic, placed his palm on the golden lid, and breathed a joyful sigh.

Huntie shuffled up, still smirking, as he stretched to touch the box. When his finger made contact, a powerful surge suddenly jolted his body, dropping him to his knees.

Cyst shouted, "Son of a bitch!" and scooted away in fear.

From a safe distance, in a darkened corner, Cyst sat in the dirt and panted from the pain.

The two men stared at the golden box that, they knew, had remained hidden since the time of the Prophet Jeremiah. They were staring at the Ark of the Covenant.[131]

"Give me a light that I might tred safely into the unknown."
He replied, "Go out into the darkness
and put your hand into the hand of God.
That will be, to you, better than a light
and safer than a known way."
King George VI's 1939 Christmas Address,
reading from a poen
as Nazi victory loomed over Europe.

Chapter 25
Rome, Italy
December 30

Meanwhile, after a restful flight, John arrived at Rome's Fiumicino Airport, alert and happy to return to the place where he most felt at home. Heading out to ground transportation, the Apostle smiled when he was met at the gate by a man who was holding a sign that read, "Mr. Thunderson." It was a sly reference to the nickname that Jesus had given him and his brother, James: "Sons of thunder."

Like the best of travel agents, John's angels had covered every detail. It wasn't long, however, before John realized that this was going to be one of those trips that required supreme faith, especially when he realized that his driver was actually blind.

Still, he confidently directed, "To the Abbey of Monte Cassino, please."

WHEN JOHN'S CAR ascended the steep road that led to the imposing mountaintop abbey, 80 miles south of Rome, John was proud of this invincible monument to the faith. Just as

Christ had promised that "the gates of hell shall not prevail" against His Church,[132] likewise it seemed that this monastery would never be erased... no matter how hard Satan tried.

It had been destroyed four times since its founding by St. Benedict in 529 AD. Around 577, the monastery had been razed by the Longobards of Zotone. Pope Gregory II, however, refused to accept the religious community's demise and commissioned the rebuilding in the eighth century. Then, in 883, Saracens invaded, sacked and burned the abbey causing the death of its saintly Abbot. Still, monastic life soon returned to the mountaintop, and was fully resumed by the middle of the tenth century. But Satan's work was not finished. The splendid building that had replaced the old one was nearly leveled by an earthquake in 1349. Yet, barbarian invasions and natural disasters could not stop persistent men of faith from rebuilding it. However, in 1799, French troops pillaged the abbey. Then, after almost fifteen decades of relative peace, the grand monastery found itself on the front line of a World War. Evil, once again, was on the march. On February 15, 1944, this holy home of prayer and study – shielding hundreds of defenseless refugees – was suspected of housing Nazis. In a span of three hours, Allied warplanes dropped 500 tons of bombs and reduced the massive abbey to a heap of rubble, with the civilians inside.

Satan's deceptions had succeeded, at least temporarily. Not only were there no Nazis in residence during the bombing, but Hitler's forces overtook the remains of the strategic mountaintop, soon after. The ruins, however, have been rebuilt to their former grandeur by the Italian government, but not without a visible tribute to lost lives. Across from the abbey, more than 1000 Polish soldiers are buried in a cemetery that memorializes the ultimate price they paid in the battle to finally liberate the abbey, just three months later.

John had been residing here, shortly before the first Allied assault and had assisted in the frantic transport of the Monte Cassino's precious and sacred contents to the Vatican, for safekeeping. The holy collection had accumulated at this abbey for over fourteen centuries. However, Church authorities had begun to fear that, with Nazis occupying a nearby town, the abbey might soon succumb to the blind crossfire of war. It was not a time that the Apostle wished to remember, but a time he could not forget.

Still, as John's vehicle pulled up to the front door of the monastery, he felt happy that his old home had been rebuilt to its former glory. As he slid out of the car and stood next to it, John turned to look over the scenic Italian hills, fading to the far horizon in shades of blue-gray. Then he was greeted by the doorman like any other cleric who had been granted permission to stay.

Before John entered the massive complex, however, he thanked his driver, knowing that the man – or angel – could only imagine John's smiling appreciation. Then he offered him a blessing before the mysterious blind man drove away, without expecting compensation.

The doorman, a humble Canadian monk, politely welcomed John to the abbey and directed him to the front desk where he would arrange his accommodations. Though John had visited here dozens of times, over the centuries, almost everything was new, since the time of the bombings. The only part of this massive complex that had survived the destruction of 1944 was the crypt that is the resting place of St. Benedict of Nursia, who died at the abbey in 547.

As John was led to his cell – from the Entrance Cloister, through the Refectory, and across to the small bedrooms on the perimeter – he admired the Benedictine monks that he passed in the hallways. For fifteen centuries, the Order's undying determination to adhere to the Rule of St. Benedict[133] and preserve his monastic and Spiritual wisdom had resulted in a religious community based on mutual Christian love and service. John fondly remembered being here in the 11th century when the abbey had reached the apogee of its excellence, housing 200 monks and providing an outstanding theological and intellectual outpost, preserving Western heritage against the debilitating barbarian onslaughts of the Middle Ages.

Even with all his experience, John still could not understand how anyone, with any degree of Spiritual maturity, could persecute or even ridicule those who had sacrificed their lives to God by a life-long commitment to poverty, chastity, humility, virtue, moderation, service and obedience?[134] Yet, too many people continued to cling to their invincible ignorance.

John remembered Jesus' warning: *"If the world hates you, realize that it hated me first. If you belonged to the world, the world would love its own; but because you do not belong to the world, and I have chosen you out of the world, the world hates you. Remember the word I spoke to you, 'No servant is greater than his master.' If they persecuted me, they will also persecute you."*[135] The Apostle realized that he had never known a time when clever critics had not belittled such harmless saints as either fools or hypocrites, and that those cynics always had been determined to amuse themselves to death.

AS HE CHANGED CLOTHES, in his sparse cell, John was pleased to remove the decorated pilot's uniform that had made him feel so deceptive when he walked through this honest community. He would feel much more comfortable in the plain, black Benedictine habit he had been given, consisting of a tunic under an apron-like scapular that had a small hood attached to the back. John had never taken the vows of the Benedictine Order, but who else here could claim to have been a friend and confidant of St. Benedict himself?

When he finished changing, John knelt and thanked the Lord for his safe journey. It had been such a comfortable and effortless trip that the Apostle suspected that this mission must be very important in God's eyes.

John decided to go out and enjoy the fresh air and sun while walking the familiar grounds, in prayer. He left his cell, went across the hall and down the first steps he found, looking for his favorite place of meditation, here, the Cloister of Bramante. But as soon as he exited into the courtyard, John encountered a group of French tourists who sounded so clueless that he felt obligated to converse with them in French in order to clear up some of their misconceptions. Quickly, they gathered that he must be a tour guide and fired questions at him, without reserve.

He explained to them that the abbey had been built over an ancient temple of Apollo, which is now long-forgotten, and he reflected on how much this invincible abbey reminded him of Jesus Christ and the Church He founded. To make his point, John recollected for them the Biblical story that, shortly after the crucifixion of Jesus Christ, the Sanhedrin had debated whether to execute the Apostles because neither imprisonment nor flogging would stop them from preaching the Gospel. Gamaliel, a truth-seeking Pharisee who had been honored by all, intervened in defense of the Apostles by offering the Sanhedrin advice: *"If their purpose or activity is of human origin, it will fail. But if it is from God, you will not be able to stop these men; you will only find yourselves fighting against God."*[136] Through the millennia, John explained, many opponents have tried to destroy Christianity, destroy Christ's Church, and destroy this abbey. They have all come and gone, and they have all failed.

One Frenchman asked, "Why don't Catholics believe in the Rapture?

John responded, in French, "By that, I assume you are referring to a removal of Believers prior to the Great Tribulation."

The Frenchman nodded.

John continued, "So, when Jesus spoke of the time of Great Tribulation by saying *'one will be taken and the other left behind,'*[137] what did He mean? He said that it will be like in the days of Noah.[138] Well, what happened in the days of Noah? The good remained alive in order to rebuild the world according to God's principles. Jesus also said it will be like in the days of Lot.[139] Then, again, the evil were taken and the good left behind. So, do not presume that you will be spared from the trials of the coming Chastisements. Yes, Jesus promised, *'I will keep you safe in the time of trial that is going to come to the whole world to test the inhabitants of the earth.'*[140] But notice that He said the *whole* world. If believers will escape the final test, why does the Book of Revelation warn, *'Hold fast to what you have, so that no one may take your crown.'?*[141] Why did Jesus say, *'Those whom I love, I reprove and chastise.'?*[142] What about *'...the souls of those who had been slaughtered because of the witness they bore to the word of God'* who *'were told to be patient a little while longer until the number was filled of their fellow servants and brothers who were going to be killed as they had been.'?*[143] In Revelation, why would Jesus describe, *'the ones who have survived the time of great distress,'* saying, *'they have washed their*

194

robes and made them white in the blood of the Lamb,'[144] and add *'God will wipe away every tear from their eyes.'*?[145] Why would He warn that the Beast will be *'allowed to wage war against the holy ones and conquer them.'*?[146] How much more emphatic could Jesus be than when He said, *'Whoever has ears ought to hear these words. Anyone destined for captivity goes into captivity. Anyone destined to be slain by the sword shall be slain by the sword. Such is the faithful endurance of the holy ones.'*[147] If believers will be Raptured away before the Great Tribulation, what about *'those who had been beheaded for their witness to Jesus and for the word of God, and who had not worshiped the beast or its image nor had accepted its mark on their foreheads or hands.'*?[148] So, live without presuming how God will treat you and, wherever you find yourself, *'continue to work out your salvation with fear and trembling, for it is God who works in you to will and to act according to His good purpose.'"*[149]

An elderly woman lamented, "I don't know if my faith can overcome all that."

"Do not fear uncertainty. But when it hits you, remember that God is true, and will not let any test come on you which you are not able to undergo.[150] Never forget that Jesus Christ purchased your redemption on the Cross. Victory is for all, if only we will accept it to the end."

John studied their faces. "It is a blessing that you are being forewarned and that you can now go out and warn others. A time of darkness is coming. A time like no other in human history. Though others will cower with fear, rejoice, because the time of great joy is near."

A Frenchman asked, "What do you mean?"

John responded, "Isaiah prophesied, *'For the stars of the heavens and their constellations will not give their light; the sun will be dark at its rising and the moon will not shed its light... Therefore I will make the heavens tremble, and the earth will be shaken out of its place, at the wrath of the Lord of hosts in the day of his fierce anger.* '[151] And Blessed Anna Maria Taigi[152] warned, *'There shall come over all the earth an intense darkness lasting three days and three nights. Nothing will be visible and the air will be laden with pestilence, which will claim principally but not exclusively the enemies of religion. During the darkness artificial light will be impossible. Only blessed candles can be lighted and will afford illumination. He who out of curiosity opens his window to look out or leaves his house will fall dead on the spot. During these three days the people should remain in their homes, pray the Rosary and beg God for mercy.'* And in even greater detail, Marie Julie Jahenny of La Fraudais[153] foresaw, *'There will come three days of continued darkness. The blessed candles of wax alone will give light during the horrid darkness. One candle will last for three days, but in the houses of the Godless they will not give light. During those three days the demons will appear in abominable and horrible forms; they will make the air resound with shocking blasphemies. The lightning will penetrate the homes, but will not extinguish the light of the blessed candles; neither wind nor storm nor earthquake will extinguish it.... The earth will tremble to its foundations; the ocean will cast its foaming waves over the land; the earth will be changed to an immense cemetery; the corpses of the wicked and the just will cover the face of the earth. The crisis will come all of a sudden and chastisement will be worldwide. "'* [154]

The elderly woman said, "That is quite alarming."

John agreed, "It is. But never forget: With God, all things are possible. The answer is not fear, it is prayer. Suffering is only allowed by God to perfect the good or to convert or condemn the wicked."[155]

Another man asked, "How will we know when the time is near?"

John said, "No one knows the day nor the hour because our prayers and sacrifices can delay or mitigate the coming chastisements.[156] However, the Three Days of Darkness will be a supernatural event, preceded by man-made disasters in the form of wars, revolutions, apostasy and other evils.[157] The times have been described like this: '*Mankind will offer the highest regard for advanced knowledge, but no principle – however holy, authentic, ancient, and certain it may be – will remain free of censure, criticism, false interpretations, modification and delimitation by man*[158] *And the Church of Jesus Christ will undergo it greatest test. The Evil One will attack the Church, depositing great weakness of faith in hearts. There will be a denial of religion and, for a time, Satan will gain control of everything.*[159] *Confusion will be everywhere and the Holy Sacrifice of the Eucharist will be forbidden.*'"[160]

A young woman said, "The three days of darkness that you mentioned is all new to me."

"It may be new to you," John responded, "but it is not new to God. He has chosen to display His displeasure like that before, telling Moses, '*Extend your hand toward heaven. And may there be darkness upon the land of Egypt, so dense that it may be felt. And Moses extended his hand toward heaven. And a horrible darkness occurred in all the land of Egypt for three days.*'[161] And, of course, during the crucifixion of Jesus Christ, '*there was darkness over the entire earth' for three hours.*'[162]

From behind him, John heard a French voice interjecting, "Just don't forget that there is a wonderful and glorious reward for all who remain faithful to the end."

As he turned, John responded with slight irritation, "Yes. I already said that.... But it is worth repeating."

The French priest who had corrected John was sitting on the edge of a fountain near the middle of the courtyard. He was a tall, imposing figure in his black, Benedictine robe. He had more the look of a retired professional athlete than that of a priest, and his calm expression reflected not only peace but certainty.

"That's right, Father," John affirmed. He turned back to the French group. "Life is a trial, but one with a fabulous reward for victory. Spread the word. Save yourselves and those you care about. Sadly, however, you cannot save those who choose to remain lost."

The French group thanked John for his comments and then continued their tour.

John walked to the fountain to introduce himself to the Benedictine priest. "Hello, Father. I am John."

"Your French is impeccable," the priest observed while shaking hands but neglecting to introduce himself by name.

John smiled, "I am pretty good with languages."

"What about Hebrew?" The priest asked.

"Uh, yes. I speak Hebrew."

"So, then you know what 'John Eben Malek' means."

John's response was noncommittal. The priest no longer smiled.

The Benedictine repeated, "John Eben Malek? The name you checked in with. You know what it means?"

"Yes," John responded slowly.

"'John, servant of the king'," the priest filled in the blanks. "However, I am guessing that it is not your real name."

John shrugged.

"So, my first thought was to throw you out on your ear."

"I'll leave. I don't want to cause any trouble."

"No, you will not leave," he commanded.

John asked, "Have you called the police?"

The Benedictine drew a deep breath, exhaled and responded, "No." Then the priest's penetrating stare continued studying the intruder. "You don't look special."

"What do you mean?"

"When I reported to the Abbot that I suspected that another imposter had attempted to check in, he was very upset … that is … until I told him your name."

"What did he say?"

The priest shook his head. "He couldn't say anything…. He was nearly choking on his excitement."

John shrugged, as if he were clueless.

"So, I think that you will have to stay here … at least until the abbot returns."

"Returns from where?"

"The Vatican."

Now it was John's turn to study the Benedictine. He had distinctive features: large dark eyes, a broad forehead, and an eagle-like nose. "You look very familiar. Have we met?"

"No," he answered curtly.

John pushed harder. "I am very good with faces."

"We have not met."

"Perhaps …" John stared.

Now the priest was uncomfortable.

John asked, "What is your name?"

"It does not matter!" the Benedictine snapped.

Immediately, it hit John. The certainty, the clarity and the commanding authority with which those four words were spoken, brought back a memory.

It was true that they had never met. However, John was looking at a face that, twenty years ago, half the world would have recognized.

It was the face of Henri Blanc.

We wander for distraction,
but we travel for fulfillment.
Hilaire Belloc

Here, at the Hotel Negresco, Tim Lassiter wondered if this was as close as he would get to an American-style sports bar. *Brasserie La Rotonde* was a bit too foo foo for his taste, displaying a cheerful carousel décor, with colorful, painted, wood horses separating every booth. But at least the French wine was tasty. When stumped by the wine list, he just told the waiter, "Surprise me." Now, he was on his second bottle.

The waiter – like most of the French people, here – did not seem to like him. Already, they had been through some testy exchanges, once when Lassiter complained to him that nobody was serving French fries in France, and again when he complained that he couldn't find real football anywhere on TV. The menu was in French, and every time Tim asked the server about an entre' his description sounded appalling. So, when the waiter approached for the third time, Lassiter felt he had better order.

Lassiter raised the menu and pointed at the *Carpaccio de bœuf.*

"Oui monsieur."

Then when Lassiter added, "Medium well," the waiter rolled his eyes and the American erupted. "Oh, forget it! Just bring me another bottle!"

†††

NOW HE WAS WANDERING ON to Italy, glad to be leaving France.

Man, Nice is the last name I would give that place!

He had liberally indulged his unlimited expense account over the holidays but wanted to find a more suitable place for New Years. Sooner or later, he knew he would have to get back to the hunt. For now, however, on his leisurely journey to Monte Cassino, he planned to stop wherever the urge hit him. He had rented a convertible and as he maneuvered the mountainous *corniche* that overlooks the scenic Mediterranean, he dreamed of sunning himself in Monaco for a while. Perhaps, even a while longer.

Along the way, Lassiter scanned the radio dial, looking for an English-speaking news channel. Finally, he found one in which the newscaster spoke almost breathlessly. She was reporting on the historic devastation that had resulted from yesterday's catastrophic California earthquake. She said that nature's ravages had been so great, there, that words could not adequately describe it, and the mind could hardly comprehend it.

Tim was intrigued by the story but distracted because he had not yet mastered the sports car's manual gear shift. Complicating his trip, even more, was the fact that over a thousand cyclists had clogged this narrow, windy road along the cliffs. Obviously, this was the land of the *Tour de France* and today it seemed to Lassiter that every Frenchman was preparing to someday eclipse the record of Lance Armstrong. More ominously, however, Tim remembered that this was the dangerous road on which Princess Grace of Monaco had crashed and died.

The radio reporter continued to another mysterious American tragedy: the lifeless, naked body of the Vice President of the United States had been found in a dumpster.

Man, Lassiter thought, *what's this world coming to?*

He wanted to pay attention to the details of the story, but an impatient Frenchmen, behind him, honked. So, Tim could not play it safe any longer by following the slow moving cyclists up the hill, along the curves and through the tunnels. Whenever the opportunity opened up, he was forced to pass them – five, ten or fifty at a time. Then, when the cyclists yielded, he would slip back into their pack and wait for his next opportunity.

The radio reporter then offered what she called "the good news of the day." She said, "Dr. Evan Thas – the brilliant, young billionaire philanthropist who now leads XCyst Industries – has announced major restructuring at the multi-national conglomerate. According to Thas, 'From improving the quality of life with the new Titan immunization inoculation project, to extending the length of life with the Eden Village organ and tissue replacement program, to improving the nature of life around us with advanced applications of hybrid and synthetic organisms, XCyst's new mission will be perfecting life itself.'" The reporter added her own editorial comment, "Thank God for Evan Thas." Then she signed off, saying her name and her standard closing line, "This is the XBC Global Radio Network."

Just then, Lassiter grinded his gears as he tried to pass a pack of cyclists. Out of frustration, he clicked off the distracting radio.

While passing, however, a couple of cyclists caught his eye. He tried to check them out in his rear view mirror but had to jerk the car back onto the road when it veered too close to the cliff. It was the two riders at the rear of the pack who contrasted with the rest of the bunch. They were older cyclists, desperately struggling to keep up. In fact, they looked exactly like two witnesses from John Malek's trial.

"Father Alonzo and Ricky Zipp?!" Lassiter thumped his fist to his head and laughed at himself. *"Man, too much French wine!"*

Good things come
to those who wait.
Proverb

Chapter 27
Vatican City
December 30

The lumbering old man limped across the grey cobblestones of the Vatican's *Cortile di San Domaso* and stormed into the Papal Palace. As he made his way toward the central offices, the Swiss Guards did not dare try to stop the determined monk-priest. They knew well the Holy Father's respect for the Abbot of Monte Cassino. They could only slow him down by making him sign in.

Inside, sitting at the head of his conference room's long mahogany table, Pope Innocent XIV had been conducting difficult meetings with Catholic, Jewish and Muslim clerics from the Holy Land. The Imams were demanding that the Vatican immediately support a Palestinian state and that the region's two-state solution be implemented within six months. The implicit threat was that a Vatican denial would trigger a war. Still, everyone but the Muslims chafed at the idea of dividing Jerusalem, as demanded. They knew that it was not possible to reconcile the two propositions that the Bible is the inspired Word of God and that the Promised Land can be divided.[163]

The old Shepherd was wearied from the bickering that he had witnessed at this table for the past two days. He no longer possessed his renowned stamina and was frail from relentless assaults by the Evil One, both physically and emotionally.

There seemed to be no solution here that could please everyone. In these negotiations, there were doubters and pretenders regarding the proposal of land for peace. But, even among those who offered the proposal, no one truly believed that conceding Israel's land would actually bring peace from its enemies.

The stalemated negotiation was just one more cross on the pontiff's shoulder. Leading the largest church in the world – truly a global collection of faithful followers – had become almost overwhelming.

In the West, the Church had been battered by the outrageously evil acts of a small minority of lost clergy. Their sexual abuses had left innocent victims and billion dollar lawsuits strewn in their wake. The pontiff feared that rebellion against the Church, now, was becoming so widespread in the West that the scandal would undermine God's precious institution and the social and Spiritual safety nets that had elevated mankind for two millennia.

In the East, radical Islamists and Hindus had been persecuting Christians to such an extent that a growing number of countries had become Christian-free zones. And across Asia, Africa and South America, instigators were fanning dormant anti-colonialist embers, threatening another wildfire of atheistic revolution.

While radical Muslims demanded a global Caliphate to rule the world, another evil had resurfaced, also bent on global conquest. Authoritarian government was re-establishing control of Russia and again starting to plant the seeds of revolution and rebellion around the world. Because of that, civil wars and foreign wars were becoming too numerous to count,[164] weighing heavily on the heart of the pontiff who was truly a prince of peace. Everywhere he looked, it seemed the Catholic Church was suffering from affliction, desolation, humiliation and poverty.[165]

So, Innocent was irritated when his friend burst through the door, unannounced. Throughout the room, in fact, the intrusion was universally unappreciated.

"Ohhh, Abbot," the pontiff groaned with a sigh, "not now. Please wait until we are finished."

But the monk would not be deterred. "I am sorry, Holy Father. This news cannot wait."

The pope slumped in his chair and was barely able to raise his hand so that the Abbot could kiss the ring of St. Peter. Then, as the monk leaned to his ear, the pope closed his eyes, preparing for bad news.

The clerics around the table studied the holy man's face as the news was whispered to him. Suddenly, his eyes popped open and he gasped. His face blushed and his mind seemed to be racing as he jumped out of his chair.

"I'm so sorry. Something very important has come up." The pope's right hand waved a Sign of the Cross as he urgently shuffled toward the door. "Please, please ... uh ... continue with your discussions. I'm sorry ... I'm sorry ..."

And, to the astonishment of the guests, the two old men bolted out the door as fast as they could hobble away.

We forge the chains that bind us.
Ralph Waldo Emerson

Mercedes Dare was flattered by the VIP treatment she and her date were receiving. *Café' L'Europe* was Evan's favorite, but this was her first time, here. Her previous suitors had not risen to this level of sophistication ... and probably never would.

Sitting across from him, she mused at how unique Evan was. He loved to charm people but, unlike the other men in her life, he had shown almost no interest in intimacy with her. Though Evan's office artwork presented the image of a playboy, only once had he shown any amorous interest. That night, on their first date, he plied her with too much alcohol. Then, as she started to doze on the sofa, he seemed to lose control of himself. The event was clumsy, almost forced, and was over before she could comprehend what was happening to her. Then, to her surprise and disappointment, he never touched her that way again.

The dazzled, young lawyer soaked in the pianist's soothing refrain of Pachelbel's *Canon in D*, as she savored another taste of lemon souffle', closed her eyes and swayed to the music. Smirking to herself, Mercedes thought about the appetizer Evan had ordered, earlier this evening. His 1 ounce serving of Iranian Osetra Caviar had cost more than she typically paid for a week of groceries.

But this was New Year's Eve, so, why not?

Now, he was off socializing while she finished her dessert. *Just like a man!*

Mer – as Evan liked to call her – gazed across the darkened restaurant, fascinated by the well-known Palm Beach regulars who seemed determined to elbow their way to Evan's side at the bar. As she watched the serious men converse with Evan, she observed that some were old enough to be his grandfather. Still, they were mesmerized with his every word. She did not realize that it was all business, disguised as pleasure. But she knew that times were tough, and anyone who could afford to eat here had to be a major player.

Occasionally, she heard snippets of conversation. The men commiserated over the shocking murder of Vice President Blight. They asked Evan whether he thought the brutal crime had been committed by anarchists, communists or Islamists.

"I'll let you guys solve that one," Evan demurred as he left the bar and returned to Mer's table.

"Did you miss me," he asked, plopping down and almost spilling his cognac.

"Of course," she smiled. "I always do."

Then, as she took her last bite of desert, Mercedes decided to delicately spring the news.

"Evan," she hesitated to gather her thoughts. "I have had the most amazing time of my life, with you."

"Yeah," he nodded.

"I'm ... well, I'm hoping that we have a serious relationship."

"Sure ... I guess so," he said as he distracted himself by signing the tab.

"I'm really happy to hear that."

"Okay." Evan changed the subject: "Are we ready to go?"

"No, Evan." She reached across the table and grasped his

hand. "I need to tell you something." She didn't delay for fear that she might lose her nerve. "I'm pregnant."

He pulled his hand back. "What?"

"Today…. I just found out today."

He responded enthusiastically, "That's great!"

She offered, "Are you sure? I'll do whatever you want with it."

"No," he smiled, "don't get rid of it."

"Oh, I'm so happy."

"Yeah, That's great news."

For the rest of the evening, however, he did not say much. He drove her back to her apartment rather than to his Jupiter Island estate, as was usually his practice.

Still, as Mer prepared for bed, she was joyful over his response. After all, before she got out of the car, Evan had invited her to join him on his upcoming trip to Nauru. That would be their first romantic getaway, together.

ON THE WAY HOME, Evan took a shortcut on a rural road and soon noticed a car in his rearview mirror. After a while, he slowed to twenty miles under the speed limit, expecting the car to pass him on the long, dark road. But it didn't. So, he gunned his engine hoping to leave the follower in his dust.

Immediately, he saw blue lights flashing, heard a siren screaming, and realized that four cars were following him. He did not want to stop on this deserted stretch but quickly realized he would have no choice. One of the cars passed him and started to slow while the others neared to the side and rear. So, surrounded and lacking a place to pull over, Evan slowed to a stop in the middle of the road. Then the flashing lights and sirens stopped.

A big, uniformed man got out of the car in front. Evan studied the officer in his headlights and did not recognize the uniform. He certainly wasn't from Florida Highway Patrol. Evan could see that all four cars were black and unmarked. Then he realized that eight men had surrounded his car, with their handguns drawn.

Familiar with this drill, Evan casually removed his seatbelt, pulled out his wallet and rolled his window down. "Can I help you, officer?"

But the cop did not respond in a typical fashion. He just said, "Get out."

"What's this all about?" Evan asked.

The officer stepped back and two even bigger men reached in, grabbed Evan's Brioni jacket, and violently removed him through the window.

"Hey, what are you doing?!" Thas protested as they held him in the air.

Then they turned him around and shoved Evan's chest against the car. They twisted his arms behind his back and handcuffed him. They dragged him to the fourth car, threw him onto the front passenger seat and slammed the door.

"Hey, moron, I'm supposed to be in the back seat!"

"No you're not," came a voice from the rear.

Evan jerked his head around and, through the metal grate, saw Angela Concepcion.

"The handcuffs are for my protection. I'm beginning to realize just how dangerous you really are."

"I assure you, Angela, you're in no position to start screwing with me."

"Is that why Blight is dead?"

"I don't know what you're talking about."

"You're becoming impossible to work with."

"No, Angela, *you* are becoming impossible to work with."

"Look, Evan," she warned with an icy tone. "You taught me to meet one-on-one whenever I might incriminate myself. That is why it's just the two of us, here." She bolstered her courage and added, "I can tell you, with absolute certainty, that if I don't have your complete cooperation by the time I leave, that big man, in the lead car, will bury you alive in this field."

Evan was completely unfazed. He knew, from her Titan psychological profile exactly what Angela was – and was not – capable of ordering.

He mimicked a star-struck country boy. "Gee, that's scary stuff. Did you see that in a movie, or something? I can't wait to see how the hero escapes in the last scene."

"Evan!" she shouted. "I went to a lot of trouble to arrange this meeting. Those men out there are not Secret Service. They work black ops. You're gonna disappear tonight, if you don't cooperate!"

"The same way your birth certificate will disappear?"

"I'm warning you, Evan, I will commandeer those satellites!"

"If you do, there will be nothing left to protect you."

"You're insane! You murdered the Vice President of the United States!"

"How can you possibly know that, Angela?" Evan asked with amusement. "You don't know how your security forces and systems were breached.... Do you? You don't know the cause of death.... Do you? You don't even know if your life is now in..."

"Are you threatening me?!" she screamed through tears of desperation.

He chuckled softly. "Angela, I am protecting you." She

snorted her disbelief, but he continued, "You're such a dreadfully dull, slow learner. How do you think you got here? A pathetic minor office-holder rises to the most powerful post in the land? How do you think you surged ahead that last month in the New York Secretary of State's race? Do you suspect it had anything to do with polling booths made by XCyst Industries?[166] From nowhere to the presidency, your success was engineered by Evan Thas and Huntington Cyst, thank you very much. We put you on third base, but now you have the audacity to pretend you hit a triple? You fool, you won't make it off third base if you don't learn humility."

She was barely listening. Her mind raced with images of the unprecedented natural disasters and the economic and social crises that were enflaming America and destabilizing the world. Everything was spiraling out of control. No one seemed willing to compromise for the greater good. Almost everyone was choosing a side and an enemy to blame. The same barbarian fury that previously had propelled mankind into the Dark Ages was now devolving twenty first century civilization into a nihilistic cesspool of jungle impulses. Now, if Evan's scientists could be believed, a global pandemic could be on the horizon. It seemed the Age of Anarchy had arrived.

Angela started to hyperventilate, overwhelmed by anxiety, nearing a breakdown.

"What do you want from me?!" she screamed, seething with resentment.

He turned and offered her a searing stare. "You delayed the immunization program."

Angela's presidency, in fact, her world was crashing down around her and she felt completely impotent to stop it. Her naïve dream of controlling the transcendent transformation of mankind had turned into a hellish nightmare.

"Dammit, what do you want from me?!"

Evan barely whispered, "I want obedience."

Then he placed the removed handcuffs on the dashboard and exited the car.

Angela was too stunned to try to stop him.

She and her eight bodyguards watched as Thas got into his car and drove away, into the darkness.

THE NEXT MORNING, a young messenger insisted on hand-delivering a letter to Evan at his office. Though various intermediaries assured him that they would personally see that Dr. Thas would receive it, the messenger refused to give the letter to anyone but Thas, himself.

So, when he was finally escorted into Evan's office, he handed the letter over and said, "Dr. Thas, please read it now. I have to witness that you read it."

Thas chuckled at the mysterious messenger as he ripped open the plain white envelope. He pulled out a single white sheet, without a letterhead, and with only three words typed on it: "I will obey."

The race is not to the swift
or the battle to the strong,
nor does food come to the wise
or wealth to the brilliant or favor to the learned;
but time and chance happen to them all.
Ecclesiastes 9:11

Chapter 29
Cassino, Italy
January 6

While Tim Lassiter pumped gas into his rented Alfa Romeo, he continued reading an English language newspaper, holding it with his free hand. The alarming news report speculated that Pope Innocent XIV may be ill or possibly even dead. The pontiff had rushed out of a meeting three days ago and had not been seen in any of his scheduled appearances, since. Lassiter was not Catholic but he knew the reputation of this holy man and realized that his passing would sadden people around the globe.

As he mulled the possibilities, Tim lowered the paper and frowned at the imposing edifice of Monte Cassino, elevated in the distance. On the heels of wild romps along the French and Italian Rivieras, his energy was trailing off. He no longer felt the thrill of attempting to exhaust an unlimited expense account. It was he, himself, who had become exhausted. Lassiter missed the simplicity of American bar food and he thought that his adventure was beginning to seem like a wild good chase. Maybe he would never find John Malek and collect the rest of the money.

Nearby, at another pump, a buck-toothed old Englishman was filling his tank. "The abbey is quite impressive, don't you think, mate?"

Lassiter wasn't up for conversation. He just answered, "Sure."

The Brit glanced at Lassiter's three day beard, his tattered jeans and flip flops. "Ah, yes. American?"

Lassiter nodded.

"Let me tell you a tale, old chap. During the war I stood not far from here, watching that monastery with another American. We thought the Nazis occupied it."

Lassiter thought, *Oh boy. Geezer with a story.*

"We looked up at that abbey realizing that Monte Cassino was an objective hated by every Allied soldier anywhere near it. So when we saw 250 Flying Fortresses buzzing up from the south on that perfectly clear February day, we thought, 'Wouldn't it be marvelous if they dropped the whole lot on the monastery?' Then whoosh, down came 500 tons. There was a colossal cheer, you could have heard it all the way to Naples.... All except this one very close friend of mine, who said, 'What are you thinking of, Douglas? Are we in this war to destroy monasteries?' And then I had a huge double take. I thought, 'My God, what are we up to?' I saw that in the last year and a half we had become literally barbarized. We had become indistinguishable from any other army, the German army, the Russian army, the army of Genghis Khan, part of the great marauding horde whose instinct is to destroy."[167]

Tim wasn't listening. He replaced the nozzle and then the gas cap. He started to walk toward the gas station but stopped when he heard the Brit say, "Tim?"

Lassiter thought, *I didn't introduce myself.* He turned slowly.

"Give it up, old chap."

Lassiter studied the suddenly serious, bucktooth

Englishman.

"Give what up?"

"Don't bother John. He has important work to do."

The weary American contemplated the request for a moment, but his mind was too addled by the unlimited expense account that he had been enjoying.

"What are you talkin' about?"

"You've had some tough times, mate. But you've always protected the innocent. Don't become what you despise. It won't go well for you."

It was all a bit more than he could comprehend. So, not in the mood to discuss or debate, Lassiter simply turned back to the station and went in.

Soon, Lassiter emerged from the station, cursing himself for fumbling his cell phone into the toilet. But when he looked around, the Englishman was gone.

THIRTY MINUTES LATER, Lassiter was stuck in traffic on the winding road that rose to the abbey. He had come to a complete stop and had not moved for five minutes.

He got out of his car and asked the taxi driver behind him, "You speak English?"

"*Si.*"

"What's happening up there?"

"The traffic … uh … always stop when … uh … big shot come or go."

Just then, a small motorcade of four cars appeared, barreling down the hill. Lassiter jumped between stopped cars to avoid getting hit. As he turned back to the motorcade, he glanced into the back seat of the third vehicle and, sitting next to a man dressed in white, Lassiter thought he saw John

Malek.

The people in the stopped traffic applauded and cheered, shouting *"Papa ... Papa!"*

Lassiter yelled at the taxi driver, "Hey! Can you back up a little?"

The Italian nodded and complied with the request as the American jumped into his car and maneuvered back and forth, until he had completed a U-turn and sped down the hill in hot pursuit of his prey.

A few minutes later, the former detective had caught up and was following at a discrete distance. The motorcade drove almost eighty miles until they left the highway, maneuvered through Rome, and entered Vatican City.

Lassiter followed more loosely as they entered a narrow, cobblestone street along the fortress wall of the Vatican. Still, he tried not to lose sight of the vehicles. Then, suddenly, massive black doors in the wall opened, the fleet drove through, the doors closed, and they were gone.

"Son of a..." he growled as he slowed to a stop.

Lassiter considered his options until a car behind him honked. He looked around and noticed an open parking space in front of a *Trattoria*. As he pulled into the space, he decided that he would maintain surveillance of the gates while having dinner. Then he noticed an American-style bar next door.

That would be even better.

BY THE TIME THE FOOTBALL GAME WAS OVER, Lassiter was in a good mood. While sitting at the bar and occasionally glancing out to the Vatican doors, across the street, Tim had become the life of the party, buying drinks for everyone, at Jane Marconi's expense.

He had struck up a friendship with a young Nigerian immigrant. She was one of the only women in the tavern and the only fan who had rooted against *Roma*. Lassiter admired her spunk, suspecting that she just liked to stir the pot, so to speak. Then, after *Fiorentina* won by a last minute goal, two bar patrons shuffled over, paid off their bets, and grumbled racial epithets at her as they left in a huff.

The tall black woman wasn't upset. She examined her winnings at the bar and mumbled, "I can always use a little extra cash."

As she counted the cash, Lassiter studied her thin features, her large brown eyes, and her pronounced cheek bones. Fueled by liquid bravery, he mentioned, "By the way, I'm Tim."

"Kikelomo," she said, looking up from her stash of Euros. "Nice to meet you."

"Unusual name. What's it mean?"

"Pampered child," she snorted. "Believe me: that, I am not."

"Yeah, it's tough out there. Where do you work?"

She rolled her eyes as she answered, "I drive a garbage truck."

"You're kidding?" Lassiter imitated an ape. "I figured they're all burly guys with hairy backs."

She laughed, realizing that her new friend had drank a bit too much. "Not all of them."

"Well, everybody's gotta put food on the table."

"I'm just doing it 'til I can find something better."

She stuffed the cash in her jeans pocket and then added. "At least I got a good route."

"Yeah?"

"The pope, himself."

"Really?"

"My route's the Vatican."

"Sweet. How'd ya land that gig?"

"My uncle's a cardinal. I'm the black sheep of the family. No pun intended…. You think I could make money off papal garbage?"

Lassiter snickered, "I bet you could." Then something occurred to him. "Hey, you picking up trash tonight?"

"Yeah."

Lassiter slurred, "So, ya wanna make a quick hundred bucks?"

She frowned. "I'm a black sheep, but I'm not that kind of girl."

"No, no, no…. I'll pay you a hundred dollars if you just let me drive in with you."

"Hmmm."

When written in Chinese,
the word "crisis" is composed of two characters:
one represents danger
and the other, opportunity.
John F. Kennedy

An hour before dawn, the old garbage truck rumbled down the cobblestone street, along an ancient wall of the Vatican, and up to the black doors. When the nearby security camera scanned Kikelomo at the wheel, an unseen guard approved entry and the doors powered open.

For Lassiter, the excitement of being so close to capturing John Malek had prevented him from sleeping. His judgment was still clouded from the alcohol. He had come prepared, but tried to carry as little as possible. Inside a large pillow case, he had brought a flashlight, a rope, some duct tape, a knife, a towel, and a bottle of chloroform.

As they bounced along an alley, inside the walls, Tim saw a back door that was propped open.

"Where's that go to?"

"That's the kitchen for the Papal residence."

"Okay, stop here."

"What?"

"I'm getting out."

"You didn't tell me that … and you haven't paid me yet."

Lassiter pulled out an American hundred dollar bill. "I won't be long. If you're still here when I come out, there'll be another hundred in it for you."

She took the bill and smiled as he jumped out of the truck, with his sack, and disappeared through the kitchen door.

Inside Tim smelled smoke. When he turned into the kitchen, he saw a chef battling a small grease fire. The cook slapped a lid on the pan and waved his hands in the smoky air.

Acting as if he belonged there, Lassiter said, *"Scuzi?"*

The startled chef jerked around, embarrassed that his fiasco had been witnessed.

Lassiter held up his sack and said, "John Malek?"

The chef wanted to get rid of him. Assuming the bag contained a delivery, he pointed at a staircase and mumbled words in Italian. The American had a limited knowledge of the language but managed to understand, "Top of the stairs. Second door on the right."

Nonchalantly, Tim said, *"Grazie,"* and bounded up the steps.

When he reached the top, he entered a dark hallway.

Second door on the right, he remembered.

He pulled out the flashlight, clicked it on and slid down the hallway. When he reached the door, he put his ear to it. All was quiet.

Lassiter reached for the doorknob and smiled when he realized it was unlocked. His heart pounded as the door slowly opened with a faint squeal. Inside the dark room, the former detective cast his light on the bed. He could see that, under the covers, his target was sound asleep.

Lassiter clicked off the light and fumbled around in his bag until he had poured the chloroform onto the towel. Then, he slipped quietly closer to the bed and hesitated until he could build up enough nerve to spring the attack.

Suddenly, he pounced on the bed and slammed the wet towel into place. Quickly, however, he realized that he had landed a choke hold on a pillow.

Then, behind him, a light clicked on and he heard, "Hello Tim."

"What the…!" Lassiter whispered as he scooted until his back was against the headboard.

Near the window, in a reading chair next to the lamp, he saw John Eben Malek.

John said, "Don't be too loud or Swiss Guards will come. They're not as harmless as they appear, especially when someone has broken into the papal residence.

"What are you gonna do to me?"

"Just explain something, Tim."

"Okay," he said with caution.

"Why haven't you checked your voice mails?"

"What? I … uh … dropped my cell in a toilet."

"Jane Marconi has been trying to reach you for three days."

"Jane Mar… How do you know her?"

"The Vatican employed her after they lost touch with me in India. That's why she hired you. But, unfortunately, your services are no longer needed. As you can see, they found me first."

"Am I gonna get paid?"

"Of course … everything you're entitled to. But your contract expired three days ago when a certified notice was delivered to your home."

"Certified notice?"

"That was all that was required under the agreement. But being the considerate person that she is, Miss Marconi also tried to reach you by phone. She wanted to make sure you didn't run up unnecessary charges that you'll be responsible for. Tim, I hope you haven't been spending unnecessarily."

He responded without enthusiasm. "Of course not."

"Now," John said with an air of finality, "if you don't mind, I need to rest until dawn. I didn't get any sleep, last night. I expected you'd be here much earlier."

Lassiter studied the man's calm demeanor. It seemed that nothing shook him up. Whether in prison or the Vatican, Malek responded to every moment with the same quiet confidence.

As John reached for the lamp switch, he said, "You look like you haven't gotten any sleep, either. Why don't you rest for a while? Miss Marconi will put you on a flight back to America tomorrow. She'll take care of those expenses."

The light clicked off and Lassiter sat in the dark for a moment. Then he slid his feet down and stretched out on the bed. But his mind would not stop racing.

I guess Marconi is tapped out.
I'm gonna owe a fortune on those credit cards.
Yeah, but I still have my contract with Mercedes.
I bet Malek doesn't know somebody else is after him.
That's $80,000 just waitin' for me!
Man, Mercedes looks good.
Ohhh, my head's throbbin'.
Why does everybody want this guy so bad?
Seems harmless enough.
He's just a kook.
Who cares, screw it!

Lassiter thought about the first time he met Mercedes Dare. When they shook hands and he visibly noticed that she wore no wedding band, he remembered exchanging sly smiles. She was probably way out of his class. But that didn't stop him from dreaming.

Mercedes ... Lassiter?

Ahhhh, that's nuts! She wouldn't go for me.
Kikelomo is probably out there waitin'.
If I can get to that chloroform, I can still pull this off.

Lassiter breathed loudly in the dark, pretending to sleep. Within a few minutes he also heard John's heavy breathing. He slid out of the bed and fumbled with the contents of the pillow sack, on the floor. Soon, he had soaked the towel with chloroform and crawled next to John's chair. Suddenly, Lassiter leaped up and shoved the towel in John's face. The holy Apostle flailed his arms in the air until they dropped to his side.

Lassiter's eyes widened as he realized that he just might pull this off.

Five minutes later, he had managed – with great difficulty – to carry the big man over his shoulder, across the hallway and down the steps. Fortunately, the kitchen, was empty when he got there. Then, as Tim exited the building, he quickly spotted the garbage truck, nearby.

Kikelomo whispered angrily out her window. "You didn't say anything about this. That isn't worth a hundred dollars. You're on your own, now."

Gasping for air, exhausted from the weight of his burden, Lassiter whispered, "Is it worth a thousand?"

Kikelomo thought for only a second. "Throw him in the back."

Unceremoniously, Lassiter dumped John in with the garbage and then hopped into the passenger's seat.

When they pulled up to the fortress wall, the truck stopped. They sat silently as the cameras observed them.

Moments passed.

Kikelomo whispered, "It usually doesn't take this long."

Seconds later, Lassiter said, "Look, this truck is big

enough to bust through those doors. But you gotta get a running start. Back up."

She whispered angrily, "I can't believe I let you get me into this."

"Back up!"

She shifted the truck into reverse and rolled back about fifty feet.

"Rev it up, before you pop it into gear."

Holding the stick shift in neutral, Kikelomo started to gun the engine. "This is crazy."

"Do it!"

She shifted into first gear but kept her foot on the clutch. "Maybe we can explain our way out of this."

He yelled over the roar of the engine, "Take your foot off the clutch!"

"I don't know…"

"Look, if I go down, you're going down!"

"This was all your idea!"

"I'll blame you! I'll say you made me do it!"

Tears rolled down her pronounced cheeks. "I can't believe you got me into…"

Red faced, he screamed again, "I swear, if I go down, you're…"

Then the motorized black doors smoothly started sliding open.

Kikelomo backed off the gas pedal, released the clutch and, together, they slowly drove away.

The snake said,
"I promise I won't bite you,
if you carry me across..."
The Beginning of a Fable

Chapter 31
Private Chapel of the Papal Residence
January 7

Pope Innocent paced the room and wept as pangs of guilt stabbed his heart and soul. In the chapel that extended from his bedroom, the pontiff moaned so loudly that a Swiss Guard rushed in without knocking. Innocent ignored him and continued his loud laments.

"Oh, Lord Jesus Christ, I beg Your forgiveness for failing to protect Your Beloved Apostle. Almighty God, please help me find John before any harm comes to him. Holy Mary, mother of God, I plead for your intercession. Bring my unworthy prayers to the feet of your beloved Son. Have mercy on us. Have mercy on us. Have mercy on us all, Lord God."

He dropped to his knees and lowered his face to the cold stone floor. Tears pooled beneath his cheeks. *How could I be so stupid? How could I let them kidnap him from under my protection?*

Just then, someone knocked on the thick oaken door of the chapel. When the Swiss Guard opened it, the pope raised his head and nodded slowly at the guard, authorizing admittance. An odd looking pair entered: the short, heavy abbot followed by the lean and muscular priest, Henri Blanc.

For the priest, so much had happened in such a short period of time that he still was trying to sort it all out. Yesterday, Blanc had been briefed on the amazing identity of John

Malek. When he finally comprehended who he had been bad-gering, Henri begged forgiveness from Christ's holy Apostle. John laughed at his heart-felt humiliation, welcomed the man with a loving embrace and informed him that Henri was about to begin his most important ministry.

Father Blanc did not understand why he had been privi-leged to share the long-protected secret that few others knew. Of course, his extraordinary life story had always contained surprises and of particular note was when, at the height of his technological success, he denounced his career and renounced all of his possessions to seek Spiritual fulfillment in the priest-hood. Still, meeting a living Apostle topped everything.

Now, he realized he would follow the stream, wherever the current took him. So, imitating the lead of the pope, he dropped to his knees and leaned his face to the stone floor. But Henri found it hard to pray. Instead, his calculating mind remained focused on what might be expected of him, here.

Blanc wondered if the pontiff expected to make use of the fortune he had accumulated in his earlier years. But Henri discarded that idea, thinking, *Surely he realizes I gave it all away.*

Then Blanc considered whether they were counting on his reputation as a genius of modern technology. However, Henri knew that in the fast paced world of technological change, he was now far behind the curve.

Why me? he kept wondering instead of praying.

Henri did not know that Pope Innocent had Spiritually discerned his crucial role, in these times, from prophecies.[168] The pontiff understood that Henri Blanc's mission would be unique ... even more consequential than his own.

Through private revelation, Innocent also realized that the emergency immunization program that was moving ahead in

America, full throttle, had been foretold as the Mark of the Beast in the Book of Revelation.[169]

Momentous events appeared to be developing quickly.

Only yesterday, the four of them – the pope, the abbot, the priest and the Apostle – had sped to the Vatican with the joyful hope that God's grand plan was unfolding and that they, somehow, would be part of it all.

The excitement of meeting the Beloved Apostle was exhilarating. Then came the chilling report, this morning, that John was missing. Upon hearing the news, Pope Innocent rushed to central security and insisted on personally supervising the review of the night's surveillance videos. Complying with the pontiff's wishes, a Swiss Guard zipped through the moments, until he suddenly slowed the tape to normal speed.

A shadowy figure was in the hallway of the residence. He entered into John's bedroom and, later, emerged with man slumped over his shoulder. Pope Innocent almost fainted when he realized that John was being carried out, unconscious or dead.

Innocent frantically wondered, *What can we do?* They could not call the police. John was an escaped convict, wanted for murder.

As the three men continued to pray over the hopeless situation, a happy tapping resonated from the door. When the guard opened it, an old, buck-tooth Englishman poked his head in and greeted Innocent with, "Hello, old chap!"

Henri and the abbot lifted their faces, shocked at the jovial impudence of the Brit.

"I just thought I would take Father Blanc for a lovely little stroll."

Wiping his tears, Innocent laughed excitedly. "Yes. Yes! Father Blanc, follow him wherever he takes you!"

Baffled, the priest rose to his feet and walked to the door where the friendly Englishman put his arm over the priest's shoulder and said, "Let me tell you, mate, about the Battle of Monte Cassino."

IN TRASTEVERE, less than two kilometers from the Vatican, John's back ached as he regained consciousness. He tried to straighten himself until he realized that his wrists and ankles were tied to the legs of his chair. So, he had no choice but to remain slumped over, as he studied his surroundings in Kikelomo's dreary, unfinished basement.

Above his head, a small light bulb dangled from a wire, casting light and shadows around the cluttered, damp room. John sniffed the stale air and then attempted to free his hands, unsuccessfully. Then he shouted, "Hello?"

Within seconds, a door at the top of the stairs opened, casting a bright light into the basement. Then a man bounded down the rickety wooden steps. It was Tim Lassiter.

"Hello, detective."

"I had to piss," Lassiter mumbled, as he slid a chair nearer to John and then sat down. "You just sit tight." He added more firmly, "I'm gonna keep an eye on you."

"Until when?"

"Until they pick you up."

"Who is 'they'?"

"None of your business."

"I doubt it would be Thas, so it must be his brothers."

Lassiter recoiled, "How'd you know that?"

"Tim, I know more than you realize."

"Then you realize they'll be here soon. We're gonna just sit quietly until then."

"No problem," John said. "But, Tim, if you don't release me now, it won't go well for you."

"Yeah?" Lassiter snorted a laugh. "I know about 80,000 reasons why it *will* go well for me." But then Tim remembered the similar advice of the Englishman at the gas station: "Don't bother John. He has important work to do.... Don't become what you despise. It won't go well for you." The former detective pushed back on those words, attempting to drive them from his consciousness. He assured himself that he was on the side of the law. After all, Malek was an escaped convict.

Doubts, however, continued to nag him. So, he chose to focus on other things. He remembered how lucky he had been to convince Kikelomo to let him use her home for a day. Lassiter had gained her trust by presenting to her a press clipping of himself, from his detective days, and another one on John' escape from prison. Then, to seal the deal, he offered her another thousand dollars. She was thrilled. Still, to protect herself from possible incrimination, the Nigerian left the two of them in the house, alone, so that she could claim that they had broken into her home when she was away, if any official asked questions later.

Unable to continue sitting quietly, Lassiter broke his own rule after six minutes of silence.

"So, why does Thas want you so bad?"

"You'll have to ask him.... But I suspect that he knows I can stop him from achieving his ultimate goal."

Lassiter laughed, dismissing the suggestion that this crazy drifter could somehow thwart the strategies of the rich and powerful. "I'm serious. Why? This may be the end of the line for you."

John smiled. "There is no end of the line ... only new beginnings."

"You sure have a crazy take on reality."

"Perhaps.... Can I tell you more about what I think?"

Lassiter exhaled, audibly. "Sure. As long as you don't bore me."

"Tim, the world is returning to the way it was."

"Like how?"

"You've read the Old Testament. Genesis? Exodus?"

"Sure. When I was a kid."

"Those stories of the past point the way of the future."

"So, what's your point?"

"Before the Tower of Babel, for example, the people said, *'Come, let us build ourselves a city, with a tower that reaches to the heavens, so that we may make a name for ourselves and not be scattered over the face of the whole earth.'*[170] Today, what do we see? Cities around the world, vying to construct the most awesome skyscrapers. Why? Because those monuments to man's achievement are magnets to those who wish to make names for themselves. They dream that they will find fulfillment in luxurious, high rise penthouses but, instead, they often encounter crime, poverty and Spiritual rot in the shadows of those towers. However, it doesn't take long before they are too busy to notice."

"Wow. I guess you're not a big city guy."

"There are good people almost everywhere. But that which dazzles the eye or the ear, distracts us from the Spirit. Before the Tower of Babel, for example, everyone could communicate with each other. Likewise today, anywhere, anytime, we can communicate. We even have technologies that bridge the language gap. But what are we saying to each other? Supposedly, progress has brought us snippets of tweets. Are we communicating anything that has lasting importance? Just scan what entertains us in movies, television shows, music and the

Internet. Is our entertainment communicating anything that does not dismiss or offend God? Yet it makes its way around the world."

"Can we talk about something else?"

"Then, as we move toward the beginning of Scripture, we read about the Ark of the Covenant, which I assure you, will surface again. We will witness God reaffirming His gift of the Promised Land. We will see many of the plagues of Egypt again, even the Three Days of Darkness.[171] Then the Divine Chastisements will be remembered for a time, but not long enough. Soon after, we will experience the widespread reawakening of the murderous envy of Cain. Brother will betray brother to death, and a father his child. Children will rebel against their parents and have them put to death. All men will hate Christians because of me.[172] Then, because of our hardened hearts, a Great Tribulation, worse than the Great Flood and unlike any other, will be necessary to convert sinners. And when mankind is purified of those who choose to be enslaved by the evil one, the world shall return to the holy simplicity of the Garden of Eden."

"Dude," Lassiter said, sarcastically, "you think you got this trip all mapped out?"

John got serious. "Look, Tim, I just want you to do one thing for me."

"You're not in a position to make requests, but go ahead."

"Accept Jesus Christ as your Lord and Savior."

Lassiter laughed. "Man, you just don't give up."

THE OLD ENGLISHMAN led Father Blanc through a maze of streets and alleys. He seemed to know exactly where he was headed during their brisk walk from the Vatican to Trastevere and for half and hour, now, the affable Brit had elaborated on the history of Monte Cassino and the battle that destroyed it. Henri suspected that there must be something very special about this man, or Pope Innocent would not have responded to him so happily. But the point of this one-sided conversation was not easily discerned.

The buck-tooth gentleman rambled about the history of the abbey and how a principled defense might have saved not only the holy site but, more importantly, many lives. He seemed to be lecturing on legitimate reasons for a just war.[173] He argued that public authorities have the right and duty to impose on citizens the obligations necessary for national defense.[174]

These were points that Blanc had always accepted. So, to bolster the man's argument, Henri inserted one of his favorite quotes: "All that is necessary for evil to triumph is for good men to do nothing."[175] But the old fellow was not listening. He was focused on continuing to reassure Blanc that lives lost in battle, sometimes, are sacrificed for a noble cause.

Finally, it seemed the Englishman was summing up when he declared: "There are times when aggressive evil must be confronted." Then, suddenly, the Englishman stopped, pointed across the street to a small cottage, and said, "There."

Henri was baffled. "There … what?"

"He's in there."

"Who's in there?"

The old man laughed. "Blimey O'Reilly! You think I've been walking and talking for the last half hour because I've got nothing else to do?" Henri did not know how to respond. So, the Brit stressed, "John ... John's in the basement." Then he took the lead, darting across the street and up to the front door.

When they stepped onto the stoop, the old man said, "Don't knock. We need the element of surprise."

"Are you going to break in?"

"No, no," the man dismissed the suggestion. "I'm not allowed."

"So, how do we get in?"

The fellow smiled, exposing two bulbous incisors, pulled a mother-of-pearl pocket knife out of his pants, and handed it to the priest.

Astonished, Henri examined the object that looked exactly like the knife he had carried for years, the one he had used when he broke into the archives of the National Library of

Israel with Huntington Cyst, decades ago.

Henri's eyes rose from his hand, to that smiling mouthful of teeth, and then to the door jamb. There, he recognized an XG-1 card reader. It was the same electronic lock that he once had found so easy to compromise, at the archives.

"Okay," the priest said with a grin. "I guess I know what to do."

Then he popped the cover off the card reader, shorted two terminals, and nodded when the door lock buzzed open.

"Hurry," the Englishman warned. "You don't have much time." Then, before Henri stepped in, he whispered, "Element of surprise, mate. Element of surprise."

The first step in community organization
is community disorganization....
An organizer must stir up dissatisfaction and discontent;
provide a channel into which the people
can angrily pour their frustrations.
Saul D. Alinsky[176]

Chapter 32
Over the Pacific Ocean
January 7

Shortly after leaving American airspace, another minor eruption occurred. It was one of those episodes that baffled Mercedes Dare but, still, made the enigma known as Evan Thas all the more intriguing. She could only decipher that the flight attendants had arranged the appetizer silverware in cross patterns on the plates. When Thas noticed it, he scolded the girls, complaining that flatware should always be placed parallel. It seemed like such an overreaction to a minor infraction that Mer suspected it had been a convenient ruse to make them disappear for the rest of the trip. So, when the baffled flight attendants retreated to the aft cabin, the cozy couple were free to converse, privately.

Recently, there had been infrequent communication between them. Thas had been maintaining a grueling pace with little sleep or food. To her, it seemed that his metabolism had been inexhaustible. So, she was thrilled to regain his full attention.

Typically, Evan was a careful man who guarded a fortress full of secrets. Today, however, he lectured for over an hour while Mercedes marveled at his every word. They imbibed a sea of expensive alcohol, together, blending it with generous portions of mutual infatuation. It is a cocktail that sometimes makes smart people stupid and fortresses vulnerable.

While the Gulfstream 550 headed for the Island Republic of Nauru, Thas and Dare had nestled into their plush leather recliners, enjoying the long trip. He had become increasingly excited as he talked about his recent accomplishments, and the triumphs still to come. In private, the young lovers did not need to restrain their enthusiasm.

She was proud to share these serene hours with him. In fact, as her hand gently slid across her pregnant waist, Mercedes imagined spending the rest of her life probing the brilliant mind of this fascinating man. Ever since she had given Evan the big news, a week ago, Mercedes had planned a very fortunate future for herself and their child.

Thas had detailed how his grand strategy was beginning to bear fruit. President Concepcion, for example, had gone through a rebellious period, but she was now under control. However, she had always displayed an independent streak. So, he had purchased additional insurance by engineering the rise of Senator Laugherly from Appropriations Committee Chairman to Vice President. Evan complained that the maneuver had not been easy but worth the effort.

"Purchased insurance?" she asked with a smile.

"Nothing as crass as shoveling cash, of course." Thas shrugged. "We just sprinkle a bit of inside information here, a bit there, and before you know it, our friends in Washington are proving to be brilliant investors ... and cooperative legislators."[177]

The frowning lawyer added, "They get re-elected while others get convicted."

Evan waved it off, "They're protected against prosecution for insider trading ... Very convenient."

Mercedes gave a tipsy giggle as she finished off the last sip of *Chateau d'Yquem* that Evan had been serving her. He took her Baccarat glass and went to the bar to pour more. Studying his steady confidence, she marveled at how quickly her priorities had changed. The dream of a successful legal career now seemed a distant memory.

When he returned, Mer gulped her wine and he continued. "Laugherly's a good soldier. At least when you buy *him* off, he stays bought. He's not as high-maintenance as Angela."

Then, as he sipped his cognac, Evan asked, "Any reports from Lassiter?"

"Yeah. He says he's been on Malek's trail along the Rivieras. He started in Nice and then headed east through Villefranche Sur Mer, Eze and Monaco. Then, in Italy, he hit Comogli, Santa Margherita and now he's investigating a lead in Portofino."

"Strange. I don't picture Malek strolling along moonlit Mediterranean beaches."

"I know. Lassiter says Malek's been deliberately moving through resort communities because that's where the police wouldn't think to look. But I'm starting to wonder about that guy. He sure knows how to entertain himself."

"Tell him he's got two weeks. If he doesn't come up with something solid, by then, we'll find someone else."

Mer finally asked what she had wondered for weeks. "What's so important about Malek? Why do you and your mother care so much?"

"She knew him years ago." Evan sighed. "I have higher priorities on my list, right now, but she keeps pushing it hard."

"Business matter?"

"No," Evan responded, flatly. "It's personal."

Then he took her crystal wine glass and went to the bar to

refill their drinks.

Mercedes didn't want to pry into the details, so she moved on. "I still feel sorry for poor Vice President Blight."

"Horrifying," Evan commented without the slightest sarcasm. "Simply horrifying."

He changed the subject. "You know, we really took it on the chin with our Global Warming and Cap-And-Trade agenda." Evan laughed. "No matter how hard we beat that horse, we just couldn't get it across the finish line. It's a real shame because there were trillions at stake."[178]

She nodded, sympathetically.

"But we've always got other irons in the fire. The United Nations has embraced our proposal that free broadband access should be a fundamental human right.[179] Now, our lobbyists can push through international funding that will assist the world's poorest countries. It's a win-win for everybody."

He did not mention that the move also would promote Evan's growing monopoly on routing Internet traffic. Soon, the global information flow – among Evan's friends and enemies alike – would be through the CyBot search engine, securely under Evan's control and supervision.

Evan explained that the world today had been unimaginable just a hundred years ago. Through the efforts of Cyst, Thas and other geniuses of their generations, modern alchemy had been accomplished. Though their forefather alchemists had dreamed of changing base metals into gold, this enterprise had been infinitely more ambitious. The incomprehensible volume of today's information flow is brought to us by the lowly grain of sand. Silicon[180] is the building block of the computer chips that process today's information, entertainment and rejection of God.

Perhaps it was the cognac, but Evan was holding very

KENNETH E. NOWELL

little back from Mercedes, trusting her more like his lawyer than his girlfriend. Some of what he had said would have disturbed her just a few months ago. Love and luxury, however, had dulled her conscience. Now, she felt more worldly and wise. She was starting to realize: *Everybody does it.*

Just then, an exotic beauty approached with a satellite phone.

"Dr. Thas, I apologize for bothering you," the flight attendant said. "This is the call you said you'd take."

Evan took the phone and answered suspiciously, "Yes?"

He listened intently for a moment, then grinned and mouthed to Mercedes the words, "Speak of the devil." Mer smiled, taking that to mean, "Lassiter."

"Excellent," Evan chortled as Mer admired that his red-headed boyish charm had returned.

Thas rose from his seat and walked to the far end of the cabin, now mumbling into the receiver. Clearly, he did not want her or the flight attendant to hear his conversation. But over the rumble of the jet engines, she could make out, "… keep him tied … Malphas and Pruflas are on Corsica…"

Then she watched as he disconnected and dialed for someone else. By the time someone answered, his smile had transformed into a sinister scowl. She could see that he was giving orders and assumed it was to one of his brothers. She listened carefully to his impassioned whispers, but the only words she could make out were "slow" and "painful." Then, before he hung up, she also thought she heard the word, "suffer."

WHEN EVAN RETURNED to his seat, his eyes flared with proud defiance. Mer's enthusiasm elevated with his. After all, his victories would now be hers.

Together, tonight, they shared a feeling of invincibility. So, Mer decided to delve deeper than she ever had before. She boldly inquired about one of his most closely held secrets. "Tell me about Titan."

He played dumb. "That's my nickname: 'The Tech Titan.'"[181]

"You know what I mean," she responded flatly. "That mind reading ... gadget ... thing."

"Ohhh, I don't know," Evan groaned playfully. "If I told you, I'd have to kill you."

"Stop it, silly," she slapped his knee.

Cryptically, he answered, "Titan is for everyone."

"Oh, come on!" she begged.

Reluctantly, he gave in. "What do you know about endorphins and adrenaline?"

"Not much."

"Well, adrenaline is a hormone that is secreted into our bloodstream when we are preparing for a "fight or flight" response. Endorphins, on the other hand, are polypeptides. They're endogenous opioid biochemical compounds."

"Holy cow!" she laughed.

"Let me ask you, what is modern man's most pervasive drug addiction?"

"I don't know, uh, heroine, cocaine, alcohol?"

"No, not at all. Those are exogenous drugs, administered from outside the body. The most pervasive drug addictions are endogenous, coming from inside our bodies."

"What do you mean?"

"You know, adrenaline junkies, for example. They're the ones who love to skydive, zoom around on loud motorcycles, watch scary movies, perhaps even rob banks or start bar fights. They get an endogenous fix of adrenaline whenever they give in to their need. Endorphins, on the other hand, are natural pain killers, like opium."

"I remember: distance runners get a sense of calm from endorphins."

"Right. Runners become addicted to that high. But, for my purposes, I prefer the addiction of pornography."

She giggled, "Ewww."

"Not for myself, but to control people, of course.... Thanks to modern technology, we have it all in abundance. For example, the Internet and the sexual revolution of the 20th century brought us the most sex addicted society in history. The computer is the new needle for endorphin-dependent sex junkies. And though that's the big one, other media also contribute to our lesser adrenaline and endorphin fixes. Whether we want a thrill, or a laugh, or a cry, or a sexual release, it's always available from a screen near you. Unlike any people in human history, we experience life vicariously, with instant access to gratification from man-made absurdities that we call reality. Think about it: 'Reality TV?' What's real about it? It's nothing more than a prescription for an endogenous drug high."

"So, what's this have to do with Titan?"

"Titan has two capability levels. First, we can identify and track anyone who is implanted."

"Implanted?"

"It's not a big deal. We use nanotechnology,[182] so it's basically like getting a shot. It's not painful, just bothersome. So, we need incentives in order to get people to willingly submit."

"Where does it go?"

"The identification element works in concert with an individual's brain waves. So, it is best to inject the implant as close to the frontal lobe as possible. That's where most of our dopamine-sensitive neurons are contained in the cerebral cortex."

She laughed. "I'm sorry I asked."

"No, it's an important question. The dopamine system is associated with reward, attention, short-term memory tasks, planning, and drive. Those uniquely individual characteristics enable us to differentiate and identify every implanted person. So, Titan should be implanted into the forehead."

"You're kidding. Does it leave a scar?"

"Just a little red mark: three concentric circles, kind of like a bulls eye."[183]

"That sounds like those weird influenza shots they're wanting everybody to get."

Evan just smiled as he took another sip of cognac. "The tracking element of Titan works much like a highly sensitive GPS locator. Once the program is universal, we'll be able to track everyone. Criminals would no longer get away with lying about where they were at the time of the crime. Terrorists would have nowhere to hide. Think about it. In less than a second we could track down John Malek and his gang.

"But it's about more than just security. In recent years, we have become pretty good at developing psycho-social profiles based on data mining people's CyBot search engine activities on the Internet. But now, when one submits to a Titan Analysis, even greater benefits are added. Each time we conduct a study, we closely track the patient's heart, lung and blood responses to a wide variety of sensory stimulants – you know, pictures, videos, sounds, songs, words, even smells. We closely track brain activity during the analysis and learn exactly what sensory inputs trigger the release of adrenaline or endorphins. So, we uncover every addiction, fear, or motivating influence in a person's life."

"Why do you want to know that?"

"You're so cute," Evan teased, "when you're naïve."

She frowned, playfully.

"Mer, an addicted or fearful man is a controllable man. I don't want him to exercise free will. I want him to exercise *my* will."

She found herself laughing, uncomfortably. "But how will you get everybody to go along?"

"They'll go along. You know, security is such a big concern, these days. In fact, the first round of implants are being done now, as a mandatory measure for civil servants with security clearances. That has been initiated discretely, without any fanfare. The camel's nose under the tent, so to speak. Next, it will be rolled out for every government employee. People will submit, if they want to keep their jobs."

"That's still not most people."

"Slow down. Measures like this have to be done incrementally … progressively." He took another sip. "Do you realize that 48.6% of all American households now receive government assistance?[184] That's the obvious next step. You wanna stay on the Gravy Train? Here's the price of a free ticket. Get your shot and shut up."

"Still…"

Evan thought for a moment, then added, "Let me tell you a little secret. Whenever I deal with people, I like to use a technique I call 'the progressive choke.'"

"What?" she asked with a startled laugh.

"I do my homework and discover their needs or, better yet, addictions. You'd be surprised at how needy people have become."

"Like how?"

He smiled. "Even simple things. Contrast, for example,

society now versus a hundred years ago. Some people today would absolutely freak out if they lost access to the Internet, or TV, or their family car. Those subtle pressure points didn't exist a century ago. Even better, what if your son might need a heart transplant? Once health care has a centralized controlling authority, people will want to cooperate. You see, just the possibility of a major health issue for yourself or a loved one will bring the population under control."

"I see what you mean."

"But I'm not just focused on health care. There are so many needs and, step by step, I convince decision makers to let me control the need pipeline. You need entertainment and information from the Internet? I'll take care of it. You want to stay informed? I'll supply the news coverage for you. You're worried about national defense? We've got the perfect weapons for you. You see, I'm the friendly man with the plan, and I will gladly assist as long as I am in control. I don't go for government by consensus."

"So, where are you doing all this?" she asked, cautiously.

"I like to focus on the coddled elites who spend other people's money. Angela's a good example. The bigger the institution, the better. In some organizations – like the UN, the IMF or the US Congress — you can finagle billions. Typically, their projects are so burdened with bureaucracy and their funding flows so long and circuitous that even the IRS tax code is easier to decipher. Nobody will lose any sleep if the audit trail gets bogged down in minutia."

"Yeah, but those auditors get paid to do a job."

"Mer, think about it: Let's say Mr. Bureaucrat is a $60,000 a year accountant. He can choose the easy and comfortable route by letting the messy details sink into the bog of barely remembered history.[185] On the other hand – if he chooses to be uncooperative – then Mr. B., his dear wife, and lovely children will have to worry about our journalists, our private investigators, or whoever else we deem necessary. God help Mr. B. if he's been too friendly with that charming young lady at his fitness center. Or, maybe he's a volunteer coach at the Boys' Club and one player seems to think he's been a bit too friendly. It would be a real tragedy to have all that nastiness dredged up in the news. He doesn't need that kind of headache." Evan took another sip. "So, anyway, you get the picture."

Mercedes, again, was uncomfortable with the conversation.

"In fact, we're using the progressive choke to fight terrorism."

"Okay, you've got my attention again."

"Well, you want to stop air travel terrorism, don't you?"

"Of course."

"That's why our political leaders passed laws and regulations that now require the crotch police to feel you up, along with the grannies and kids that you travel with. They're a terrible threat, you know. More importantly, TSA was mandated to screen passengers with XCyst's latest technology for imaging. It's a win-win for everybody: XCyst gets a massive boost to sales revenue, the politicians get to say they're keeping you safe, and the groper patrol not only get to feel you up but they are also scrutinize every square inch of your gloriously naked body."

"Yeah, airport screening has gotten about as intrusive as a gynecological exam."

"All according to plan," he smiled, "and it'll get even worse."

"Worse?" she asked with mock anger.

"Until people finally demand a stop to it." He studied her

response. "Let's face it: people are asses." She laughed as he continued. "I'm referring to donkeys, of course. They stubbornly resist moving without a carrot or a stick."

"So, why do you want airport check-in to be so difficult?"

"Titan," he smiled, "that's why."

She shook her head. "You lost me."

"The Big Daddy of all progressive chokes. Mer, like I say, Titan is already being implemented secretly. Federal , state and local government security clearances are now requiring the full Titan analysis. But that's just the start. Eventually, we'll evolve into the full implementation of Titan technology with everyone submitting to the full analysis. You see, Titan can track individuals because it can identify each one as effectively as fingerprints or DNA. However, it can do it from a distance and in real time."

"What kind of distance?"

Evan smiled, sheepishly.

"Are you saying, from your satellites?"

He continued smiling but did not answer directly. "So, we'll first sell it as a benefit for the privileged few. You won't be able to fly without it. Eventually, though, it will be mandatory for all. We'll herd them in like sheep for the innoculations. But the advanced phase – the analysis – requires you to submit to an hour-long evaluation wearing an encephalographic cap."[186]

"Count me out."

"That's the problem. Too bothersome."

"All that, just to get on an airplane?"

"No, not just for flying. Titan will become an indispensable convenience in every aspect of your life. That's the beauty of it. Once Titan is implanted, you will just walk right through any security line in which you are classified for access: the airport, a military base, even the White House. Increasingly, those who are Titanized will be given preferential treatment as standard procedure. No need to wait in lines with the masses."

Mercedes thought about how security was becoming a dominant concern in America. After a variety of mall bombings, even shopping centers had begun inconvenient inspections of customer bags upon entry. This seemed like such an improvement.

"Pretty cool," she said.

"Even your medical history will be stored in our databanks, allowing you easy access to health care. Also, your bank account will be tied to your Titan identity. For example, when you go to a movie, walk right in. Your implant will transmit your identity to the theater and the correct ticket price will be automatically debited from your bank account. Walk into a car lot, pick a car, tell them your preferences on financing, and drive away. Your application information, credit report, insurance and driver's license information are all automatically reported and stored. Buying a house will be just as simple. Automatic computer entries will account for every economic transaction, whether from work income, purchases at a store, or whatever. Think about it: The Titan system will eliminate credit card fraud and identity theft because no one can imitate your brain waves. Even counterfeiting cash will become a thing of the past, because we will become a cashless society. Every transaction will be secure and safe. No more tax evasion. Criminals and terrorists will have nowhere to hide, no way to survive, on the run."[187]

"So, you're thinking that if security screening becomes so uncomfortable and intrusive, and if identity theft and credit card fraud keep increasing ..."

"That's right. If we progressively choke off conveniences that people have learned to expect, they will accept the changes that our solutions require. Mer, with Titan, I can accomplish fundamental change."

"I know, but people like my parents won't want to go along."

"Christians?"

"Big time. They'd be screaming, 'Mark of the Beast! Mark of the Beast!'"[188]

"Yeah, there are a few like that. But, of course, you have to crack a few eggs to make an omelet. Still, believe me, the world will be an amazingly better place when I'm through. However, the task is large. We have to re-educate in order to fundamentally change mankind. We must deconstruct every traditional belief, trust, hope, and love. Faith in God, in the family, in private enterprise, in personal freedom, in Constitutional rights, they are holding us back. Individual freedoms have brought chaos. Intelligent design is the answer. Our human relationships and beliefs must be redefined and realigned, intelligently, for the good of everyone. Re-education is not as hard as it sounds. We will discredit and replace the failed ideologies of the past. Even faith in the almighty dollar has to go. So, we will move to a global monetary system. Now is the time, because daily struggles for the average individual have become so burdensome that there is a hunger for a better world. People are yearning for revolutionary change. They will be open to the promise that their every pleasure, comfort and security can originate with Titan. It's just a matter of education. We'll show them the benefits that Titan will offer – the carrots, so to speak."

"But what about people who refuse the implants."

"Well, then," he smiled sheepishly, "there's always the stick."

†††

ON THE OTHER SIDE OF THE WORLD, Malphas and Pruflas stood on Kikelomo's front porch, knocking. When no one
answered, Pruflas kicked the door open and the two casually
walked in.

"Help! I'm down here," Lassiter shouted from the basement.

When the twins descended the rickety wood steps, Tim
recognized them immediately. Though he had never met the
dark pair, he knew them from the many media reports he had
seen regarding Evan's famous family.

"Ahhh, thank God," Lassiter said while uncomfortably
bending over, with hands and ankles tied to the feet of his
chair. "I had no idea how long I'd be stuck here."

Malphas and Pruflas stood silently, staring at Lassiter, as
if waiting for an explanation.

"You just missed Malek! We can still catch him!"

Squirming to get free, Tim was agitated and anxious over
how close he had been to victory. He watched their faces
tighten, but he was frustrated that they were not springing to
action.

"Untie me and I'll tell you what happened."

Neither of the twins moved.

"Okay. I'll tell you anyway. See, I captured Malek – kidnapped him right out of the Vatican. Pretty cool, huh? And
then I had him all tied up, down here."

The twins did not appear to appreciate Tim's accomplishments.

"Don't worry. I can get him back."

Still, no response.

Aching from crouching, he reminded them, "Guys, I could explain it better if you'd just free me."

Malphas nodded and stepped up to Lassiter's chair.

The grateful prisoner raised his head to thank the man, saying, "Okay buddy, I really appre…" until he stared into the void of Malphas' deadly, dark eyes.

Suddenly, he understood.

Tim Lassiter accepted Jesus Christ as his Lord and Savior just before his neck snapped.

The Christian ideal has not been tried and found wanting.
It has been found difficult, and left untried.
G. K. Chesterton

A ngela slid the box out of her bedroom closet. She sat
on the floor, ripped open the taped top, and started
removing its contents, spreading them on the Orien-
tal rug. It contained all of what had been her mother's most
prized possessions.

One clipping after another described Angela's accomplishments throughout her life. Some of her childhood awards
and trophies were stuffed in there too. Displayed most beauti-
fully, however, was Angela's first Holy Communion picture.

She was just eight, at the time, and radiated an innocence
that had left her long ago. She had worn a beautiful white
gown with a delicate lace veil on her head.

That was a different person from a different world. It was
before everything had turned into a competition to rise above,
even if by pushing others down. The horrors of earthquakes
and nuclear fallout and economic depression and assassina-
tions had never entered that child's mind.

Instead, she feared the soap ogre in the car wash and the
invisible alligator under her bed. Still, she knew that those
frightful monsters could not harm her as long as Mama or
Papa were around to shoo them away.

After his death, long ago, and hers last year, Angela was
on her own. It seemed strange, now that they were gone,
realizing they were no longer out there, somewhere, cheering

252

her on. Angela's memories filled with regrets.

In the picture, her white-gloved hands were folded prayerfully and her eyes shone brightly the excitement of encountering Jesus Christ in a very special way.

Ahh, that sense of peace and joy. Grownups don't have it.

But then she corrected herself: *Except Mama.*

She remembered how her mother had displayed a loving spirit even when everything was going wrong. And Angela remembered that a lot of what went wrong had been her own doing.

Shameful, she thought of her own selfishness.

What gave Mama that peace?

Deep down, she knew the answer. It had always been there, just too obvious for her to pay attention to it.

As Angela grew into her rebellious teenage years, she felt that she was far too special to pray to the God of her parents – the God of simple people. Her god had to be extraordinary, very special. Something that only intelligent people would understand. Something that only artists could truly appreciate. Yes, her god would attract only interesting people.

Ashamed of herself, Angela dug around in the bottom of the box and pulled out her mother's most prized possession: her Rosary.

That was what had sustained her through every difficulty: the Sacraments and the Rosary.

The little *Chiquita* sighed fondly, missing the simplicity and love of her parents.

Suddenly, Fred burst in. "Hey, get moving. Your buddy's speech starts in an hour. You don't wanna be late for that one."

"Fred," she groaned at his sarcasm. They both knew that Israel's Prime Minister had been scheduled to speak before a Joint Session of Congress, at this time, to detract from

Angela's upcoming State of the Union address. It was a way for her congressional enemies to stick a thumb in her eye, knowing that the President of the United States could not say no.

"Oh, don't be so down in the dumps. Israel has to give in. The pressure's on." He looked down at her digging into the box. "So, what are you doing?"

"Oh, just going through some of Mama's old memories."

"Don't worry about it. I'll have 'em throw it out tomorrow."

Angela did not protest. She knew that every piece of presidential memorabilia should be saved for her eventual presidential library. Right now, though, she did not feel worthy of honor. So, she put all the clippings, pictures and trophies back into the box and slid it in front of the closet.

Tomorrow, it would be trashed.

Before she got up, Angela gently stroked her midsection and then slipped the red Rosary into her pocket.

It is sort of a disease
when you consider yourself some kind of god,
the creator of everything.
But I feel comfortable about it now
since I began to live it out.
George Soros[189]

She had dozed for a few hours. The wine had made her drowsy. As the jet neared Nauru, Mer stretched her arms into the air and observed that Evan had not rested. He seemed intensely focused on a problem.

"Your mind's still working. Give it a rest."

He almost smiled, but did not respond. So, she let him think for a while longer.

To her, the past few months had seemed like a dream as her fate had become so closely intertwined with that of one of the most powerful leaders in the world. She wanted to know more about this mysterious man. She finally asked, "What's your secret, Evan?"

He did not pause. "I excel at identifying what people want."

"Oh, yeah?" she teased. "Like, what do I want?"

"You, my little Mer, want a life of luxury."

"That's terrible! You think I'm a gold-digger?"

"Look, I know I'm a geek. If I lost my fortune tomorrow, you'd be on your way by sundown."

Mercedes turned her head to the window, as if pouting. However, she did not deny his assertion.

"Don't be angry with me for having a firm grip on reality." Evan added, "I also excel at *giving* people what they want."

With that reassurance, she offered him a reluctant smile. Then Mercedes asked, "What about President Concepcion?

"She is a child who wanted a peak at what she's made of, then didn't like the view."

"So, what does she want in life?"

"She wants attention, favorable attention. It doesn't matter whether she is being noticed for wearing the right gown or for brokering a Middle East peace breakthrough, just fawn over her and she's happy."

Free from interruptions and hangars-on, Mer felt that this private, quality-time had strengthened their relationship and allowed them to bond on a much deeper level. She smiled as she stroked her own tummy and reflected on the future of her fortunate child.

She had rarely seen Evan this relaxed and radiating contentment. For the past month he had been maintaining a torturous pace, immersed in his work, focused on training his twin brothers.

They're such an odd bunch, she thought of the strange pair and their mysterious mother. The silent twins seemed harmless enough, but Mer resented the relentless pestering that Faridah offered Evan. Though the attorney had only overheard bits of conversations – often discretely veiled with codewords – Mercedes had come to believe that Evan's mother was obsessed with finding John Malek and with getting Evan to complete some strange project in Capernaum Israel. Then, also, there was the weird claim that Faridah had made in an interview on XBC News. With no hint of humor, she said that Evan was the product of a virgin birth.[190]

The tabloids ran with the story and many people became

fascinated with the idea.

Mer concealed her smile. *Attractive people, but very, very strange.*

Evan served her another glass of wine as the pilot announced the beginning of their descent into Nauru International Airport.

"Drink up. We're almost there."

She sipped quickly, but could not stop wondering if she would ever feel comfortable around his family. However, she knew that Evan respected them all. He had worked so hard on his brothers' training that it seemed that he viewed them as vitally important to his efforts. Still, Mer could not imagine that they would ever be able to manage people as effectively as Evan had.

The dark pair[191] had inherited Faridah's regal Middle Eastern features, the only qualities that Evan seemed to lack. However, the twins made most people very uncomfortable with their air of superiority. The one seemed arrogant, taking for granted that he was in charge of everyone except Evan and Faridah. The other's facial expressions were so disagreeable that Mercedes wondered how anyone could tolerate working with him. Still, the brothers were quiet, so much so that many thought that they did not understand English. Mer, however, had come to believe that they were not only fluent in English but also very intelligent. They were extremely observant and they had an unspoken way of communicating with Evan – almost intuitive. The twins seemed to cater after, and even predict, Evan's every need.

So, encouraged by too much wine and reassured that Evan had been very friendly in the family's absence, Mercedes joked, "And what about the Brothers Grimm? What do they want?"

"Who?"

"You know, Sneaky and Creepy."

He inhaled deeply and asked, without amusement, "Malphas and Pruflas?"

Suddenly uncomfortable, she nodded slightly.

He paused and studied her more closely.

"My brothers want whatever I want."

The temperature in the cabin seemed to chill.

The chloral hydrate began to take effect.

She squinted at Evan, to focus. Her throat tightened. She began to choke.

"Mer," he added, seriously, "it's not wise to mock my family."

Then she rubbed her bleary eyes and passed out.

I denied myself nothing my eyes desired;
I refused my heart no pleasure.
My heart took delight in all my work,
and this was the reward for all my labor.
Ecclesiastes 2:10

Chapter 35
Nauru Airport Tarmac
January 7

The medic slammed the ambulance door shut. In the back, Thas sat next to the white-coated doctor who checked Mer's blood pressure. She was stretched out on the gurney, unconscious. Then the island's quiet night ended when the motorcade sped away, with lights flashing and sirens screaming.

Outside the airport gate and along the road to Eden Village, the islanders gathered and watched. They had never seen such a spectacle. It seemed that every emergency vehicle on the island had been engaged and the XCyst security officers had forced all traffic to yield to the speeding fleet.

Worrying that he may have caused an overdose, Evan shouted up to the driver, "Don't let anybody slow you down."

"Her vital signs are okay," the doctor said. "She'll be fine."

Evan sighed his relief.

Still, the driver radioed ahead, requesting that all perimeter protection systems be disengaged so that the patient would not be slowed on the way to the hospital. As the security forces responded, the motorized carbon fiber gates opened, the heat and motion sensors powered down, and the emergency roadway bollards lowered into the pavement. Perimeter sharpshooters watched as the emergency motorcade sped through. For the first time, an exception to Eden Village's security protocols had been approved and the patient's transport had proceeded flawlessly, just as it had been planned, over the past week.

Inside the gate, on the way to the hospital, they sped past each Tower Building while Evan looked up and admired the seven massive structures that contained his most prized possessions. Each Tower housed a variety of enormous tanks, and inside each Tower tank floated the crops that almost everyone would someday need.

On this island, Evan's genius and his reported return on investment had become legendary, as Eden Village routinely shipped body parts to the world's wealthiest, everywhere.

However, all had not gone well here in the past. While the Village's pampered residents had successfully followed Evan's commandment to "Be fruitful and multiply,"[192] he had not been as fortunate, himself. Though Thas had spent the night with every female in the Village, he had impregnated none of them. That misfortune had not only become a source of whispered jokes at Eden but, more importantly, a threat to his longevity.

Uniquely, Evan's unusual DNA prevented him from taking advantage of XCyst's organ and tissue replacement program. Evan's doctors and scientists had concluded that his extraordinary body would only accept transplants and grafts from his own offspring.

So, while he had promoted the concept of the immortal man, around the globe, Evan had realized that his own prospects were limited.

Then, a week ago, Mercedes Dare announced that she was expecting Evan's baby. Finally, he had fathered the offspring he needed. He knew that just a few years of chemical nurturing in Eden's tanks would produce the spare set of body parts that he someday would use. The realization that his work could go on indefinitely had reinvigorated him, and he understood that Mercedes would be a necessary partner in insuring his immortality with additional offspring.

As the medics rolled the gurney through the Emergency Room doors, Thas paused to look out over the grounds. He could see that the constant flow of air traffic had resumed, shipping human organs around the world. Then he gazed, admiringly, at the distant Towers and took pride in their awesome size, dwarfing everything else in sight.

Some day, this island will be full of Towers.

He could not see, however, that in the shadows of Tower 7, an angry islander was hiding. He had snuck in before the security gates had closed.

THE ISLANDER knew that he would be caught. In fact, he realized that he might not see tomorrow's dawn. But he did not care. He wanted justice and, even more, revenge.

Since the age of ten, the small but sturdy Micronesian had worked under the scorching sun, strip mining Nauru's phosphate. He was proud of his work ethic but he wanted much more for his only child.

She had always hoped to become a doctor, and when the XCyst facility was being built he had encouraged her youthful enthusiasm, saying that she certainly would work there, some day. Then, XCyst had been viewed as a savior of Nauru's faltering economy. The company spokesman promised jobs and prosperity on the island, saying that the next generation of islanders would be free from the difficult and dangerous work of strip mining.

Before long, however, rumors began to circulate that the company was engaged in scandalous activities. Inside the twelve foot high chain link perimeter fence, many islanders believed that gruesome rituals were being performed. Their simple minds did not understand how profitable human experiments and fetal farming could be.

At first, the man refused to believe the gossip. Then a neighbor girl was accepted into the program. Though she had been kept from her family, word leaked out that she was enjoying a life of pleasure and becoming wealthy, by island standards. Soon, the lure of a luxurious lifestyle was becoming hard to resist for every young islander who could meet Eden's genetic standards.

Rumors continued to spread and the Micronesian heard some disturbing details. They were so sensational that he could not imagine greater evils, even if a coven of witches had moved onto the island, performing ritualistic sexual offerings and human sacrifices. The islanders would never have tolerated such rituals. This facility, however, operated with the blessing of island leaders, under the innocuous sounding label of "scientific progress."

Then, shortly after his daughter had turned 16 – the youngest age for Eden recruitment – she disappeared. She had not been kidnapped or deceived. She was an enthusiastic volunteer.

That was four months ago, and since then the man had tried daily to gain entrance to Eden Village so that he could convince her to return home. But, every day, he had been turned away. There was nothing more he could do, legally. XCyst Industries now exercised dominion over the entire island and all of its inhabitants.

With just a claw hammer in his hand, the man slithered

along the darkened lawn, anxious to get into position before the heat and motion sensors powered up again. He climbed over a six foot interior fence to the back side of a Tower, just as the field he had crossed lit up with crisscrossing infra-red beams. He slid along the side of the building until he came to a window. His eyes widened when he saw the enormous acrylic tanks, inside, that were filled with fluid and floating black bags. The image confirmed for him that the rumors were true: Incubating in those bags were thousands of human fetuses and at least one of them, he imagined, could be his own grandchild.

What can I do? The Micronesian fretted. *I have to stop these monsters!*

Then he saw on every tank, in six different languages, the notice: "DANGER – EXTREME FIRE HAZZARD – USE UTMOST CAUTION."

WHEN MER'S EYES SLOWLY OPENED, she saw nothing but bright white. Coming into focus … white lights… white ceiling… white walls.

She wondered, *Am I dead?*

Then Evan's red head leaned into her view.

"What happened? Where am I?" she asked as she raised her arm to inspect an intravenous tube that was taped to it.

"Don't worry. You're okay. You must have had some kind of reaction to the alcohol."

Mer propped herself up on her elbows and her eyes nervously wandered the room. Near the door, a nurse busied herself with reading a clipboard. But when their eyes met, the nurse wiped a tear from her cheek and turned away.

Mer was not comforted. "I don't feel good. My whole

body …"

"Shhhh," he tried to quiet her. "We'll talk about it later."

"Talk about what? Where *am* I?"

The nurse, next to the bed, asked, "Do you want me to leave, Dr. Thas?"

Evan shook his head. "No, Ashley, just wait."

To Mercedes, the woman appeared overwhelmed by anxiety.

Thas firmly attracted the patient's attention with comforting words. "Mer, you're in the Eden Village Hospital. You're okay, so don't worry."

"I don't feel okay." Her hands slid across her stomach. "What about my baby?"

"Later, we'll talk about it later."

She shouted, "I don't want to talk about it later. Is my baby okay?!"

He nodded softly at the nurse and she injected something into the IV tube.

Evan sighed, "Mer, you lost it."

"What do you mean. I lost what?"

"The baby. You had a miscarriage."

The fear in her eyes melted into sadness.

He added, "But we'll keep trying. There'll be more."

She was disquieted by the strange smile on Evan's face. When Thas recognized her increasing emotion, he summoned, "Nurse Adams, please help her calm down."

The medical assistant obediently slid over to the bed. As she started to inject a clear liquid into the intravenous tube, Mer tried to make eye contact, but the nurse quickly averted her gaze.

Mer studied the woman's face. "Nurse Adams, will I see my baby?"

Her only response was a trembling upper lip.

Mercedes Dare did not realize that, by now, the fetus already had been bagged in a synthetic uterus and immersed in a hormonal solution.

Thas reassured, "Don't worry about it. Everything will be fine."

Then, as Mer's eyes became too heavy to keep open, alarms pierced through the island night.

EVAN WAS RUSHED to the standoff at Tower 7, hanging on the side of a speeding fire truck. He hopped off as the vehicle skidded through the mud and firemen hurried to connect their hoses, just in case.

Thas frowned as he sniffed familiar fumes. He yelled "Hey," at a security officer. The man looked surprised to see the boss on site and, as he walked over, Thas demanded, "Brief me!"

The officer answered, "Dr. Thas, we got at least one islander in there. He broke in through a back window."

"Has he damaged anything?"

"He crashed two tanks."

Now Evan realized what he was standing in. "We have to move quickly," he shouted, knowing that none of Eden's fetuses could survive for more than three minutes without chemical immersion. "As soon as possible, crowd the drying sacks into the remaining tanks."

The officer reassured him, "It won't be long. Village SWAT is closing in. They're inside now. They'll take the guy out."

"Take him out," Evan repeated with alarm. "Take him out with what?"

"Don't worry Dr. Thas. They got enough firepower to …"

The explosion was the most destructive force the island had ever experienced. Flying debris shot high into the sky and the surrounding Tower buildings were assaulted with shrapnel that penetrated through the siding of the surrounding structures, making the tanks inside vulnerable. For the next 45 minutes, roaring flames and continuing explosions assaulted the tanks that were filled with flammable chemicals and 36,000 innocents. The emergency crews were powerless to stop the raging inferno as each of the 72 massive tanks – one or more at a time – exploded.

Evan did not witness the fury. With a crushed right hand and an eighteen inch sliver of steel shrapnel through his right eye, the great Dr. Evan Thas could do nothing more than lay there, unconscious, in the flaming mud.

Chapter 36
US House of Representatives
January 7

Rebekah Emunah was frail, serious and highly controversial. Some of her critics labeled her paranoid. Her
supporters, however, saw her as the last effective defense against the proliferating hordes who resented Hitler,
only because he had not finished the job he started.[193]

After 43 tumultuous years, Prime Minister Emunah's intense eyes were starting to wrinkle, and her long, dark hair
was displaying strands of grey. Still, she never succumbed to
the vanity of makeup or hair dye. Her beauty was conveyed
by her indomitable spirit.

She would speak before a highly anticipated Joint Session of Congress, which had been scheduled for a prime time
airing because of its importance. Congressional leaders had
extended the invitation knowing that the honor would put additional pressure on the Prime Minister to make concessions
regarding the division of Jerusalem. Also, the appearance
would highlight President Concepcion's floundering Middle
East strategy. For Congressmen, this was a no lose event, offering the perfect venue for American politicians to present
a public spectacle in honor of the pretense that they would
never abandon Israel.

As she mounted the podium, Emunah was solemn.

Emaciated from fasting, she was often soft-spoken, yet always firm. She realized that this standing ovation for her meant nothing, just as words without substance had meant nothing for her besieged state, in the past. Israel was now confronting an existential threat that could only be placated by unthinkable concessions.

Though never proven, Israel was still widely suspected of causing the biological attack on the Saudi Royal Family that had triggered the sabotage of the Saudi oilfields and the subsequent tsunami of global instability.[194] Those suspicions, along with a natural hatred for the Jewish state, sparked an unusual alliance. Only a few years before, no one would have foreseen a coalition between revitalized communists and Islamists who would take to the streets and seize power around the globe. Now, the unlikely partners coalesced around a secret shared goal: bursting the bubble of American supremacy.[195] Consequently, Middle Eastern oil-rich nations fell in line behind Russia's increasingly radicalized leadership, which fell in line behind Vasily Melnikov's increasingly secretive control. It was a disturbing development for Evan, causing concern that his Russian partner might be maneuvering too independently, these days. Thas knew that the agenda for the Legion of Babylon was meant to be global, not fractured into regional interests.

Together, however, the breakaway alliance felt secure under Russia's aging, but still potent, nuclear umbrella, and they rallied with strategic partners, like China, who offered not only a booming economy, but also an exploding population that could put two million soldiers in the field.

The demand for a Palestinian state from a divided Israel had become today's litmus test for loyalty, and fears of petroleum supply shocks were forcing each nation to choose sides.

Oil or Israel?

President Concepcion, previously, had delegated a significant behind-the-scenes role in crafting American foreign policy to Thas who had moved quickly to initiate significant changes. Since then, his minions in the press and in the administration had effectively dominated the national debate regarding Israel which, increasingly, had become isolated as the focus of America's blame for all the world's ills. On issues ranging from oil prices to human rights to economic stagnation to nuclear proliferation, Israel had been labeled the poster child for bad behavior. "Land for peace, NOW!" had become the slogan for talking heads in the Administration as well as at the United Nations, where Evan had, but Israel lacked, allies.[196]

For Angela, the delegation of duties to Evan had been welcomed. After all, she had been reading his scripts for so long that she might as well give him a more visible role.

These days, she resented her workload and, increasingly, her thoughts centered on her developing baby. Still, the world knew nothing about it, and she was not sure that she would choose life. Right now, however, the idea of changing the White House's west bedroom into a nursery intrigued her. So, she began jotting notes on the possibilities.

Angela was seated in a special section in the House chambers to signify the importance of her Middle East peace initiative. As the lengthy applause and ovation ended, the Prime Minister offered the President a serious glance. Immediately, however, Angela nervously diverted her gaze to papers in front of her. Then, when the Prime Minister cleared her throat, the hall became quiet in anticipation of hearing whether Israel would bow to the unanimous will of the global community.[197]

"Thank you ... thank you very much.... Madame

President, Vice President Laugherly, Speaker Gitt, distinguished senators, members of the House, honored guests, I am deeply moved by this warm welcome. And I am honored that you've given me the opportunity to address Congress a second time. Israel has no better friend than America."

When the ovation began, again, the Prime Minister reflected on the long, tumultuous path that had brought her here. She had been the eldest child of a charismatic father who, himself, had risen to become Israel's Prime Minister, two decades earlier. Sensing that this daughter possessed the intelligence and talents of the father, the family encouraged and supported her advanced studies abroad, at Oxford. But shortly before the end of her time in England, her popular father fell victim to a suicide bomber's attack. On the eve of an early national vote – in which the Prime Minister was highly favored to win reelection – the assassin strapped explosives to himself and detonated them as he bicycled past the official motorcade. The subsequent investigation revealed extensive tentacles into a variety of enemy countries but justice was never served.

After the tragedy, Rebekah never publicly displayed anger, shock or emotion. But she evolved much more deeply into a quiet woman of profound faith. The cruel blow to the Emunah family only strengthened their resolve to protect their country and the lives of their fellow citizens. After all, they were God's chosen people.

Over the next two decades, Rebekah fearlessly went on to accumulate the titles of "first female …" for a dozen different honors, many of them humanitarian. Today, however, the Prime Minister was not receiving another honor. She was being battered into submission. Almost every traditional ally had deserted Israel – demanding a forced partition of its country and capital. That reversal of American foreign policy would force a redrawing of Israel's national borders, leaving it indefensible. These specific border changes would certainly encourage enemies to deliver the long-awaited death-blow to the Jewish state.

The Prime Minister continued, "In an unstable Middle East, Israel is the one anchor of stability. In a region of shifting alliances, Israel is America's unwavering ally. Israel has always been pro-American. Israel will always be pro-American."

Another ovation began but she interrupted it, tiring of fake admiration.

"An epic battle is now unfolding in the Middle East, between tyranny and freedom. A great convulsion is shaking the earth from the Khyber Pass to the Straits of Gibraltar. The tremors have shattered states and toppled governments. And we can all see that the ground is still shifting. Today, the Middle East stands at a fateful crossroads. Like all of you, I pray that the peoples of the region choose the path less travelled, the path of liberty. Israel has always embraced this path, but the Middle East has long rejected it. In a region where women are stoned, gays are hanged, Christians are persecuted, Israel stands out. It is different."

Again, the assembled dignitaries interrupted her, with applause. Angela, however, was distracted. She knew well the Prime Minister's arguments, and didn't agree with them. So, Angela began a list of names in two columns: one for baby boys, the other for girls.

The address continued. "We're proud that over one million Arab citizens of Israel have been enjoying the rights of liberty for decades. Of the 300 million Arabs in the Middle East and North Africa, only Israel's Arab citizens enjoy real democratic rights. I want you to stop for a second and think about that. Of those 300 million Arabs, less than one-half of one-percent are truly free, and they're all citizens of Israel! This startling fact reveals a basic truth: Israel is not what is wrong about the Middle East. Israel is what is right about the Middle East."

President Concepcion did not bother to clap. She had tired of baby names and started reviewing her notes from the last time Faridah Shabaan had read her palm. Angela kept underlining the words, "He will destroy you."

The Prime Minister continued, "Militant Islam threatens the world. It threatens Islam. I have no doubt that it will ultimately be defeated. But like other fanaticisms that were doomed to fail, militant Islam could exact a horrific price from all of us before its inevitable demise. Those who dismiss it are sticking their heads in the sand."

She paused so that the silence would be remembered. Angela looked up from her notes and wondered what she had just missed.

"In much of the international community, the calls for Israel's destruction are met with utter silence. It is even worse because there are many who rush to condemn Israel for defending itself against Iran's terror proxies. If history has taught the Jewish people anything, it is that we must take calls for our destruction seriously. We are a nation that rose from the ashes of the Holocaust. When we say never again, we mean never again. Israel always reserves the right to defend itself."

The room remained mostly quiet.

"We must also find a way to forge a lasting peace with the Palestinians. This is not easy for me. I recognize that in a genuine peace, we will be required to give up parts of the Jewish homeland. This is the land of our forefathers, the Land of Israel, to which Abraham brought the idea of one God. No distortion of history can deny the four thousand year old bond, between the Jewish people and the Jewish land.

"But there is another truth: All six Israeli Prime Ministers since the signing of Oslo accords agreed to establish a Palestinian state. So why has peace not been achieved? Because, so far, the Palestinians have been unwilling to accept a Palestinian state, if it meant accepting a Jewish state alongside it. You see, our conflict has never been about the establishment of a Palestinian state. It has always been about the existence of the Jewish state. I have said, 'I will accept a Palestinian state.' It is time for us to hear, in response, 'I will accept a Jewish state.' Those six words will change history. They will make clear to the Palestinians that they are not building a state to continue the conflict with Israel, but to end it."

A few idealists cheered during tepid applause from others.

"Peace must be anchored in security. In recent years, Israel withdrew from South Lebanon and Gaza. But we didn't get peace. Instead, we got 12,000 thousand rockets fired from those areas on our cities. Missiles fired from a future Palestinian state could reach virtually every home in Israel in less than a minute. Would you live that way?"

Then Emunah touched on the subject everyone was waiting for. "And as for Jerusalem, only a democratic Israel has protected freedom of worship for all faiths in the city. Jerusalem must never again be divided.[198] Jerusalem must remain the united capital of Israel. I know that this is a difficult issue for Palestinians. But I believe with creativity and goodwill a solution can be found."

Those words of optimism were greeted with silent disappointment and anger. Watching, Angela Concepcion folded her notes and closed her binder. She and her allies fumed, knowing that Israel's refusal to divide Jerusalem would be portrayed as another foreign policy defeat for her administration.

Then, when an aide slipped in behind the president and whispered into her ear, the alarm in her eyes signaled to observant legislators that something big had happened. So, many of them quickly pulled out their smart phones and dialed up news sites that were reporting: "Nauru disaster – Thas believed dead."

Barely noticing the increasing rumble of muffled conversations, the Prime Minister continued, "My friends, you don't need to do nation-building in Israel. We're already built. You don't need to export democracy to Israel. We've already got it. You don't need to send American troops to defend Israel. We defend ourselves. You've been very generous in giving us tools to do the job of defending Israel on our own. So, I speak on behalf of the Jewish people and the Jewish state when I say to you, representatives of America, thank you. May God bless the United States of America."

Few in the audience were still paying attention to her.

While the world was starting to focus on losing Nauru's promise of human immortality, most of these legislators now had a more immediate concern on their minds: reelection without Evan.

Angela's gamble to manipulate concessions from Emunah had failed. However, the president was the one politician in the room who felt a strange sense of relief from tonight's news about Evan. It was as if a burden had been lifted from her shoulders.

The others, however, were filled with questions and anxiety. Caring little that the Prime Minister of Israel was receiving a world class snub from congress, the legislators immediately emerged from their seats to find or call their campaign strategists in attempts to get ahead of the news cycle.

Emunah had made clear that she would not willingly participate in national suicide, no matter how popular the concept had become, globally. She had expected that her speech would be met with scorn and ridicule. However, she had not anticipated distracted indifference. While some in the audience refused to applaud out of anger, most forgot to applaud out of disinterest.

They gave no thought to the alarming circumstances that Israel's enemies already had mobilized, that the dogs of war were being unleashed and that, consequently, Israel would be attacked and Israel would be blamed. The world's community of nations had come to accept that if the Jewish state was not ready now to give, its enemies were ready now to take.[199]

Here, in the legislative chamber of Israel's closest national ally, the self-absorbed American dignitaries – whether rooted in ignorance or evil – refused to consider Israel's existential threat. Most would simply continue to recite the naïve mantra, "land for peace," without bothering to consider two certainties:

If the Palestinians would lay down their arms, soon the nation of Palestine would exist.

If the Israelis would lay down their arms, soon the nation of Israel would not.

Silence in the face of evil is itself evil:
God will not hold us guiltless.
Not to speak is to speak.
Not to act is to act.
Dietrich Bonhoeffer

The morning after the Nauru disaster, Faridah Shabaan arrived and took charge. Within view of the smoking fields where Towers once stood, she hustled Mercedes across the tarmac and onto Evan's Gulfstream. She warned the young woman that it would not be safe for her to stay and requested that the pilot deliver her back to her parents in Montana. Mer wanted to remain by Evan's side but she was so dazed by the drugs and the tragedies that she was in no shape to argue.

On the long flight back from Nauru, Mer could not sleep. Her body felt violated and her thoughts were agitated. She knew that focusing on her own physical pain and the emotional pain of losing her baby would only make her feel worse. So, she tried to occupy her mind with news reports, hoping to learn the latest developments on the Nauru disaster and Evan's condition. But little was being reported on the satellite news channels, apparently because reporters' planes were not being allowed to land, there.

In search of answers, Mer channel surfed through one bad news story after another, frustrating her all the more.

One report explained how the global economic crisis had led to an "every man for himself" breakdown in once-valued virtues.[200] International trends indicated that the family structure also was disintegrating as partners shunned marriage and traditional commitments to each other.[201]

She clicked to another channel and listened to political news for a while, learning that Vice President Blight's murder was still considered a crime without clues, and that the N1656 virus was destabilizing the governments of Russia, Italy and Spain as major population centers had been struck by the deadly contagion.[202]

Switching again, she discovered that this year's natural disasters would be the most expensive on record.[203] Still, disaster relief for the California earthquake was not only proceeding at a painfully slow pace but large areas of the state would be forever uninhabitable either because scenic land had slid into the sea or because of radiation exposure. Elsewhere, off the coasts of Ireland and England, another earthquake triggered a major tsunami and casualties numbered into the tens of thousands.[204]

Throughout the flight, even the commercial breaks depressed Mer, from the popular mega-church pastor, Brother Daniel Mitchum, suggesting that tithing to his church was the best way to cash in on God's promise of prosperity, to a famous television psychic who was hawking ridiculously expensive "healing crystals." The only commercials that disgusted her more were the ones in which young, beautiful women purred with delight because their balding, middle-aged men had found the secret to their libido problems.

It seemed that people, today, would be unrecognizable to their ancestors.[205]

To Mer, it was beginning to appear that faith had become greed and love had become lust.[206]

She had reached the limits of her disgust, and was about

to turn the television off, when a story caught her eye that was truly alarming.

The anchorwoman reported: "The body of an American tourist was found today in the Trastevere section of Rome. Police have ruled murder as the cause of the death of Timothy A. Lassiter, a former police detective from a small town in New York State."

Mer gasped when she heard the name.

"The victim was found in the home of a Nigerian immigrant, tied to a chair, with his neck broken."

"Oh, no." Mer moaned from a mistaken conclusion. "Malek killed him."

"Officials are seeking information on two suspects who are wanted for questioning."

The television displayed two renderings by an artist that looked vaguely familiar.

Then the anchorwoman continued, "The men were seen leaving the scene of the crime. Witnesses say that the suspects have dark hair and complexions, with Middle Eastern features. They wore matching dark suits and resembled each other to such an extent that they appear to be twins."

"No!" Mer screamed while clutching her cramping waist. Then she quickly clicked the television off and threw the remote to the floor, not wanting to touch it.

However, it was too late. Now, she would forever blame herself for luring an innocent man to his death. Still, she refused to consider an obvious conclusion.

Evan couldn't have known!

It added just one more cause for confusion.

In every generation,
there are those who wish to destroy
the Jewish people.
Israeli Prime Minister
Benjamin Netanyahu

Three Secret Service agents surreptitiously ushered the Prime Minister of Israel past the dumpsters and into the White House, through a darkened side entrance. Angela had finally given in to Emunah's pestering, hoping that a short meeting would placate the Prime Minister. However, Angela agreed to the meeting only on the condition that it be kept off the record. She did not want to stir up any more animosity from Israel's oil-rich enemies. Also, she did not wish others to think that she was accepting Emunah's obstinacy.

When the agents escorted her down the center hall and into the Vermeil Room, Angela was there, waiting. Pointedly, she did not rise when the Prime Minister entered. From her Empire sofa, the President continued pouring hot tea that had been placed on the table in front of her. Then she looked up and waved at an upholstered chair, nearby. "You may sit there."

The agents remained outside and closed the door.

Rebekah Emunah knew her time would be limited, so, she sat down and quickly started in.

"Madame President, I appreciate that you agreed to meet with me. I want to bring to your attention a few…"

279

"No," the President interrupted. "I will bring to *your* attention a few important points."

Then Angela put her teacup down, without offering any to her guest.

"I never asked that we be tied together in this alliance. I'm stuck with it. But you seem determined to turn our bond into a noose around my political neck. Do you have any idea how much heat I'm taking, just for being your friend? Divide your land, dammit![207] Your unwillingness to compromise is going to cost me my oil suppliers!"

Rebekah's eyes tightened on Angela. Then she spoke with a soft, measured cadence. "Are you through, you petty, venal, worm?"

"How dare you!" Angela shouted. "I will have you thrown…"

"You will not," the Prime Minister interrupted softly but forcefully. "Because I have information that you desperately need. Frankly, I'm tempted to leave without telling you. However, that would not be true to our alliance."

Angela fumed, but she privately admired something in this determined woman. It was not false bravado – an abundant commodity around town – but principled conviction. So, the president did not shut her out. "If you have something to say, say it."

"You want oil? We have it."

"What are you talking about?"

"We have discovered that the Shfela Basin, just a half-hour drive south of Jerusalem, holds as much oil as sits under Saudi Arabia … times two."[208]

"What?"

"It is not only abundant but premium quality as well, the equivalent of Saudi extra-light."

"How can ..."

"Together, our alliance now controls enough oil to fuel our two countries' needs for the next 200 years."

"Why don't I know this?"

"Because my country is better at keeping secrets than yours."

"Why keep it a secret?"

"Please tell me you are only pretending to be ignorant."

Angela just gasped her frustration, but let her guest continue.

"Are you not aware that enemies are plotting against Israel, as we speak? No matter what we do or say, they are hell-bent on taking all of our land and driving us into the sea. We do our best to delay the inevitable war, but how can we stall them any longer when a sea of oil is added to the spoils? So, we choose to reveal our secrets only to ... trusted partners."

Angela stood, signaling the end of the meeting. "Well, I certainly can't just take your word for it. I'll have to verify your claims."

"I'm not through. Sit down."

Angela recoiled with resentment, but returned to the sofa.

"I have two more things to discuss. Where is John Eben Malek?"

"Who?"

"Don't play stupid," Rebekah sneered. "It is fitting but not credible, at the moment."

Angela pouted. She was willing to listen, but not to share any information.

"We know that Evan Thas operatives are running your administration and we know he is obsessed with killing Malek."

"What makes you say that?"

"You make me repeat myself: my country is better at

keeping secrets than yours."

"Why are you interested in Malek?"

"I will tell you, only because I now have the threat of oil hanging over your head. But I warn you that America will never see one drop of our oil if you betray this trust."

Enticed but skeptical, Angela moved to the edge of her seat. There was nothing she liked better than a good secret and, for some reason, Malek had always fascinated her.

"The history of the Jewish people is replete with possible myths and legends. One of the most persistent, however, is the reappearance through the centuries of the Mystical War Counselor."

"Now who's sounding stupid?"

The Prime Minister seemed to change the subject. "Do you know about General Moshe Gideon?"

"Of course, Israel's hero of the Six-Day War ... the commanding general."[209]

"Correct, and how did he win that war?"

"I don't know. I guess he had the bigger army."

"Oy vey," Rebekah sighed her frustration. "Almost a half million Arab troops from Egypt, Jordan, Syria, Lebanon and Iraq amassed on our borders, backed up by the armies of Algeria, Kuwait, Sudan and the whole Arab nation."

"Okay," the President said, impatiently. "So, how did he win?"

"He acted instead of reacted. While your President Johnson insisted on continuing pointless negotiations, enemy troops were amassing on our borders. Their stated goal was the annihilation of Israel and negotiations were simply giving them the time they needed to prepare their attack."

"So you struck first."

"Correct. On June 5, 1967, while Egyptian pilots were

eating their breakfast, we sent almost our entire Air Force to pound their airfields. In less than two hours, we destroyed nearly 300 of Egypt's planes. Then we hit Jordanian and Syrian air forces and an airfield in Iraq. By the end of the first day, we had destroyed almost all of the Egyptian and Jordanian air forces, as well as half of the Syrians'. Then, over the next five days, The Holy One protected our troops, making them invincible. In just six days, Israel more than tripled its territory and unified Jerusalem."

"So, by sending your Air Force on an attack mission, Israel left its air defenses vulnerable."

"Yes. It was an act of faith. We won the war, however, it was not without pain. In fact, as a proportion of our population, Israel lost twice as many men, in those six days, as America lost in eight years of fighting in Vietnam."

"So, are you saying that General Gideon is this ... Mystical War Counselor?"

"Please, bear with me a moment longer. You will see that I am not wasting your time."

The Prime Minister's polite response helped to ease Angela's distrust. Then, Rebekah continued, "Recently, I met with General Gideon in the nursing home where he now resides. His short term memory is going, but his reflections on past battles are as flawless as ever. He had urgently requested a meeting with me and I, naturally, was honored that he had."

"Of course."

"He briefed me in detail on the circumstances that led to that victory. Then he explained quite revealing facts about our war in 1973."

"Like what?"

"On Yom Kippur, the holiest day on the Jewish calendar, Egypt and Syria opened a coordinated surprise attack on

Israel. By every logical analysis, regarding the balance of power, my people had little chance of survival. Nine Arab states had aided the Egyptian-Syrian war effort and even the Soviet Union supported the invasion. On the Golan Heights, for example, our tanks were outnumbered almost eight to one. Even worse, along the Suez Canal, our troops were outnumbered 1,200 to one. Still, with God, all things are possible."

"Yes, and General Gideon led you to another seemingly miraculous victory."

The Prime Minister paused to size up the sincerity of the President. "It does seem a miracle, doesn't it?"

"So, what was his point?"

"He said that, before he died he wanted to correct the historical record. He said he felt compelled to reveal a long-kept secret, now that dark forces are again surrounding Israel."

"Okay... and..." she urged, with anticipation.

"He told me that he does not deserve praise for the victories."

"Was he just being humble."

"No," Rebekah laughed. "He is not a humble man."

"Then what?"

The Prime Minister breathed deeply, as if pondering whether to proceed. Then she answered, "He said that the Mystical War Counselor came to him before each of those battles and explained how each would be won. The General said that he had been adamantly opposed to what he heard and, each time, even argued with the man. But, eventually, General Gideon became convinced of the element of surprise behind each strategy. So, he followed the Counselor's advice, calling it an act of faith."

"Well, who is this guy?"

The Prime Minister reached into her pocket and pulled

out a newspaper clipping. "This is an article from one of your American newspapers. The General has carried it with him for some time."

Rebekah dropped the clipping on the table, in front of Angela. Then she tapped her finger on the picture of a man, standing trial.

Angela immediately recognized John Malek.

"He is the Mystical War Counselor."

"Ohhh," Angela groaned. Her mind reeled from trying to piece together the puzzle of the mysterious man named Malek. If this information had come from almost anyone else, Angela would have immediately dismissed it as fantasy. But Rebekah was not one to fantasize.

"So, even you believe him? You really think ..." Angela laughed at the absurdity of it all, "that he is John the Apostle?"

"I don't know." Rebekah sighed. "I can only tell you that General Gideon is not someone to doubt."

Angela's wall of invincible ignorance began tumbling down. *Dear God, whose side have I been on?* The president mumbled, "Evan will despise hearing this ... if he's still alive."

"I do not mean to be rude, but I pray that he is dead. However, if he survives, Madame President, this information must remain secret. Evan Thas is the last person who should be told."

"Hmmm ..." Angela nodded, "I understand. So, why are you telling me all this?"

"I must speak with John Malek, and you have the resources to find him."

"Why do you have to speak to him?"

Again, the Prime Minister paused to weigh her words. Then she answered, calmly, "I must prepare for what you Christians call ... Armageddon."

†††

MOMENTS LATER, Secret Service Agents scrambled as Angela unexpectedly escorted Rebekah out the front door with all the graciousness that the Prime Minister of Israel deserves. Tonight, a trust had developed that had never existed before.

At the curb, a car was waiting. But before Rebekah stepped into it, she turned and gently held the President's hand.

"Madame President, I also must make an urgent request."

Angela regretted letting her guard down. The disappointment showed in her tone. "Yes … what do you want?"

Rebekah motioned the president away from the driver at the car door and whispered, "I must urge you to keep your baby."

Angela blinked her surprise that the secret was out. She was stunned silent.

"With all due respect, I know that we sometimes feel that we are important. However, I assure you that your daughter will be greater than either … than both of us."

Angela was pleasantly surprised. *A girl?* It was a confirmation of what she already felt.

As they gently shook hands, Angela did not know what to make of such a strange comment. Still, she admired the twinkling in Rebekah's smiling eyes and marveled at the thought of who her daughter might become.

To Angela, the woman seemed to have unfathomable qualities. As she peacefully prepared to defend against the war that could take the lives of her people and herself, she became the defender even of Angela's own child.

Then, as the driver opened her door and Rebekah slid into the back seat, Angela asked, "How did you know I'm … that way?"

Rebekah Emunah grinned. "You make me repeat myself."

The President watched, thoughtfully, as the door shut and the limousine pulled away.

Perhaps Momma Laudie had been right. Four people had advised Angela on the life or death of her baby. Fred, Evan and Faridah had insisted that she terminate the pregnancy. Now, a woman that Angela hardly knew advised her to choose life. Unlike the others, she had given advice that resonated with unselfish truth.

Angela rubbed her tummy and imagined her child, full of life, happiness, and loving virtue. Then the word "Armageddon" reverberated in her head and the old fears and uncertainties surfaced that had always pushed her in the wrong direction.

This time, however, she pushed back.

No, she admitted to herself, *this baby will not be convenient. They never are. But my baby will be born ... and my baby will be loved!*

She always had been defiantly pro-choice. This time, however, she would choose life. This time she would choose to accept God's calling for her mission in life. Her true purpose had never been to become famous, or powerful, or admired. God's purpose for her was to have this baby. That is why the demons had focused on her, so enthusiastically, to convince her to embrace the culture of death.

For as long as she could remember, a rebellion had crept into her soul and the more she rebelled, the more she seemed to be rewarded by the world. So, day by day, brick by brick, Angela's pride had built a wall between herself and God.

Then, suddenly, it was gone. Her childlike faith returned and she no longer felt defensive or protective against God's advances.

On the White House steps, Angela dropped to her knees and humbly asked Jesus Christ to guide her and her child to become shining lights for this darkening world. She prayed fervently and, with the joy of newfound faith, believed He heard her.

Tonight, even when the words could have caused fear or alarm, there had been something comforting about the determined Rebekah Emunah. She had the certainty that President Concepcion lacked, and she could not be bribed or flattered into submission. In a world where agendas are always hidden, Angela found her directness very refreshing and judged her as a rarity in politics: a person worthy of respect.

Strange, Angela thought as the car drove away, *that I would be brought back to Christ by a devout Jew.* She laughed at her own foolishness. *But, then again, He was one too!*

THE NEXT DAY, reports headlined that the President of the United States was thrilled that a baby was on the way and the American public welcomed the good news, for a change. This would be one more first for Angela Concepcion's record book.

Unreported, however, was that Fred, Evan and Faridah despised anything that might disrupt their plans, including this baby.

There is no neutral ground in the universe:
every square inch, every split second
is claimed by God and counterclaimed by Satan.
C. S. Lewis

The sensation of dull, throbbing pain slowly grew as Evan became conscious.[210] Laying motionless in his intensive care bed, his mind searched for memories of where he was and why. Evan's one remaining eye circled to find whatever clues might help, but a neck brace prevented him from turning his head.

Then Pruflas nudged Faridah who was dozing in a nearby chair. With a gasp she woke, rose and moved to her son's bedside. Like always, the silent twins slid in behind her.

"Evan, wake up." Her tone was harsh. "Do you hear me?"

Almost imperceptibly, he nodded and then winced in pain. "Where ... am I?"

"You're in the hospital. There was an accident."

Evan felt the heaviness of immobility, being burdened by the bandages that covered his entire body, except his left eye and mouth. His pain was manageable, but only because of the narcotics. "How long have I been ..."

"Four weeks."

Thas sorted his foggy thoughts, attempting to reassemble the puzzle. He remembered flying with Mer to the island and the doctors successfully transferring her fetus to the lab. Then he recollected his fire truck ride to Tower 7 and the smell of chemicals that covered the ground when he arrived.

"Explosion?"

"Yes."

"How much damage?"

She did not want to say it, but finally answered, "Burns on ninety percent of your body, extensive damage to your right hand, and you lost your right eye."

"Not that," he groaned.

"You're lucky you survived."

"Not that," he repeated. "The Towers. How much damage?"

"Substantial."

"How much?!" he shouted.

Faridah resented his demanding tone. She sighed audibly and then said, "The Towers are a complete loss."

Evan's bloodshot eye widened.

"That end of the island is just charred remains."

Thoughts and questions flashed through his mind: Eden's immortality project, wiped out; his long-awaited offspring, lost in the fire; the possibility of a life with pain and disability. Then another memory hit him. He recalled that John Malek had been captured and that the twins had been ordered to finish him off.

Evan's eye tightened and he exhaled audibly. "He's not dead … is he?"

She knew who her son meant. "You need your rest," she stalled. "We can talk about this …"

Defying his pain, Thas jolted upright in bed, ripping out his intravenous tube and causing an alarm to sound.

"Answer me!" Evan screamed over the beeping alarm. "Is he dead?!"

Just then a nurse rushed through the door.

"Get out!" Evan shouted.

"No sir, I've gotta get that tube back in …"

Then, with heartless precision and surprising strength, Malphas grabbed the woman by the collar, dragged her to the door, opened it with his free hand, and slung her out.

The alarm continued beeping.

Faridah answered angrily, "He escaped."

Evan's eye rolled back into his head, until only his blood-shot white sclera showed. He panted like a caged animal and foam drooled from the corner of his mouth.

A secondary alarm sounded with a high pitched squeal.

"I told you, but you would not listen," Faridah hissed, incensed that Evan had resisted her warnings. "You should have killed him long ago! You will never have what is yours until he is dead and the ritual is finished!"

Evan raised his face to heaven and cursed God in a dozen different languages. Then, when his profanities and blasphemies finally transformed into English, he screamed, "You think You can cause me pain without consequence?"

Faridah and the brothers stepped back in fear.

Then, with a deep, guttural cacophony of utterances, Thas exhausted his fury: "I will cause pain, too! And I will destroy every one You love!"

I expect to die in bed.
My successor will die in prison,
and his successor will die a martyr
in the public square.
American Cardinal Francis Eugene George
2010

Chapter 40
Various Locations
The Next 4 Months

As the global economy continued to deteriorate, Evan Thas consolidated his power with unprecedented speed and determination. However, his physical recovery had not advanced so well. He still had limited use of his right hand, his right eye was missing, and his face was burn scarred. But none of that had diminished his ambition.

However, a major source of frustration for Evan surfaced from the fact that the Legion of Babylon had elected a new leader during his extended absence. Even worse, they chose Evan's sneaky business partner, Vasily Melnikov, to replace him. The change eased the concerns of many Legion members who felt Thas was becoming too popular, too fast. It also allowed them to keep the resources of XCyst Industries at their disposal since Melnikov was the corporation's largest shareholder. Still, Evan chose to continue his membership, determined to exert his influence, wherever possible.

In America, though, his grip was tightening. Consistent with Evan's wishes, Angela continued to play the role of subservient figurehead. She read her lines well and smiled at all the right times, while reams of Executive Orders were issued in her name, but without her input.

His deceptions did not upset her, anymore, because she had abandoned the fantasy that she, somehow, could get America back on track. The problems confronting the world were almost too big for her to comprehend and, certainly, too big for her to solve. She had no choice but to bank on Evan and his cadre of experts. Surely they could come up with answers.

However, her nervous partnership was dominated by lingering fears. She realized that if she ever defied Evan's wishes, she might someday share Vice President Blight's fate.

Angela's catch phrases and talking points for this major new initiative resembled those that she had used in her campaign for president. So, her rhetoric seemed a natural evolution of her governance. The buzzwords were all methodically polled and focus grouped. Since almost everyone responded favorably to variations of the word "perfect," it became the cornerstone of their rhetoric. Any one who spoke against any of Angela's proposals was attacked as being "out of touch" and "standing in the way of achieving perfection."

The kickoff of the new Perfective Program was announced in a major national address where Angela designated that a new path to economic empowerment would be available to those who not only agreed to Titan implantation, but also scored well on Titan testing. Those federal jobs were so lucrative that citizens flocked to apply. Consequently, from those growing ranks, Evan developed an army of loyal foot soldiers who were free of religious or moral reservations about implementing his aggressive agenda.

The Perfective Patrol, as Angela dubbed them in that national speech, was being promoted as the vanguard of the Perfect Society. They would be the government-approved watchdogs, shepherding the sheep to a Perfect World and fighting off the wolves of Imperfection. Likewise, Legion of Babylon members had organized similar Patrols and agendas in their own countries.

Evan eventually took a visible role, for a change, in leading this effort. Consequently, Angela named him America's "Perfect World Ambassador." His oversight responsibilities included every policy promoted by the Executive Branch, every bill advanced in congress, and every regulation promulgated in America.

The old rhetoric of "Change and Reform" were now deemed *passé*. Today's imperative was to "Create and Recreate."

Media reports soon praised Angela's wise appointment of Thas and credited his brilliant work with the Legion of Babylon. He had already received high praise for spearheading the Legion's efforts in its global war against the N1656 viral pandemic. His minions in the media always emphasized the insupportable claim that the death toll would have included millions more, if not for Evan's genius. Still, Thas sought to avoid complacency, so he warned that much work was left to be done in order to completely eradicate the virus.

Now, on the heels of what was proclaimed as unprecedented philanthropic charity, Thas and the Legion would partner again to broaden their commitment to mankind. The Perfect World Union, or PWU, would be the most ambitious philanthropic commitment the world had ever witnessed … reportedly.

Evan's continuous push to control the agenda of the Legion irked Melnikov. After all, he was its new leader. However, no one could argue that Thas was not effective. It seemed his accomplishments would be virtually limitless.

With that sense of entitlement, Thas applied his legendary

organizational skills, with a whirlwind of initiatives around the globe. By design, nothing was sacrosanct, except Evan's leadership. Laws were changed, calendars adjusted, fashions introduced, and progress redefined. Wherever people welcomed "in with the new," however, they also feared "out with the old," as private property was redistributed, families were regulated, and expressions faith were not tolerated.[211] Consequently, people quickly learned that Perfect Cooperation was the only virtue that would protect one's job or business.

Melnikov resented being shunted aside, but wisely chose to bide his time.

To his Legion troops, Evan insisted that a day should never pass without substantial movement and activity. He wanted to keep minds focused on how to implement the constant barrage of changes rather than why.

His Perfective Patrol consisted of those with the most malleable principles, as evaluated by Titan analyses. Whenever they received a promotion, it was without regard for their credentials or competence. In fact, Evan often advanced undeserving underlings, counting on the fact that their obvious inferiority would insure their undying gratitude. So, devotion to Evan's agenda became the PWU's highest priority. Loyalty oaths were administered and loyalty was not only expected but demanded.

Perfectives began to infiltrate their ideals into every level of society. Federal grants funded projects that incorporated the Perfective agenda and social scientists produced a wave of studies that validated the new science of Perfectionism. School curricula infused endless propaganda on the benefits of centralizing power and the dangers of individual freedoms. The Perfective agenda became a religion for the masses.

Media commentators, particularly on XBC News, often

pointed out that people of traditional faiths interfered with the goals of the PWU because they believe in an imperfect God. The logic of that argument was that since the world is undeniably imperfect, then the God that they believe created it must also be. Following that line of thought a step further, religious Imperfectives were deemed by many to be a hindrance to all society because they reject perfection today by living for an imaginary perfection after death. Consequently, many forms of discrimination developed against those without the mark of Titan on their foreheads. Even some "justifiable" crimes against Imperfectives were now being ignored by police and judges.

Still, around the globe, happy faces accompanied every public service ad that promoted the loving family of The Perfect World Union. Conveniently ignoring the Church that Jesus Christ had founded, the PWU cheerfully promoted itself as the first universal movement in which every human being was truly welcome.

AROUND THE WORLD, John's devoted followers had become true Apostles of the Latter Times[212] as they quickly moved from country to country. To them, Jesus Christ gave eloquence and strength to work wonders and to convert His enemies. They travelled wherever the Holy Spirit called them, resolved to seek the glory of God and the salvation of souls. They lived without money and without concern, finding lodging with responsive people of faith in whatever town they arrived and, especially, in Church rectories and monasteries.[213]

As true disciples of Jesus Christ, they imitated His poverty, His humility, and His contempt of the world. With holy anger and ardent zeal burning in their hearts, they thundered against sin and stormed against the world, striking down the devil and his followers with the power of their words. Revealing pure Truth, they pointed out the narrow way to God, according to the holy Gospel, and rejected the ways of the world. So, with the Peace of Christ in their hearts, they were never troubled, and refused to fear or prefer any man.

The Apostles were blessed with the two-edged sword of the God's Word in their mouths. They carried the crucifix in their right hand, the Rosary in their left, and the holy names of Jesus and Mary in their heart. The simplicity and self-sacrifice of Jesus Christ was reflected in their whole behavior.

By the will of God, and through the intercession of the Blessed Virgin Mary, they warned everyone – even mocking, impious unbelievers – to prepare for Jesus Christ's Second Coming. Yet, the Apostles left behind them, wherever they preached, the treasure that is more precious than gold: love, which is the fulfillment of the whole law.

Through the fruits of their labor, the prophecy was fulfilled that in the End Times, "Almighty God and his holy Mother will raise up great saints who will surpass in holiness most other saints as much as the cedars of Lebanon tower above little shrubs."[214] These great souls were filled with grace and zeal, and chosen to oppose the enemies of God who were raging on all sides.

With exceptional devotion to the Blessed Virgin, they were illumined by her light, guided by her spirit, and sheltered under her protection. From her guidance, they never condemned an error without offering a Truth. They saw her as God's chosen role model for mankind, our helper and assistant. So, by word and example, they drew all men to a true devotion to her and, though this provoked many enemies, it gained many victories and much glory to God.

However, because of their zeal for Jesus Christ and his Blessed Mother, they became targets of Satan, experiencing crosses and persecutions, and fulfilling St. Louis de Montfort's prophecy: "True it is, indeed, great God, as you yourself have foretold, that the devil will lie in wait to attack the heel of this mysterious woman, that is, the little company of her children who will come towards the end of time.... You have appointed this humble Virgin to crush this proud spirit under her heel."[215]

MEANWHILE, at the Vatican, John had developed a close relationship with Pope Innocent and Father Blanc, and the two eager students had learned many important lessons from the ancient Apostle.

John had enlightened them on the Spiritual history of modern times. He explained that mankind had experienced greater change during the previous century than during any previous millennium, and that the change had not been for the better. So-called improvements in communications, transportation and technology had served as distractions from the Faith. Even the entertainments of the average person, today, demonstrated the growing rebellion of mankind.

Pope Leo XIII was correct, John said, when he predicted a century of Satan, unchained. The era had begun around the time of the warnings from Our Lady of Fatima.[216] Then, she predicted the rise of a great evil from Russia just months before the Bolshevik Revolution spawned a global movement that promoted the illusions that the state must replace God, that the collective good required the trampling of human rights, and that power grows out of the barrel of a gun.[217]

Perhaps as a sign that we should never ignore her messages,

she had offered a way to avoid much of the revolutionary conflict that eventually scarred mankind's bloodiest century. However, the Church delayed following her instructions for 67 years before properly consecrating Russia, consistent with her directions.[218]

John said that, as the 20th century had progressed – or, more appropriately, digressed – Blessed Mother's warnings had become more numerous and urgent. In Heede, Germany, when Hitler was coming to power, she declared to four little girls that "The world will have to drink the dregs of the chalice of divine wrath for their innumerable sins through which they have wounded the Sacred Heart of Jesus."

Two decades later, she warned an Italian stigmatist, Sister Elena Aiello, that "The world is flooded by a deluge of corruption. The governments, of the people, have arisen as demons in human flesh and even though they speak of peace, they prepare for war with devastating weapons that can annihilate whole peoples and nations.... Innumerable scandals carry souls to their ruin, especially the souls of the youth. They have given themselves to the pleasures of the world which have degenerated into perversions."[219]

Then, for seven years after 1975 – three decades before an earthquake and tsunami devastated the area, causing the worst nuclear power disaster in history – Blessed Mother also appeared in Akita, Japan, warning, "In order that the world might know His anger, the Heavenly Father is preparing to inflict a great chastisement on all mankind."

Blessed Mother appeared in Kibeho Rwanda, warning of what a visionary described as "...rivers of blood..." and a "...reality where people killed each other, blood running, fire burning on the hill, mass graves, skulls, beheaded bodies, skulls put apart." That was a decade before a hideously genocidal war broke out in 1994, in which nearly a million men, women and children were murdered using little more than machetes. The Virgin Mary also warned that, "There is not much time to prepare for the Last Judgment."

Then, starting in 1981, she appeared to six children in the village of Medjugorje[220] in the former Yugoslavia, warning of future chastisements. Here, just like in most other messages, Blessed Mother implored us to convert to God, to pray continually with the heart, to turn to the Sacraments and to sacrifice through fasting and other forms of self-denial.

Not long after the apparitions began, a vicious civil war broke out in the region, killing 300,000. Though violence rocked everywhere around it, Medjugorje remained protected during the conflict. The visions continued throughout the war and, even after the hostilities ended, they have continued to this day, over 30 years later. They compile the largest collection of Marian messages in history.

Of course, Pope Innocent and Father Blanc knew these apparitions and prophecies. However, they found that John spoke with such conviction and clarity that the urgency of the messages resonated with his every word. Because of that, they understood these horrible tragedies were but minor chastisements compared to what is to come.

Apparitions and miracles and prophetic warnings had not been enough to draw the attention of modern man. Many people had never even noticed these 20th century messages from heaven. So, what would it take to prompt us to invite God back into our lives? What would it take to stop us from harming ourselves and others as we embrace sin?

We were created in God's Image and, because of that, He would always respect the free will that He had given us. However, anyone who would refuse to pass through God's door of

Mercy would have to pass through His door of Justice.[221]

Throughout the 20th century, around the world, Blessed Mother had become the greatest of the prophets. Like them, however, she had been mocked and ignored.

Before Christ's first coming, Isaiah proclaimed and John the Baptist repeated what Blessed Mother is passionately pleading today: "I am the voice of one calling in the desert, 'Make straight the way for the Lord.'"

Time is running out.

Urgent change is required.

Still, John assured the attentive pope and priest that conversion, prayer and sacrifice can restrain God's hand of justice.

TONIGHT, THEY PLANNED a modest meal, together, breaking their fast at sundown. John, Pope Innocent and Father Blanc realized that tomorrow's news would forever change their lives.

They sat at a small dining table in the papal residence discussing many of the economic and Spiritual problems that were turning the world's once civilized citizens into barbarians, abiding only by the law of the jungle. It seemed that the more people perceived that even basic needs like food and shelter were at risk, the old rules and laws were increasingly irrelevant.

John emphasized that God's justice moves slowly, from our perspective, but certainly. He encouraged the Church to redouble its message that if we lose sight of God, we do it at our peril, because He never loses sight of us.

Then a monk-valet entered with a telephone, in hand.

"Please forgive the interruption. Your Holiness we

received a call on the private line."

"Yes … it must be important." He reached for the phone.

"Uh, no, Your Holiness. I mean to say that it is not for you … The call is for Father Malek. The Prime Minister of Israel says she urgently needs to speak to him."

The pope waved his hand John's way. "Yes, go ahead."

The men around the table knew the extreme danger that was confronting Israel at this very moment. An unprecedented coalition of troops from Russia, China, Iran and a dozen Arab countries were amassing on Israel's border.

John took the phone and immediately began speaking fluent Hebrew.

Innocent listened intently, but understood little. Blanc, on the other hand, understood the words, but was baffled by their meaning.

He heard John say that he, too, was honored. Then the Apostle listened for a period of time and finally warned the Prime Minister that the advice he would offer would be very hard to accept. In fact, he explained, that he, himself, would be reluctant to follow such guidance from almost anyone. However, he said, whether comfortable or not, true prophecy is true. He listened for a moment more and then told her to read the book of Mark, chapter 13, verse 14.[222] Then, just before he hung up, John assured her, "God is with you … and your people."

Dealing with the media
is more difficult than bathing a leper.
Mother Teresa

Chapter 41
Vatican Press Office
June 15

Journalists and cameramen pressed tightly into the Vatican press office. Never before, had such an unruly group assembled, here. Some grumbled curses at each other when they were forced to listen from the hallway, outside the packed room. The apparent urgency of this announcement signified that historic news would be conveyed. By Vatican standards, press conferences were never this hastily arranged. Consequently, the journalists who had been fortunate to be assigned to Rome, at this time, were ravenous for the breaking story.

Some journalists speculated that the Vatican would officially condemn the increasingly belligerent, multinational threats of war against Israel. Others suspected that this major announcement would reveal something more immediate. In fact, since the pontiff had cancelled a number of scheduled appearances, over the past few days, rumors were beginning to circulate that Pope Innocent XIV had died.

Near the front of the press office, four of the Swiss Guards stood at attention, with their ceremonial halberds at their sides, offering a tribute more to the bygone weapons of the past than the realities of papal protection in the present. They prevented the rowdy crowd from pushing too close to the podium from where the announcement would be made. Some reporters whispered wagers with each other on whether the pontiff had expired. However, the guards paid no mind to the angry, elbowing journalists who were now standing on chairs in order to get a clear camera shot when the announcement came.

Suddenly, however, the room became quiet when six more Swiss Guards entered, carrying Heckler & Koch MP5 submachine guns. The reporters had never before witnessed such an overt display of firepower at the Vatican. Now they knew that the news must be more dangerous – more urgent – than they had realized.

Did somebody assassinate the pope?

The guards took their positions, a few feet behind the podium, on each side of a large projection screen. Then Innocent entered briskly.

"Beatisimo Padre!" some of the Italian reporters whispered excitedly, while crossing themselves.

The press corps had expected the papal spokesman. They had never witnessed a pope who personally conducted press conferences, here. Closely behind the pontiff, a man followed that one reporter recognized.

"That's Malek!" the journalist whispered loudly.

The pope nodded. "Yes. I proudly stand with John Eben Malek."

Quizzical stares turned to the man at the pope's side. He showed no emotion, only a serene independence from the churning confusion of the audience.

"I will speak to you in English since the first part of my message is directed at American legal authorities." Innocent continued, "I want you all to know that I have immense respect for the American system of justice and that I admire their constitutional commitment to equality under the law. However, justice was not served when John Eben Malek was convicted."

Pictures flashed and video cameras continued filming as the reporters mumbled their misgivings about such a sweeping statement.

"My friends, I beg your understanding for a truth that will be hard to comprehend. I have taken the name of Innocent. John Malek, however, has lived a life that is innocent. So, as Bishop of Rome and head of state for the sovereign city-state of Vatican City, I hereby extend temporary Sanctuary protection to John Eben Malek."

One cynical reporter could not restrain his disbelief. "Your Holiness, on what grounds of international law?"

"Religious and civil Sanctuaries have been recognized throughout the centuries, particularly in England and across Europe. In America, even now, some cities are offering Sanctuary to illegal immigrants. However, in order to make a permanent determination, I hereby call for an emergency conclave of the College of Cardinals to convene. Then, we shall decide all matters regarding John Eben Malek."

"This is unprecedented," a young, female reporter commented.

"What we are dealing with is unprecedented."

For a normally reserved press corps, the cynics began to show an extraordinary level of agitation in the presence of Pope Innocent, head of Church and state. John's presence had always enticed the rage and ridicule.

Another reporter: "Holy Father, he murdered a nun!"

"No ... he did not."

From the crowd: "How do you know?"

"Because I know who he is."

Someone shouted from the back, "Who is he?!"

John answered, from the pope's side, loud enough for

everyone to hear. "I am John, son of Zebedee and Salome, brother of James the Greater."

Those who understood, laughed. One mumbled, "He tried to pull that crap at trial. It didn't work then, either."

"Let me ask you," John boldly continued. "What language am I speaking?"

The journalists looked at each other. Some smiled, others offered puzzled glances.

"You are gathered from countries scattered around the world. You speak scores of languages. Yet each of you understands me."[223] There was something about John's calm tone that brought a sense of peace to each of the listeners. "So, now that I have your attention, I must warn you."

Pope Innocent yielded to John, moving away from the podium, and John stepped up to the microphone.

"This message is from Jesus Christ, King of His people, Savior and Just Judge."[224]

Some in the audience responded with suppressed laughter.

John continued without embarrassment. *"The speed at which the prophecies are unfolding is becoming evident for all to see. Watch the changes that will become apparent with my Church, as one of the first signs. This is when The Deceiver will lead my disciples astray.*

"The second sign will be seen in the way many of you will no longer be in control of your own country. This includes all material control and the military. They will be like a boat with no rudder. This boat they steer will be aimless, and they will be lost.

"My children, you must pray hard now to loosen the grip these evil groups of people will exert over you. They are not of God's Kingdom and through the cunning deceit of their exterior, you will not realize that this is a powerful force that

is careful not to reveal itself.

"Rise up, My children, now. Do not accept the Mark. If more of you do not accept, then you are stronger in numbers. This mark, the Mark of the Beast, will be your downfall. It is not what it seems. By agreeing, you will be removed further and further away.

"Beware of the plan driven by the Deceiver to remove all signs of My Eternal Father and the teaching of Scriptures from your life. You will see this in schools, colleges, hospitals and in the constitution of your countries.

"The biggest abomination, which causes Me deep pain, is the abolition of the teachings of scripture from those who practice their adoration of Me, their Divine Savior. Very soon, you will see that My word and the teaching of the truth will be abolished and punishable.

"You, My dearly beloved children, will suffer greatly in My name. These evil forces are responsible for this. They are led by Satan. You will find them everywhere, and especially in those leaders in authority whom you depend upon to survive.

"Children, do not be frightened for yourselves. Rather, be frightened for those poor misguided souls so infested are they with the Deceiver, that they find it difficult to pull away; such is the grip they hold. These people are not to be trusted. You will find it difficult to fight them as they will control even your bank, your property, your taxes and the food you need to survive.

"But this will not last long, for their days are numbered. Should they abide by their slavery to evil, they will plunge into an abyss of such terror that to describe their fate would be too terrifying and so frightening that man would drop like a stone, dead, were he to glimpse just one minute of the torment they will endure.

"The Battle is about to begin and unfold, as the hand of my Eternal Father will fall swiftly in punishment for their sins, which is about to be witnessed on this earth, the sins which I died for.

"No man is a child of God who bears witness to, or colludes in this sinister, but orderly, army of destruction. This evil army filled with the demons from the pits of Hell perform acts of such evil magnitude that innocent people could not possibly fathom.

"I have no wish to frighten My children, but the truth will be exposed for what it is, in time. Rise up now, My children. Fight the forces of evil before they destroy you. Be wary of Global rule in any shape, size, form or code. Look at your leaders carefully and those who control your daily access to money, which will feed you and keep you alive. You need to stockpile food now.

"You have not received this message in a way that reflects my teachings, but hear Me now. These prophecies have been foretold. My children must listen carefully. The spirit of Darkness is growing, and you, My followers, must stay strong. Keep your belief in Me alive through prayer. All of My followers, must say the prayer, The Divine Mercy,[225] each day. It will strengthen souls and will help them find favor at the moment of death.

"My children, please do not let My message frighten you. My followers have a duty to Me now. Let Me say this. Remember you will be filled with the Holy Spirit, as soon as you accept My word. Do not fear, because you have been chosen. You, My army of followers, will lead to the defeat of the Evil One. To do this, you must pray.

"I come with a message of pure love. Do you not realize that you will experience Paradise when heaven and earth join

as one? There is nothing to fear, for you. My followers will be lifted body, soul and mind into the realms of the Divine Hierarchy. You will see your loved ones; those loved ones who have found favor with my Eternal Father.

"Do as I say. Pray, talk to Me, love Me, trust in Me. In return, I will give you strength. Pray for protection through the recital of the Most Holy Rosary given to you with blessings from My beloved Mother. This prayer must be said to help protect you from the Evil One on the one hand, on the other hand you must ask for protection for those people with whom you come into contact, so that they cannot contaminate you or diffuse the faith you hold in your heart for Me.

"Pray for My visionaries and prophets, so that they are protected. Pray for My beloved sacred servants, those holy devout servants sent by me to guide you. They, just like My followers, suffer torment by the Evil One. He will never stop trying to blind you from the truth and will use every devious tactic to convince you that your faith is false.

"Hear Me. He, the Deceiver, will use logic and reasoning, couched in a soft gentle manner, to convince you he brings hope into your lives. He will, through the Anti-Christ, strive to make you believe he is the Chosen One.

"Many of My followers will fall prey to this despicable deceit. Be on your guard. He will be seen as the messenger of love, peace, and harmony in the world. People will fall to their knees and adore him. He will show you his power and you will believe it is of a Divine source. But it is not. He will instruct you in a manner that will seem odd at times.

"True believers will know he is not of the light. His boastful, pompous demeanor will be hidden behind pure evil. He will strut and show what will appear to be true compassion and love for all. Behind this facade, he is full of hatred for *you, My beloved children.*

"My children, he will confuse you terribly. He will appear powerful, confident, humorous, caring, loving, and will be seen as a savior.

"He will wreak havoc in the world and will murder many. His acts of terror will be clear for all to see. Many will die for their faith in Me. No, do not fear, because if you suffer for Me, in Me, with Me, you are chosen. Pray, pray not to submit to his reign of terror. Stand up, fight for Me.

"Do not let the Anti-Christ, for all his convincing charm, win over your souls. Let me hold you in My arms, cradle you with My Divine Grace now, to give you the strength to fight for the truth. My love for you will never die. You should never choose this route, or you too will be lost to Me. It will be hard, but help will be given to my children in many, many ways, to ease your suffering. Go now and prepare for the final battle."

The journalists were now dividing into two groups: those who continued listening, still planning their reports, and those who were sending ridiculing emails and tweets on their smart phones. Regardless of the outcome, this story would be big news. Most reporters, however, had not yet decided whether to present Pope Innocent as a dupe or a lunatic.

One crafty reporter played along, "So, how will people know when the time is near?"

John continued with Jesus Christ's words:[226] *"The Warning is close now. It is with great sorrow that I must tell you that many souls will not heed these messages about The Warning. My word falls on deaf ears.*

"Why won't they listen? I am not only giving them My great gift of Mercy, when I will shower My graces over the whole world, I am also trying to prepare them for this event. Many millions of sinners will rejoice when they are shown My

great mercy. Others won't get a chance to redeem themselves in time, because they will die of shock.

"Pray, My beloved followers that your brothers and sisters can rejoice when they too are shown the proof of My existence. Pray that they will accept that this is their chance to redeem themselves in My eyes, that this great act of Mercy will save their souls if they will allow Me to help them.

"You will be shown what it is like to die in mortal sin. The Warning will be a purifying experience for all of you. It may be unpleasant in part, especially for those in grave sin, because for the first time ever you will be shown what it feels like when the light of God disappears from your life.

"Remember, it is important that I allow all of you to feel this emptiness of soul. For only then will you finally understand that without the light of God in your souls, you cease to feel. Your soul and body would be just empty vessels. Even sinners feel the light of God because He is present in every one of His children on earth. But when you die in mortal sin, this light no longer exists.

"Replenish your souls. Rejoice now, for The Warning will save you and bring you closer to My Sacred Heart. Welcome the Warning, for then you will be given the proof of Eternal Life and know how important it is."

The crusty reporter interrupted. "Why should we believe you?"

John looked back at Pope Innocent and nodded. Then he stepped aside and let the pontiff take the podium. Innocent picked up a remote control and clicked it, projecting a faded, black-and-white image of two men on the large screen behind him.

"This is Pope Leo XII with John Malek. The picture was taken in the earliest days of photography, on January 6, 1829."

311

Innocent could see disbelief in the eyes of the audience, so he continued the slide show in rapid-fire succession. "This is John Malek with Pope Pius VIII in 1830 ... with Gregory XVI in 1845 ... with Pius IX in 1874 ... with Leo XIII in 1901... with Pius X in 1913 ... I could continue, but we have assembled a package of pictures, information and data for each of you."

A humble cameraman could not endure the humiliation of Pope Innocent any longer. "Holy Father, please forgive me, but those images have been doctored. This man's picture has been digitally inserted into each of these photographs. It's obvious for anyone who understands the technology behind it. It doesn't prove anything."

By now, most of the video cameras had stopped taping. Some of the journalists were dozing in their chairs. Many in the hallway had left.

"But this does," Pope Innocent said, decisively. He clicked the remote again and a large image of a discolored scroll appeared on the screen. Only two journalists suspected correctly that the words printed on it were in ancient Aramaic.

"Eight months ago," the pontiff continued, "I commissioned a secret investigation into the verifiable characteristics of this scroll. Each of the members of the team we assembled has world-class credentials, among the best in their fields. We will provide you with complete informational background. Today, this historic scroll is stored in the Vatican archives. Miraculously, it has been preserved since it was received in 69 AD by Pope Saint Linus, the Church's second pontiff. It is the oldest extant message received by the man at my side."

Disbelieving smiles spread through the audience.

"Over the past two millennia, the Church has registered a total of 1782 of these messages from Our Lord Jesus Christ, through John Eben Malek."

One reporter stuffed his notepad in his briefcase and walked out of the room, mumbling, "What a waste of time."

Pope Innocent ignored him, continuing, "Carbon dating of a double-blind, random sampling of 40 of these scrolls has verified, with 99.876% certainty, that each scroll is from the time period in which it is claimed."

"So you've got some old parchments," the crusty, old reporter moaned. "That proves nothing regarding Malek."

Innocent clicked the remote again, displaying a close-up image of the brownish-red smudge at the bottom of the scroll.

"Every message ends with this mark, all of which also were carbon dated."

Now the old reporter showed interest. "What is it?"

The pope turned to recognize John. "Our DNA profiling experts tell us that it is this man's thumbprint, in this man's blood."

The room became quiet.

All eyes focused on John Eben Malek.

With those words, Pope Innocent XIV broke the most sensational news story in modern history.

The fourth beast is a fourth kingdom
that will appear on earth.
It will be different from all the other kingdoms
and will devour the whole earth,
trampling it down and crushing it.
Daniel 7:23-25

Chapter 42
Cyst/Thas Estate
Jupiter Island, Florida
June 16

Evan's doctors were pleased with the pace of his continuing recovery at home. However, Thas still felt scarred and crippled and was not happy with the pace of the changes that he had been demanding for Titan's implementation.

Complicating matters even worse, yesterday's shocking Vatican announcement meant that his existing deadlines for performance metrics were out the window. A new urgency existed and timetables would have to be collapsed. Without a doubt, John Malek's revelation necessitated a rapid response that would squelch any momentum he might gain in public acceptance.

By now, nearly a third of all Americans had voluntarily accepted Titan implants because of a variety of incentives that the federal government had offered. But that still left two thirds of the American population untrackable and, consequently, uncontrollable.

During the methodical process of Titan implementation, Evan had planned a progressive choke, as he liked to call it. But, now, he had lost all patience. The tragedy at Nauru had instilled in him a sense of urgency, and he worried that his window of opportunity might be closing.

Surprisingly, some aspects of the program had proceeded more easily than expected. For example, people were not objecting to the minor pain of implantation, using a modified syringe. Also they did not seem to mind that each inoculation left a mark consisting of three concentric circles, like a small bulls eye on the forehead. In fact, a massive cultural campaign effectively promoted that the bulls eye had become a wildly popular fashion statement.

Through the miracle of nanotechnology, the tiny Titan transmitters had become reputed to be the only foolproof method of identifying individuals in this age of rampant insecurity. Since no other means could recognize an individual's unique brain wave patterns, every other form of ID had been deemed suspect by U.S. officials. Less known, however, was the fact that each implant included an extraordinarily precise global positioning chip.

So, implants had been required before an individual could receive any form of government job or benefit. Then, the right to vote was coupled with Titan identification. Next, it was mandated that non-cash purchases must be validated with Titan ID. So, many people resisted by paying for everything in cash. Now, Evan was pushing his biggest step yet in Congress: making cash transactions in excess of $100 illegal.

The introduction of each restrictive measure had been preceded by widespread news coverage of a crisis, such as uncontrolled identity theft or widespread tax evasion in the underground economy. Then, after each crisis rollout campaign, the Titan program had been promoted in media reports as the convenient solution to the problem.

So, the noose was tightening, but not fast enough for Thas.

His goal included more than America. He wanted the world. However, foreign governments had been slow to support an American company's agenda. They did not react to warnings about identity theft and tax evasion with the urgency of pliable American politicians.

Even Evan's influential business partner, Vasily Melnikov, claimed to be having difficulty getting the Russians to comply. However, Evan suspected that Melnikov might be slowing his progress by freelancing different agendas with other ambitious and restless members of the Legion of Babylon. Thas wished he could act more forcefully against Melnikov but the Russian had become too unpredictable to provoke.

Evan's uncertainty in handling Melnikov stemmed from the fact that, without his knowledge, Cyst had shared Evan's Titan Analysis with the Russian. Now, Vasily could and would exploit the young man's psychological weaknesses. It was a dangerous game that patient Melnikov liked playing ... at least for now.

They had never been close but had to tolerate each other as co-owners of XCyst Industries' vast industrial and technological empire. The tubby Russian was wise to let Evan have free reign in running the companies and, as long as record profits rolled in, Melnikov would not complain. Even meeting together had become problematic, based on their well-founded concerns. Vasily would not travel to America because he valued his freedom. Evan would not travel to Russia because he valued his life.

Evan's greatest frustration, however, was that Angela had believed her own scientists, rather than his, and refused to publicly link the viral immunization program to the deaths of the Saudi Royal Family.

She stood up to him, for a change, arguing, "I see no

reason to cause a panic. My scientists don't agree with what you are claiming."

She changed her tone when he responded, "Madame President, planned obsolescence is not a wise strategy for your future."

Consequently, one impediment after another had been frustrating for Thas. But the delays actually worked in his favor, allowing XCyst Industries the months it needed to produce enough Titan implants for the world's population.

Now, a new motivator had to be found. Panic would serve Evan's purposes better than complacency.

Until a few days ago, the XCyst satellite known as "Glass Andalusian" had patiently awaited its orders. Today, however, Phase 2 would begin.

NEW YORK NEWS TRIBUNE
PUBLISHED: JUNE 16, 10:14 AM

Killer Virus May Spark Global Chaos

ATLANTA – Top secret U.S. documents have surfaced on a little-known, watchdog, Internet site claiming that a frighteningly aggressive and adaptive new strain of virus is baffling health care officials and threatening to cause widespread death and panic around the globe. Health care officials have confirmed the authenticity of these documents.

The virus, dubbed N1656, presents initial symptoms of intense skin reddening, blistering and ulceration. Quickly following, however, are symptoms that resemble acute radiation toxicity, including headache, nausea, vomiting, tremors, seizures, and hemorrhaging of internal organs. No victim has survived more than 90 minutes after the onset of symptoms.

Health officials are investigating 46 similar outbreaks that have occurred in 12 countries. The contagion is responsible for the deaths of at least 921, over the past 48 hours and scientists project that the death toll will likely increase exponentially over the coming days.

In order to discover the origin of the virus, health officials are investigating common patterns of travel, diet, or behavior among victims. At present, however, no such commonalities have been detected. Anyone with potentially helpful information regarding a victim's health history is encouraged to contact the Centers for Disease Control and Prevention in Atlanta, Georgia.

NEW YORK NEWS TRIBUNE
UPDATE: JUNE 16, 2:21 PM

Thas to Explain Deadly Contagion in Urgent Announcement

NAURU – Billionaire industrialist, Evan Thas, has hastily scheduled a live video feed to "explain the alarming viral outbreak that is ravaging parts of the globe," according to an XCyst Industries spokesman.

> The CEO of XCyst Industries will make the announcement from his Florida estate where he is recovering from severe injuries that he recently sustained in an industrial accident at the company's Nauru Island facilities.
>
> Thas is reputed to be one of the most important technologists of our time and is believed to have information that will save lives and possibly overcome the outbreak before it reaches pandemic status.
>
> The announcement will be broadcast, live globally, at 6 pm EST on the XBC News Networks.

EVAN'S FACE was covered with makeup, but little could be done to hide his blistered mouth and patched right eye. He blinked back tears as he focused on the camera lens that projected his image around the world. From a Nauru hospital bed, the Tech Titan spoke with apparent pain, not only in his body, but from his heart.

"I will never be able to fully describe my feelings regarding the viral outbreak that is threatening to ravage communities around the globe. To say I am angry is an understatement. But I am also saddened to my soul. This looming tragedy was completely avoidable. But for one evil man, it never would have happened."

Thas motioned for a tissue and when the nurse handed it to him, he wiped a tear from his eye.

"Bear with me, though, I will get to that in a moment. What we are witnessing is the same aggressive virus that wiped out most of the Saudi Royal Family. We call it N1656.

You heard me right. The Royal Family was not killed in a biological attack. The deaths were caused by a killer virus, the most lethal ever encountered. Those facts were kept secret in an attempt to preclude the possibility of mass panic.

"My company, XCyst Industries, was successful in isolating the virus after the Saudi incident and that is why the world has been relatively free from the contagion, until now. But, recently, a saboteur attacked our facilities on Nauru. He destroyed much of the unprecedented biotechnological progress that Dr. Huntington Cyst and I have accomplished there."

Evan handed the tissue back to the nurse.

"Our work was bringing hope to millions. We supplied the organs that made their lives full again. We offered the promise, some day, of the immortal man. But that has all gone to waste … at least for now."

Thas sighed deeply and gathered his thoughts.

"We have conducted an extensive investigation with Cyst-Blanc supercomputers scanning surveillance video footage, from each of our facilities, over the past decade. Using facial recognition software, we have discovered highly incriminating evidence."

Evan picked up a remote from his bedside table and clicked it. The XBC video feed then isolated a picture of a dark haired man near a launch pad. Around and across his face were lines and dots that indicated a computer-generated facial recognition.

"This intruder was spotted at one of our sites in Russia just four hours before our rocket launch malfunctioned, destroying one of our surveillance satellites."

Thas clicked more pictures.

"Here he is, again, just 30 minutes before a nighttime fire at one of our biological weapons facilities in central Africa.

Here he is shortly before a forklift crashed into our computer system at XCyst's Advanced Radiation Weaponry lab. And, again, we seem him just before a water line broke and flooded the supercomputer at our stealth drone plant. As you can see, the incriminating pictures go on and on."

Evan began clicking through slides in rapid-fire succession.

"Each of these incidents cost untold expense and delays. But make no mistake; these were not industrial accidents, they were terrorist strikes. We were lucky we didn't lose any lives."

The video feed returned to Evan's face.

"The man I have shown you, over and over again, is the same terrorist that we believe caused the disaster at Nauru. We don't have video footage because the surveillance cameras there were destroyed. But I know it was him, and this time people died!" Then, seething anger tinged Evan's voice. "In fact, I lost my newborn son in the attack."

Thas paused, for dramatic effect, and then began to weave a fine tapestry of lies.

"That terrorist's name is John Eben Malek. He is a convicted murderer who escaped from prison in New York. He is also a suspect in the vicious, Saudi viral attack that triggered the collapse of the global economy.

"Now, that leads me to today's threat of a viral pandemic. With deepest regret, I am confirming that the recent terrorist attack on Nauru caused a breach in the containment of N1656. The virus that wiped out the Saudi Royal Family is now airborne and Pacific air currents are transporting the virus around the globe. Unfortunately, we have never discovered a deadlier strain.

"I realize that this news is incredibly disturbing, but please do not panic. If you follow my leadership, I have a three-fold solution.

"First, I am committing all of the resources at my disposal and my entire fortune, if necessary, to eradicate this virus before it eradicates humanity. Take comfort in the fact that XCyst scientists have discovered an immunization formula that will protect each of you from the deadly virus, and it is being manufactured at break-neck speed, even as we speak. I have restructured every division of XCyst Industries to assist in this vital effort and I have mobilized the support and resources of the Legion of Babylon for our global immunization blitzkrieg.

"Second, the scale and scope of this looming pandemic is potentially so overwhelming that an effective response will require a unified world structure. Laws in countries, around the globe, will have to be changed in order to expedite our crisis procedures. We are blessed to have the Legion of Babylon managing the emergency response from ten regions, around the world. Do not hinder their efforts. The stakes are so high – the death toll potentially so great – that any country or individual that attempts to delay or disrupt our emergency response will be treated as a threat to the common good and an enemy of war. I do not have time to debate every petty politician and bureaucrat. Our survival strategy will require the assistance of not just them, but also journalists, bankers, legislators and judges. So, I say this not as a threat, but a promise: Our limited resources will be allocated to the most cooperative, first.

"Third, and equally important: Justice must be served. I cannot sufficiently describe for you my outrage when I discovered that the Vatican is providing sanctuary protection for John Eben Malek. Why protect a murderer?

"Why? Because the church of Rome has been the focus of

evil for two thousand years. Why? Because the man who calls himself Pope Innocent XIV is a False Prophet. Why?" Thas paused and then declared: "Because the terrorist he protects is the prophesied Antichrist."

Evan let that dramatic announcement linger in the minds of listeners.

"The facts I am telling you will be denied. But the time of deceit is ending. Make no mistake: your politicians and pastors have been lying to you."

Then, fighting back pain, he sat up in bed. "They tried to kill me, but God would not let them. Now, to shield you from his evil, I must put an end to John Malek.

"To those of you who are watching, I want you to know that I love each of you like my precious child, my son who was sacrificed on the altar of Malek's madness. My righteous anger is for your benefit.

Then, firmly, he added, "The tribulation that you have been put through is from the hands of John Eben Malek. The economic depression, the viral pandemic, even the murder of a living saint has been orchestrated by his diabolical evil.

"To the renegade pope and his council of evil I say: Leave now. I give you fair warning that I will gladly sacrifice your guilty lives before I will allow you to continue sacrificing the innocent."

"Today, prophecy is fulfilled. Antichrist has arrived to destroy mankind. However, I have been sent to save you."

Chapter 43
Choteau-Agusta, Montana
June 20

ercedes Dare slumped in her chair. She had not bathed for a week nor eaten for two days. Vodka and cigarettes had become her only sustenance.

Though Mer's parents had worried for her safety, they knew she needed time to sort everything out. So, they offered her the use of the family hunting lodge, hoping that, there, she would spend a few days finding her way back to happiness.

But that was four months ago.

Now, Mer spent her days in the darkened cabin rewinding the memories, over and over, hoping to discover what went wrong. She had abandoned her professional dreams for Evan Thas only to find that, now, he had abandoned her.

Nothing seemed to make sense, anymore.

After the accident, Evan's mother had rushed Mer off the island. Then, for the next few weeks, Mer stayed with her parents, depressed about her miscarriage and worrying over Evan's recovery prospects and the future of their relationship.

Finally, one day, she got through to him, by phone, at the hospital. Evan seemed pleased to hear from her but was extremely bitter about the disaster and his injuries. She told him how much she missed him and that she did not care how bad his injuries were. She still loved him.

The conversation went well. So well, in fact, that

Thas even reassured her that he still wanted her to bear his children. She was ecstatic.

So, when he returned to his Jupiter Island estate to recuperate, Thas called to ask Mer to join him for dinner at their favorite restaurant. With his usual flair for extravagance, he arranged a private jet to fly her from Montana. Then, a driver picked her up at the Palm Beach airport and brought her straight to *Café L'Europe*.

The long-awaited reunion was emotional. Though she had tried to prepare herself for the worst, the extent of his injuries almost turned her stomach. Evan now wore a black patch over the right eye that had once admired her beauty. His face was still partially bandaged, but obviously burn-scarred. His singed red hair was returning to its early state but his right hand could hardly grip a fork.

Still, Mer made the best of it and kept the conversation light and happy. She was pleased that nearby diners were polite enough to pretend that they did not notice his injuries, although whispers made it clear that they did.

Evan seemed excited about future prospects as he described to her the rebuilding of Eden Village and how he planned to get operations moving ahead as soon as possible. He had drank a bit too much, but she was pleased to see that his spirit had not been broken.

Then, as dessert was being served, he expressed optimism, again, about having children. At that point Mer saw no reason to delay telling him the unfortunate news.

She explained that her doctor had recently informed her that the miscarriage had come with complications. She would not be able to bear children.

Mer watched as a strange expression transformed his scarred face. Evan's breathing became labored and his eye blinked and darted around as if seeking to clarify confusion.

She reassured him, "Don't worry, silly. We can still adopt."

"What?" he shouted. "What are you talking about?"

The outburst stunned her into silence.

He grabbed his head with both hands and moaned.

"Dr. Thas," a waiter asked, "is everything okay?"

Evan looked up. "Are you insane? Of course not!"

The nightmare was as clear as if it had happened yesterday. Now, sitting in the darkened cabin, Mercedes remembered how Evan noticed that diners were staring at him.

"Eat your dinner, dammit!" he growled at an elderly lady.

"Bring my car to the door," Thas demanded.

"Yes, sir. Right away."

Mer whispered, "Evan, shhhhh."

"Don't you shush me!" he screamed.

The manager quickly slid next to their table and whispered, "May I help you?"

Thas ignored him.

Mer begged, "Evan, please…"

Thas stood and bellowed to the stunned patrons, "You all think you can fool me, don't you?"

The manager said, "Dr. Thas, we're not trying to fool anyone."

"Oh, come on!" he groaned as he pushed over his half-filled glass of pinot noir.

Mer squealed, "Evan!"

Now, everyone was watching him. "You look at me with disgust, but you all want what I have."

At the door, the waiter said, "Sir, your car is ready."

"You can't fool me and you can't stop me," Evan growled to his shocked audience. "None of you!"

Thas started for the door but then backtracked to Mercedes.

Looking down on her, he hissed, "And you ... you're the worst."

Then he stormed out of the restaurant, leaving her to find her own way back to Montana.

THE FIRST KNOCKS did not wake her. The person outside, however, was persistent and pounded even louder.

This time, Mercedes roused out of her drunken slumber. From her chair in the darkened living room, she could see slivers of bright light around the draperies.

It must be morning.

But she still made no attempt to answer the door.

"Ms. Dare?" a female voice beckoned from outside. "Ms. Dare, I know you're in there. Your parents told me how to find you."

Mer growled a vulgarity and ran her fingers through her tangled blonde hair.

"Go away," Mer shouted. "I don't want to see anybody!"

The woman continued knocking. "It's important, Ms. Dare. I have to speak to you."

Mer groaned as she shuffled over to the window. She figured that her parents had sent over another psychiatrist but, when she peaked out of the drapes, she saw a woman who looked oddly familiar.

There was nothing particularly unusual about her, nothing that might spark a clear memory. Just a white, middle-aged lady, carrying her baby.

"What do you want?" Mer shouted through the door.

"I have to speak to you," the woman said. "It's urgently important."

Dare did not respond.

The woman raised her voice. "I am not leaving until I speak with you!"

The baby started crying.

The door opened.

MERCEDES WARMED the woman's formula in a pan on the stove.

Good enough, she thought as she dipped her finger into the milky liquid.

Then, as Mer poured the milk into a bottle, she cautioned, "Okay, I didn't invite you in so I can play Mother Teresa. You've got five minutes to speak your mind and feed your baby. That's it."

"Do you remember me?" the woman asked.

"No ... uh ... maybe ... I don't know."

"I was your nurse at Eden Village."

"Oh, yeah. I remember now. Nurse ... Adams."

"Yes, that's right: Ashley Adams."

Mer handed her the bottle and, suddenly embarrassed by her appearance, ran fingers through her hair, again. "I'm sorry, I ... I shouldn't be so rude. You seemed ... moved, that night. I appreciated your sensitivity."

Ashley nodded and began feeding the infant.

Mer watched, sadly, and suggested, "I guess you identified with my circumstances, being pregnant, yourself."

"Well, that's why I'm here." Then the nurse explained what few people knew about Eden Village. She described a medical establishment that, to Mer, sounded like a house of horrors where human body parts had been treated like lucrative crops, fertilized for rapid growth, harvested, and then sold at market. Life, there, was a manufactured commodity, conceived, tortured, modified and disposed of without concern. The contrast was nauseating: In Ashley's arms was a living example of pure innocence, but out of her mouth poured descriptions of sadistic evil. Listening to the gruesome details, while the infant sucked loudly on the warm bottle, caused Mer to want to sit down.

"You should have told Evan about all that," Mer complained. "He would have put a stop to it."

Nurse Adams responded with a hollow laugh. But her eyes reflected sadness. "You really don't know, do you?"

"Know what?"

"That everything, there, was done at his request."

Now, Mer laughed. "Don't be ridiculous. What you described is a death camp."

"It *is* a death camp ... at Dr. Thas' request."

Mer was stunned. *She looks believable.* Then, slowly, the veil of self-delusion dropped. Realizing that she had been deceived, Mer moaned, "Oh, how could I have been such a fool?"

"So," the nurse asked, suspiciously, "are you still seeing him?"

"No... He never wants to be with me again."

Ashley Adams looked up from the baby and offered Mer a baffled stare. "You're lying."

"What? How dare you!"

The infant cried.

"I'm sorry," Ashley said as she placed the empty bottle on the table. "I just know that Thas would never leave you. He still wants children."

"Yeah, don't we all," Mercedes said, sadly, as she reached across the table and quieted the baby with strokes to his tummy. "But I can't have children, anymore."

"Ohhhh," the woman breathed a long sigh. "I see."

"Not that it's any of your business," Mer complained.

"I apologize. I don't mean to be insulting or prying." Then she held the boy up and asked, "Would you like to burp him?"

"Sure," Mer said, gladly taking the infant. She raised and bounced him in the air as she admired his snug cotton jumper, clear blue eyes, and fresh crop of wavy red hair.

Then, as Mer caressed the boy over her shoulder, the nurse asked seriously, "So, you don't think you will ever see Dr. Thas again?"

"No … never."

"Ohhhh," the woman sighed once more. "Then I want to tell you what happened that night … the night of the disaster."

"I'd appreciate that. I was so drugged up, I don't remember much." Then, softly patting the baby's back, Mer asked, "What's his name?"

For a moment, Ashley studied Mercedes and the infant in her arms. Then she answered, "What would you suggest? He's your son."

A baby is God's opinion
that the world should go on.
Carl Sandburg

Chapter 44
Eden Village Hospital
Twenty Three Weeks Earlier

The hospital administrator assembled his top professionals for an emergency meeting. On Nauru, however, pleasure was always prioritized higher than professionalism.

For a week, now, he and the head doctor had prepared for this project, but the rest of this team had not been briefed on the importance of today's delivery. So, looking like actors from a movie set, three attractive doctors and four lovely nurses shuffled into the conference room, clowning and flirting, with their usual good humor.

Adding contrast, however, Nurse Ashley Adams followed them in, always more serious, more competent, and more homely. She and the beautiful residents of Eden Village knew that her appearance scored no points on this island. It was her intellect that had landed her here and the research paper she published in nursing school that had caught the eye of Evan Thas.

In fact, it was more than a little irritating to her that some of her research conclusions on speed-breeding the perfect race had been adopted here on the island, without compensation or even acknowledgement. Her research proposals had become like her job: On paper, they both seemed utopian; In practice, however, they were far messier.

The Administrator tapped on the conference table and

attempted to bring the group to order with, "Let's get serious, now."

The medical professionals settled into their conference room chairs, still snickering about last night's raucous party at The Garden restaurant.

"Come on, straighten up. We're clearing the decks for an extremely important patient who will be arriving in a half hour."

"A local or an import?" a nurse inquired.

"She's flying in with Dr. Thas."

Some of the staff raised eyebrows.

A doctor blurted out, "And you think she's pregnant?"

Others chuckled, "Nah ... No way!"

A younger nurse asked, "What's the big deal?"

A doctor answered, "He's one of the horniest hound dogs on the planet. I bet he's bedded thousands of women. But never got one pregnant."

"Maybe he wants it that way."

"No, not Thas. He's got this weird DNA thing going on that causes his body to reject organ transplants that are not from his own offspring. Kinda freaky."

"That's right," the Administrator said. "So this delivery is both tricky and extremely important." He continued, "Dr. Thas will be watching. If all goes well, after hormonal growth stimulation, he'll have adult organs available in 42 to 46 months.... Jim, you want to lay out the game plan?"

"Sure," the head physician responded. "Look, we've got just 38 days of gestation. So there's no room for error." Some of the staffers frowned. "We're dealing with an active brain, two heart valves pumping, and rudimentary organs such as lungs, pancreas, stomach and liver. But the entire object is only the size of a sesame seed.[227] So, I'm handling the hysteroscopy. I'm not gonna let one of you clowns screw this up."

"Oh, come on!" staffers laughed and booed him, around the table. "That's not fair."

"Once I make the extraction, though, it's your turn. I want the object positioned in its synthetic uterus and immersed in hormonal solution within 45 seconds of delivery. Any problems with that?"

"Jim, you know that's not standard protocol. We should conduct the immersion at the Tower."

"That's the way Dr. Thas wants it. Any of you gonna argue with him?"

In unison, they all emphatically shook their heads.

Then he startled Ashley. "Nurse Adams, I'm putting you in charge of delivering the immersion jar to the Towers. But, first, Dr. Thas wants you in the recovery room with him when the patient comes to."

"Why?"

The doctor dismissed her resistance with a laugh. "You know how he is: always delegating the dirty work."

A nurse suggested, "Probably wants you to break the bad news to her."

Adams groaned and rolled her eyes.

The head physician continued, "Anyway, as soon as you get her sedated, Tower 3 will be expecting you."

FORTY THREE MINUTES later, Nurse Ashley Adams was in the parking lot, sitting in her golf cart and staring at the seven Towers in the distance. Even though she was learning to despise them, the massive monuments to man's genius still inspired awe in herself as well as fear in island residents. Tonight, they were so brightly lit against the dark sky that they resembled seven luminous mountains, unnaturally dominating the Pacific waters that surrounded this once primitive island. To her, the Towers had become symbols of scientific defiance, clawing toward heaven and daring God to respond.

Ashley still hadn't started her cart. She looked down at the large glass jar in the passenger seat and thought about what she had never before allowed herself to admit: Floating in two gallons of synthetic hormonal solution was a black sack that contained a boy; he will grow quickly, needing only his nurturing chemicals; and he will endure a world without love, light or sound until the day that Dr. Evan Thas decides to carve him up.[228]

She mumbled, "What am I doing?"

The nurse thought about how the delivery had proceeded flawlessly. But she could not shake the sadness that she felt for Mercedes Dare. Until now, it had been tolerable to work with informed volunteers who were having the time of their lives and getting paid handsomely for their services. Each of them had been pre-screened by Titan to assure that they would have no moral or religious reservations about their work on the island. However, Ashley felt it was quite another matter to secretly steal a wanted baby.

Such a horrible deception, she thought.

But that was how Dr. Thas wanted it and, on the island, he got everything he desired. Ashley was not brave enough to rock the boat, here. She knew that people who left on bad terms were never heard from again. Perhaps they had all willingly forgotten their friends at Eden Village. Or, perhaps not.

Suddenly, alarms across the island shattered the nighttime quiet. Oddly, but instinctively, Ashley picked up the jar and protected it in her arms as her heightened senses attempted to discern the danger.

Floodlights scanned the Towers and the fields, nearby, as security vehicles raced away from her, toward the Towers. She saw Dr. Thas, running out of the hospital and into the parking lot. She watched as he leaped onto the side of a slow-moving fire truck as it left the parking lot and then raced to the Towers.

For a few moments, Ashley anxiously wondered what all the activity meant. But, soon, she found herself amused at the indifference of the immense monoliths. From this distance, it was obvious that the cold, uncaring Towers shared no sympathy nor concern for the frenzied ants below.

Then she jolted when the island was lit by the most breathtaking explosion she had ever seen. The bright flash forced her to close her eyes but that did not protect her face from the hot gust of wind, nor her ears from the thunderous burst.

Shocked and amazed, she sat motionless, with eyes glued on the horizon.

For forty five minutes, she tried to comprehend one explosion after another. But she never stopped clutching the jar at her chest. And, when the last Tower was gone, she started her cart, drove to her home, and hid the jar in a suitcase.

... of course I bit you.
I'm a snake.
The End of a Fable

Chapter 45
Cocoa Beach, Florida
June 23

D r. Trip Weston despised having to answer today's call. In the warm surroundings of his home office, he watched through an open door as his nurturing wife read a fairy tale to their little princess in the living room.

Then the phone rang, on cue, but he tried to resist it. The young scientist recollected how thrilled he had been the day of his appointment to head XCyst's Aerospace Technologies Division. He had been promoted from relative obscurity to work at the side of The Tech Titan, Dr. Evan Thas. He promised his wife that this career path would change their lives, forever.

Now, however, his prestigious position had become a burden, a disgrace, a reason for self-loathing.

Finally, Weston answered with a mumbled, "Hello Dr. Thas."

"Trip, do you have a pen handy?"

"Yes, go ahead."

Thas then read six sets of GPS coordinates."

Weston wrote them down. "Got it," he affirmed.

The young scientist knew that Thas would never reveal his reasons for each day's coordinates. However, he had conducted his own private research and discovered that each location was from where John Malek's followers had been spotted, around the world.

The End of the Age Apostles were no longer anonymous preachers. They had become favorite subjects of gossip, praise, scorn and media reports as they railed against accepting the inoculations that they believed represented the Mark of the Beast. Travelling in pairs, they surfaced unexpectedly, stirring up communities around the globe with their uncompromising warnings, healings and demonic deliverances. So, wherever they went, the Internet would quickly relay amazing stories of miracles and conversions for Evan's CyBot search engine to find.

However, the Apostles had been trained never to linger at a location. So, by the time Evan could track them, they had always moved on. Even after exhaustive efforts, Evan's brothers had failed to catch up with the Apostles. With God's grace and a mission to fulfill, the prey always managed to stay one step ahead of the predators.

However, Thas knew that the Titan program, once fully implemented, would eliminate forever the need for this kind of manhunt. Coordinating a sophisticated network of satellite surveillance systems, Titan would allow unprecedented tracking and control. No one would be able to hide.

His four most powerful satellites had been given unusual code names. Each had been matched with a color and an equestrian breed because Thas and Cyst thought they were like powerful stallions, ready to break out of the starting gates. More importantly, Evan saw them as the Four Horses of the Apocalypse and himself as the Horseman. Whoever controlled White Appaloosa, Red Thoroughbred, Black Arabian and, especially, Glass Andalusian could control the world. He alone would become the ultimate arbiter of conquest, war, famine and death.[229]

With those tools at his disposal, Evan had become capable

of dispensing god-like justice whenever he willed it. So, naturally, he punished every community that welcomed the Apostles. Wherever the men reportedly had preached – whether in churches, hospitals, orphanages or schools – Thas ordered a deadly strike from the satellite known as Glass Andalusian.

Inevitably, news stories reported that in each of those communities another outbreak of the N1656 virus had hit. Few realized that the so-called viral pandemic was a fraud. Those who suspected deception were either shouted down or silenced in other ways.[230]

Soon, even the normally atheistic XBC News began reporting that the viral outbreaks may be indicating "God's dissatisfaction with any community that harbors the heretics." For some of the faithful, and even non-believers, the media warnings sparked fear, dread and anger wherever the Apostles surfaced. Now, the fugitives were not just wanted by authorities for their prison escapes, but were hunted by many in the population at large.

When Trip finished repeating the coordinates back to Evan, the scientist hesitantly asked, "Dr. Thas, may I ask you a question?"

Thas did not answer, but Weston proceeded.

"Why are you doing this? I mean, I understand using the satellites to find sunken treasure. But your salvage teams have already located $50 billion of it. When's enough enough?"[231]

Still, no response.

The scientist continued, "And I realize that inoculating everyone will protect the world from the pandemic. But what we're doing is a big deception. It's not only causing unnecessary deaths but, actually, creating a panic to get the inoculations."

Thas answered flatly, "Just do your job."

Weston knew he had gone too far. "Fine."

"Wait a minute," Thas added. "I have one more." Then Evan read a lengthy alpha-numeric string, while Weston scribbled it on his notepad.

"What's this last one?" Weston asked. "Looks like somebody's Titan ID code."

"No big deal. We're just experimenting with focused accuracy."

"Okay... I'll talk to you tomorrow."

"No, Trip. I want you to do it now, while I'm on the phone."

Weston sighed.

He slid his notebook computer closer, engaged its Titan identification software and connected to the Cyst Industries secure and encrypted satellite communications and control site.

A moment later, Thas nudged, "Trip?"

"Yes, yes. I have Glass Andalusian now."

After Titan approval, Weston entered the coordinates slowly. "Why do you want me to do this? You know how."

"I have my reasons."

Another moment passed.

Thas asked, "What's taking so long?"

"I don't know. System's slow, or something."

Thas wasn't buying it. "I hear your keystrokes. Stop stalling."

"Okay. Okay. I'm just ... I'm just reviewing the coordinates.... Uh oh, I must have entered something wrong."

Evan reached the end of his patience. "Trip? How's that toddler of yours doing?"

The question deserved no answer. Weston pressed "Send."

†††

NINETEEN MINUTES LATER, the ambulance arrived. Weston's hysterical wife answered the door, holding her sobbing daughter in her arms and babbling about what had happened.

The two medics rushed into the office, observed the body, and immediately ordered the wife and daughter out of the room.

Then the younger medic radioed his superior. "Code Red. Code Red. We have a suspected case of N1656. Request guidance."

The superior responded, "What? Did you say…"

"Yes, dammit! What do we do?"

"Uh, look, you've gotta quarantine the house and everybody who had contact with the subject."

"Roger that. Please get Team Alpha over here immediately."

The two medics ordered the wife and daughter to close themselves off at the far end of the house. They turned the air conditioning system off, put on latex gloves and covered their lower faces with breathing masks. Then they returned to the office where Dr. Weston's body was still slumped over his desk.

They cursed their bad luck as they studied his burnt, hemorrhaging and blistered face, still resting on his keyboard.

The older medic said, "Strange."

"How's that?"

"Look how rapidly initial symptoms progressed to death."

"That's typical with this virus."

"But just a few feet away, the wife and kid weren't even affected."

"Weird."

Then they cursed their bad luck again.

The two observers knew that they, too, might not have long to live. This virus was defying what most scientists and doctors thought they knew about viral infections. The only comprehensive investigations on N1656 had been conducted at the XCyst facilities on Nauru, before the disaster. These medics trusted those scientific conclusions.

Instead, they could have prayed to find a clue that would contradict their initial prognosis. But they didn't. So, they never noticed that Weston's notebook computer also had been fried.

This century is under
the power of the devil,
but when the secrets confided to you come to pass,
his power will be destroyed.
Our Lady of Medjugorje

From the hills of Medjugorje to the mountains of San Sebastian de Garabandal, visionaries began announcing that long-awaited prophecies would be fulfilled soon.[232] The urgent calls implored praying, fasting and converting our lives back to God. The seers made clear that, with those protections, no one should fear God's Justice, but without them, no one would escape God's Justice.

The announcements caused the Latter Day Apostles to redouble their evangelizing efforts, around the world. Each pair, however, had encountered difficulties in staying "off the grid" while moving from country to country. However, somehow, they always found a way to stay on the move.

Their greatest rewards were from watching the joy of the many thousands who were newly converted. Their greatest sorrows were from watching the rejection of their life-saving ministries.

In India, Samir and Rodney had been confronted, repeatedly, by radical Hindus, intent on purging Christianity from their midst. They had witnessed an orchestrated campaign of lies against Christians that resulted in churches and cathedrals being burned, sometimes with Christians inside. Priests had been falsely accused and pastors killed. Even the sisters who had worked alongside of Mother Teresa were attacked after being blamed for kidnapping and forced conversions. Many thousands of believers had been forced to flee their homes but they found no protection from persecution, even in refugee camps.[233]

In Mexico, Worthington and Pedro had expected that the land of Our Lady of Guadalupe would be welcoming. However, they quickly found themselves entangled in a raging drug war. Teaching the liberation of Christianity clashed with the slavery to addiction that the drug lords sought.

The evils that the pair had witnessed seemed too shocking to be happening so close to home. In just five years, the drug war had claimed over 47,000 lives, along the American border. Cartel attacks had become increasingly brazen, brutal and frequent. Targeted individuals, including journalists and bloggers, were frequently murdered. Others counted themselves lucky if they had only been kidnapped, robbed and tortured.

One day, Worthington and Pedro even found themselves stuck in a massive traffic jam after dozens of bodies were dumped on a busy Veracruz highway during rush hour.[234] Still, even frequent beheadings failed to gain the attention of the American public.

Father Alonzo and Ricky Zipp had made their way across Europe, too often finding churches empty[235] but streets filled with demonstrators. In some places, they saw that many Europeans simply gave no thought to God, anymore. From England, through France, then in Spain, Italy and Greece, they saw a spirit of rebellion in protesters who seemed eager to eventually plunge into violence.

In the Middle East, Booker and Qurban confronted radical Islamists, and in Africa, they found that their Christian message was often attacked by a resurgent anti-colonialist bigotry. However, across Australia and on to the Pacific Islands Ozzy found that his biggest obstacle had been convincing Jin to press on. The Aussie felt a profound sense of fulfillment from his evangelizing efforts but wished his dispirited partner had felt the same.

Finally, as Chippy and Henry traversed North America, they found something even worse: prideful ignorance. Here, even the poor were wealthy, by world standards. Yet, all their technological luxuries and conveniences had only brought them farther from God. There was no better place to witness the fulfillment of the 1884 locution of Pope Leo XIII, than in America. Truly, the past century had proven that Satan had been allowed greater influence over those who would give themselves over to his service. His century was running out, but his evil seeds had been planted, and his greatest attack against Christ's Church was coming to fruition.

Chippy and Henry realized that God's Judgment against the incorrigible people of Semiazas, as horrible as it had been, was only a warning. Something much bigger was coming.

With each passing day, the Apostles contemplated that their time, also, was running out.

IN FLORIDA, Evan Thas realized that the announcements from the Medjugorje and Garabandal visionaries meant that tumultuous times were coming. Those warnings, along with the increasing activities of the Latter Day Apostles, were causing a frenzy on the Internet and, even with all his control of the Worldwide Web, Evan had been unable to stop such a burst of communications. So, helplessly, he studied Internet traffic reports that attested to the fact that millions were being converted to God.

At first he was perplexed. But then the solution came to him. Like any good politician who sees a parade, he would jump out front and pretend to lead it.

With the help of the XBC News global radio network, Thas arranged an audio announcement that would be broadcast around the world. It was brief, but abundantly brazen.

With messianic fervor, Evan warned that there would be an extreme price to pay if the Catholic Church refused to surrender Malek, and if they continued to condemn the N1656 viral inoculations.

In times past, most observers would have been put off by such outrageous hubris. These days, however, nothing was more entertaining than real, larger-than-life characters in either attack or, better yet, self-destruct mode. So, most of the world cheered Evan's antics no matter how agitated, impatient or irrational his public dictates became.

Like moths to a flame, people naturally gravitated to his bold, brash behavior. He always gave them something to talk about and had become a source of supreme amusement for those who hoped to fill their empty lives with his unique formula for emptiness.

To most observers, Thas represented science over superstition.[236] Still, with the help of a compliant media, many of his pronouncements had been given saintly significance. In fact, his outspoken opposition to Christianity, in general, and Catholicism, in particular, had elevated him to the status of a spiritual leader, warning that self-deprivation for delayed gratification was one of the world's greatest evils.[237]

People had been yearning for the spiritual transcendence that they had never found in traditional faith. So, likening eternal truths to the latest diet soda, they responded enthusiastically to Evan's new and improved god.

Thas offered novelty because his Perfective agenda always turned traditions upside-down with a variety of alluring deceptions. Every virtue had been deconstructed into its Perfective equivalent. Faith was encouraged, not in God, but in football teams, for example. Love had been reduced to the sex act. Courage was assigned to anyone who tore down time-tested traditions. Individuals felt charitable when they demanded that other people's taxes be raised. Kindness, humility and temperance were mocked. Chastity was shunned like a mental illness.

From Evan's teachings, those who had never embraced faith-based sacrifice imagined themselves holy for accepting his pursuit of pleasure principles. Still, while adopting that deception, they ridiculed those who had given themselves to God, expecting nothing more in this life than poverty, celibacy and service.

Today, to a global audience, Thas proclaimed: I and the Father are One.[238] He explained that God demanded obedience to Evan's requests and he cryptically promised that cooperation would insure safety, but defiance would invite destruction.

For the Vatican, the world had become difficult to understand, these days. However, Evan knew how to communicate with his amused global audience.[239] They loved it when he ended his Vatican condemnation with the shout, "Penance! Penance! Penance!"[240]

My Son's Vicar will have much to suffer,
because for a time the Church will be
handed over to great persecutions:
it will be the time of darkness;
the Church will undergo a frightful crisis....
Civil and ecclesiastical authority
will be abolished ,
all order and justice will be trampled underfoot.
Only murders, hatred, jealousy,
lying and discord will be seen,
with no love of country or family.
Our Lady of La Salette

Chapter 47
Vatican City
July 5

Cardinals from around the world converged on Vatican City after dutifully responding to Pope Innocent's call for an emergency conclave. Upon arrival, each was escorted to the *Casa di Santa Marta*, the housing complex where cardinals resided during more recent conclaves. Though relatively modest, these accommodations were a vast improvement over the makeshift housing, next to the Sistine Chapel, that had been used for this purpose since the 1400s.

However, these holy men would not have been deterred, even if they had been forced to sleep in the streets. They understood the historic importance of this assembly and the unprecedented votes that they would cast.

They also understood the Darkness that the world was now confronting.

The recent bluster of Evan Thas did not merit a significant level of attention or concern from Pope Innocent and his cardinals. They were focused on the historic news that was yet to be announced: the pontiff would voluntarily step down and, in his place, Jesus Christ's Beloved Apostle would lead the Church that Christ had founded.

So, 120 elector cardinals were chosen from those assembled, the maximum number allowed. No one could say, however, how many of those electors doubted John's story.[241]

On the morning of the election, the cardinals entered the Sistine Chapel, in solemn procession and in full red regalia. Pope Innocent XIV, alone, wore white vestments. Once inside, the last cardinal-deacon closed the doors. Then, all entry points were locked from within[242] so as to avoid any contact with the outside world.

The Pontifical Swiss Guards, 110 in number, verified that no one remained inside who was not allowed to vote and then placed themselves in guard positions at all access points around the Chapel. The pope and cardinals were safe inside.

From above the conclave of cardinals, Michelangelo's masterpieces observed their procession, reminding each of them that God also is watching. However, those Biblical images – from the Garden of Eden to The Last Judgment – were not the complete story of God's creation. Today, another chapter would be added: The celebration of the rise of the Beloved Apostle to lead Christ's Church.

From an altar, rising seven steps above the floor, Innocent offered High Mass and led recitations of the Rosary, the Litany of Saints, and the Chaplet of Divine Mercy. Then he secured a large, consecrated Host between glass plates in an ornate, gold monstrance. He placed it at the center of the altar and requested perpetual adoration during the election of the new Vicar of Christ. Then, humbly, he descended the steps and joined the electors where they sat together, quietly contemplating the Holy Eucharist on the altar, the large crucifix behind it and the moving backdrop of the famous Renaissance fresco known as the Last Judgment.

Not far away, at *Castel San Angelo*, John waited patiently in prayer with Father Henri Blanc. He had not been allowed to enter the conclave because he was not a cardinal and, consequently, not permitted to vote. However, any Catholic in good standing is eligible to be elected to head the Church. So, John's non-cardinal status was not a hindrance to his leadership.

Once the balloting began, the proceedings moved quickly. Each cardinal wrote a name on the ballot under the Italian words for, "I elect as supreme pontiff." Then, one by one, each folded his ballot twice, held it in the air and declared, "I call as my witness Christ the Lord who will be my judge, that my vote is given to the one who before God I think should be elected." Then each placed his ballot on a gold patten plate that rested on a large, gold chalice. Next, the elector cardinal picked up the plate, and slid the ballot into the chalice.

When the voting had ended, three scrutineers were chosen from among the electors. They ascended the steps, sat at a table, next to the altar, and counted the ballots.

Once it was determined that 120 ballots had been submitted, the first scrutineer removed a ballot, noted the name on it, and passed it to the second scrutineer. He, then, noted the name and passed it to the third scrutineer. Then the third scrutineer read aloud the name, pierced the ballot with a needle at the top, and slid the ballot onto a string of thread.

Sitting below, each elector noted each name that was read. Then, once all ballots had been revealed, the scrutineers wrote down the official count on a separate sheet of paper, tied the ends of the thread together to preserve the vote, and placed the string of ballots in a receptacle.

Though no one spoke, all were joyful. For perhaps the first time, a unanimous vote had occurred on the first ballot.

No cardinal had doubted that John was truly the Beloved Apostle.

Outside, a smaller than usual crowd had gathered at *Piazza di San Pietro*. They were the faithful few who ignored the ridicule and endured the persecutions that had become so common, these days. Soon, consistent with ancient custom, all of the electors' ballots and notes were burned, causing white smoke to rise from the Chapel's famous smokestack.

All had proceeded according to tradition.

At this point, however, Innocent broke with standard protocols in order to explain to the world the momentous change that had occurred. While John Malek was being rushed through the enclosed passage from the *Castel*, Innocent stood at the back of the Chapel, speaking from behind a podium. Before an unmanned camera that had been installed for this purpose, he explained that he had never before experienced the joy that he felt today. Though his body had been wracked by disabilities and disease, in recent years, he would have continued in office if not for the arrival of God's promised messenger. So, with a peaceful soul and a loving heart, Innocent expressed his delight in relinquishing the Keys of the Kingdom to John Eben Malek.

His words were both optimistic and encouraging, and they were broadcast, live, around the world, until tragedy struck.

... *BREAKING NEWS ... BREAKING NEWS ...*
NEW YORK NEWS TRIBUNE
PUBLISHED: JULY 5, 6:14 AM

KILLER VIRUS STRIKES VATICAN CEREMONY

VATICAN CITY – Eyewitnesses report that a horrifying tragedy occurred during the transfer of Roman Catholic papal authority at the Sistine Chapel today. During the ceremony in which Pope Innocent XIV planned to transfer leadership of the Roman Catholic Church to a controversial successor, an outbreak of the N1656 virus struck the conclave of cardinals before his replacement could be named.

During the pontiff's live broadcast, after the balloting, he suddenly appeared ill. At that point the camera did not capture the pope's actions, but a live microphone recorded sounds in the Chapel of agonizing pain.

The New York News Tribune has compiled eyewitness accounts from stricken survivors who felt compelled to describe details of the tragedy now if, in fact, they too are dying.

They reported that Pope Innocent could have exited quickly through the Sistine's back door. But he seemed determined to go to the altar. He trembled as he slowly offered the Sign of the Cross while blessing those who were suffering around him. With halting steps, he continued staggering forward, even as he stumbled over cardinals' bodies in the aisle.

One witness cried when he said, "The Holy Father, alone, was wearing white, a symbol of purity, wading through a sea of red death."

At the altar steps, Innocent fell to his knees and slowly crawled up them. Around him, everyone had been affected. Some already were dead and most were dying from the mysterious killer.

The pontiff struggled to raise himself to the altar and then reached for the monstrance at the foot of the Crucifix. He removed the large Host from its glass casing, broke it and offered the pieces to the cardinals around him who had not yet expired. Four of them were able to receive and then the pope consumed the last piece, himself.

Eyewitnesses have offered no further details.

Though Roman Catholics around the world pray for a miracle, experts predict that the virus normally claims its victims' lives within hours of the onset of symptoms.

The Vatican Press Office has not responded to repeated requests for more information.[243]

> Man holds in his mortal hands
> the power to abolish all forms of human poverty
> and all forms of human life.
> President John F. Kennedy

Evan's burn-scarred face was reasonably presentable for this television appearance, thanks to liberal applications of makeup. However, his right arm was still in a cast and he had boldly added a black patch over his right eye that proclaimed Titan's mark: three concentric circles. True to form, he would turn even the Nauru disaster into a cause for self-promotion.

From a makeshift studio in his home, Evan hoped to soothe the concerns of a fearful and confused world. So, he started his address with soothing words.

"Be not afraid, for I shall bring you comfort."

His words proceeded in a calm, deliberative tone.

"However, I have no sympathy for the imposter church. I warned them of their sins, but they would not listen. They chose to follow the diabolical guidance of the Antichrist known as John Malek. Now, the penance that they would not freely offer to God was taken from them, against their will. The penalty of sin is death.

"How foolish they have been. I warned the heretics that they were vulnerable without inoculations. But they rejected science for superstition. Even worse, they placed many

353

millions of lives in danger by advising them also to reject science. How cruel and evil. They are the ultimate symbols of Imperfection.

"Now, to all of you in other parts of the world. I realize that the viral attack at the Vatican has alarmed many. So, riots have broken out in the rush to get vaccinated. I want to assure you that anyone who remains orderly will receive protection. However, I am instructing the Legion of Babylon and those in the Perfective Patrol who are implementing the inoculation program, that anyone who exhibits disorder will be forever barred from vaccination. I am confident that a potential death sentence should be sufficient to motivate each of you to maintain order. Cooperation insures safety. Defiance invites destruction.

"All of Vatican City must be evacuated now because no one, there, had heeded my warnings and received the inoculations. Until we can clear out the virus and declare it safe, they are all potentially vulnerable to viral attack in those contaminated buildings.

"Tomorrow, I will lead my scientific team into Vatican City to evaluate the continuing danger that the N1656 virus poses, eliminate the threat, and return the Church back to the people it has failed to represent for far too long."

Then Evan stared deep into the camera lens and added, "God will not tolerate mockery."

This is a deep mystery,
and an inexhaustible subject of meditation,
that the salvation of many depends
on the prayers and voluntary penances [of the few.]
Pope Pius XII
Mystici Corporis Christi

Chapter 49
On an Italian Rail Line
July 6

The freight train that rumbled north out of Rome appeared to be making just another typical run. One of its 312 freight cars, however, was anything but typical. It was part of a meticulous plan that had been carefully protected.

That intermodal freight container was equipped with an air conditioning system that could filter chemical and biological agents out of the air. Its exterior was shielded to prevent even the penetration of armor piercing bullets. Its medical facilities, inside, were state-of-the-art.

The nondescript rail car had been designed for just this purpose: emergency medical evacuation of the pope. Today, though, it was transporting away from Rome the leadership of the Roman Catholic Church, past, present and future.[244]

Pope Innocent and three other cardinals occupied the two bunk beds. One more cardinal, however, had to rest on the floor, between the beds, as the two doctors tried not to disturb him while they tended to the patients. The pain and nausea of the patients had receded, thanks to modern narcotics. The doctors prayed that they had enough medicine to comfort the patients for the entire trip.

At the foot of the beds, John Malek and Father Henri Blanc sat on the floor, praying for miraculous recoveries. Though they had entered into close proximity of the conclave, neither of them had felt any symptoms.[245] Just as Jesus Christ had not feared touching the lepers[246] neither would they fear contracting the virus.

John reflected on the last scroll he had delivered to Pope Innocent. It warned him to "Remain in Rome and prepare to carry your cross." However, he hardly wished to interfere with the pope's emergency evacuation. The holy man was in agony. Now, in the absence of the pontiff and with the College of Cardinals wiped out, John realized that extreme evil would rush to fill the vacuum of sanctity at the Vatican.[247]

After an hour of prayer, John spoke up. "Henri?"

Father Blanc roused from his meditations, "Yes?"

"You know, the Vatican is in chaos."

"Who leads the Church, now?"

"The authority has not yet passed to me."

"Then what should we do?"

"Pray for Pope Innocent, his cardinals and the Church. I had prayed that he would never leave Vatican City. His departure has created a vacuum that will attract a vicious evil. So, there is an urgency now, like never before."

"Tell me what I need to do. I will follow wherever you lead."

"But you are not meant to follow me. You are a man of war."

"Oh, no. There was a time when I could scratch my way to the top of any heap. Those days are long past, now."

Pope Innocent coughed, rousing one of the doctors out of his chair. The physician rushed to the pontiff's side, lifted his head, and pressed a cup of water to his blistered lips. Soon, the pontiff rejoined his fellow patients in the unconscious numbness of their sedated struggle to live.

The two doctors did not question that the N1656 virus had struck at the conclave. They agreed with the scientific community, around the world, that had embraced the research conclusions of Thas-subsidized scientists.

Occasionally, though, researchers or reporters would come upon evidence that brought doubt to the consensus view. Before their criticisms could be widely circulated, however, those skeptics always succumbed to the virus.

Still, no one in this rail car protected himself from the contagion. Each would accept God's will, whatever the outcome.

When the physician returned to his seat, John asked Henri, "Are you aware of the prophecies regarding the Great Monarch?"[248]

"No, I don't think so."

"He will be a descendent of Charlemagne, Pepin, and Clovis … the French Kings."

"And?"

"You fit that description."

Blanc smiled, slightly. On any other occasion, he would have laughed. "You must be listening to my mother. She told me such fairy tales."

Henri fondly remembered those peaceful and secure moments, a lifetime ago. He was an imaginative boy urged on by his loving mother. Each evening, putting him to bed, she would tell another tall tale of Henri's heroic ancestors and his own heroic future. Undoubtedly, the absorbed mythologies later contributed to his relentless ambition, as a young man, to improve the world through computer advancements. Over time, however, he learned that his own inventions were no longer a force for good. They were furthering the cause of centralized power and the suppression of individual liberties. Eventually, he realized that there can be no heroic future, without God.

John persisted, "Amongst the birch trees of Westphalia, the Great Monarch will fight his greatest battles."

"There, you see? I've never even visited Germany."

"His symbol will be the lily, a white lily."

"Yes, of course, Blanc means white."

"And the *fleur de lis* was the symbol of the House of Bourbon, of which you are also a descendent."

"Again, fanciful stories to make a little boy feel like a king. Today, I only wish for God's favor."

"The Great Monarch will put down the revolt in France…"

"What revolt?"

"… and be lame afoot."

Blanc sighed. "I don't understand your point. Surely you must be thinking of someone else. I am fit from top to toe, and I am certainly not a warrior."

"You are probably right. I am just struck by the coincidences. However, the Great Monarch will be lame … and with that disability, he will discover his greatest abilities and produce his greatest accomplishments."

"Accomplishments?"

"He is predestined by God for the defense of the one, holy, catholic and apostolic Church, and he will submit all other kingdoms to his scepter. He will be victorious and prosperous as long as he remains faithful to the Holy Roman See, but he will be rudely punished every time he becomes unfaithful to his vocation.[249]

"He shall extend his dominion over all, and assist the pope with the reformation of the whole earth. Many princes and nations that are living in error and impiety shall be converted, and an admirable peace will reign among men because the wrath of God shall be appeased through their repentance, penance and good works. But after a time, fervor shall cool, iniquity shall abound, and moral corruption shall become worse than ever. This shall bring on upon mankind the last and worst persecution of Antichrist."[250]

Henri Blanc thought for a moment, absorbing all that those prophecies revealed. Then he said, "As a prayer warrior or a battle warrior, I am prepared to follow wherever you lead me, because I know that path leads to Christ."[251]

AS THE 677 MILE JOURNEY neared its end, the train rolled through the birch tree forests of Westphalia and eventually into a rail yard in Cologne Germany.[252] Though it was after midnight, a crane operator was there, ready to lift the intermodal rail car from the train and lower it onto the flatbed of a truck that immediately rumbled out of the yard.

A half hour later, they arrived at their destination: The historic Cathedral of Cologne.

The truck driver backed up to one of the rear doors in a darkened corner of the church grounds. Then a group of doctors, priests and nuns rushed out to help make the transfer as quickly and inconspicuously as possible.

To John and Henri, it appeared that the Germans knew what they were doing and the patients were stable but unconscious from the doctors' sedatives. So, they simply stayed out of the way as the sick were transferred to a secret bunker in the basement of the cathedral.

Last out, Henri jumped from the back of the trailer. In midair, however, he was struck by an awesome vision. Blessed Mother appeared before him, in all her beauty and grandeur.

He was overwhelmed with joy when she reached out to him, saying that she recognized his purity.

He hardly noticed an angel approaching until he touched the sinew of Blanc's hip, just as he had done to Jakob. Immediately, a flash of intense pain radiated through Henri's side.

When Father Blanc hit the ground, he almost screamed, but he did not want to draw attention to himself. He could have called out for a doctor to assist. But he didn't.

Henri struggled back to his feet, realizing that the visions were gone, the pain remained, and he would never walk the same again.[253]

Oh, what a horrible v sion I see!
A great revolution is going on in Rome!
They are entering the Vatican...
Oh God! Oh God!
What a horrible scene! How dreadful!
Blessed Elena Aiello

Chapter 50
Vatican City
July 7

From the steps of St. Peter's Basilica, Evan Thas proudly gazed through his acrylic face mask and out over the *piazza*. The area was empty because the residents of Vatican City had fled in panic, after the horrific tragedy at the conclave of cardinals. Without a pope to protect, even the Pontifical Swiss Guard Corps had taken flight.

To most people, it seemed that no one in the world could conquer this ravaging pandemic except Dr. Evan Thas. So, no one argued with him when he promised that he would rid the Vatican of the virus and return the Church to the people. But he also warned that he would not tolerate interference from anyone. So, just in case, he and his 1,400 Perfective Patrollers carried firearms.

Evan has insisted that they all wear haz-mat protective clothing and breathing equipment for the benefit of the viewing audience because his every move, today, would be taped and broadcast to a global audience that was hungering for answers.

And Evan now had all the answers he needed from mining the massive data banks of the Cyst-Blanc supercomputers.

There, neatly tucked away, he had accumulated information on everyone who had used the CyBot search engine and everyone who had submitted to Titan analysis. Now, he knew that a third of the population had reached a breaking point. They were ready to follow a military dictator, a political king, or a religious savior. Better yet, they could follow Evan and get all three in the deal.

With just a third of the population, committed to him, Evan would have the critical mass that was necessary for a successful rebellion. Even though another third might rise up against him, Evan could count on the final third being afraid to commit to anything except fear. So, using the elements of surprise and ruthless execution, Thas felt that the world was ripe for the picking.

Just one last ingredient was needed for his explosive mixture: a focal point of blame. So, like an arsonist with a magnifying glass, focusing the sun's rays on forest leaves, Evan began igniting the wildfire.

THAS GAVE A NODDING SIGNAL and four of his men began pounding the Basilica's historic, bronze Holy Door with a battering ram. It would have been easier to use another entrance. After all, the Holy Door was ceremonially bricked on the inside because it is only opened every 25 years. But this grand entrance would add significance to Evan's grand conquest. He also wanted to make the point that it was useless to try to lock him out of anything.

So, the Patrollers battered the repeatedly before it opened. In the process, most of its priceless bronze panels, that depicted various Biblical scenes, were pummeled beyond recognition. It was a fitting preview of what Thas planned to do to all things Biblical.

Once the door had been pounded open, Evan strutted into the largest church in Christendom, with his cameraman following. Exhibiting the confidence of a king at court, he strolled through the aisles, unimpressed with Michelangelo's *Pieta'*, sneering at Cambio's bronze statue of St. Peter, but then admiring Bernini's immense Baroque *baldachino* over the main altar.

Thas mounted steps and quietly stood behind the pontifical altar, allowing time for his 1,400 soldiers and lone cameraman to take their positions in the pews. Then, when all were seated, Evan removed his haz-mat head gear, shocking many of his followers. His face displayed supreme confidence, demonstrating that he did not fear the virus. But his heavy makeup was beginning to give way to his perspiration.

"Do not worry for me," he shouted from the altar. "Already, I have purified this place. In fact, you also are safe."

Evan's not-so-bright soldiers removed their breathing masks, smiling and nodding to signal their complete amazement at the boss's abilities.

"I made two promises before I arrived: First, that I would make the Vatican safe again. You see how easy that was for me?"

His compliant audience nodded and laughed.

These 1,400 men were top leaders in the Perfective Patrol, not because of their abilities or accomplishments, but because of their Titan-tested weaknesses. In fact, they would never have lasted in any disciplined military. They were lovers of themselves and of money, boastful, proud, abusive, ungrateful, unholy, loveless, unforgiving, slanderous, without self-control, brutal, haters of good, treacherous, rash, conceited, and lovers of pleasure rather than of God.[254] They followed

Evan, religiously, because he alone promised to feed their every addiction.[255]

Holding up a Bible with his left hand – his good one – Evan proclaimed, "I swear by this Bible that I have been sent to chastise a corrupt age, and I cleansed this corrupt temple of its viral affliction because God is with me, God is in me, and God is on my side.[256] This heretic church has propagated lies for two thousand years. So, I want to leave no doubt that I speak for the Holy Spirit[257] when I tell you that God struck down the diabolical leadership of this church of thieves."

The Patrollers applauded and cheered as Evan wiped some of the sweat from his brow.

"That leads me to my second promise: To return the church to the people. But how can that be accomplished? After all, these pious bandits have been fleecing the flock for thousands of years. How can it all be returned to the people?"

His audience hooted their approval. They did not care that, sweating profusely, Evan had lost almost all of his make-up and his face now revealed repulsive burn scars.

The camera tightened on Evan's ravaged face. "Anyone who has ears to hear, let him hear that I have been sent to those who have less than they want. In fact, I have been sent to proclaim a new Commandment."

Thas smiled as he scanned his Patrollers.

"Take!" he shouted. "Take what was stolen from you!"

When the cheering subsided, Evan focused his eyes deep into the camera lens, knowing that an estimated two billion people were watching, around the world.

"The Jews await the coming of Messiah … the Muslims, the return of the Twelfth Imam … the Christians, the Second Coming of Christ."

Then standing at the papal altar – directly above the grave

of St. Peter – the Abomination that causes Desolation[258] proclaimed: "I am who I am!"[259]

With those words, Evan Thas unleashed his diabolical
army on St. Peter's Basilica and all of Vatican City. For three
days, everything of economic value was stolen; everything of
artistic value was destroyed; everything of Spiritual value was
desecrated.[260] The demons that had inspired the sack of Rome
in 1527 returned to finish the work they had started.[261]

Consecrated Hosts were tossed into toilets, priceless artworks were hammered, and apostolic relics were trampled
upon. Pews in the Sistine Chapel were piled high and set on
fire. The papal residence became a brothel and urine and ex-
crement covered all that was once pure.

With its flames fanned by greed and envy, diabolical nihil-
ism became a raging wildfire. Immediately, around the world,
Catholic churches, schools, monasteries, convents, and even
hospitals came under attack by looting hordes.[262] All Catholic
property was considered free for the taking, and the spiritual
contagion spread quickly to attacks on Protestant churches and
Jewish synagogues. Good people cowered in fear as evil ones
took control. Even the twelve Apostles of the Latter Times
went into hiding, recognizing that now was not the time to
confront the demonic forces that had become unleashed. It
was the beginning of The Warning[263] to the world that had
been prophesied.

Within three days, almost every Christian and Jewish
place of worship had been ransacked and robbed. Most had
been burned.

Across Europe, a lawless spirit of disorder reigned supreme with overthrow as its primary goal. The blood of priests
and religious soaked the Italian soil.[264] France descended into
frightful anarchy and civil war in which even old men took up

arms.[265] Around the world, the young rose up against the old, and the base against the honorable.[266]

XBC News covered the mayhem, around the clock. They emphasized that the outrage of the masses finally had come to a boil because Christianity is anti-science and, consequently, the antithesis of Perfection.

Evan's reporters claimed that the people had come to the realization that their pastors, priests and rabbis were not seeking a Perfect World at all. That was evident from the fact that many of them had even fought the inoculation program that was designed to save lives.

Instead, it was claimed that religious leaders had always oppressed the people and that religion had become one big money grab. Consequently, giving to the church was no longer considered virtuous. Taking from it was the new virtue, and a small but significant portion of the population immediately embraced the opportunity to effect a virtuous redistribution of wealth.

Those crimes became so numerous that many were classified as "justifiable" and given a low priority for prosecution. Still, adding another element of fear and uncertainty, most people who had gained notoriety by denouncing the looting had been struck down by the virus. So, it seemed that Evan was right when he claimed that God was on the side of the takers.

However, property crimes were not the only ones being committed. Here and there, priests and nuns were tortured, rabbis were murdered, pastors were beaten, and all of them were made destitute.[267] There was no limit to the diabolical frenzy, and clergy members were forced to go into hiding. Around the world, the holy Mass could only be offered in secret.[268]

For a century, communists had slaughtered based on class, Nazis had slaughtered based on race and, now, Perfectives would slaughter based on religion. Every act of violence, destruction or theft was being done in the spirit of Evan's teachings: Clear out the Imperfect, to make way for the Perfect.

When three days of global attacks against all things sacred had expired, Evan convened his newly named college of cardinals.[269] He was aware of a substantial public backlash against the violence because he always monitored information flows on the Internet. So, Thas broadcast a global call for peace on XBC News, claiming that the excesses had been committed by evil opponents who were trying to discredit his rise so that the world would return to the old, failed beliefs of the past. As planned, rising above the fray and playing the peace-making victim effectively exonerated him from culpability in the public eye.

Now, in total control of Vatican City, his band of barbarians convened a mock conclave of cardinals and elected the successor to St. Peter. Then Thas designated himself "Universal Bishop," thus negating the authority of every other bishop,[270] and announced that the Sacramental duties of priests, around the world, were no longer honored by God.[271] The sacrifice of the Mass by mere priests, now, was outlawed.[272] He also forbid public prayers,[273] proclaiming that the Good Shepherd, alone, would be responsible for prayers and Sacraments,[274] and that he would lead the flock with the only appropriate name: Pope Jesus II.[275]

They rush upon the city;
they run along the wall.
They climb into the houses;
like thieves they enter through the windows.
Before them the earth shakes,
the sky trembles,
the sun and moon are darkened,
and the stars no longer shine.
Joel 2:9-10

Chapter 51
Various Locations
July 10 – The First Day

nside the Cave of Secrets, Evan studied Huntington Cyst's
lost look as the reflected flames wavered in his vacant blue
eyes. *He doesn't seem to care. Maybe, this is what Huntie
wants.* Still, Evan's crippled right hand did not tighten its grip
on the knife.

"Do it," Faridah urged, revealing the sinister instructions
of her inner voices.

Evan turned to examine her wide-eyed intensity. Then he
remembered Cyst's warning: "Once I am gone, she will attempt to find and control you. Do not trust her."

Unexpectedly, the three of them heard, from above, men
shouting angrily at each other.

One of the Perfective Patrollers – the leader with the
bulls-eye tattoo around his eye – had felt threatened when he
heard Faridah tell Evan, "They don't matter anymore." He
had witnessed Evan's standard operating procedures in which
expendable people were … expended. So, after Evan, Huntie
and Faridah descended into the cave, he confronted Pruflas

with angry questions.

That was a mistake.

Evan and his mother looked up to the oculus when they heard the shouting.

Then they heard a shot.

Suddenly, like firecrackers on New Year's Eve, a deafening hail of rapid-fire gunshots – dozens, then hundreds – echoed from outside the cave.

Huntington Cyst did not notice the blasts, nor the knife at his chest, nor the golden Ark in the corner of the cave. His mind was too numbed by his diet of narcotics.

"Do it!" Faridah screamed. "Do it now, dammit! Conjure the demons!"

Evan froze, still mesmerized by the bright oculus and the unseen violence above. Then he felt her hands around his. Evan did not fight her, but neither did he want this. She groaned the growl of a ravenous predator, shoved with all her might and, together, they plunged the dagger into Huntington Cyst's heart.

Evan focused on Cyst's weary blue eyes, as life left them. He released his hold on the knife and his adoptive father collapsed on the dirt floor.

Taking a moment to absorb what he had done, Evan then inhaled deeply and, as he exhaled, whispered, "It is finished."

The little humanity that was left in him felt repulsed. Of course, by now, Thas had murdered many thousands of innocent victims. This act, however, was much more personal than wiping out anonymous people with a few strokes on a keyboard.

"We did it!" Faridah shouted.

Evan was not listening.

She was ecstatic, screaming her ignorant assumptions into

the shining oculus. "We killed the Apostle. We destroyed the Church. We completed the ritual. I fulfilled my promises to you, Satan! Now, fulfill yours to me!"

A promise from Satan.

She should have known.

Suddenly, she saw a spectacular burst of light and heard a jarring, thunderous roar. Then the oculus darkened, the candle flames extinguished and – unlike any event in human history – the light of the world vanished.

God's warnings and merciful patience ended.

The prophesied Three Days of Darkness began.[276]

IN COLOGNE CATHEDRAL'S BASEMENT, moments earlier, John knelt next to a cot, holding Pope Innocent's blistered and bleeding hand while praying only that God's Will be done. Standing nearby, the German doctors, priests and nuns realized they could do nothing more, except pray. The pontiff had become unresponsive, even though his heart monitor continued to beep steadily.

At the back of the room, Father Blanc gave instructions to a priest regarding the burial of the four cardinals who already had passed away. However, he refused to mention anything about Innocent's burial arrangements, holding out for a miracle.

The interments, Blanc emphasized, would have to be done under the cover of darkness. After all, their presence in Cologne must continue to be kept secret. No one, outside this small group, knew that any of them had survived.

The secrecy was necessary because the ruthless takeover of the Vatican had signaled a new period of evil in the ascendency. If Pope Innocent died, then John would indeed rise to the chair of St. Peter. So, more than ever, he would need protection.

For three days, this group had hunkered down, locked in the basement, while looters pillaged the cathedral. The vandals did not try to burn down the church that once boasted the tallest spires and the largest church facade in the world. Instead, they took everything of economic value. They even dragged away the triple sarcophagus that is believed to contain the remains of the Biblical Magi. Certainly, the thieves were not interested in stealing it because of its reputation as the world's largest reliquary. Instead, they would certainly tear it apart, retrieving its gold and silver overlay, its 1000 jewels, and its ancient cameos. The rest of the sarcophagus and its contents then would be dumped.[277]

The ransacking of the church, however, had not been this group's most serious concern. They were more worried about the survival of their holy patients. Now, only Innocent clung to life.

Blanc made his way to John's side and patted him on the shoulder. "You need rest. I'll stay with him."

Before John could respond, Innocent coughed, drawing their attention to him. Then the pope slightly opened his eyes. He squeezed John's hand and stared, briefly, first at John and then at Henri. He seemed to strengthen and a smile broadened his lips as he said, "Soon, everything will be good."

Slowly, he closed his eyes and the heart monitor beeped erratically as he peacefully passed into eternity, smiling.

During John's long life, he had never seen anything like this. The Holy Father and the Princes of Christ's Church were no more.

A doctor disconnected the heart monitor, nodding to confirm death.

One of the nuns lost control of herself and began crying, but everyone else dropped to their knees and prayed for the souls of Pope Innocent and all those defenders of the faith who had died.

A moment later, Henri Blanc rose, realizing what must be done. He addressed the Beloved Apostle: "John, son of Zebedee and Salome, you have received the required number of votes from the college of cardinals. Do you accept your election as pope?"

John continued kneeling and holding Pope Innocent's hand. "I do."

"Then by what name do you wish to be called?"

He paused and then asked, "What is the official name of this cathedral?"

One of the German priests answered, "The High Cathedral of Saints Peter and Mary."

John bowed his head. Moments passed.

Then Blanc prompted, "Holy Father?"

Finally, John answered with confidence, "I shall be Peter II."[278]

Blanc stepped over and separated the hands of the old and new popes. Then he removed Innocent's Ring of the Fisherman and placed it on the third finger of John's right hand. He knew that there would be no need for Holy Orders nor even a consecration to be named Bishop of Rome because John had been among the first to receive those sacred honors from Jesus Christ, Himself.

Blanc turned to announce the ceremonial proclamation, *"Habemus Papem!"*[279] But before he could utter a word, suddenly, there was a spectacular burst of light, a jarring, thunderous roar, and the light of the world vanished.

†††

IN PROVIDENCE HOSPITAL, moments earlier, President Angela Concepcion's groan became a scream as she pushed even harder.

"That's good," the doctor encouraged. "You're almost there. Give me one more push."

She panted, "Give me just a minute."

This was not how Angela had planned it. She should be happy, right now. Instead, she couldn't get selfish Fred off her mind. He should have shown up for this, even if just for the appearance of it. But, true to form, he was too busy pouting that this baby would impose on his comfortable lifestyle. It was ... inconvenient.

Deep down, though, she knew she couldn't be too hard on Fred. After all, she was once just like him. Now, however, she had matured into understanding the beauty – the importance – of life. It was the gift that she had always rejected. Now, this new life had changed her life. From now on, she understood that there will be something more important than herself.

In her hand, Angela squeezed hard on a memento from her mother. "Okay," she warned. Then she heaved one more time with a grunt.

"Here she comes!" the doctor said. "I've got her. I've got her."

The nurses in the room applauded. One wiped the sweat off her brow and said, "You did great, Madame President."

The medical team went through the procedures that they had executed over a hundred times and then presented the baby girl to her mother.

Angela wiped tears from her eyes. "I can't believe I'm so overwhelmed. She's so beautiful."

Angela's embarrassment over her sentimentality disappeared. Then the proud mother said, "Look at her," as she held the naked baby up. "She's perfect!"

With a lot of nodding smiles, the nurses began to clear out equipment and clean up the facilities.

The doctor said, "Madame President, we'll get you up to your room shortly. There are some details to take care of, first. So, we'll let you and your little princess get to know each other in private for a few minutes."

Angela nodded as they left the room. She cradled the baby at her breast and could not believe her happiness. There had been times, over the past few years, when she thought she might never be happy again. Now, however, the problems of the world did not seem so intractable as she imagined how this new life in her hands might eventually make the world a better place.

Then Angela opened her right hand – the one that she had gripped so tightly during the delivery – and admired what she had been squeezing.

It was her mother's old Rosary.

Angela did not know why she had brought it to the hospital. Perhaps it was a just a good luck charm. More likely, however, she knew that, if there is a heaven, her mother was looking down with pride. After so many years of denying and defying God's gift of innocent life, Angela felt blessed.

The loving mother tickled her baby's tummy until she elicited her first giggle.

Then, suddenly: a spectacular burst of light; a jarring, thunderous roar; and the light of the world vanished.[280]

Suddenly I saw the complete condition of my soul
as God sees it.
I could clearly see all that is displeasing to God.
I did not know that even the smallest transgressions
will have to be accounted for.
What a moment! Who can describe it?
To stand before the Thrice-Holy-God!
St. Maria Faustina Kowalska

Chapter 52
Various Locations
Over the Next 3 Days

A ngela Concepcion clutched her baby and her Rosary, but she could see neither. Terror filled her heart.
She might have suspected going blind, but she knew
that she had not. The darkness was like none that she had
experienced before, so dense that it could be felt, shrouding a
malevolence that could be sensed.

Angela wanted to cry out for her Secret Service Agents
but realized that no one would heed her call. She did not believe her shouts would penetrate this sinister cloud.

If not for her precious baby, she would have felt completely alone.[281]

Is this a dream?

The darkness was too profound to describe, too mysterious for human comprehension.

Still, Angela's newborn baby felt and sounded content in
her arms, seemingly shielded by its innocence.

To Angela, it appeared that the world had come to a stand-
still.[282]

Then something jolted her and she gasped, in panic.

Angela felt a profound Illumination of Conscience, suddenly seeing herself as God sees her.[283] The experience horrified Angela, searing her conscience[284] in the burning fire of Divine Truth.[285] She felt alone with her conscience before God, exposed for all of her sins and the evils that her sins had caused.[286]

Angela experienced the Illumination as a horrible punishment – self-inflicted, not from God – because she felt excruciating shame for the unrelenting selfishness of her life. However, she had no doubt that this moment was being shared with God, whose unfathomable love had always been available to her, but always rejected by her.

Angela was overwhelmed by something more profound than sorrow because, for the first time, she could offer no charming excuses, no eloquent diversions. Deep in her heart, she judged herself guilty before God and worthy of hell.

THE FLAMES FLICKERED in front of the picture of the Sacred Heart of Jesus as John began another decade of the Rosary. Though Cologne and Germany and the world had become blanketed in black, these blessed candles illuminated the room.[287] They offered this small group not only the security of sight, but also the assurance that prophecies from God, presently, were being fulfilled.

This scene, however, was not unlike what was happening in countless homes around the world. The Apostles of the Latter Days had spread the word on what to expect, and believers had shared their messages with the faithful. Like an Internet video, gone viral, the warnings of the Three Days of Darkness had spread from believer to believer, across the globe, and each one prepared with an arsenal of Sacramentals, Bibles, blessed candles, food and water.

Here, in the basement of the Cathedral, the clerics and medics knelt, praying the deepest prayers of their lives. Their petitions to God were no longer focused on the souls of the pope and cardinals who had died from what they thought had been a viral outbreak. Those good men were reaping the rewards of their holy lives, now.

Neither were their prayers focused on themselves, because they already had received comfort. More than ever before, the Illumination of Conscience had revealed to them a sublime affirmation that they were the recipients of God's love and approval.

Instead, they directed their intercessory appeals to The Almighty for the conversion of the indifferent of the world. Though these prayer partners knew that some lost souls would forever side with sin, they understood that others had lived lives of distraction, ignorant of their God-given opportunities. Like alcoholics or addicts, hitting rock bottom would be a necessary step on their road to recovery.

God, Himself, had pronounced a stern warning against lukewarm believers, stating that, because they are neither hot or cold, He would spew them out of His mouth![288] However, these prayer warriors trusted God's Mercy and knew that He would forgive, if each would only ask. They trusted the words of St. James, when he wrote, "The prayer of a righteous man is powerful and effective."[289] They were confident in God's promise: "If my people, who are called by My name, will humble themselves and pray and seek my face and turn from their wicked ways, then will I hear from heaven and will forgive their sin and will heal their land."[290]

For the lukewarm of the world, this holy gathering prayed for the fulfillment of God's promise to Ezekiel: "I will give them a new heart and put a new spirit within them; I will remove the stony heart from their bodies, and replace it with a natural heart, so that they will live according to my statutes, and observe and carry out my ordinances; thus they shall be my people and I will be their God."[291]

So, for three days, they would remain here in prayer, because they knew the prophecies warned that no one will survive who opens their windows or ventures out into the darkness. Still, they were comforted by the assurance that those who remain where they are, pray the Rosary and beg God for mercy will be protected.[292]

INSIDE THE CAVE OF SECRETS, Faridah crawled into a corner and trembled. She did not know where Evan was and she did not care. The blackness commanded her complete attention.

Though she could not see, her wicked spirit sensed what was happening, around the world.

Not a demon was left in Hell and the atmosphere had become infested with innumerable fiends that were causing the deaths of many incredulous and wicked people.[293] Around her, spirits caused the air to resound with shocking blasphemies, and agonizing screams resonated in the dark fog. But she could not be sure of whether they were from human or demonic origin.

Then, a terrible and violent wind broke out, sounding like roaring lions, and Faridah perceived the fear of the world as furious hurricanes ravaged the earth.[294] Lightning struck so forcefully that it penetrated the cave walls and the earth, itself, thundered and trembled.[295]

Faridah discerned the distress of nations, bewildered by

the roaring of the sea and waves, shocked that, as oceans cast their foaming waves over the land, the planet was becoming an immense cemetery.[296]

She knew that even the most hardened of men were fainting from fear in expectation of things to come. She cowered in her cave's corner, knowing that the very powers of heaven had been shaken.[297]

However, while the Illumination of Conscience caused millions of lost souls to die of remorse, instantly, Faridah would not be so simply defeated. She – just like her son – had suppressed, smothered and suffocated her conscience[298] to such an extent that it no longer could restrain her rebellious nature.

Faridah was terrified, but she and Evan had prepared for this day, also.

Between the cries of 'Everything is lost,'
and 'Everything is saved,'
there will scarcely be any interval.[299]
Abbe Souffrand

Around the world, the light returned, after 72 hours of darkness.[300] It seemed brighter, clearer, purer, than before and, unlike with the dawn of past ages, it awakened no one, except Spiritually.

For the past three days, people had not slept. In every country, on every hill, in every valley, those who had called on the name of the Lord, lived.[301] Death, on the other hand, welcomed those who did not.

Each had been stunned by the sudden certainty that God truly exists.[302] However, many could not live with the shock of discovering that God's Justice is inevitable. In the light of ultimate Truth, they understood that their choices in life had rightly earned them eternal damnation.

Along the roads and on the beaches, their bodies now littered the landscape.[303] Over a three day period, the world's population had been reduced by a third – more than two billion people.[304] Still, for those lost souls, not a tear would be shed. They were among the unloving and unloved. Living selfishly, their existence had been barren, devoid of love, because they had resisted God for a lifetime. Consequently, they had not been able to bear their Illumination of Conscience. Now, He would resist them for an eternity.

Throughout their lives, they had been given countless opportunities to open their hearts. Still, they cast their lot with Satan and had loved only pleasure and money. They had been boastful, proud, abusive, disobedient, ungrateful, unholy, unforgiving, slanderous, without self-control, brutal, treacherous, rash and conceited.[305] They had brought many evils into their own lives and countless sufferings into the lives of others.

Like gold in the purifying fire, the Three Days of Darkness had separated the priceless souls from the worthless ones. Those who previously had embraced God's love, found the mysterious event to be an awesome affirmation of God's presence, bringing them even closer to Him. However, those who had knowingly and deliberately rejected God's love were irretrievably lost. Consequently, their influence had been removed from the earth so that life there might become what God desired it to be.

Still, another large group remained alive. They had wandered through life, distracted and ignorant, neither rejecting nor accepting the Lord. The Darkness had terrified them, but they emerged into the light with a blessing: the knowledge that God had been merciful.

So, their trials on earth would continue except, this time, with the undeniable comprehension of God's love and almighty power. Those who had stubbornly ignored God throughout their lives felt a deep sense of gratitude for His abundant mercies. However, with knowledge comes responsibility and, now, they knew the eternal Truth. Never again would ignorance excuse their sins and shield them from Judgment.

✝✝✝

ANGELA SHOUTED, "Anderson?"

He had been standing outside her hospital room door. However, her Secret Service agent did not respond.

"Anybody ... can you hear me? I need help."

She gently rocked the baby that rested in her arms and waited for a response.

None was heard.

Still, Angela smiled, remembering how amazingly calm the infant had remained throughout the incredible ordeal. The screams and groans in the night did not bother her. The quakes that seemed to rattle the entire earth and every building on it, did not make her cry. Born on the eve of darkness, the little one did not fear it. Instead, she remained comforted in Angela's embrace, contented to be loved, with food no farther away than her mother's breast.

The eerie quiet seemed unnatural. The president noticed that she did not hear the traffic noise outside that had seemed unrelenting before the darkness.

"Hello?" she called out, again.

Moments later, Angela sighed and asked, "Okay, God, what do we do, now?"

It would have been an unthinkable question, for her, just a few months ago. She chuckled at herself, thinking that God became her new chief of staff. *After all, who could be better qualified?*

Her three days of trials had helped her to understand the qualities that she had respected in Rebekah Emunah. For the first time, Angela felt not only certainty but wisdom. However, it was more than just a feeling, this time.

In the past, her emotions and feelings had always led her astray because they had been rooted in selfishness. Now, her concerns were not for herself but truly for others. There was a cohesion to the principles that her loving and merciful God had revealed. A communion – an interconnectedness – of all human life existed and, at the heart of it, was the most profound love.

Once, she would have questioned God's right to judge mankind. Now, however, she had glimpsed the undeniable mercy of His justice. If anything, she would have been less merciful.

Angela rolled out of the bed, slid her feet into hospital slippers, and snuggled her baby between two pillows. Then she wrapped her hospital gown around herself, shuffled to a cabinet, and scrounged until she found sanitary wipes and a disposable diaper.

Back at her bed, the president smiled as she changed a horribly malodorous diaper, for the first time, while two fascinated brown eyes watched. Never before would she have tolerated such a degradation. Now it was a joy.

As Angela rolled up the dirty diaper and tossed it into a trash can, Mercedes Dare had done the same, in a Montana cabin. Mer gently hugged her infant and cooed, "You're such a big boy."

Angela lifted her little girl and whispered, "My *chiquita*."

Cradling the baby in her arms, Angela turned to the door and took a deep breath. Then she shuffled away, in search of the remains of humanity.

WHEN THE LIGHT RETURNED to Cologne Cathedral, it welcomed the dawn of the reign of the most controversial pontiff, Pope Peter II.

John Eben Malek had been convicted of murdering of a nun. Rumors still circulated that he had been complicit in the attack on the Saudi Royal Family that had triggered the global economic meltdown. He had escaped from prison just hours before his planned execution and was now a fugitive from justice, subject to extradition in many countries around the world.

Still, those facts had not deterred Pope Innocent XIV nor the Church's College of Cardinals. They trusted that John was Christ's Beloved Apostle and they were ready to stand with him, leading Christ's Church.

For the first time in his lengthy existence, John had found a support network that could not be easily dismissed. They were intelligent, credible and holy men, capable of influencing global conversions in unprecedented numbers.

But, now, they were dead.

Rousing from their meditations in the church basement, the small group that had prayed continuously with John began to gather their belongings. They had feared nothing during the Darkness because they had prepared. But there was nothing more they could do for the deceased pontiff and cardinals. So, they would return to their families and assist the living.

When John looked down on Innocent's body, he felt a stabbing solitude. Once again, he was alone on earth. The strain was almost too much to bear.

Yet, as always, he would continue.

He knew that the vast majority of the enemies of the Church had perished in the darkness.[306] As horrifying as it had been, though, John realized that they had only witnessed a minor demonstration of the awesome power of almighty God.

So, the trials would continue, and ignorant indifference would no longer suffice. Now, the lukewarm would have to choose either to accept or reject God's mercy.[307]

There was no doubt that Pope Peter II had been chosen to

lead the Church through its most difficult days.[308] More than ever, he would need the assistance of his Latter Day Apostles. John's first order of business, however, was to arrange a simple but appropriate funeral. It would be the first of many to come.

The lonely pontiff jolted when he felt a hand on his shoulder. It was Father Blanc's. "Your Holiness, is there anything I can do?"

The Beloved Apostle turned to study the man who appeared to be flinching from concealed pain.

"Yes." Pope Peter breathed a long, deep sigh. "There is quite a lot you will do."

SUDDENLY, the oculus brightened and the cave lightened.

Faridah crawled out of her corner. "Evan?"

She heard no response.

"Evan, where are you?"

Shabaan struggled to her feet and brushed the dirt off her pants. She squinted to study her surroundings: the oculus, the rope ladder dangling from it to the altar and, in the far corner, the Ark of the Covenant. Then she thought she saw something move, in the darkness, beyond the Ark.

"Evan?"

Slowly, she crept toward the movement.

"Evan, answer me."

She inched closer to the darkness. Then she saw him on the floor, pushed against the farthest wall and curled into a fetal position. His terrified eyes were focused on the Ark.

"Are you alright?"

Evan's breathing was rapid. His body shook with fear.

"What's wrong? Are you injured?"

He curled even more tightly, into his protective ball. "It tried to kill me," he whispered.

"What … what tried to kill you?"

With the slightest motion, he pointed his forefinger at the Ark, too afraid to speak its name.

When she realized that he was only weak with fear, Faridah became angry. "Stop it!" she shouted.

Haltingly, he whispered, "During the darkness … I … I … accidentally touched it." Then, he growled, "It tried to rip out my soul."

She turned to study the gold box that, long ago, Cyst had warned her not to touch. He had told her that only Henri Blanc could handle it.

"Get up!" she demanded. "We succeeded. We lived through it all. Now, imagine what we can do."

He loosened a bit, "But our followers are dead."

"I know," she answered, "but we control the Ark. We'll find more followers."

Evan showed some reassurance. "They're such fools."

"Think of it, Evan. Our enemies are dead, too." She sneered, "Melnikov … you could never trust him. Even the Legion … backstabbers … they're all gone." She laughed, "You won't have to share the world with them. You control it all."

Evan sat up, adjusted his eye patch and wiped his sweaty, scarred face. "I still have Glass Andalusian."

"That's right." She became stern, again. "Now, get up and act like a man."

As he rose to his feet and brushed himself off, she added, "Never let anyone see you cower like that again."

Dutifully, he followed his mother to the oculus as she lectured him. "Only the weak are left. You can take what you want." Without a care, she shoved the bloody body of Huntington Cyst out of her way, slid onto the altar and began climbing the rope ladder. "You don't even need Angela. You are the most powerful force on earth."

Faridah spoke with the certainty that everything was working out, exactly as Satan had promised.

From the altar top, Evan followed closely behind her, up the ladder. When she crawled out of the hole, she turned to help pull him up. Then, on their feet, they studied the area, outside.

In and around the vehicles, all of their men lay, dead. It made little difference whether they had been victims of lethal gunfire or the deadly Illumination of Conscience, the result was the same.

Evan watched as his mother wandered through the vehicles and eventually stood over the bullet-riddled bodies of Malphas and Pruflas. She paused for a moment, but seemed unmoved. Then she turned to Evan and barked, "Let's go!"

Immediately, however, he saw her jaw drop and her face turn ashen white. "Oh, no," she moaned. Her eyes fixated on something above and behind him.

Evan turned, looked up and gasped. He struggled to catch his breath as he remembered the prophecy that foretold what he was seeing. Dominating the sky, was the awesome, permanent, indestructible sign that could only have come from God.[309]

Go now, write it on a tablet for them,
inscribe it on a scroll,
that for the days to come
it may be an everlasting witness.
These are rebellious people,
deceitful children,
children unwilling to listen
to the Lord's instruction.
They say to the seers,
"See no more visions!"
and to the prophets,
"Give us no more visions of what is right!
Tell us pleasant things, prophesy illusions.
Leave this way, get off this path,
and stop confronting us
with the Holy One of Israel!"

Isaiah 30:8-11

NOTES

1   This vision happened 33 years, to the day, before the miracle of the sun at Fatima. As a result of this disturbing revelation, Pope Leo XIII wrote the Prayer to St. Michael the Archangel and ordered that it be said after every low Mass. That practice persisted around the world for eight decades. There are many sources for this story. This one came from http://prophecy.knightsoflasalette.org/2010/10/31/the-vision-of-pope-leo-xiii/

2   This mysterious international group of fictional power-players was founded by Dr. Henri Blanc, initially as a charitable entity. Blanc was Huntington Cyst's first partner and the brains behind the development of the Cyst-Blanc supercomputers that helped Cyst Industries gain its dominant position in controlling and monitoring Internet traffic. Cyst's relationship with Blanc deteriorated and eventually collapsed as he increasingly rejected Cyst's dark beliefs. Blanc returned to his Christian roots, however, and the Legion of Babylon now has perverted its original humanitarian mission.

3   St. Hyppolytus (d. 235) and St. Irenaeus (d. 200) both suggested that "Evanthas" is a name that corresponds to 666, the number that is representative of the Antichrist in the Book of Revelation. Thas is the second "beast" of Revelation 13:11, and following. His boyish looks make him look "like a lamb" but he speaks "like a dragon." "He exercised all the authority of the first beast (Huntington Cyst) whose fatal wound had been healed." Regarding the timing of the arrival of the Antichrist, St. John of the Cleft Rock (14th century) prophesied, "... twenty centuries after the Incarnation of the Word, the Beast will be incarnate in his turn, and will menace the earth with as many evils as the Divine Incarnation has brought it graces."

4   The following prophecies, and others, were used to construct the character and background of Faridah Shabaan. Various prophecies of visionaries and saints suggest that the mother of the Antichrist will be "... born of a Hebrew nun, a false virgin who will communicate with the old serpent, the master of impurity and his father will be B." (Our Lady of La Salette, 1846). Also, it is believed that the Antichrist will have Syrian roots. (See Isaiah 10:5.) Citing Luke 10:13, St. Zenobius prophesied that the son of perdition "will be born in Corozain, will be brought up in Bethsaida and shall begin to reign in Capharnaum (today's Capernaum), according to what Our Lord Jesus said in the Gospel: 'Woe to thee Corozain ... woe to thee Bethsaida ... and thou Capharnaum that art exalted up to heaven, thou shalt be thrust down to hell.'"

5   The Antichrist will have brothers according to one of the visionaries of La Salette (1846), Maximin Giraud: "He will have brethren, who will be children of evil but not incarnate devils like himself. Soon they will be at the head of armies,

supported by the legions of hell."

6   Huntington Cyst represents the "first beast whose fatal wound had been healed," mentioned in Revelation 13:11, and following. Known as the "Prophet of Technology," he prepared the path for Evan's arrival. He is the "False Prophet" mentioned in Revelation 16:13; 19:19-20; and 20:10.

7   The Antichrist's entrance to the world stage will be accompanied by false miracles, signs and wonders.(2 Thessalonians 2:9) He will speak boastfully. (Daniel 7:8; Revelation 13:5) He will blaspheme God. (Daniel 7:25; 11:36)

8   The author recommends a review of the endnotes of Chapter One, Book One, of this Trilogy for anyone who would like a concise summary of some of the prophecies of saints that describe the coming Antichrist. Some of those, as well as many other prophecies, will be cited during the course of this story.

9   In this story, Evan's father was B. Abu Ladin, a deceased terrorist. His character was patterned after deceased international terrorist, Abu Nidal.

10   Henri Blanc's conversion from darkness to light will play a significant role in this story.

11   These incantations are the converse of various prayers of Christian spiritual warfare, as well as the Prayer of St. Francis of Assisi.

12   The Three Days of Darkness have been prophesied in Scripture and by a surprising number of visionaries. A couple of the Scriptural prophecies are as follows: "Let all who live in the land tremble, for the day of the LORD is coming. It is close at hand—a day of darkness and gloom, a day of clouds and blackness." (Joel 2:1-2) "'In that day,' declares the Sovereign LORD, 'I will make the sun go down at noon and darken the earth in broad daylight. I will turn your religious feasts into mourning and all your singing into weeping.'" (Amos 8:9-10) Mystic and stigmatist, Marie-Julie Jahenny of La Fraudais offered numerous prophecies regarding "… three days of terrifying darkness,"
including, "The earth will be covered in darkness and hell will be loosed on earth." (September 20, 1882) "The crisis will explode suddenly; the punishments will be shared by all and will succeed one another without interruption." (January 4, 1884) More Scriptural prophecies, as well as detailed prophecies of saints, will be presented in later chapters.

13   In Hebrew, his name roughly translates, "John, Servant (or Messenger) of the King." John's character was established in Book One of this Trilogy. He is the Beloved Apostle who is still alive, guarding that "the gates of hell shall not prevail against" Christ's Church. This character's life is based on Jesus' words, "If I want him to remain alive until I return, what is that to you?" (John 21:22) Of course, he

is only a fictional device for the purpose of this story.

14   See Judges, chapter13 through 16.

15   The dark night of the soul was first described by St. John of the Cross, but other saints have described it similarly, including Therese of Lisieux, Mother Teresa of Calcutta and Padre Pio.

16   In "The Story of a Soul" this is a quote from St. Therese of Lisieux who, at the time, was no more than four years old.

17   The Catechism of the Catholic Church (2280) states, "We are stewards, not owners, of the life God has entrusted to us. It is not our to dispose of." Still, "We should not despair of the eternal salvation of persons who have taken their own lives. By ways known to Him alone, God can provide the opportunity for salutary repentance." (2283)

18   The Apostles of the End Times were prophesied in the writings of St. Louis de Montfort (1673-1716) and will be presented in greater detail later.

19   The Indian River Lagoon may be the most biologically diverse estuary in the continental United States. Even though it is much smaller, it has twice the number of species that are found in the Chesapeake Bay. See: http://www.sms.si.edu/irlfieldguide/IRLBiodiv.htm.

20   A warning known as the Birch Tree Prophecy (before 1800), states, "There will come a time when the world is averse to God. Loyalty and faith rule no more. Then there will arise a general insurrection, so that the father will fight against the son and the son against the father."

21   In Book One of this trilogy, the Saudi Royal Family came under a biological attack that had been planned and executed under the direction of Evan Thas and Huntington Cyst. Fearing a coup d'etat, the royals chose to initiate a doomsday strategy known as "Petro S.E." The desperation move was designed as a "scorched earth" exit strategy in which the Saudi oil reserves would be irradiated with dirty bombs leaving the attackers nothing but Scorched Earth in the end.

22   The description, here, is very loosely based on St. Mary's School and Orphanage in Kumbakonam, India, which is real. It houses and educates 1,900 handicapped, deaf and poor children. Fr. Antony is the founder, however, he is not blind. This excellent charity can be reached at www.HelpTheHelpless.org.

23   For a sample of pictures of Rosa Mystica statues and pictures that mysteriously oil or a blood-like substance, see: http://www.google.com/images?q=rosa+mystica&um=1&ie=UTF-8&source=univ&sa=X&ei=6ZyYTfD7I4mE0QGz3KX

2Cw&ved=0CDQQsAQ&biw=1600&bih=775. The author has witnessed the Rosa Mystica statue in Sunrise Florida that exudes not only fragrant oil but pearls.

24   "The Thunder of Justice," Ted and Maureen Flynn, MaxKol Communications, p. 106.

25   Browsing the Internet for videos of the Rosa Mystica phenomenon, one often finds the vilest of comments. Perhaps, this is one of the reasons she is crying.

26   From Book One of this Trilogy, Qurban's planned bombing of a Washington Metro car could have claimed the lives of Huntington Cyst and Evan Thas. However, the terrorist had a last second loss of nerve.

27   Later, Qurban had a Near-Death experience in which he returned to life after John prayed over his dead body.

28   This surprising information is not from an anti-abortion group, but from the Guttmacher Institute itself. See: "Contraception: Short-Term vs. Long-Term Failure Rates" by John A. Ross, Family Planning Perspectives, Vol. 21, No. 6 (Nov. - Dec., 1989), pp. 275-277, Published by: Guttmacher Institute, Stable URL: http://www.jstor.org/stable/2135382

29   Zdenko "Jim" Singer, a Croatian-Canadian, claimed Our Lord revealed to him, "These very ones, these innocent ones, were intended to deliver you from the despairs from which you now suffer. These innocent souls were intended to rule and advance this world which I gifted you, in the manner that I teach you, in My love." Our Lord also emphasized to him that evil has penetrated so many organizations that we should "courageously put into question every institution which violates the family." (From Michael H. Brown's excellent book, "The Final Hour," Queenship Publishing, 1992, p. 255.)

30   Some of these suggestions are from "Hide Your Assets and Disappear: A Step-by-Step Guide to Vanishing Without a Trace," by Edmund J. Pankau, (Harper Collins, New York). It is a book that the author hid in a drawer for 12 years with a note on the cover that read, "Research for writing fiction," just in case a family member found it and started to wonder...

31   See Matthew 19:29 and Mark 10:29.

32   St. Louis de Montfort (d. 1716) prophesied, "The training and education of the great saints, who will appear towards the end of the world, is reserved for the Mother of God. These great saints will surpass in holiness the majority of the other saints like the cedar of Lebanon surpasses the lowly shrub."

33   This is the often repeated request of the Virgin Mary reported by many

visionaries, but most emphatically, perhaps, from the Medjugorje seers.

34   In "How the Catholic Church Built Western Civilization," (Regnery Publishing, 2005) Thomas E. Woods, Jr. describes how the Benedictines – boasting 37,000 monasteries, at their peak – focused on teaching both practical and Spiritual arts, like these, in preserving Western Civilization.

35   "Americans make up half of the world's richest 1%," Money.cnn.com, 1/4/12. The article points out that any individual who earns $34,000 a year, after taxes, is among the world's richest 1%.

36   The data in this paragraph are presented and sourced in Fr. John J. Pasquini's, "Atheist Personality Disorder" (AuthorHouse) pp. 60-63. Further, George Mason University Professor Walter E. Williams reminds us that popular radicals have been dead wrong on the population debate for decades. In his wildly successful 1968 bestseller, "The Population Bomb," Paul Ehrlich made a name for himself that resonates with leftists even today. He predicted that by "the 1970s… hundreds of millions of people are going to starve to death." He claimed that starvation would reduce the U.S. population to 22.6 million by 1999. Still, he was even more hyperbolic regarding England's prospects, saying: "If I were a gambler, I would take even money that England will not exist in the year 2000." ("Population Control Nonsense" Dr. Walter E. Williams, 2/19/99. http://econfaculty.gmu.edu/wew/articles/99/Population-Control.htm

37   In America, 80% of disabled children are aborted before birth according to http://www.catholicnewsagency.com/news/archbishop-chaput-urges-respect-for-life-amid-high-disabled-abortion-rate/.

38   This reference is meant to remind us that Jesus' public ministry began with the celebration at the wedding in Cana. John 2:1-11. We should remember that "Nehemiah said, 'Go and enjoy choice food and sweet drinks, and send some to those who have nothing prepared. This day is sacred to our Lord. Do not grieve, for the joy of the LORD is your strength.'" Nehemiah 8:10.

39   After Judas, every Apostle except John had been martyred for the Faith.

40   St. Hildegard of Bingen predicted, "The Man of Sin will be born of an ungodly woman who, from her infancy, will have been initiated into the occult sciences and the wiles of the demon."

41   Today, petitioners are trying to stop the sale of St. Basil's in Beirut to a Saudi real estate holding company. The convent offers social services in the community, contains a Catholic church that is open to the public, and is one of the last Christian convents in Beirut.

42   This passing character is loosely based on the deceased international terrorist, Abu Nidal. Coincidentally, Nidal's name, spelled backwards, fits the spelling for Osama bin Ladin. Finally, in 1846, in LaSalette France, the Virgin Mary hinted that the Antichrist's "father will be B." There was no explanation for what this initial represents.

43   Prophecy of St. Hippolytus (d. 235) and St Irenaeus (d. 200).

44   Prophecy of St. John of the Cleft Rock (14th century) and Sister Bertina Bouquillon (d. 1850).

45   Prophesied in Isaiah 10:5-7 and predicted by Origen (d. 254) and Lactantius (4th century).

46   Prophecy of St. John Damascene (d. 770).

47   Prophecies of Our Lady of La Salette (1846).

48   Possible name of Antichrist as suggested by St. Hippolytus (d. 235).

49   A prophecy from St. Hildegard of Bingen (d. 1179) stated: "As soon as he [Antichrist] is born, he will have teeth and pronounce blasphemies…" Also, this precise description was confirmed by Our Lady of La Salette in 1846.

50   Similar to 1 Peter 1:5-9

51   Edward Conner "Prophecy for Today" Tan Books, p. 11.

52   Conner, p. 20.

53   Conner, p. 46.

54   Conner, p. 49.

55   Richard G. Lennon, Bishop of Cleveland, has declared "that the alleged apparitions and locutions to Maureen Sweeney-Kyle are not supernatural in origin." Consequently, these prophecies, and any other unapproved predictions mentioned in this fictional tale, are not included with the intent to encourage devotion, or add credence, to such alleged visionaries.

56   Natural disaster data from http://en.wikipedia.org/wiki/List_of_natural_disasters

57   "2011 was most expensive year in world disasters" by Doyle Rice, USA Today, 1/5/12.

NOTES

58   See also, Nicky Eltz, "Get Us Out of Here!" The Medjugorje Web, p. 140, in which Maria Simma, a poor Austrian visionary, warned in the early 1990s, "Satan is everywhere today – in the Church, in the law, in medicine, in science, in the press and in the arts. But there is an area where he is for the greatest part running the entire show and that is in the banks.

59   Nicky Eltz, "Get Us Out of Here!" Walking Word, p. 140.

60   Numerous resources may be cited but proponents on each side of the debate should use caution when separating fact from wishful thinking. Some articles include: http://www.catholiceducation.org/articles/facts/fm0011.html

61   This charge is not made lightly. On ABC's "Primetime Nightline," 8/10/11, former child actor, Corey Feldman said, "I can tell you that the number one problem in Hollywood was and always will be pedophilia. That's the biggest problem for children in this industry.... It's the big secret.... [T]here are people in this industry who have gotten away with it for so long that they feel they're above the law..." As of this writing, the mainstream media have completely ignored this shocking revelation.

62   For those who fail to comprehend the apostasy around us, see, for example, "Is Ireland divorcing from the Catholic Church?" by Mary Kenny published in the U.K. Telegraph on July 26, 2011. The author writes that her homeland " once called itself a foremost Catholic nation and most loyal ally of the Holy Father." Then she describes the Ireland of today. The following are excerpts of the rest of her report: "In the wake of the sex abuse scandals, an anti-Vatican mood is sweeping the land.... One newspaper published a photograph of the Pope in full regalia, with "Persona Non Grata" superimposed on his image. The airwaves are full of bitter remarks... [attacking] the "disgraceful" Vatican, and recommending every anti-church measure from the dissolution of the monasteries to the expulsion of the Papal Nuncio and the severing of all links with the Holy See. (The recall of the Papal Nuncio this week marks the lowest point of relations between Ireland and Rome.) One correspondent wrote that it was his ardent hope that the Catholic Church would follow the example of the News of the World, and hold a "last Mass" before shutting down...."

63   See Rev. R. Gerald Culleton "The Reign of AntiChrist" Tan Books, pp. 164-165.

64   Michael H. Brown, "The Final Hour" Queenship Publisinhg, p. 259.

65   From Maureen Sweeney-Kyle's, "Heaven's Last Call to Humanity" Maranatha Enterprises, p. 259. This woman's messages have not received Church approval. In fact, the Bishop of her diocese has decreed that her alleged apparitions

395

and locutions "are not supernatural in origin." However, this set of messages appear consistent with many other Church-approved prophecies and, because of their brevity, made them of value, if only for the purposes of telling this fictional story.

66   From Luke 10:1-12

67   Mark 8:34-36

68   Ephesians 6:11-12.

69   Based on Acts 2:2-4.

70   Daniel 8:24 predicts that the Antichrist will prosper in everything he does.

71   The National Security Agency is responsible for the collection and analysis of foreign communications and foreign signals intelligence, as well as protecting U.S. government communications and information systems.

72   In an odd and shocking admission, the U.S. Department of Agriculture has claimed responsibility for the mass poisoning of tens of millions of birds in recent years. Though critics are highly skeptical of this admission, at least it provides some kind of logical explanation for all the seemingly inexplicable bird deaths that have occurred. More on this can be found at http://www.earth-issues.com/2011/12/mystery-bye-bye-blackbird-solved-usda-has-admitted-to-poisoning-millions-of-animals/.

73   In "A Life Decoded: My Genome: My Life," J. Craig Venter - one of the first to sequence the human genome and participant in creating the first cell with a synthetic genome - cites an Israeli study that isolated this gene as responsible for novelty-seeking adventurers.

74   This satellite represents the 4th horseman of the Apocalypse. For a premodern, like John, trying to describe satellites would have been an impossible task. All four of the most powerful satellites controlled by XCyst Industries are code-named with a color and a breed of horse.

75   See Revelation 13:13-14 in which we read that the Antichrist "performed great and miraculous signs, even causing fire to come down from heaven to earth in full view of men. Because of the signs he was given power to do on behalf of the first beast (Huntington Cyst), he deceived the inhabitants of the earth."

76   This is a true story. Today, however, the rights to any treasure found along a 300 square mile area of the Treasure Coast are owned by a single company as declared in a 1982 U.S. Supreme Court decision.

77   St. Ephrem (d. 375) prophesied: "The devil will help him find all the hidden treasures of the world, even those at the bottom of the oceans." (Many of these prophecies are from "The Reign of Antichrist" by Rev. R. Gerald Culleton, Tan books.) Treasure still rests off the Treasure Coast of Florida but the exact value of what remains is unknown.

78   This quote is from the ancient historian, Tertullian.

79   The one million martyr estimate is from the detailed research of Robert Royal in his book, "The Catholic Martyrs of the Twentieth Century." (Crossroad General Interest, 2000).

80   This is a list of the sufferings that Pope John Paul II endured during the last two decades of his life. See: http://forums.catholic.com/showthread. php?t=47012

81   These facts may be found at http://www.businessinsider.com/why-spain-is-a-dead-economy-walking-2010-6 and http://www.expatinvesting.org/the-worlds-most-economically-stable-countries-and-economically-unstable-countries/

82   From Tom Pyle with the Institute for Energy Research, Interview on Fox and Friends Saturday, 6/18/11.

83   See "Ethanol's Failed Promise" at http://www.washingtonpost.com/wp-dyn/content/article/2008/04/21/AR2008042102355.html

84   See "Rush to Use Crops as Fuel Raises Food Prices and Hunger Fears" at http://www.nytimes.com/2011/04/07/science/earth/07cassava. html?partner=rss&emc=rss

85   "While people are saying, 'Peace and safety,' destruction will come on them suddenly, as labor pains on a pregnant woman, and they will not escape." 1 Thessalonians 5:3.

86   This paragraph describes the actual economic transition of Russia in the 1990s, after following American-sponsored advice. The administration officials most responsible were "Russian policy czar" Strobe Talbott (State Department), Lawrence Summers (Treasury), and Vice President Al Gore. They, in turn, handed over tremendous responsibility and credibility to billionaire George Soros and his hand-picked economist, Jeffrey Sachs, in guiding Russia's ill-advised transition. More on this subject can be found in David Horowitz and Richard Poe's The Shadow Party, (Thomas Nelson, Inc., 2006, Chapter 5)

87   David Ignatius of the Washington Post wrote (August 25, 1999) in "Let's call it Russiagate," bemoaning: "...the lawlessness of modern Russia and the acquiescence of the Clinton administration in the process of decline and decay there." He concluded, "What makes the Russian case so sad is that the Clinton administration may have squandered on e of the most precious assets imaginable – which is the idealism and goodwill of the Russian people as they emerged from 70 years of Communist rule. The Russia debacle may haunt us for generations."

88   This paragraph offers brief details that mirror how billionaire "philanthropist" George Soros was behind the manipulation and fraud that pushed through the McCain-Feingold campaign finance reform bill, as described in detail by authors David Horowitz and Richard Poe in The Shadow Party, Chapter 8.

89   Rabanus Maurus Magnentius (c. 780 – 4 February 856) - Frankish Benedictine monk, archbishop of Mainz in Germany, and theologian – prophesied: "Antichrist will heal the sick, raise the dead, restore sight to the blind, hearing to the deaf, speech to the dumb..." See "The Reign of Antichrist" p. 123.

90   Loosely based on Daniel 11:8: "He will also seize their gods, their metal images and their valuable articles of silver and gold and carry them off to Egypt."

91   Source: "Nefarious" documentary trilogy found at NefariousDocumentary.com. It is a disturbing but important look into one of the great evils of our time.

92   Also from "Nefarious" and cited as sourced from the U.S. Department of Health and Human Services.

93   See: "The coming hunger: Record food prices put world 'in danger', says UN - Perfect storm of climate and oil puts world into 'danger territory'" by Sean O'Grady, Economics Editor of The Independent. http://www.independent.co.uk/news/world/politics/the-coming-hunger-record-food-prices-put-world-in-danger-says-un-2177220.html.

94   This sentence contains the description of the Internet that was given by Julian Assange, the infamous founder of the WikiLeaks whistleblower website. (See: "Internet is world's 'greatest spying machine': Assange," AFP, 3/15/11, www.breitbart.com.)

95   All of the innovations listed here are presently available in various stages of development.

96   Paraphrased from Deuteronomy 11:26-28.

97   "The ten horns you saw are ten kings who have not yet received a king-

dom, but who for one hour will receive authority as kings along with the beast. They have one purpose and will give their power and authority to the beast. They will make war against the Lamb, but the Lamb will overcome them because he is Lord of lords and King of kings—and with him will be his called, chosen and faithful followers." Revelation 17:12-14.

98   See: "38 Million Sharks Killed for Fins Annually, Experts Estimate" by Nicholas Bakalar for National Geographic News October 12, 2006, at http://news.nationalgeographic.com/news/2006/10/061012-shark-fin.html.

99   See Mark 9:29. Most translations include both prayer and fasting as Jesus Christ's recommendation for overcoming the most difficult demons.

100   Pope John Paul II believed that suffering is allowed for the purpose of perfecting the good, or converting or condemning the wicked.

101   Semiazas is the name of the chief demon of fallen angels.

102   This chapter is very loosely based on Genesis 18 and 19.

103   In folklore, Malphas is believed to be a demon who is the Grand President of hell, commanding 40 legions, and sometimes appearing as a raven.

104   Pruflas is believed to be a demon who heads 26 legions, provokes wars and quarrels, and sometimes appears with the head of an owl.

105   Pigs with human blood were produced by the researchers of the Mayo Clinic in 2004. See "Animal-Human Hybrids Spark Controversy," by Maryann Mott, National Geographic News, January 25, 2005.

106   Ibid. This was accomplished in 2003 by Chinese scientists at the Shanghai Second Medical University.

107   See: "How Engineering the Human Body Could Combat Climate Change" at http://www.theatlantic.com/technology/archive/2012/03/how-engineering-the-human-body-could-combat-climate-change/253981/

108   At www.humanityplus.org, more information on the Transhumanism movement can be found, as well as the Transhumanist Declaration that was adopted in 2009. Its advocates present the utopian ideal that, they claim, can be achieved by developing "emerging and speculative technologies that focus on the well-being of our species...."

109   Ibid. In the article, when this amazing possibility was seriously suggested, David Magnus, director of the Stanford Center for Biomedical Ethics dodged

answering the question with a supreme understatement: "Most people would find that problematic."

110   Automatic translation technology is a modern accomplishment that reminds one of the story of the Tower of Babel, when God chose to respond to mankind's arrogance with constraints on communication.

111   Ibid. Irv Weissman, director of Stanford University's Institute of Cancer/Stem Cell Biology and Medicine in California had created, as of 2005, mice with partially human brains and planned to conduct experiments soon thereafter seeking mice with completely human brains.

112   Placing Eden Village on the island of Nauru effectively protected XCyst from intruding regulations like the ones that are being called for in the Associated Press article, "UK scientists want human-animal tests monitored." The July 21, 2011 report explains, "Controversy erupted several years ago in Britain after scientists announced plans to make human embryos with the nucleus removed from cow and rabbit eggs." It goes on the say, "Among experimentation that might spark concern are those where human brain cells might change animal brains, those that could lead to fertilization of human eggs in animals, and any modifications of animals that might create attributes considered uniquely human, like facial features, skin or speech." Science fiction is now becoming fact.

113   The following facts regarding synthetic life are derived from, among other sources, a series of articles from www.guardian.co.uk which discuss this scientific breakthrough: "Craig Venter creates synthetic life form," by Ian Sample, May 20, 2010; "Synthetic life breakthrough could be worth over a trillion dollars," by Ian Sample, May 20, 2010; "Synthetic cells: It's life, but not as we know it," Editorial, May 22, 2010. Also, some details are drawn from Venter's autobiography, "A Life Decoded – My Genome: My Life," Viking, 2007.

114   In Book One of this Trilogy, we learned that the Antichrist is predicted to gain full power upon reaching the age of 30.

115   As noted before, Huntington Cyst was known as the "Prophet of Technology" and he prepared the path for Evan's arrival. He is the "False Prophet" mentioned in Revelation 16:13; 19:19-20; and 20:10.

116   In addition to suggesting the name "Evanthas" for the Antichrist, St. Hyppolytus (d. 235) and St. Irenaeus (d. 200) both suggested that the name "Titan" also corresponds to 666, the number that is representative of the Antichrist in the Book of Revelation.

117   See http://en.wikipedia.org/wiki/G-20

118   This is today's environment. Quotes are from a recent recipient of this true award as reported on the Defense Professiona_ website at http://www.defpro. com/news/details/23742/?SID=cebce1e87d9cb0f1217dfab0055c061e

119   Antichrist will rise, deceitfully, on a platform of peace, as predicted by Daniel 8:25.

120   These are the actual numbers for General Electric's 2010 fiscal year taxes as reported by the New York Times at http://www.nytimes.com/2011/03/25/busi- ness/economy/25tax.html. General Electric is, perhaps, the world's most powerful and influential international conglomerate, and is the parent corporation of NBC, CNBC and MSNBC

121   An interesting collection of articles on weapons of the future, including free-electron lasers and other directed-energy weapons, can be found at http:// www.wired.com/dangerroom/tag/free-electron-laser/

122   Venerable Anne Catherine Emmerich was an illiterate, German Augus- tinian nun. In the years before her death in 1824, she dictated an immense treasure of details regarding her visions of Our Lord's life. These ecstatic descriptions were published in "The Dolorous Passion of Our Lord Jesus Christ," which is available in an unabridged audio version by Tan Books and Publishers, Inc. and Recorded Books, LLC. More information on this amazing stigmatist is available from the Catholic Encyclopedia at http://www.newadvent.org/cathen/05406b.htm

123   In "The Prescription of Heretics," ancient historian, Tertullian, docu- mented this story, though some of the details here are embellishments.

124   From Hebrews 13:2. "Do not forget to entertain strangers, for by so do- ing some people have entertained angels without knowing it."

125   This magnitude would make it the second largest earthquake since 1900. The largest occurred in Chile in 1960 with a magnitude of 9.5. See: http://earth- quake.usgs.gov/earthquakes/world/10_largest_world.php

126   This description of hell is closely paraphrased from the first secret of Fatima, as reported by visionary, Lucia Santos, in her third memoir.

127   These three sentences are based on Pope John Paul II's clarification of the Catholic Church's position on hell, defined at a general audience on July 28, 1999.

128   Venerable Anne Catherine Emmerich prophesied that the Antichrist's mother will be "a depraved woman possessed by the devil, [and] will live as a pros- titute in the desert.... She will then be venerated as a saint by deceived people."

129   Fentanyl patch abuse is increasingly blamed for overdose deaths and robberies. The DEA has described it as having this level of potency when it is abused by improperly consuming the drug orally from the pain patch.

130   In the 17th century, David Poreaus predicted that the prophesied Great Monarch "will be of French descent, large forehead, large dark eyes, light brown wavy hair and an eagle nose. He will crush the enemies of the Pope and will conquer the East."

131   God instructed Moses to have the Israelites build the Ark of the Covenant after their escape from slavery in Egypt. It was approximately 45" x 27" x 27", made of acacia wood and covered in gold, inside and out. (See Exodus 25:9-11 and 21.) It contained, at one point, the miraculous staff of Moses and Aaron, a jar containing manna, and the stone tablets of the Ten Commandments. It was housed and revered in the holiest inner sanctuary of the first Temple, and it was for that reason, among others, that the Temple was built by Solomon. When the Jews were conquered and carried off to Babylon in 587 BC, the Temple was destroyed and the Ark was moved and never found again. In the Catholic Bible, we read, "And Jeremiah came and found a cave, and he brought there the tent and the ark and the altar of incense, and he sealed up the entrance. Some of those who followed him came up to mark the way, but could not find it. When Jeremiah learned of it, he rebuked them and declared: 'The place shall be unknown until God gathers his people together again and shows his mercy. And then the Lord will disclose these things…'" (2 Maccabees 2:5-8, RSV) After 70 years in Babylon, the Israelites returned to their Promised Land and the Temple was rebuilt. But the Ark was never found.

132   Matthew 16:18.

133   Wikipedia.org explains this as follows: "The Rule of Saint Benedict (Regula Benedicti) is a book of precepts written by St. Benedict of Nursia for monks living communally under the authority of an abbot. Since about the 7th century it has also been adopted by communities of women. During the 1500 years of its existence, it has become the leading guide in Western Christianity for monastic living in community. The spirit of St Benedict's Rule is summed up in the motto of the Benedictine Confederation: pax ("peace") and the traditional ora et labora ("pray and work")."

134   These virtues, and others, are taught in Chapter 7 of the Rule of St. Benedict, as 12 steps on the ladder to heaven. "The Rule," as it is called, is the enduring foundational document of monastic life. It consists of an additional 72 chapters and ends with the humble suggestion that the volume is chiefly intended for beginners in the Spiritual life.

135   John 15:18-20.

136   Acts 5:38-39.

137   Luke 17:34-35.

138   Luke 17:26.

139   Luke 17:28-29.

140   Revelation 3:10.

141   Revelation 3:11.

142   Revelation 3:19.

143   Revelation 6:9 and 11.

144   Revelation 7:14.

145   Revelation 7:17.

146   Revelation 13:7.

147   Revelation 13:9-10.

148   Revelation 20:4.

149   The last two clauses are quoted from Philippians 2:12-13.

150   1 Corinthians 10:13.

151   Isaiah 13:10-13.

152   Blessed Anna Maria Taigi died in 1827.

153   Marie Julie Jahenny of La Fraudais died in 1891.

154   These prophecies of saints are from "Prophecy for Today" by Edward Connor (Tan Books, Rockford IL) pp. 26-28.

155   This explanation was offered by Pope John Paul II.

156   See Mark 13:32.

157   Prophecy of Blessed Anna-Maria Taigi.

158   Prophecy of Venerable Bartholomew Holzhauser, a 17th century German.

159   Prophecy of Marie Julie Jahenny of La Fraudais, a 19th century French stigmatist.

160   Prophecy of Marie Julie Jahenny of La Fraudais. Also see Daniel 12:11.

161   Exodus 10:21-23.

162   Matthew 27:45; Mark 15:33; Luke 23:44.

163   As was footnoted in Book One of this trilogy, see Exodus 32:13: "... I will give your descendants all this land I promised them, and it will be their inheritance forever." Also, for those who believe the Bible is the Word of God yet doubt Israel's claim on the Promised Land, the author recommends studying the following verses: Hebrews 11:9, Deuteronomy 19:8, Deuteronomy 34:4, Exodus 12:25, Exodus 3:17, Joshua 22:4, Numbers 14:16, Numbers 14:23, Acts 7:5, Ezekiel 30:5, Joshua 23:5, Genesis 28:15, Genesis 50:24, Nehemiah 9:23, Nehemiah 9:8, Ezekiel 20:42, Psalm 47:4, Leviticus 20:24, Jeremiah 32:22, Jeremiah 2:7, Isaiah 58:14, 1 Chronicles 11:10.

164   The prophecy of Premol (496) predicted, "Ah! The dragon has appeared in all countries and has brought terrible confusion everywhere. There is war everywhere. Men and people have risen up one against the other. War, war, war – civil war and foreign war. What frightening onsets."

165   This sentence is paraphrased from a prophecy by Venerable Bartholomew Holzhauser (17th century) that described the end of the fifth period of the Church, which began circa 1520. At this time, he claimed that the "Holy Pope" and the "powerful Monarch" will arrive on the scene.

166   The rush to introduce technology into the voting process has been responsible for compromising the ballot beyond what most believe is credible. For just a small look into the system's vulnerabilities, see "Researchers Hack Voting Machine for $26." The short but revealing and disturbing expose' can be found at http://www.foxnews.com/scitech/2011/09/30/researchers-hack-voting-machine-for-26/print#.

167   After the words "Monte Cassino," this is a quote from British veteran Douglas Lyne, from the book "Monte Cassino: The Story Of The Most Controversial Battle Of World War II" by David Hapgood and David Richardson. General Mark Clark of the U.S. Fifth Army ordered the bombing believing that the site was occupied by the Nazis. However, that suspicion later proved false. The massive

structure, with all of its historic, cultural and religious significance, was wiped out. The Vatican could only complain that the military operation was a "colossal blunder" and a "piece of gross stupidity." The so-called "Monuments Men" were later employed, after the war, to help insure that historic monuments would never again be destroyed so carelessly.

168   The prophecies regarding the Great Monarch will be presented in future chapters.

169   The Mark of the Beast is mentioned in Revelation chapters 13, 14, 15, 16, 19 and 20.

170   Genesis 11:4.

171   Mark 13:23-25 reads, "So be on your guard; I have told you everything ahead of time. But in those days, following that distress, the sun will be darkened, and the moon will not give its light; the stars will fall from the sky, and the heavenly bodies will be shaken."

172   The last three sentences are from Mark 13:12-13.

173   The Catechism of the Catholic Church accepts the "just war" doctrine "subject to rigorous conditions of moral letitimacy." (See 2309.)

174   This responsibility is from Catholic Catechism 2310.

175   This quote is often attributed to Edmund Burke though its actual origin is in dispute, somewhat.

176   From Saul D. Alinsky's "Rules for Radicals," Vintage Books, 1989, p. 116 and 117.

177   See "House members in the know score 'abnormal' stock profits, study says" by Valerie Richardson, Washington Times, 5/25/11. http://www.washingtontimes.com/news/2011/may/25/house-members-stock-market-success-questioned/. At the time of this writing, legislation has been presented to curb this abuse.

178   The evidence is abundant that the global warming and Cap-And-Trade agenda, if successful, could have become the largest fraud in world history. At the forefront of that runaway propaganda train was Former Vice President Al Gore who won a Nobel Prize, and an Oscar for his film, "An Inconvenient Truth." Gore compared skeptics of man-made global warming to racists and flat earthers while jetting around the globe and consuming 20 times the average usage of electricity in one of his mansions. On his way, reportedly, to becoming the world's first "Eco bil-

lionaire," however, he got sidetracked when the conclusions of so-called "scientific" studies lost credibility as agenda-biased research became exposed. As reported in February of 2009 on CBS' "60 Minutes," Gore proclaimed that man-made global warming is a "moral and spiritual issue" and urgently warned, "This is about survival." However, more clear-headed research now suggests that Gore's crisis agenda had been hijacked by a global network of self-interested parties. Newer research suggests that, in fact, the world may be headed for a mini-ice age, as reported at http://www.dailymail.co.uk/sciencetech/article-2093264/Forget-global-warming--Cycle-25-need-worry-NASA-scientists-right-Thames-freezing-again.html.

179   Self-serving entities have developed a global push for private and public sector alliances that will bring about universal broadband access. One report is at the UN News Centre in the article, "UN telecommunication official warns of widening Internet broadband divide."

180   For the process of turning sand into silicon, see http://pcplus.techradar.com/2009/05/21/how-silicon-chips-are-made/

181   As noted before, in addition to suggesting the name "Evanthas" for the Antichrist, St. Hyppolytus (d. 235) and St. Irenaeus (d. 200) both suggested that the name "Titan" also corresponds to 666, the number that is representative of the Antichrist in the Book of Revelation.

182   Lending credence to this fictional account of the miniaturization of such technologies, scientists have reportedly developed transistors consisting of a single atom. (See: http://www.sfgate.com/cgi-bin/article.cgi?f=/g/a/2012/02/20/bloomberg_articlesLZNZ0D07SXKX01-LZO0R.DTL)

183   In Revelation 13:16, regarding the Antichrist, we read, "He also forced everyone, small and great, rich and poor, free and slave, to receive a mark on his right hand or on his forehead. No one could buy or sell unless he had the mark, which is the name of the beast or the number of his name." Though it is impossible to know what the Mark of the Beast will be, this symbol is drawn from two traditions: 1) Just as the Trinity represents holy perfection, the number 3 often symbolizes a type of perfection; 2) The circles are meant to represent the number zero or the concept of nothingness. Therefore, the three concentric circles are meant to convey the number of a perfect nothingness, lack or void.

184   Source: The Wall Street Journal, http://blogs.wsj.com/economics/2011/10/05/nearly-half-of-households-receive-some-government-benefit/

185   A modern example is the case of Jon Corzine (former US Senator, NJ Governor, and CEO of Goldman Sachs) who led the collapse of MF Global in which investigators say that much of the firm's customers' missing $1.2 billion will never be found because it simply "vaporized" in the frantic trading of the company's last

days. However, the author suggests that if just one percent of discovered funds was offered to investigators, then every last dime might be found. See: http://www.nypost.com/p/news/business/mf_global_client_money_feared_gone_cH697L-FiURrTtKEQvrzjdI

186   Book 1 of this trilogy described, in Chapter 37, how Angela Concepcion submitted to a Titan analysis. The resulting evaluation identified her hopes, her fears and even her inner-most secrets.

187   See Revelation 13:17 in which "no one could buy or sell unless he had the mark, which is the name of the beast or the number of his name." (Titan)

188   For the Mark of the Beast, see Revelation chapters 16 and 19.

189   George Soros quote is from The Independent, June 3, 1993.

190   Faridah's character is based on a variety of prophecies, some of which were cited in Book One of this Trilogy, but also the following: Melanie Calvat, one of the visionaries of La Salette, said in 1851, "Lastly, hell will reign on earth. It will be then that the antichrist will be born of a Sister, but woe to her! Many will believe in him, because he will claim to have come from heaven, woe to those who will believe in him!" Later, in 1879, she elaborated, "It will be during this time that the antichrist will be born of a Hebrew religious, of a false virgin...." Much earlier, in the twelfth century, Saint Hildegard prophesied that the antichrist's mother "will maintain that her son was presented to her by God in a supernatural manner, as was the Child of the Blessed Virgin."

191   In 1879, the La Salette seer also prophesied that the antichrist "will have brothers who ... will be children of evil.... They will each be at the head of armies, assisted by the legions of hell."

192   God's first commandment to Adam and Eve, found at Genesis 1:28.

193   Seventy three percent of Palestinians in the Gaza and West Bank agree that Jews should be killed wherever they hide. The poll, which has a margin of error of 3.1 percentage points, of 1,010 Palestinians in the West Bank and Gaza, was conducted in partnership with the Beit Sahour-based Palestinian Center for Public Opinion and sponsored by the Israel Project, an international nonprofit organization that provides journalists and leaders with information about the Middle East. See: http://www.jpost.com/DiplomacyAndPolitics/Article.aspx?id=229493

194   In Book One of this Trilogy, the Saudis initiated a "scorched earth" retaliation against what appeared to be a decapitation strike on the royal family. The royals initiated "Petro SE" in which their oil reserves intentionally were irradiated, thus rendering them useless.

195   This expression was popularized by George Soros in his 2003 article, "The Bubble of American Supremacy" found at http://www.theatlantic.com/past/docs/issues/2003/12/soros.htm

196   In 1975, a voting coalition of Communist and Muslim nations united their political clout at the United Nations, targeting Israel. As a result, almost 40% of all U.N. Human Rights Council resolutions now condemn the only democracy in the Middle East: Israel. Contrary to any rational standard of fairness, the Jewish state has received more human rights condemnations than all other repressive countries, combined. The world's worst human rights abusers are many of the member states that sit in judgment. An informative, short video can be seen at: http://www.youtube.com/watch?v=j7Mupoo1At8&feature=player_embedded

197   The following speech is excerpted, almost verbatim, from portions of Prime Minister Benjamin Netanyahu's excellent speech before a join session of the US Congress on May 24, 2011.

198   See Exodus 32:13: "... I will give your descendants all this land I promised them, and it will be their inheritance forever." Also, for those who believe the Bible is the Word of God yet doubt Israel's claim on the Promised Land, the author recommends studying the following verses: Hebrews 11:9, Deuteronomy 19:8, Deuteronomy 34:4, Exodus 12:25, Exodus 3:17, Joshua 22:4, Numbers 14:16, Numbers 14:23, Acts 7:5, Ezekiel 30:5, Joshua 23:5, Genesis 28:15, Genesis 50:24, Nehemiah 9:23, Nehemiah 9:8, Ezekiel 20:42, Psalm 47:4, Leviticus 20:24, Jeremiah 32:22, Jeremiah 2:7, Isaiah 58:14, 1 Chronicles 11:10.

199   Probably written at least 25 centuries ago, Psalm 83:4-9 describes well the ancestors of Israel's enemies today: "With cunning they conspire against your people; they plot against those you cherish. 'Come,' they say, 'let us destroy them as a nation, that the name of Israel be remembered no more.' With one mind they plot together; they form an alliance against you—the tents of Edom and the Ishmaelites, of Moab and the Hagrites, Gebal, Ammon and Amalek, Philistia, with the people of Tyre. Even Assyria has joined them to lend strength to the descendants of Lot."

200   2 Timothy 3:1-5: "There will be terrible times in the last days. People will be lovers of themselves, lovers of money, boastful, proud, abusive, disobedient to their parents, ungrateful, unholy, without love, unforgiving, slanderous, without self-control, brutal, not lovers of the good, treacherous, rash, conceited, lovers of pleasure rather than lovers of God— having a form of godliness but denying its power. Have nothing to do with them."

201   St. Senanus (d. 560) prophesied: "Women will abandon feelings of delicacy, and cohabit with men out of wedlock; they will follow those practices without secrecy, and such habits will become almost unsuppressable. All will rush into in-

NOTES

iquity against the will of the Son of the Blessed Virgin Mary."

202   Blessed Anne Catherine Emmerich (1774-1824) described one of her many visions this way: "A pale faced man floated slowly over the earth and, loosening the cloths which wrapped his sword, he threw them on sleeping cities, which were bound by them. This figure also dropped pestilence on Russia, Italy, and Spain."

203   See USA Today's "2011 was most expensive year in world disasters" by Doyle Rice (January 5, 2012) in which a record was not only set but exceeded the previous record by a whopping 44%.

204   St. Columbkille predicted, "Seven years before the last day, the sea shall submerge Ireland in one inundation." That prophecy also was made by St. Nennius, St. Patrick, and Leabhar Breac. Also, regarding England, Fr. Balthassar Mas (1630) said, "I saw a land swallowed by the sea and covered with water, but afterwards I saw that little by little, the sea retreated and left the land visible and the upper parts of the towers and turrets of the cities rose and appeared more beautiful than before being swallowed by the sea, and it was told me that was England."

205   St. Nilus (430 AD): "After the year 1900, toward the middle of the 20th century, the people of that time will become unrecognizable. When the time for the Advent of the Antichrist approaches, peoples minds will grow cloudy from carnal passions, and dishonor and lawlessness will grow stronger. Then the world will become unrecognizable. Peoples appearances will change, and it will be impossible to distinguish men from women due to there shamelessness in dress and style of hair. These people will be cruel and will be like wild animals because of the temptations of the Antichrist. There will be no respect for parents or elders, love will disappear, and Christian pastors, bishops, and priests will become vain men, completely failing to distinguish the right hand way from the left. At that time the morals and traditions of Christians and the Church will change. People will abandon modesty, and dissipation will reign. Falsehood and greed will attain great proportions, and woe to those who pile up treasures. Lust, adultery, homosexuality, secret deeds and murder will rule in society."

206   The Didache (ca. 100 AD) predicted: "In the last days false prophets shall be multiplied, and such as corrupt the word, and the sheep shall be changed into wolves, and love into hatred: for through the abounding of iniquity the love of many shall wax cold."

207   Joel 3:2 says, "...I will enter into judgment against them concerning my inheritance, my people Israel, for they scattered my people among the nations and divided up my land." Exodus 32:13 says: "... I will give your descendants all this land I promised them, and it will be their inheritance forever." Finally, for those who believe that the Bible is the Word of God, yet doubt Israel's claim on

the Promised Land, the author recommends studying the following verses: Hebrews 11:9, Deuteronomy 19:8, Deuteronomy 34:4, Exodus 12:25, Exodus 3:17, Joshua 22:4, Numbers 14:16, Numbers 14:23, Acts 7:5, Ezekiel 30:5, Joshua 23:5, Genesis 28:15, Genesis 50:24, Nehemiah 9:23, Nehemiah 9:8, Ezekiel 20:42, Psalm 47:4, Leviticus 20:24, Jeremiah 32:22, Jeremiah 2:7, Isaiah 58:14, 1 Chronicles 11:10.

208   This little-known discovery is reportedly true. Regarding the possible game-changing ocean of oil under Israel, these facts and data are taken from http://www.theglobeandmail.com/report-on-business/with-its-oil-treasure-israel-gets-a-shield-from-tyranny/article2078985/

209   General Gideon is a fictional character, however the data below, regarding Israel's Six-Day and Yom Kippur wars, can be found in a variety of sources but are conveniently summarized in "The Complete Idiot's Guide to Middle East Conflict" by Mitchell G. Bard, Pearson Education, Inc., 2003.

210   Predicting Evan's head wound, Revelation 13:3 says, "One of the heads of the beast seemed to have had a fatal wound, but the fatal wound had been healed. The whole world was astonished and followed the beast."

211   "He will speak against the Most High and oppress his saints and try to change the set times and the laws." Daniel 7:25.

212   Perhaps the reader, here, will detect a writing style that is more elevated and inspiring than before. The following descriptions of the Apostles of the Latter Times are paraphrased from the prophecies of St. Louis de Montfort (1673-1716) in his classic work, "True Devotion to the Blessed Virgin," and others.

213   In "True Devotion ...", Montfort writes, "... true Apostles of the End Times [will live]... in the midst of other priests, ecclesiastics and clerics."

214   Ibid.

215   Montfort, "Prayer for Missionaries." See also Genesis 3:15.

216   Our Lady of Fatima appeared to three children on the 13th of each month, from May through October of 1917.

217   The last clause is a famous quote from Mao Tse-tung.

218   At the time of the Fatima messages, Russia was a Christian nation. When the Blessed Mother asked them to pray for Russia, the uneducated children thought she was referring to a lady. A couple weeks after the sixth and last month's message, the Bolshevik Revolution started and began the bloody and ruthless reign of Soviet communism. The Virgin Mary had predicted, "If my requests are heeded, Russia

will be converted, and there will be peace; if not, she [Russia] will spread her errors throughout the world, causing wars and persecutions of the Church. The good will be martyred; the Holy Father will have much to suffer; various nations will be annihilated." Her request to consecrate Russia was not accomplished until Pope John Paul II properly consecrated Russia -- according to the last surviving visionary -- on March 25, 1984. Seven years later, the Soviet Union collapsed. The attempted assassination of Pope John Paul II is believed to have been plotted by Soviet leaders and it occurred on the anniversary of the last Fatima message, May 13, 1981.

219   Sister Lucia of Fatima said Blessed Mother warned, "The devil knows that when religious and priests fail in their beautiful vocations they carry along with them many lost souls into hell."

220   At the time of this writing, the alleged apparitions of Our Lady of Medjugorje are being investigated by a special commission at the Vatican.

221   This sentence is paraphrased from the Diary of St. Maria Faustina Kowalska (1146).

222   "When you see 'the abomination that causes desolation' standing where it does not belong--let the reader understand--then let those who are in Judea flee to the mountains." Mark 13:14.

223   This was one of the many amazing Gifts of St. Vincent Ferrer (d. 1419). For over 30 years, he spoke in a miraculous manner so that everyone who heard him understood clearly in their own native tongue. At his canonization investigations, more than 100 witnesses attested to the miracles.

224   The following message that John delivers is excerpted from a November 15, 2010 message, allegedly from Jesus Christ to a woman who chooses to use the name Maria Devine Mercy. Reportedly, she is a European mother of a young family who began receiving allegedly Divine messages on November 9, 2010. She seeks to remain anonymous for reasons family privacy and personal humility. Also, she claims that her messages are being delivered under Church supervision and that, though there has not been time for a Church investigation to conclude, she will remain submissive to the Magisterium of the Church. She warns that all so-called "Divine" messages must be evaluated with extreme caution. The author cannot know what a Church investigation might conclude, regarding these messages, but chose to use these excerpts because they demonstrate a consistency with many other prophecies regarding The Warning, The Illumination, and The Three Days of Darkness. Her reports of allegedly Divine messages can be found at www.TheWarningSecondComing.com.

225   The Chaplet of Divine Mercy is a devotion, instructed by Jesus Christ, as reported by the 20th century saint known as Sister Faustina Kowalska.

226   The following is the June 5, 2011 message reported by the alleged visionary who is described in the note above.

227   These are some of the characteristics of a five week old fetus as described at http://www.livestrong.com/article/81426-week-fetus-look-like/

228   This is not far from the gruesome reality in which human fetal organs are harvested and sold internationally. Planned Parenthood and other organizations are reportedly very active in the practice. The abortion industry's "dirty secret," as it has been called, has been reported on ABC's 20/20 and other expose's like the following account about an insider, eyewitness: He "and his colleagues would turn up at the abortions that offered the best donor prospects to begin dissecting and extracting what they needed before decay set in…. 'We were taking eyes, livers, brains, thymuses, and especially cardiac blood…even blood from the limbs that we would get from the veins….' [He] told of seeing babies wounded but alive after abortion procedures, and in one case a set of twins 'still moving on the table' when clinicians from [his company] began dissecting the children to harvest their organs. The children, he said, were 'cuddling each other' and 'gasping for breath' when medics moved in for the kill." The full report can be found at http://www.investigatemagazine.co.nz/Investigate/?p=2451

229   Loosely based on Revelation 6:1-8.

230   If this silencing sounds far-fetched, one only need to review the many man-made global warming skeptics who were shouted down and silenced for a decade. One former proponent of the theory admitted that he eventually felt "duped on climate change." See: http://www.spiegel.de/international/world/0,1518,813814,00.html

231   The total value of the world's sunken treasure is estimated to be $60 billion, as reported in http://www.popularmechanics.com/technology/engineering/gonzo/whats-the-total-value-of-the-worlds-sunken-treasure?src=soc_fcbks

232   Though investigations continue, the Catholic Church has never issued an official pronouncement condemning either of these alleged sets of apparitions.

233   Each of these tragedies is from recent, true stories described at http://miracle-witness.blogspot.com/2011/08/christian-persecutions-you-dont-know.html

234   These Mexican drug war facts can be found at a variety of sources, such as http://www.examiner.com/immigration-in-tucson/mexican-gov-t-47-000-murdered-drug-war-last-five-years

235   In Nice, France, the author found a church in which 8 priests were offering the Advent evening prayer service of Vespers for their parishioners, but none of them attended.

236   Daniel 11:37 predicts that the Antichrist will not believe in the God of his fathers.

237   Antichrist will oppose God and exalt himself above God (2 Thessalonians 2:4), and will speak marvelous things against God. (Daniel 11:36)

238   John 10:30.

239   Revelation 13:7 predicts that the Antichrist will be given power over all kindred, tongues and nations. Daniel 7:23 predicts that he will devour the whole earth.

240   The words of the enraged angel in the third secret of Fatima.

241   The following general procedures for electing a pope are accurate.

242   The word "conclave" is derived from the Latin "cum clave" which means "locked in."

243   This part of the story is very loosely based on a number of prophecies, including the following:
> •   The Third Secret of Fatima described: "a Bishop dressed in White" who was believed to be "the Holy Father" with other clergy "going up a steep mountain, at the top of which there was a big Cross." He was "half trembling with halting step, afflicted with pain and sorrow, he prayed for the souls of the corpses he met on his way; having reached the top of the mountain, on his knees at the foot of the big Cross he was killed…"
> •   Brother John of the Cleft Rock (1340) prophesied: "The pope, with the cardinals, will have to flee Rome under trying circumstances to a place where he will be unknown. He will die a cruel death in this exile. The sufferings of the Church will be much greater than at any previous time in her history."
> •   John of Vatiguerro (13th century) predicted: "The pope will change his residence; the Church will not be defended for the duration of twenty five months, and more, because during all this time there will be no pope…"
> •   Finally, even before the Fatima prophecies, Pope Pius X (d. 1914) prophesied: "I saw one of my successors by name fleeing over the corpses of his brethren. He will flee to a place for a short respite where he is unknown, but he himself will die a cruel death."

244   "Rome will lose the faith and become the seat of Antichrist, the Church will be in eclipse." Our Lady of La Salette (1846)

245   The Third Secret of Fatima prophesied that the Virgin Mary would shield some of the rays of the avenging angel's flaming sword.

246   See Mark 1:40-45.

247   Venerable Anne Catherine Emmerich explained a vision, "… As we came nearer, however, the fire abated and we saw the blackened building. We went through a number of magnificent rooms, and we finally reached the pope…. He was very ill and weak; he could no longer walk…. I told him … that he must not leave Rome. If he did so, it would be chaos. He thought that the evil was inevitable and he should leave in order to save many things beside himself. He was very much inclined to leave Rome, and he was insistently urged to do so."

248   The Great Monarch is foretold in many prophecies of saints. The following descriptions of the Great Monarch can be found in Rev. R. Gerald Culleton's "The Prophets and Our Times," Tan Books and Publishers (1974), in numerous prophecies cited on p. 70.

249   From the prophecies of St. Remigius (d. 535).

250   From the prophecies of St. Caesar of Arles (469-543).

251   Finally, regarding the Great Monarch, Blessed Anne Catherine Emmerich predicted that his name will be Henry.

252   Helen Walraff (d. 1801) prophesied: "Some day, a pope will flee from Rome in company of only four cardinals and come to Cologne."

253   For story simplicity, this account does not accurately portray every detail of the prophecy of Anne Catherine Emmerich regarding the Great Monarch: "I had a vision of the holy Emperor Henry. I saw him at night kneeling alone at the foot of the main altar in a great and beautiful church … and I saw the Blessed Virgin coming down all alone. She laid on the altar a red cloth covered with white linen…. Then came the Savior Himself clad in priestly vestments…. The Mass was short. The Gospel of St. John was not read at the end. When the Mass had ended, Mary came up to Henry, and she extended her right hand towards him, saying that it was in recognition of his purity. Then she urged him not to falter. Thereupon I saw an angel, and he touched the sinew of his hip, like Jakob. Henry was in great pain; and from that day on he walked with a limp …"

254   A description of people in the last days, as described in 2 Timothy 3:2-4.

255   St. Ephrem (d. 375) prophesied, "Antichrist will use worldly goods as bait. He will entice many Christians with money and goods to apostasize. He will give them free land, riches, honor and power."

256   John of the Cleft Rock (1340) predicted, "This Prince of Liars will swear by the Bible and pose as the arm of the Almighty, chastising a corrupt age.... He will be a one-armed man with innumerable soldiers resembling legions of Hell whose motto will be 'God with us.'"

257   "So I tell you, every sin and blasphemy can be forgiven--except blasphemy against the Holy Spirit, which will never be forgiven." Matthew 12:31.

258   "So when you see standing in the holy place 'the abomination that causes desolation,' spoken of through the prophet Daniel—let the reader understand— then let those who are in Judea flee to the mountains. Let no one on the roof of his house go down to take anything out of the house. Let no one in the field go back to get his cloak. How dreadful it will be in those days for pregnant women and nursing mothers! Pray that your flight will not take place in winter or on the Sabbath. For then there will be great distress, unequaled from the beginning of the world until now—and never to be equaled again. If those days had not been cut short, no one would survive, but for the sake of the elect those days will be shortened." Matthew 24:15-22.

259   This is the name that God gave Himself in Exodus 3:14. Also, consider, "At that time [the end of The Age] if anyone says to you, 'Look, here is the Christ!' or, 'Look, there he is!' do not believe it. For false Christs and false prophets will appear and perform signs and miracles to deceive the elect—if that were possible. So be on your guard; I have told you everything ahead of time." Mark 13:21-23.

260   St. Bridget of Sweden (d. 1373) said, "Rome will be visited by sword and fire and plowed under."

261   The Cure of Ars (d. 1859) prophesied, "They will attempt to kill all the priests and all the religious. But this shall not last long. People will imagine that all is lost; but the good God shall save it all."

262   Johannes von Lilienthal (date unknown) reportedly predicted, "At that time, the Church will suffer severe pressure, will practically lose all its wealth and will be severely oppressed by internal and external enemies..." Also, Father Jerome Votin (d. 1420) predicted, "... after the end of five centuries (the 20th century) the servants of the altar will weep and suffer persecutions for the sake of justice. [This may refer to past communist persecutions.] The shepherd (Pope) will be smitten and the fold scattered..."

263   Among others, the prophecies from Garabandal, Medjugorje and Akita predict The Warning in the End Times. Though their descriptions sometimes vary, somewhat, they also predict are a permanent, visible sign, and the Illumination of the Soul during a time of chastisements.

264   Two prophecies from Sister Rose Asdenti of Taggia (1847).

265   Prophecy of Blessed Maria Taigi (d. 1837).

266   Isaiah 3:5.

267   John of the Cleft Rock (1340) prophesied, "[Antichrist] will massacre the priests, the monks, the women, the children, and the aged. He will show no mercy, but will pass torch in hand, like the barbarians, yet invoking Christ!" With the sacrificial nature of a victim soul, St. Theresa of Liseaux said, "My heart thrills at the thought of the frightful tortures Christians are to suffer at the time of Antichrist, and I long to undergo them all." Blessed Maria Taigi (d. 1837) prophesied: "Religious shall be persecuted, priests shall be massacred, the churches shall be closed, but only for a short time; the Holy Father shall be obliged to abandon Rome."

268   "His armed forces will rise up to desecrate the temple fortress and will abolish the daily sacrifice." Daniel 11:31.

269   Anne Catherine Emmerich prophesied, "Whole Catholic communities were being oppressed, harassed, confined, and deprived of their freedom. I saw many churches closed down, great miseries everywhere, wars and bloodshed. A wild and ignorant mob took violent action. But it did not last long …"

270   Pope Gregory the Great wrote that the Antichrist will be the man who proclaims himself Universal Bishop.

271   "From the time that the daily sacrifice is abolished and the abomination that causes desolation is set up, there will be 1,290 days." Daniel 12:11.

272   Daniel 11:31 predicts that the Antichrist will abolish the daily sacrifice.

273   Sister Marianne (d. 1804) prophesied, "So long as public prayers will be made, nothing shall happen; but a time will come when public prayers shall cease. People will say, 'things will remain as they are.' It is then that the great calamity shall occur."

274   A prophecy of Daniel 12:7 says that the Antichrist will scatter the power of the holy people.

275   Blessed Joachim (d. 1202) predicted, "Towards the end of the world, Antichrist will overthrow the pope and usurp his See." St. Francis of Assisi prophesied, "There will be an uncanonically elected pope who will cause a great Schism." Venerable Bartholomew Holzhauser (d. 1658) said, "Antichrist and his army will conquer Rome, kill the Pope and take the throne." Sister Mary of the Nativity (Jane Le Royer, d. 1798) predicted, "… a great power arising against the Church. It despoiled, plundered and laid waste to the vineyard of the Lord… [T]his power boldly confiscated the properties of the Church and at the same time usurped the powers of the pope, whose person and laws they condemned…. Antichrist will kill the pope…" Finally, Nicholas of Fluh (d. 1487) prophesied, "The Church will sink still deeper until she will at last seem to be extinguished, and the succession Peter and the other Apostles to have expired. After that she will be victoriously exalted in the sight of all doubters."

276   As mentioned earlier, the Three Days of Darkness have been prophesied in Scripture and by a surprising number of visionaries. A couple of the Scriptural prophecies are as follows: "Let all who live in the land tremble, for the day of the LORD is coming. It is close at hand—a day of darkness and gloom, a day of clouds and blackness." (Joel 2:1-2) "'In that day,' declares the Sovereign LORD, 'I will make the sun go down at noon and darken the earth in broad daylight. I will turn your religious feasts into mourning and all your singing into weeping.'" (Amos 8:9-10) Mystic and stigmatist, Marie-Julie Jahenny of La Fraudais offered numerous prophecies regarding "…three days of terrifying darkness," including, "The earth will be covered in darkness and hell will be loosed on earth." (September 20, 1882) "The crisis will explode suddenly; the punishments will be shared by all and will succeed one another without interruption." (January 4, 1884)

277   The relics of the Magi were originally situated in Constantinople and transferred to Milan in 344 and then Cologne in 1164.

278   St. Malachy, who died in 1148, famously compiled a list of short descriptions of every pope from that date until what many believe will be the final one. Though there is some dispute regarding the first 400 years of these predictions being authentic (because it was not discovered until after that time) there can be little doubt about the authenticity of the surprisingly accurate predictions since the time of that discovery. The description that fits Pope Benedict XVI is listed as second to last. The final pope listed is Petrus Romanus, or Peter the Roman. Since no pope has ever taken the name Peter - out of respect for the first pontiff - that would make him Peter II. He is described as follows: "In the final persecution of the Holy Roman Church there will reign Peter the Roman, who will feed his flock among many tribulations; after which the seven-hilled city will be destroyed and the dreadful Judge will judge the people."

279   Translation: "We have a pope!"

280   Garabandal visionary, Conchita Gonzalez, predicted something "like two stars... that crash and make a lot of noise, and a lot of light... but they don't fall. It's not going to hurt us but we're going to see it and, in that moment, we're going to see our consciences."

281   Description by Garabandal visionary, Conchita Gonzalez.

282   Prophecy of Garabandal visionary, Mari Loli-Mazon.

283   Also called the Illumination of the Soul, this event has been prophesied by Blessed Anna Maria Taigi (1836), as well as St. Catherine Laboure in 1830, St. Faustina Kowalska in the 1930s, and to the four young seers of Garabandal, Spain in the 1960s. Some claim that the secrets of the Medjugorje visionaries may also include this phenomenon.

284   A description from Garabandal visionary, Conchita Gonzalez.

285   This prophetic description is from the recently deceased mystic, Father Stephan Gobi.

286   Paraphrased from description of Garabandal visionary, Conchita Gonzalez.

287   As cited previously, prophecies predict that only blessed candles (some say they must be beeswax) will shed light during the Three Days of Darkness. They also advise that believers should pray the Rosary and venerate the Sacred Heart of Jesus during that time.

288   Revelation 3:15-16.

289   James 5:16.

290   2 Chronicles 7:14.

291   Ezekiel 11:19-20.

292   Paraphrased from prophecies of Blessed Maria Taigi (d. 1837).

293   Prophecy of Palma Maria d'Oria (d. 1863).

294   Paraphrased from prophecy of Venerable Isabel Canori-Mora (d. 1825).

295   Paraphrased from prophesy of Marie Julie Jahenny of La Faudais (1891).

296   Prophesy of Marie Julie Jahenny of La Faudais (1891).

297   Paraphrased from Luke 21:25-26.

298   "Antichrist will be born near Babylon. He will win the support of many with gifts and money. He will sell himself to the devil and thereafter will have no guardian angel or conscience." St. Jerome (d. 420).

299   A very similar prophecy was also made by Sister Marianne (d. 1804).

300   Most prophecies say "three days," some say "72 hours," one says "70 hours."

301   A promise from Joel 3:5.

302   Father Bernard Maria Clausi, O.F.M. (d. 1849), predicted, "Before the triumph of the Church comes, God will first take vengeance on the wicked, especially against the Godless. It will be a new Judgment, the like has never been before and it will be universal."

303   Again, Father Clausi prophesied that God's Judgment "will be so terrible that those who outlive it will imagine that they are the only ones spared.... Before that, evil will have made such progress that it will look like all the devils of hell were let loose on earth..."

304   The mind boggling concept of two billion deaths actually substantially understates the predicted death toll. Some prophecies claim that the world's population will be reduced by three-quarters after the Three Days of Darkness. Sister Mary of Jesus Crucified of Pau (d. 1878), for example predicted, "During a darkness lasting three days the people given to evil ways will perish so that only one-fourth of mankind will survive." For the purposes of this story, however, the author chose to limit the death rate to one-third of the global population.

305   Paraphrased from 2 Timothy 3:2-5.

306   Blessed Anna-Maria Taigi prophesied, "All the enemies of the Church, secret as well as known, will perish over the whole earth during that universal darkness, with the exception of a few..."

307   From the Diary of St. Maria Faustina Kowalska, Christ said: ""Before I come in glory, I will throw open the doors of My mercy. And all those who pass through the doors of My mercy I will protect as My own at the hour of death. Those who refuse the opportunity to pass through the doors of my mercy must pass through the doors of My justice."

308   Interpreting St. Malachy's prophecies, the final pope will be the one who

succeeds Pope Benedict XVI. He is called Petrus Romanus (Peter the Roman) and is described as follows: "In the final persecution of the Holy Roman Church there will reign Peter the Roman, who will feed his flock among many tribulations; after which the seven-hilled city will be destroyed and the dreadful Judge will judge the people."

309   The permanent, indestructible and beautiful sign from God has been foretold by the Medjugorje and Garabandal visionaries. It will be presented in greater detail in Book Three of the Trials and Triumph Trilogy.

The Trials and Triumph Trilogy:

The Rise

The Rebellion

The Return

by

Kenneth E. Nowell

www.VeroHousePublishing.com